GO PHISH

Also by Geoffrey Mehl...

Fiction (Tommy Kane/Mandy Owens)
  STRAY CATS
  NINE LIVES

Landscaping/Sustainable Design
  PENNYSLVANIA NATURALLY

  PERENNIALS: HABITAT AND CULTURE

  A GARDENER'S GUIDE TO NATIVE PLANTS
  OF NORTHEASTERN PENNSYLVANIA

Learn more at www.geoffmehl.com

ISBN-13: 978-0-9862766-6-8
ISBN-10: 0-9862766-6-9
Printed in the United States of America

GO PHISH

by Geoffrey Mehl

CHAPTER ONE

Corrientes, Argentina

Tap. *Splash*. Tap. *Splash*.

Mandy Owens shivered. Freezing from head to toe, she crossed her arms to ward off the chill. And avoid peeking at what remained of an original David Aire gown, hanging limp on her body. The toe of a Jimmy Choo pump slammed into her very own puddle, one of hundreds scattered across the tarmac.

An icy trickle of water snaked through her hair and onto her back. Breathing came easier and her tone calmed. "Tommy, I don't want to sound negative, but I'm just not very enamored with Plan B."

In the cool night air filling the wake of the thunderstorm, he looked unperturbed, like it was routine to be soaked to the skin while awaiting rescue. Hector's private army was closing in. Walter's chopper was late. And so was the jet that would whisk them away.

He said, "There was no Plan B."

His tailored dress shirt clung to his torso, every inch of his skin visible, and a flutter of lust revived her heart rate. "You made it up as you went?"

"Well, yeah. Totally improvised, on the fly. Things go side−ways sometimes."

"Ah, of course. I should have guessed. Well, more like ex−pected." Mandy shifted her weight to splash the other foot. It didn't matter now. A favorite pair of shoes was a lost cause. "Look, I, well... Hm. Okay. Don't take this the wrong way, be— cause tagging along on one of your little capers is the sort of thing every woman dreams about doing —"

"You're upset about the dress."

"Gosh, no, I was simply thinking that if we're going to be partners on burglaries and stuff, we need to communicate better. Have a well-organized Plan B for times like when it takes too long to break into the vault. Or when the half-drunk girl barges in looking for a toilet and reacts the way she did. That's all."

He nodded and passed the aluminum case from one hand to the other. About twenty-four by thirty inches and six inches thick, it was undamaged and sparkled with every flash of depart— ing lightning from the east. "So you'd like to have some input on planning. Or is it actually about the dress?"

She drew a deep breath. Time to accept reality. An hour ear— lier the flowing silk fashion triumph by David Aire was worth at least thirty-five hundred dollars. Now it was destined for a dumpster. "Well, perhaps indirectly, but—"

He chuckled satisfaction. "Knew it all along. Sorry, but kitchen doors are unpredictable. Sometimes you just have to ac— cept —"

Mandy again shifted to toe-tap with the opposite foot. "It was more about no Plan B, Tommy. We were *supposed* to quietly slip out of the side entrance of Hector's mansion, settle into a very snuggly limo with Sergei and Charlie and... Oh, gosh, I hope they're all right."

"They'll be fine. Running interference. Probably creating chaos somewhere between Hector's and the airport. They're both good at it. So what would you have done differently?"

Mandy's foot paused. "Well, if we had a good Plan B, I prob— ably would have packed a black turtleneck, maybe dark yoga pants and one of those masks terrorists seem to prefer. Couple of throwing knives and some sort of gun, maybe."

His tone was defensive. "But we got here all right, didn't we? Shortcut. Straight line path, right to the spot where Cesar will turn the jet for takeoff. Hector's guys will take the long way around, just to lug all their weapons."

Mandy sighed exasperation. "So we traveled light, through the string of pastures, with considerable effort, Tommy, because heels stick in mud. Heaven knows what I was stepping in, all that squishy."

"Until I broke off the heels. I suppose there's no applause for that."

"Not at six hundred dollars a pair. Plus the barbed wire. Men have no appreciation for what happens to a favorite silk gown when going through barbed wire fences."

"Sorry about that. Maybe Ella Spence at the —"

"She's a Jacks Ford dry cleaner, not a Garment District seamstress. And we're talking *shredded* fabric. Dozens and dozens of rips and snags. Not to mention soaking wet. We have to promise never to tell David Aire. He may be king of runway, but he'd weep, knowing one of his best originals is a rag. Trust me on that."

"So, you're really upset about the dress."

"Okay. Now that you mention it... Do you have any idea how cold this gown gets when saturated with rain water? Not to mention hair, laying across bare shoulders like a dead snake? Men have no clue." She resumed toe-tapping, trying for more splash to emphasize the the severity of the storm, the sheets of water just fallen. "And the only reason I'm not seriously angry is because you let me have your jacket. Which, by the way, has a rip most of the way down the left arm."

"The second fence line." He hoisted the case. "So, do you want to see the painting?"

"No. I'd rather have some idea when the jet will be on the ground to gather us up with warm clothes, hot sandwiches and a scotch, double at least. And then we would swoop away into some really comfy time off." She held a cell phone aloft and her tone darkened. "But I have no way of knowing since I dropped it in that drainage ditch. Sorry, just static, no Lucy to reassure us."

"Everyone'll be along. These things always work out."

Mandy shook her head. "Tommy, everyone includes half the police force and all of Hector's private army. Just thinking about jail in Argentina... well, I'm not sure if I should be scared to death or just frightened out of my mind."

A trickle of water scampered across Tommy's forehead and onto his nose. "For being cornered in a forbidden-access area of a South American airport after a major felony? I'd probably go with scared. But it's an individual thing."

"Scared works for me. Are you —"

Tommy pointed. "Nah. Reinforcements just arrived. Charlie and Serge. Only one vehicle, no lights, no sirens. Hector's people will be a major swarm." The case hung tantalizingly high in the air. "Care for a peek?"

"No. I'm sure it's too warm and humid."

The proposition *was* tempting. Missing for seven decades, it was one of the most hunted masterpieces ever. Tommy released the catches on the case, letting the muggy November air of Argentina pour all over an oil painting that should never be separated from climate control.

She lunged to assist. "Careful! You'll drop it!"

The painting slid into her hands, lighter than expected, the colors muted in the semi-darkness. Her breath went shallow as reverence blossomed and a soft shiver rippled through her body. Not from the cold. Raffaello Sanzio da Urbino. *Portrait of a Young Man*, 1513. *Raphael*, in what some scholars thought was a Renaissance-style selfie. Caught up in the Nazi art thefts, vanished from a Polish castle in 1945. Probably worth between a hundred and hundred and twenty million dollars.

And stolen. Again.

"Okay, this is just wrong. Let's put it away, Tommy. Open

the case and hold it underneath my arms so I don't drop it."

The vehicle stopped and Charlie called out. "You got the goods okay? Damn. You two look like something drug in by a barn cat."

Tommy said, "She's upset about the dress."

Mandy tugged the jacket tight around her. Sergei was clearly enjoying the view. "No, I'm not. It's about the lack... never mind."

Tommy beamed pride. "We got the painting, Charlie. You guys want to see?"

Sergei's grin was way too lecherous. "I have already enjoyed small moment to admire."

She clutched the jacket tighter. "I meant the painting, Sergei."

Charlie shook his head. "Nah. Just some picture rich folks get excited about."

Yenchenko towered over Charlie and echoed the gesture. "Most seriously agree, Koshka. Take care not to damage picture, make deduction from my share, *da?* Where is contact?"

Tommy followed instructions and closed the case around the painting. "Late. We lost our comm, so we're running blind."

Charlie scowled and Yenchenko rolled his eyes.

Mandy raised a confession hand. "I dropped the phone in a drainage ditch."

Yenchenko chuckled, shifted an AK-47 from one paw to the other, and pulled a plastic bag from a bulging pocket on the leg of his combat fatigues. "Sergei always prepare for poor weather of South America. *Koshka*, of course, never learn."

Tommy chuckled. "I never carry a phone, Serge. Give it to Mandy, not me."

Yenchenko laughed as he passed the phone to Mandy, who immediately pressed the number two button.

Lucy's instant voice sounded anxious. "You okay?"

"Just a, um, technical glitch."

"Wait. You're on Sergei's unit. Oh, crap. You've lost the —"

"Dropped it. In a puddle. So it sort of doesn't work."

Lucy sighed. "Wow. Dad's tight about that shit. It's gonna cost Tommy five grand."

"Never mind. Where is everybody?"

Lucy said, "A few minutes late because of the storm. Looked pretty nasty on satellite. Hope you didn't get too wet."

"We'll be fine, Lucy. So?"

"Walter's coming in now. Cesar is fifteen miles and closing. You guys better haul ass. Half the law enforcement people in Argentina have mobilized."

A helicopter's landing lights burst to life a few hundred yards away.

"He's here, Lucy. Sergei and Charlie are carrying rifles, so —"

"I'm not worried about Charlie, Mandy. Just try to keep Sergei from killing anybody. Don't need the hassle."

The chopper hovered for a moment before the nose lifted and the aircraft plopped onto to the tarmac.

"Got it. Catch you later."

The lanky frame of Walter Campos bounded toward them. He wore the usual rumpled khaki, long-billed fishing cap and ear-to-ear grin.

"Sorry to keep you folks waiting. Bit of weather, had to go around the squall, you see."

Tommy held the case aloft and Walter rubbed his hands to-gether like a child encountering a mountain of gifts.

"Splendid, Kane, just splendid. Anyone hurt? No? Excellent. You looked soaked to the skin, Mandy. You'd better get changed before you catch a cold."

Tommy said, "She's upset about the dress."

Walter's laugh boomed across the pavement. "I'll buy you another. Two, if you like."

Mandy mustered a smile. "Thank you, Walter. Nice to work

with a gentleman. Take good care of that painting. It's —"

"Priceless. I know." He accepted the case from Tommy. "My contacts in Poland will be glad to see it home at last. It's taken decades to track it down to a vault here."

Charlie grunted. "Seems to me they coulda worked it out with some of them diplomat types."

Campos nodded. "Been dragging on for too many years. Time to square things once and for all. Take the initiative, you see."

Charlie said, "And o'course, you're just a good citizen and art lover."

Campos chuckled. "Business, Charlie. *Quid pro quo.* Scratching the back, you know."

Yenchenko sighed. "Capitalists."

Campos ignored the point. "Well, I'd buy you all a round at the nearest bar, but I'm informed that Hector Suarez's people are rolling up the ol' *Ruta Nacionale* as we speak."

Tommy glanced at Charlie and Sergei.

Charlie snorted. "Yeah, well, we got us a little time. Sergei wanted to blow up the first gasoline tanker headed toward town, but I talked him into a couple of cattle trucks. So they got a hundred head of cows millin' around on Route Twelve and *then* they gotta deal with a pair of jackknifed rigs."

Yenchenko shrugged. "I prefer big fire, melt asphalt, make more delay. But we are team, *da?*"

Tommy nodded. "Good call, Charlie."

Lucy's voice came alive in the earbud. "Okay, Mandy, Cesar's on final with clearance. You've got maybe ten, twelve minutes tops. No time for a refuel. We've got their communications down outside of A-T-C, but I suggest you get out of Argentinian airspace as quick as you can."

To the south, the bright landing lights of the jet came on just as Lucy said, "He's at minimums and descending. Where are you guys, exactly?"

The ball of brilliant white settled to earth, at first a shining star with tiny green and red escorts and a low rumble on the horizon.

Mandy repeated the tarmac location called out by Tommy. "Thanks, Luce, we've got visual."

Ground lights outlined the fuselage, and the tail and cabin took their individual forms. Wingtip strobes popped flashes of balled lightning amid engines hissing thunder.

Lucy said, "Hector's people are about nine minutes and clos-ing. I can get you an extra minute or two by jamming the gates, but don't linger, okay?"

Touchdown. Reverse thrusters. Screaming down the runway.

"Got it, thanks."

"No prob. Have a nice flight."

Walter's chopper lifted and rolled away into the darkness.

The jet crept toward their little corner of the airport. Every-one scanned horizons for the police, the army, the guy who was not happy about someone lifting an incredibly important paint-ing given to his wife but could never admit to owning. Ground lights from the front tires of the jet put them in a spotlight. No hiding the dress now. All dignity evaporated. "You know, Tom-my, Mrs. Suarez did lay out a great spread of *hors d'oeuvres*. Those little cookies were very nice. I wonder if we could have Karen round some up for the flight back... No, probably not."

The Gulfstream rolled onto the alley, huge and loud, the il-luminated tail soaring skyward like an immense sail.

Tommy said, "You seem more relaxed. No regrets?"

Charlie snorted. "We got no time for touchy-feelie. That mob of cutthroats'll be here anytime. Let's get out of Dodge."

Sergei said, "*Da, da*. Like agile wolf, we make our way quick-ly through forest."

Tommy began to speak, but she raised a hand to silence him. "It's only a dress, Tommy. It was a couple of years old and just occupying space in the closet. But you owe me. Holding the masterpiece wasn't enough."

Charlie and Sergei strolled toward the unfurled steps of the aircraft and Tommy gestured for them to get going. "Karen's got some great sandwich fixings and 25-year-old Macallan single malt aboard."

"Not enough."

After Charlie and Sergei passed, Karen's usual welcoming smile dissipated into a concoction of shock and sympathy as the wet, ragged couple followed.

Tommy brightened. "Couple of weeks off on the island?"

"My island. Doesn't count."

"There must be something —"

"I'll think about it." At the base of the steps, her voice mellowed. "Hi, Karen. Hope there's a warm and dry outfit aboard. It's been a very long evening."

"Yes, m'am. Plus sandwiches and scotch. Cesar already has clearance for takeoff, so let's get you aboard and comfortable."

Tommy gestured a go-ahead and smiled at Karen. "She's upset about the dress."

Karen's smile was patient and understanding. "No Plan B again? I'm not surprised."

Halfway up the steps, Mandy turned to see Tommy reply with the wince of a mischievous boy trapped into a cookie-jar confession.

"Exactly, Karen. *Exactly*." She laid out a maternal smile of her own. "C'mon, Tommy, let's go home."

CHAPTER TWO

Billy's Tavern, Jacks Ford, Pennsylvania

Clean shirt, clean pants, clean shaved, shoes all shiny. A first-rate bar with first-rate food and music. Saturday night. And Mandy. Unable to keep a grin in check, Tommy reached for the door.

She paused to ask, "You really think I'm okay in this outfit? I feel as self-conscious as an orange in a bowl of apples, Tommy."

He tugged the door open. "*Very* fine. Trust me, that kind of gorgeous is illegal in nine, ten states. Maybe more. You'll turn a lot of heads, hear a lot of sigh." Carhartt was never looking so good. Soft plaid shirt, just loose enough to give a hint, jeans just tight enough to leave no doubt. He caught the scent of spring flowers as she stepped past, calling in the marker from the air–port. It might be a small-town square dance, but it could have been a whole lot worse.

She hesitated again at the portal. "You're really sure?"

He tossed her a bouquet of reassurance. "Oh, absolutely."

"I don't want to — "

He chuckled. "Sure you do. Deep down, every woman does."

"And you're really willing to do this?"

"Not much choice. I owe you, so, yeah. Let's go pass some good time."

Her eyes sparkled and her smile went warm and wide. "Yes. I've always thought square dancing was a good way to spend a

Saturday night. Well, since this morning, anyway."

As he followed her inside, his grin mellowed into cool smugness. Heads at the bar did turn, like a stadium wave, with unabashed admiration, the kind when your friend gets a really nice fish into the net.

High fives. Fist bumps. Thumbs up. Eighteen, maybe twenty, good drinking buddies at the bar, the kind who've been there, are there, bend an ear, tell good tales and know when an outrageous lie is just part of the fun. Solid sound from a genuine jukebox. Up tempo. Truckin' music, rubber on the road, doin' seventy-five. Fish and fries, two-stepping in deep fat. Introducing the prettiest gal in town, lookin' really fine. *Catchin' some trash talk Go ahead, I don't mind. Talking to me but looking at her, wouldn't have it any other way. Dang, if she doesn't have a smile that'd melt glass.*

"Hey, Billy, where y'at?"

"Not too bad, Tommy. Too bad about the election. You'd a made a good mayor. Better luck next time."

"Never was a first time, won't be a next. And that's just fine with me. Nice crowd."

Billy finished drying a glass and tossed the towel over his shoulder. "Decent. Hiya, Mandy. Don't you believe a word this guy says, eh?" Billy's eyes took the lecher's tour. "Damn, Tommy, I always said you sure could pick 'em."

Mandy turned. And there it was. The Look. *Caught ya.* Eyebrows up. *Don'tcha dare.* But there was a twinkle in her eye, and she was trying to keep a straight face.

"Okay, Tommy, you can leave that one alone."

He raised his arms in submission. "Yes ma'm. No trouble at all."

Billy reached for glassware. "What can I get ya's?"

"I'm thinking we'll head into the hall, maybe get a little supper, see what's going on." He felt a light jab in the ribs. "And maybe do a little square dancing."

Billy grunted. "No shit? Damn. Anyways, good luck with that. Not the best of nights. Terry and the Haystackers is out of town."

"You don't say." Tommy turned to Mandy, who smiled sweetly. Her eyes said he was not off the hook.

Billy wiped his hands with the edge of his apron. "Tonight they're working some event up to New York State, Ithaca, some kind of college, Core-something or other."

She nodded. "Cornell? Pretty famous university, big reputa—tion, Ivy League."

"Yeah, well, college, university, high school, I don't much care. Terry knew damn well this was square dance night but took the gig anyway. Said they tossed a whole bunch of money at 'em for some reunion thing. I can't compete with top dollar, Tommy. You know that. Everybody knows that."

"So what happened?"

"I one time got a card from some booking guy passing through, give him a call and a touring group was available, cheap o'course, and I figured we could sorta fudge it out for one night, see? Problem is they don't know proper dance music, and Jack Miller — he's the caller — is chewin' on my ear every few min—utes about it."

"What kind of band?"

"I dunno. Inexpensive. They got some kinda little accordion and an electronic piano instead of a slide guitar and banjo. Shit. Here comes Jack again. Why don't you folks find a table in the hall and I'll fetch a couple of platters. Beer okay with you, Mandy?"

She nodded. "Whatever Tommy's drinking."

Tommy gestured for calm. "Don't fret over Jack. He's just excitable, that's all."

"Yeah, yeah. Tell me about it. I'll bring them beers."

The dance hall was a sea of smiles, waves, hellos, handshakes, finger points. She worked the crowd like a princess on a rope line. The band struck up a tune that to Tommy's ear had a distinct Cajun edge to it, not quite a bayou two-step, but definitely not square dance. No one left their chairs, conversations or dinnerware and Mandy's expression began to wither.

A wave to join them, a big grin, an old friend framed a destination.

Frannie's called out, "Wow, look at this couple! Prince Charming and the Belle of the Ball. Mandy, you look just terrific."

Mandy blushed. "Gosh, that makes four of us looking great, then. Hi, Chet, so nice to see you."

Chet's usual easy grin looked more like a polite smile through a case of indigestion. "Hey, Mandy, Tommy."

If Mandy noticed tension, she didn't show it while greeting Frannie with a polite hug. "Have I told you that Chet's our most favorite customs and border guy? A credit to Homeland but just the nicest gentleman..."

"About a zillion times," Frannie said. "But I know he likes to hear it. Isn't that right, Chet?"

He feigned embarrassment. "Yeah, yeah, whatever you say."

Chet Towers was a half a foot and fifty pounds bigger than Tommy, carried himself like a former tight end, and wore a close-trimmed flat-top hair style over a leathery complexion that could peg him as a badass Marine drill instructor or no-nonsense cop if it wasn't for his easy-going grin and relaxed style of speech. Both of which were missing tonight and Frannie seemed to be working patiently around it.

Chet stood and hitched up his thick belt around a trim torso. "If you'll excuse me, I gotta call a guy. Back in a couple of minutes."

Maybe he was dealing with some sort of problem with his ex-wife. It had been a nasty divorce and somehow Frannie was involved. But because Frannie owned the Puffin Diner, gossip was kept away from the social hub of Jacks Ford, an unwritten rule of small town manners.

Tommy said, "Yeah, sure, Chet. But don't linger too long. Got a pitcher of Black and Tan on the way, and we'll need a whole bunch of help."

Chet nodded, gave a little wave and began to weave through the thicket of round tables. The song from the bandstand began to lose heart. Billy was probably getting an earful from Jack Miller.

Frannie leaned and spoke so softly that she could barely be understood in the room noise. "Um, Tommy, can I sorta bother you with something?"

"Yeah, sure, of course. Chet?"

"Yeah. I think he's kind of in a jam. I mean, you're like *guys* and all, and this might be one those guy things that guys don't like to talk about to girls."

"Sure thing." Time for a subject change, and Mandy sensed it.

She said, "The hall looks very nice. Sort of a shame the dance floor is empty."

Frannie chuckled. "Honey, this is only a pole barn with a concrete slab covered with wood flooring, just a step above a tractor barn. But Billy makes a killing off it every Friday and Saturday night, so I've got to respect that. And ain't nobody dancing because they got a bum band nowhere's near Terry and the Haystackers."

Billy arrived with a tray supporting two platters of beer bat–tered fish, fries and onion rings and a pair of tall glasses and an pitcher of Yuengling draft. On the opposite side of the table, Mandy's smile went wider and her dark eyes sparkled with ex–citement.

"Oh, my," Frannie laughed. "We've got the owner himself waiting tables. What's up, Billy? Too cheap to hire waitstaff?"

Billy scowled. "Don't gimme none of your shit. Otherwise, I just might start considering opening my kitchen for breakfast, show the diner a thing or two."

Her laugh deepened. "Billy, your customers aren't even out of bed until noon. And then only to nurse a hangover."

Billy appealed to Tommy. "See? I got a tough business, a lousy band, and now I gotta catch shit from Miss Puffin Diner herself. I'm tellin' ya, Tommy, this is a rotten way to make a living."

Tommy reached up and patted Billy's shoulder. "But you're a sturdy guy, Billy. You'll be all right."

"Say, you talk some of that French, don'tcha? These people don't know hardly no English and I'm thinkin' that they might be talkin' French or something. Ain't Spanish. I've heard that. Gotta be French. Maybe."

Tommy smiled. "*Que voulez-vous que je leur demande?*"

Frannie sighed. "I just love it when Tommy talks French."

Mandy glanced at Tommy, then Frannie and returned her gaze to Tommy. "*Beaucoup de personnes parlent le français, Tommy. Peut-être que vous pourriez leur demander d'où ils viennent — mais je ne pense pas qu'ils viennent de la Louisiane.*"

Frannie jaw dropped. "I'll be damned."

Billy stared, too. "So you'll gimme a hand with this?"

Tommy lifted his glass to Mandy. "Sweet. What makes you think they're not from Louisiana?"

"The music."

"Ten dollars?"

Her expression turned mischievous. "Twenty. Plus a round for our table."

"You're on. Billy, I think we maybe got us a ringer here." He studied Mandy's frisky eyes. "Yeah. A ringer for sure."

Billy seemed unimpressed. "Yeah, well, I got a bar to tend. See what you guys can do, okay? I'll knock something off your tab." He jerked his head toward the bandstand. "And ain't nobody gonna dance to sad stuff like that."

Mandy's attention had kept turning to the bandstand at the

far end of the hall and a simple, melancholy tune that whispered across the floor. She succumbed to the call, and in a soft voice, excused herself to follow the notes of the button accordion to its source.

Frannie and Tommy exchanged looks and shrugs.

"Did you know she spoke French?"

Tommy shook his head and watched Mandy cross the floor.

"She's perfect for you, Tommy. Perfect."

Tommy stood, feeling warmth in his ears. "Let me go talk to Chet."

Frannie nodded and looked at the empty chairs. "Thanks, Tommy. I'll hold the seats. Not that anyone's rushing in..."

Tommy found Chet at the quiet end of the bar, poured a double bourbon to gently shovel away a defensive layer of em-barrassment, and heard the tale.

Chet sighed. "Y'know, for a couple of seconds, I thought it was my ex that did it. She's a mean bitch. But no. Bottom line is I was plain, doggone, dumb with a goddamn email and gave the bastards all my account stuff. By the time I reached the bank, they cleaned me out and there wasn't nothing they could do ex-cept freeze it or close it."

Tommy nodded. "Phishing. Happens to a lot of smart guys, Chet." *Like a couple of executives at Penn State and the New York Federal Reserve we used.*

"Yeah?"

"Yeah. Trust me on that one."

Chet shook his head, and turned a mournful expression back toward Tommy. "Maybe so, but my ex is gonna come after me with a lotta legal shit, and that gets me into deep trouble with my supervisors at Customs and Immigration. Be my luck that I'll wind up being a rent-a-cop at some goddamn mall somewhere." He tossed the bourbon into his throat, wiped his lips with the back of his hand and grunted. "So I'm a smart guy. Only I don't have fourteen grand and change no more."

"I can fix that."

"Don't need no loan, Tommy. Couldn't pay it back, any—how."

Tommy chuckled. "No, I meant — "

Chet waved him off. "And no charity, neither. Word gets around about that stuff."

Tommy poured another splash of whiskey into Chet's glass. "How about justice?"

Chet gathered up the glass and swirled it. He cocked an eye—brow. "You know somebody?"

Lucy Tramanian. "Yep. I surely do."

"Yeah?"

"Yeah."

Chet sighed again. "Be my guest, buddy. I got nothin' to lose."

"We oughta rejoin the ladies. Their night and all. Besides, Mandy shanghaied me into dancing."

Chet laughed. "No kidding? You? Aw, man..."

"Yeah, well, a friendly face in the crowd would be good, buddy."

Chet nodded his way through a snicker. "You got it."

CHAPTER THREE

When the men slid back into their chairs, Frannie asked, "You boys good?"

While Chet poured beer, Tommy said, "Yep, believe so." He pointed toward the makeshift stage. "What's going on?"

"No idea. The accordion player played some sort of forlorn waltz, then Mandy caught his attention and they began to talk some, all kind of relaxed and friendly-like."

A younger woman with blonde hair and a maroon blouse was at the center of a semi-circle of guys. Interpreter, maybe. The guys backed away, some picking up instruments, playing quietly, without amplification.

Mandy's toe picked up the beat, then went into a heel-toe combination. The blonde gestured approval. Together, they be—gan a more extended dance, similar to a jig, not quite like Irish folk and much more subtle than clogging. The impromptu dance abruptly ended after a minute. The blonde woman moved to an pile of instrument cases and returned with a pair of black shoes, about ankle high. Mandy took a seat on the edge of the bandstand to change footwear.

"Gee, Tommy, I do believe Mandy's — "

The button accordion guy was lanky, fifty-ish, with greying hair combed straight back. He smiled, started to play, and both women stepped to the rhythm. A guitar player picked up the song, and then the fellow with the electronic keyboard. Two men in dance shoes watched with nods of approval while the women worked out some steps.

Wearing a stern expression, Jack Miller returned from the bar and began to cross the room.

Tommy waved him to proximity and pointed to Mandy's chair. "Do everyone a favor, Jack, and just take a little break."

"What?"

Frannie's tone was blunt. "Put your ass in the chair and shut the hell up."

Miller looked startled and meekly complied.

At the other end of the floor, tempo and volume rose and became more organized. Tommy listened to several bars and said, "No doubt about it — that's a reel and it's not from Louisiana. It's folk music. From Quebec."

Mandy and three troupe dancers tinkered with a step pattern, polishing the moves. After two experimental starts, the band uncorked a full-blown reel, loud enough to catch the attention of everyone in the hall.

In a square in front of the stage, all four dancers took solo turns, followed by group stepping in a line. Jack Miller might have had his arms crossed on his chest, but his knee echoed the tapping of his foot in time with the frenetic tempo of the reel. And it went on. And on. And on.

Frannie could contain herself no longer and jumped to her feet. "Holy shit! Did you know she could dance like that?"

Enchanting. Absolutely enchanting. "No, no way."

"That's amazing, Tommy. Look at her feet! Look at her freaking feet!"

Tommy nodded. *Feet, yes. But her face...* Concentration. Assurance. Joy. Utter abandon, as though she had been possessed by childhood. Her first steps might have been reticent, but now were carefree, heel-toe, toe-heel, flat, sometimes looking like she was trying to tangle her legs but proving she wouldn't. Looser, ever looser.

The band changed key and cranked up the tempo. The

dancers launched an intricate pattern that made square dancing look like slow motion, but their feet continued tapping heel and toe. The crowd drifted toward the dancers, hands clapping to the beat.

The performance finally shifted back into a single line. The band added a final flourish and heels hit the floor in unison on the last note.

The audience burst into applause, hoots, whistles and hollers. Holding hands, the line of dancers beamed and took a bow, then another. At the end of the line, Mandy let go, stepped forward and turned to join the ovation.

Billy had delivered a round of beer and stood next to Tom— my to watch. "Pretty fair show," he conceded. "But I don't think it's gonna get folks on the floor."

Mandy bounded back to the table, still out of breath. "Gosh, that was *so* much fun! And I am *so* out of shape."

Frannie laughed. "You go, girl. That was just — well, I've never seen anything like that. Where'd you learn those steps?"

"My mother taught me, when I was a child. It's wonderful music, part of the whole folk culture of Quebec."

"Quebec?"

"Mom was French-Canadian, from a little town called Saint-Honoré, near Saguenay. The leader of the band, Louis Boulanger — the fellow with the button accordion — and his niece, Dominique — who is a *very, very* good dancer — are orig— inally from there, too. So we kind of hit it off. The band, by the way, is now from Montreal and were touring, trying to make their way back home, but they're struggling. It's a group of seven altogether, and the tour has not gone well. Very few people out— side Quebec understand the culture."

Mandy extended a hand, palm up. "Twenty bucks and a round, right?"

Tommy dug into his pocket for folding money. "Well, you certainly got everyone's attention. Looks like these folks really enjoyed the show. You were magnificent. For true."

Billy agreed. "But nice as it was, it still didn't get folks on the floor."

Tommy's attention clung to Mandy's expression. Pumped up, running on adrenalin, premium grade. "It doesn't —"

Mandy interrupted. "Tommy's twenty that I can."

Frannie's crossed her arms and lifted her chin. "And thirty more from me to make it fifty."

Billy chuckled with a cynical edge. "A hundred and you're faded. But it's got to be everybody in the hall. Well, most, any—way."

Tommy cocked his head. "Let's make it a *thousand*, Billy. A thousand for the band."

Mandy's eyes widened. "Tommy — "

Frannie leaned in close to her. "You can do it. I just know you can."

Mandy looked back to Tommy, who nodded. She drew a breath. "You won't be angry if this doesn't work out?"

"Not even a little bit. I'm with Frannie on this one."

Billy rubbed his chin, but Mandy ignored the anxiety. She had already turned to cross the floor. She spoke to Louis, then picked up a microphone from the bandstand, clicked it on and tapped it twice to make sure it was live. Mandy turned, stepped into the center of the floor and faced the audience.

"Bonsoir, mesdames et messieurs. Puis-je avoir votre attention, s'il vous plaît? Merci. Mon nom est Mandy Owens." She paused and cleared her throat. "Oh, gosh, forgive me. When you hear the marvelous music of Quebec, you almost forgot what country you're in."

Supportive laughter rippled through the crowd.

"Again, hello, I'm Mandy Owens. Sort of new to town, and I just wanted to welcome everyone to a very special program tonight."

Throughout the room, smiles, attention, interest.

Tommy whispered, "You're gonna lose, Billy."

Billy crossed his arms and grunted. "I ain't complaining."

Mandy's voice filled the hall as she introduced the band and then the dancers, now joined by the road manager of the troupe. "And we are going to need some volunteers to get us started on learning a *quadrille*, one of the wonderful dances of Canada. I see Frannie and Chet over there."

The crowd responded with encouraging applause and the couple tentatively entered the dance floor.

Nice. Nice move.

Mandy kept on. "Anyone else?" She looked around and ignored several raised hands, finally pointing toward her table. "Ah, yes. My good friend, Tommy Kane."

More applause and laughter.

Aw, man...she got me.

The silence of anticipation swept through the hall. A couple of distant calls of encouragement. Frannie and Chet and especially Billy — smiles way too smug.

Mandy's grin teased, welcomed, comforted, all at once. "Well, Tommy Kane, do you want to dance or not?"

A blinding flash of *deja vu* shot through his mind. Her name was Belle, the girl with the darkest eyes and the prettiest smile. Most everyone thought she was the loveliest in all of St. Tammany Parish. On a warm Saturday night long ago, the band began a slow tune, a waltz, *"Les Grande Bois."* He was thirteen, hanging out in the bullpen, trying to fit in, when Belle came out of nowhere, put her hands on her hips, the reminiscence as clear as if it was five minutes ago. And Belle said, "Well now, Tommy Kane, do you want to dance or not?"

Thirteen stupid. Clumsy. Unsure. Out of place, and certain that no girl in St. Tammany would ever want anything to do with a kid out of St. Martin, on the Teche. He tried, too hard, and blew it. Thirteen stupid. The guys said she was like that, a flirt. But the look, the smile, the softness of her hand. The scent of her hair...

A moment of second chances. To Mandy's look of curiosity and encouragement, he said, "This is about the dress. You're still upset about the dress and now you're —"

"Absolutely."

"Been a while. A long while."

She laughed and waved him forward. "It's like riding a bike."

"With a flat tire."

She laughed again, freely and easily, unrestrained and unashamed, fire in her eyes. "Hah! You see, Tommy? We're not so different after all."

* * *

Tommy was just so adorable with that helpless look in his eyes. Garnished with a touch of panic.

He asked, "So you're going to teach me this? You're sure it's gonna work?"

"Absolutely. It had better. Because I have no Plan B."

"Well, okay, then." He grinned and joined a growing class of students, accepting the role of being an example. She walked them through the steps and moves of a culture that an hour earlier none of them had heard of. But they'd come to dance, itching to get out on the floor, and within minutes the tables and chairs were empty. With each new tune, she patiently exhibited the moves and after an hour and a half the floor began to thin out as older dancers began to slip away.

Tommy passed a tightly folded packet of currency to Mandy. "This oughta about cover it."

"It's the right thing to do, Tommy. Thanks for being a good sport. Where'd you guys go earlier?"

"Had to have a talk. Couple of issues, nothing we can't help with. Favor to Frannie."

Her shoulders drooped. "Please tell me we're not getting in—

volved in Frannie's love life. It's just too complicated and not a safe place to go." The crowd from the dance hall began to thin out while the band packed gear. "I'll just go pay the band. It was worth it, don't you think?"

"Absolutely."

She beamed a smile, turned and strolled toward the musicians, who welcomed her like family. And she returned with the shiny dance shoes that she returned after the performance was done.

Tommy said, "Can't quite give them up? Souvenir?"

"Nikki — well, Dominique — insisted that I should take them."

"That's nice."

Mandy glanced at Frannie, whose expression faded fast into serious when she read Mandy's expression. Then back to Tommy. "It was the oddest thing. I handed the cash to Louis, thinking he'd be very pleased that they could pack up and head home with a full wallet. But he almost blew it off, like it wasn't necessary, like he was bothered by something. And Nikki looked, well, kind of panicky."

"People react in funny ways, sometimes."

"Something's not right, Tommy."

Frannie had crossed her arms and nodded agreement. Chet cocked an eyebrow. A scrap of white in the right shoe. Mandy's fingertips entered and returned with a scrap of paper, a scribbled note.

"Help me. Please."

Turning her back to the band, Mandy passed to Tommy to read, then chose her most plaintive expression when they reconnected.

The faintest nod. The faintest smile. The twinkle in his bright blue eyes. And while his surface expression looked placid, he was probably already organizing something while he passed the note to Chet. Frannie leaned in for a peek.

Tommy said, "Maybe we could separate them somehow? Get everybody on the road but her, hold hold her on some kind of an immigration beef?"

Chet shook his head. "Thin to start with, buddy. Besides, they're Canadian and there's all kinds of conveniences that go with that. They can pretty much come and go as they please."

Frannie went to her toes to peer over Mandy's shoulder. "Well, whatever you're gonna do, you boys best do it quick. They're almost ready to go. And that gal Nikki's lookin' scairt as hen at a butcherin' party."

Tommy returned his gaze to Mandy, cocked an eyebrow and produced the grin he used just before he was about to do some-thing terribly unpredictable. "Plan B?"

"I just knew you'd turn this into a tit-for-tat. Just knew it."

Tommy turned to Chet and Frannie to explain. "She's still upset about the dress."

Chet nodded knowingly. Frannie was suppressing a chuckle.

Heat filled Mandy's cheeks. "I'm not, darn it. It was about Plan B, Tommy, about..." Like all those awful teenage moments of embarrassment, the impulse to politely flee for a moment to get collected, to reset. Powder the nose, check the makeup. Sanctuaries that guys never challenged.

A flash of inspiration. "No. Well, sort of. It's about re-strooms."

CHAPTER FOUR

Frannie laughed aloud. "Honey, about the *last* place you want to use in Billy's is the women's can. I'd drive back to town before—"

Tommy interrupted. "It might be a tight fit, but you'd be able to get some solid intel on what's going on, make some space we could work with, mostly time."

"Like the thing in Tel Aviv, with the Palestinian woman?"

"Yep. Chet and I'll can do a little blocking while you decide what to do."

Mandy said, "I get the sense that Louis is some sort of guardian or minder, but more than a leader. The kind of guy that can make a fuss. The others seem like regular musicians and shouldn't a problem."

"And Chet's conveniently with immigration. So he can squeeze and it won't seem out of place. Worst possible scenario is I can assure him that we'll get Nikki back to Montreal on a direct flight tomorrow. So yeah, go for it, adapt as needed, I'll catch up later."

Mandy nodded and turned to march toward the band. Nikki was trying to look calm, but the tension in her jaw gave her away and her eyes widened as Mandy casually strode forward. Louis noticed, too, and eased close to Nikki.

They were nearly touching when Mandy got near enough to display a warm smile and say, "Hi. Nikki, before you folks leave,

I just wanted to thank you again for the shoes. It was very sweet of you and I definitely promise to practice."

Louis's eyes narrowed. Maybe he didn't approve of her giving away shoes. Nikki flushed, looked up and said, "It was my pleasure. And, um, all of us are very grateful for, well, helping us tonight. *Merci.*"

Mandy nodded and turned to Louis. "And I just adored you and your group. I haven't heard those tunes in a very long time and it was such a delight. It's an excellent band, and I'm certain that you're quite successful."

He bowed and put on a stage smile. "*Merci beaucoup, mademoiselle.* You dance very well, and for us it was a great pleasure to entertain everyone tonight." He shrugged and extended his right hand. "But alas, the hour is late and now we must — "

Mandy shook hands, taking care not to rush the gesture. "Of course. I shouldn't hold you up much longer. Nikki, if you'd like to freshen up before you leave, the tavern has a really nice restroom just over — "

Louis interrupted. "I'm sure. But we — "

Nikki bit her lower lip. "Uncle Louis, I really could use..."

Louis loudly exhaled and raised his hands in submission. "Very well, but — "

Nikki looked down and murmured, "I won't be long. I promise."

Mandy stepped between them and gathered Nikki's right arm in her hand to guide her away, reaching for anything light in the way of conversation to cross the dance floor as if it were the most normal thing. "Nice big smile," she whispered to Nikki.

"I'm trying. But this is not so easy."

"Gets easier with every step. My father always told me, *steady, strong, serene.*"

"I think your father was very wise. But my knees feel like —"

They had taken more than a dozen steps. "Don't worry. Here come the guys. When we pass them, you'll be safe."

Nikki's smile stretched a bit further, but there was anxiety in her eyes. "They are two, and the band has — "

"My guys can handle it. Stay calm."

Tommy and Chet were within ten feet when Nikki said. "I can't. I have a son. In the van, probably asleep."

Plan B? How about C, D and F? Steady, strong, serene myself. "That's lovely. Is his father — "

"No. In Montreal. Louis is his brother-in-law and watches me. Mandy, this is too dangerous for me. My husband is a very powerful man..."

Mandy brightened when Tommy and Chet were close enough to speak in whispers. She looked back at Louis and the others. Watching intently. Louis gestured to the keyboard guy and he began to trail them. An escort. A guard.

"Tommy, Nikki's got a son traveling with them. I'm sorry, Nikki, I didn't catch his age."

"Just six years old. And he is the world to me..."

Tommy glanced at Chet, who nodded and pulled a portable radio from his belt, spoke a soft command, listened, and report-ed. "We'll have Kenny and Jamaal check on the boy's safety."

Ken Pollard. Chief of Police. Jamaal Emerson, a no-non-sense rookie patrolman who was bigger than Chet and Kenny's right hand man on the town force. Plan B was coming together better than expected. She spoke up, loud enough for witnesses to hear. "We're just on the way to the ladies room. Back in a flash, Tommy."

"Great. We're on our way to express our thanks to the band ourselves. Gotta show some of that small-town hospitality, you know."

Mandy beamed and pointed. "Louis Boulanger is the guy in charge. I'm sure he'd like to show off his passport, or whatever."

Chet nodded. "I'll be glad to check their documentation."

Nikki had found courage. "We'd better get going, Mandy, I really need to — "

Maybe she did. Or maybe it was a sense of resolve taking hold. Either way, a broad gesture to move ahead. "Ah, of course. Right this way." A few paces further. "Just stay relaxed, don't look back."

Nikki smile seemed terse as they encountered audience stragglers eager to say hello. "I'm trying. Hi... Hello... Oh, *merci*, thank you so much. You're so very kind. I'd love to chat but — "

Mandy interrupted. "It's been a lovely evening, but the band is eager to be going and — "

"Of course," one of the older women said as she leaned in and lowered her voice into confidentiality, "but, my dear, personally? If it were me I'd wait for the first gas station or mini-mart. Billy's facilities are..." she shrugged and seemed to struggle to find some way to say it politely.

Mandy said, "Exactly, Muriel."

Muriel retreated to a look of satisfaction, probably trying to organize a way to keep the conversation alive.

Enough. The hall was almost empty, and Louis was checking his watch as Tommy and Chet closed the gap to keep the band occupied. "Please excuse us, but — "

Muriel gave up. "Oh, yes. Of course. Don't mean to — "

Nikki smiled and began to move on. "Quite all right. Thank you for coming. *Bonsoir et merci encore.*"

Crossing the portal into the bar, Mandy began a census. Billy, who kept a bat under the bar and was rumored to have an unregistered pistol stashed near the register. Two old-timers she didn't know, lost in a drunken stupor and staring out into space. A couple of familiar faces, focused on a nightcap before trying to make it home before encountering a Breathalyzer. It would have been helpful if some of the hunting crowd had lingered, but luck was running thin. There was always the window above the toilet. If it had been opened sometime in the last ten years. If it was big enough to get through.

Nikki looked over her shoulder. "It's my only chance. If they take me back to Canada, my husband will never let me leave again. You can't imagine — "

Mandy pushed a sympathetic smile. "Don't worry. We'll fig—ure something out. How close is the van, your son?"

A rush of cool evening air raced across the floor. Kenny Pol—lard. And Jamaal, right behind. Hurried introductions, scamper—ing through a recap, the wait for sanctuary.

A squat man with a rounded belly pushing hard against a lot of black leather, Pollard studied Nikki while he shifted his cap higher onto his forehead and adjusted his glasses against the bridge of his nose. His skin seemed pale against the black uni—form, but his eyes said he was focused and all business. "Ma'm, that your boy in the van out there?"

"*Oui, oui.* He is very young, but — "

Pollard hoisted a hand to signal pause. "Awful young to be left alone in Billy's parking lot, this time of night, this kind of weather."

Nikki almost laughed. "Oh, I'm very sure he's all right — "

Mandy shook her head. "Kenny — "

"*Chief* Pollard, Miss Owens. This is a regular investigation, based on a complaint we got." He pointed toward the mike pinned to the left shoulder of his uniform. "We do things proper around these parts."

"Of course." Mandy cleared her throat and spoke louder and with emphasis on enunciation. "Just for the record, *Chief,* we have reason to believe that Mrs. — um..."

"Dominique Savage, officer. I'm very certain that if I depart with the others in the band, my life will be in great danger."

Jamaal had moved around the huddle to observe. And he leaned away to measure how many people were in the dance hall. The three fans came through the door and turned quickly to exit. Jamaal offered a pleasant smile and semi-salute. Chet and Tommy appeared to be involved in guy talk, but Louis kept looking at his watch.

Pollard cocked his head. "That so. You got any sort of pro—tection order or maybe you want to put in for one? But first, you from town or nearby?"

Mandy sighed impatience. "She's Canadian, Ken...er, Chief."

"From Canada?"

"*Oui, monsieur, Montreal. Quebec.*"

"Got some kind of identification?"

Nikki reached for where a bag should hang and wore a help—less expression when she looked up. "My bag. I left it with our equipment."

Pollard nodded. "Seems kind of strange. Most women, the first thing they'd take, if they were running, it'd be their purse. Isn't that right, Jamaal?"

Jamaal shrugged and glanced toward the women. "Seems logical."

Billy had drifted close to eavesdrop and would probably be a good option for an endorsement of innocence. The drunk guys paid no attention, and the lingering boozers struggled to pre—tend sobriety.

Mandy rolled her eyes. "It seems even more logical that if you're concerned about the unattended child in the van, you'd have someone — "

Pollard motioned her into silence again. "Already taken care of, Miss Owens. We're a small force, but we're professionals here."

Mandy looked into Nikki's anxious eyes. "Don't worry."

"But they think I'm neglecting my son. They think I'm some kind of monster!"

Pollard's voice remained even. "Now, let's just calm down. Probably some sort of misunderstanding. Maybe the boy got tired of the dance hall, wandered off to take a nap. Somewhere familiar. It happens."

Nikki said, "*Mais, oui. It must be so.*"

Pollard nodded and turned to Mandy. "Chet and Tommy?"

"Under control."

"Got things in hand?"

"That's not what I meant. *They're* under control. They're not going to hurt anybody."

"Ah. So. Well. Last thing we want's some sort of interna‐tional incident. Usually, I'd ask Jamaal to cuff our suspect, Mrs. Savage here, and get her comfortable in one of the units out front. But it seems to me that it'd be good to have both of us stroll on over to deal with the musicians. No need for trouble, ain't that right, Billy?"

Billy crossed his beefy arms over his chest and nodded. "Don't want no trouble, Chief."

Mandy looked at Billy's torso and was certain that the base‐ball bat was in his right hand.

Pollard rubbed his cheek with his fingertips. "Yeah. No trouble. So, Miss Owens, I want you to do me a real big favor and escort Mrs. Savage out to my patrol car, meet the matron, take a seat with her kid. That okay?"

It would have been more interesting to join what promised to be a confrontation, but it would have to do. "Of course."

Pollard shifted his attention to Nikki. "That okay with you? You won't be giving me any trouble, now, will you?"

"No, officer, no trouble. I promise. And thank — "

Pollard raised his hand again. "Let's not get quite that far, ma'm. Got a way to go with our investigation, here. Night's young. Now, if you ladies'd make your way to the units outside, Jamaal and I'll join Chet and Tommy and see what's what. We good?"

Mandy and Nikki nodded in unison.

Pollard seemed satisfied, even bemused. "Well, ladies, move along, then."

Mandy grasped Nikki's elbow to steer her toward the front door. As they were slipping out the line of of sight of Louis, the men in the band became alert. There was no backing away now.

"But, my coat, my bag..."

Mandy pushed harder. "We'll get them back for you. Right now, you have to think about your son."

"Mandy, please. I must know. Can I trust — "

Mandy put her shoulder into the heavy door to shove it open. "Oh, absolutely, Nikki. You have no idea how much."

CHAPTER FIVE

Tommy grinned his way into a deep Texas hill country drawl and extended his right hand. "Hello. I'm Tommy Kane, and this here's a buddy of mine, Chet Towers. We just wanted to thank y'all for some first-rate music tonight. Yessir, first rate. Ain't that so, Chet?"

Louis leaned left and right, trying to see past Tommy toward the hall entry. In the role of an eager clodhopper, Tommy mirrored the moves, just to annoy.

Louis' handshake was weak and his focus distracted. "Yes, yes, but of course. It was our pleasure." He turned to the keyboard guy and spoke in French, discussing directions to the ladies' room.

It was more difficult than expected to pretend he couldn't understand the debate about where Nikki had gone, or plan a blocking move when the keyboard guy offered to go have a look. So Tommy plowed into the conversation in the best of good ol' boy tradition. "Well, the gals sure enough thought it was darn good. They had themselves a great time." He eased to the right to block the path of the keyboard guy, trying for an end-around.

Chet came to the rescue. "That's true, something different. We don't get many Canadian bands in here, mostly because we're off the beaten track. You boys on a tour of some kind?"

Tommy and Chet closed the ring of a corral in the narrow space between crates of equipment. Louis and the others began shifting their weight, one foot to the other, like swamp critters do when a couple of gators slither in close.

Louis' voice took on a distinct edge of impatience. "Yes, yes. It has been most pleasant to visit your country. Now if you will excuse — "

Chet nodded in a defensive way. "Hey, partner, no need to hurry. The ladies'll be along soon enough. Hey, Tommy, I for-got to identify myself to these fellas." Louis' eyes ceased flitting back and forth and narrowed in concentration as Chet pulled an identification wallet from his pocket and flipped it open to dis-play badge and credentials. "I'm a customs and border patrol of-ficer with U-S Homeland Security. So it's probably a good idea, sir, for you to understand that anything you say — "

Tommy sighed. "No need to go getting all official here, Chet. These boys are just a road band, pretty decent one, on tour."

Chet picked up the cue. "All the same, Tommy, we've been getting some alerts on smuggling — drugs, legal and not — coming in from Ontario, so we're supposed to be on the lookout for vans and similar vehicles that might be hauling the stuff."

Louis relaxed and translated for the others. "But of course I understand, officer. However, we are not only from Quebec, Montreal to be exact, but we are also enroute home. This is our final appearance before we depart, eh?"

Others in the group nodded as if they guessed Louis' re-sponse.

"See, Chet? Nothin' to worry about."

Chet tucked his credentials back into his pocket. "Maybe so, but I believe you all have identification, passports, work visas, that sort of thing."

Louis tensed. "But we are Canadian. You must surely under-stand — "

Chet cocked an eyebrow. "You got a problem with I.D.?"

Louis shook his head in exasperation and began to look for his jacket, pausing when two uniformed police officers strolled toward them. His shoulders slumped.

Tommy glanced toward the new arrivals. "Hey, Kenny, Ja—maal."

Pollard said, "Evening, guys. This the band?"

Tommy said, "Sure is. And a nicer bunch of fellas you'd nev—er meet."

Jamaal hung back a couple of steps and to the left, his right hand parked on the butt of his service pistol.

Pollard spoke in a soft but direct tone. "That so? Gentle—men, I'm Ken Pollard, the police chief here in town, and this is Officer Emerson."

Louis spoke in a tone suggesting patience was wearing thin. "Very pleased to meet you, officer — "

"Chief. Chief Pollard."

" — Yes, of course. *Chief.* We were just explaining to these men that we are merely a band of musicians, and we are return—ing to Quebec. Nothing to be concerned about. So. If you'll par—don us, we'll load our equipment and be on our way."

Chet said, "Homeland had a BOLO out, drug smuggling, thought I'd ask."

Pollard cocked an eyebrow. "You got probable, Chet?"

"Nah, just a hunch."

Tommy brightened. "It's all right, Kenny. No need for any—body to get riled. Ol' Louis here and his boys have been decent about Chet just doing his job." He turned to Louis and added, "You know how it is, what with all the crime and you boys being out-of-towners and all."

Louis said, "Of course. A simple misunderstanding while we wait for my niece, Dominique, to return. And then we will be on our way and trouble you no further, eh?"

Pollard showed a thoughtful expression and scratched the back of his head, the way he always did when he was about to lay out a platter of bad news. "So you're the uncle?"

"*Mais oui*, Louis Boulanger. Is there some difficulty?"

Pollard nodded, almost apologetically. "Yeah, well, afraid so. You boys are free to go — unless Chet's got a solid probable cause to have a look at your truck and gear — but the young lady and the child will have to stay."

Louis sputtered, "But... but, why is that?"

Tommy went for phony astonishment, "Gee, Kenny, what could a folk dancer possibly have —"

Pollard raised a hand. "Well, first off, we got a complaint about a kid left in a locked van, alone, in a parking lot and when we responded we discovered a possible warrant on the mother. So until we —"

Louis waved his arms. Chet and Jamaal went on immediate alert. "This is ridiculous. I demand that Dominique be returned immediately."

Pollard cocked an eyebrow. "You ain't demanding nothing, sir. Now, like I said, you boys can load up, get on the road, go home. Or I can cite you all for obstruction, disorderly, whole raft of stuff, and you can spend the night in the county jail. Ar-raignment'll be in the morning."

Louis crossed his arms and other members of the band took half a step back.

"I wouldn't do that," Chet warned. "Keep your hands where we can see them, sir."

Tommy seized the opportunity and stepped in. "Now, now, no need for anyone to go gettin' excited. I'll just bet there's some sort of confusion about your niece and the child."

Louis thrust his chin out and lifted his head. "Do you have any idea who Dominique's husband is? He is very powerful —"

Pollard stayed calm, bordering on indifferent. "I can add threatening an officer to the charge sheet, sir."

Louis sighed and looked away to consider options.

"It's all right, Louis," Tommy said in a soothing tone. "Tell you what. You boys head on home, we'll clear this misunder-standing up, and I'll have Dominique flown back to Montreal as soon as I can. Pay for it myself. I know my gal Mandy give you a wad o'cash for your travel expenses, so maybe it'd be best if you all were on your way, let the dust settle and such."

Louis shook his head. "Impossible. We will travel together. I demand, er, strongly request that this be resolved just now. Per— haps if you let it go, then Dominique's husband will show some kindness, perhaps make a donation to a civic purpose or some— thing like that."

Chet shrugged and turned to Pollard. "Now that sounds like bribery."

Louis muttered in French, "This is insane." He turned and described the situation to others in the band, but they responded with an anxious shrug.

Tommy pressed the reassurance button. "Louis, it's a good deal. You got a thousand bucks and I bet Billy's got a fat ol' en— velope for you at the bar. I'd take it."

Louis grunted and pulled the wad of cash from his pocket, held out his hand and dropped it on the floor. "You keep your filthy American money. We have no need for it."

Chet took half a step forward, bringing him nearly nose-to- nose with the shorter and thinner Louis. "Tell you what, pal. You guys gas up that friggin' truck and get your ass on Interstate Eighty-One. And you stay on it all the way. Follow the signs to Collins Landing, head on through, go directly to Thousand Is— lands Bridge. And get out of my country. If you aren't on that bridge in five hours, my buddies at the border will bust you on so much shit that you'll wish you never left Montreal in the first place."

Tommy said, "Five hours? Hardly fair, Chet. I'd give 'em maybe five and a half, six. Back roads and all, before you get to eighty-one."

Louis seemed briefly perplexed, but must have picked up on the offer when his expression took on the look of appeal to Chet.

"Okay, then. Six. No more. Now, just one more thing. Does

the lady have anything personal here she'd need, purse, bag, anything?"

Louis turned to one of the band members, muttered something in French, and the musician located a large leather bag and handed it to Louis, who seemed to pause for a moment while his back was turned. At last he spun around and gave it to Tommy.

"Thanks, buddy."

The band leader pursed his lips, the muscles in his jaw so tight that they might snap at any second. He lowered his voice and his eyes narrowed into ice cold. "All of you? You can go to the hell."

Tommy chuckled and picked up the wad of currency from the floor. "*Mon ami, vous êtes déjà là.*"

Louis hissed, "You're a son of a bitch."

Tommy tidied the money, folded the wad in half, and handed it to Chet. "Yeah, I know. That's what they all say."

* * *

Twenty minutes later, Tommy and Chet could at last bring their cold hands together and close to their mouths to exhale warmth into chilled fingertips. Except for Jamal, who was well-equipped with police gloves, there was no longer need for male bravado.

The turn signal of Louis' van blinked at the parking lot exit. The truck made a right and headed north, out of town.

Jamal's radio crackled to life to report Chief Pollard was enroute back to town.

The officer grinned. "All of which means he's dropped the women and the boy off at your place, Tommy. Sure hope you know what you're doing."

Chet grunted. "More than you might realize, Jamal. Okay. I'm gonna get out of here. Freezing my ass off."

Tommy asked, "Frannie?"

"Coupla friends give her a lift. Better that way."

"I reckon."

Jamal checked his watch. "Okay, I think I'm going to head north a bit myself, make sure those guys actually do leave town. We're all good here? You're okay to drive?"

Tommy extended a hand. "Yep, just fine. Thanks for coming out, giving us a hand."

Jamal waved and opened the door to his patrol car. "Any-time, buddy. You guys take care."

Just as the patrol car crunched gravel and pulled away, Billy stepped out of the bar, no jacket and oblivious to the raw chill, an envelope in his hand.

Chet lowered his voice and spoke to Tommy. "About that thing — "

Tommy nodded assurance. "No worries. We'll get it fixed." He offered Chet a wad of cash.

"No thanks, man. It's not about the money, Tommy. I want those bastards fried."

"We'll do what we can. Meanwhile, this is yours. It's the wa-ger money on the dancing. Call it a tide-me-over, for right-away expenses. You helped win it."

"You sure?"

"Yeah, I'm sure."

Chet accepted the cash, stuffed it into his jacket pocket, gave a thumbs-up sign and stepped away. "Thanks, buddy. G'night Billy. Have a good one."

Billy waved at the huge figure strolling toward a pickup truck at the end of the lot, then turned his attention to Tommy. "Got somethin' for ya." He offered the envelope.

"What's this?"

"Well, first off, it's what I owed the band. That Frenchy bas-tard didn't want it, just stormed out. Maybe the lady and the kid could use it. Plus some of the guys tossed a little into the hat to kind help out."

Tommy chuckled. "Word's out, eh?"

"Geez, Tommy, maybe this ain't exactly the Puffin Diner, but you oughta know there ain't many secrets around here."

Tommy tucked the envelope into his pocket. "I'll see that they get it."

Billy nodded. "Good. I gotta go close up. Besides, what you doin' standing around in the goddamn cold? Go home, pal, go home."

CHAPTER SIX

Near Jacks Ford, Pennsylvania

The drive to the remote cabin had been quiet, somber, and uncertain. Ken Pollard, on his own and off the clock, pretended to be aloof. Maybe this was one of those small-town things best overlooked, maybe he was doing his best to avoid perjury, or maybe he didn't want to know if he'd crossed the boundaries from rescue to kidnapping.

So, he silently focused on the drive, taking great care on the lane into Tommy's place, probably to avoid any kind of accident that would require explanation for having a police car so distant from jurisdiction.

"You'll be okay?" he asked.

Mandy glanced at Nikki, who nodded while clinging to a sleeping child in her arms. "Yes. Thanks so much, Ken. I definitely owe you one."

"Nah. We're all square." He began to slide into the patrol car. "I better get back. Have a good night."

From the moment Pollard vanished into the darkness, Mandy discarded the personal comfort zone of English, reaching for the experience of her former days as an investigative reporter. Like working a source, making them feel as comfortable and confident as possible. It worked. Nikki's entire demeanor eased to the point where she mustered a brave-looking smile.

Overwhelmed by a barrage of conversational French with a

distinct Canadian accent, Mandy apologized for her own rusty linguistic skills. *A long way from the level you'd need with diplomats at the U.N., but it'll have to do.*

Nikki's smile warmed. "*Ne t'inquiète pas. Tu te débrouilles bien!*"

Mandy sighed. Who was comforting whom? No matter. The rust on syntax was dissipating and comfort shining through with each exchange as they climbed the several steps to the front porch. Mandy unlocked the door. What was at first a dialog de‐ manding concentration had settled into casual chat with all the old vocabulary pouring forth with astonishing ease.

They were *Québécois*, with Nikki sturdy under the load of a sleeping child and Mandy tamping down anxiety about unex‐ pectedly inviting someone with whom she'd just bonded into a house that had Tommy's imprint all over it. Recollection of how they'd left the cabin flickered through her mind. Had the dishes been put away? Was the kitchen as tidy as it should have been? Were the linens on the guest bed clean, and were there items of apparel lingering in the great room?

Nikki stepped across the threshold, looking eager to gather in the lifestyle but at the same time evidently weary from the long evening, the stress of the events and the weight of the child.

Mandy surveyed the kitchen. Not too bad after all. "Follow me to a guest bedroom. Your son looks totally exhausted. Must be so past his bedtime."

Nikki accepted Mandy's help unloading the child onto the bed, removing his shoes and tucking him in, barely a stir and still young enough to be totally at peace in slumber.

"We'll have to figure out some arrangements. I'm sure Tommy—"

Nikki beamed and shook her head. "This will be fine for both of us. I don't wish to put either of you to any trouble or discomfort."

It was too early in the relationship to be sure if it was a courtesy response or if Nikki was genuinely okay with it, so Mandy left it at, "Well, okay, if you're sure..."

Nikki leaned down to kiss the boy's forehead and retreated into the hallway that connected both ends of the building. With the door to the bedroom gently closed and secure, she turned to Mandy with brighter eyes but only momentary eye contact.

Mandy said, "I can put on some coffee..."

"No, no, that's quite all right."

"Something a bit stronger?"

Nikki's expression suggested a moment of contemplation and then, a firm, "Yes, why not?"

Mandy gestured toward the great room. "The bar is this way."

She watched Nikki's gaze flit from point to point, measuring, evaluating, taking it in. *Just the way I did, the morning after I arrived. Only now I'm the hostess. Sure hope I can remember how to start a fire.*

Nikki self-toured the room while Mandy went straight to a pair of Glencairn glasses and hoisted a bottle of 30-year-old Macallan single malt, the go-to-favorite on chilly evenings.

"Scotch? We have just about everything, including wine, but it's only fair to warn you that Tommy is very big on Pennsylvania wines and they may not—"

Nikki laughed, an anxious laugh, one of unease and uncertainty. "Scotch would be very nice, thank you. You have such a lovely home. It has a sense of sturdy dignity to it, rather like a sportsman's lodge..."

"Absolutely. It's really Tommy's lair, so it's got masculine stamped all over it, I'm afraid. Every once in a while I get thinking about touches I'd make, but then..." It was, in fact, Tommy's lair and the concept of co-dependency flashed through her mind. But Tommy wasn't that way, and probably would have been amenable to any suggestion on décor.

Nikki drifted near to accept the scotch. Her eyebrow rose.

"Then, what?"

"Well, you know, I actually like it just the way it is, the sense of him, rather like being *in* him. I guess that sounds silly. I should try my hand at getting that fireplace doing what it's supposed to do."

Nikki nodded. "Not silly at all. More like you are in love with him. He seems to be a very nice person, a good man. *Pardonnez-moi, mais je suis anxieux.*"

Grateful that her back was turned to mask an overwhelming sense of embarrassment, Mandy busied herself with bits of kindling and a box of long wooden matches. "I understand your anxiety. It must have been so difficult for you to do what you did, and here you are in a strange place with stranger people." Realization of her acceptance of Tommy's lifestyle nagged again. "Oh, gosh, I'm sorry, I didn't mean to imply that Tommy—"

"It's all right. And I am so happy that you not only came to my rescue, but have found something so wonderful and remarkable."

Which was true. But impossible to acknowledge without putting Nikki down for being caught in such a rotten relationship that she grasped at the first passing straw to escape. With consequences that were not good to think about. Or maybe Nikki hadn't weighed the alternatives and was flying on impulse. Or perhaps she had, and was that desperate. The first tentative flames illuminated her face and warmed it. *Success. Tommy will be impressed.* The trick now was not to get too far away, to feed the little blaze bit by bit, let it flourish and fill the room with comfort and the magic dancing yellow light that made so many memorable evenings. Good, happy times, the kind of memorable that almost put a damper on springtime.

Mandy waved her arm at the options of chairs that circled the hearth. "Please, sit wherever, relax. You're very safe here. Trust me on that. Outside of Tommy, Chief Pollard and I, no one will have any idea."

Nikki bit her lower lip and exhaled a sigh. She chose the overstuffed field of green tartan that was always Charlie's favorite when he was in town for trout or whatever other finny option presented itself at the lake a couple of hundred yards down the hill. Charlie's chair, close to the fireplace, where he could shamelessly park his boots on the coffee table and sip bourbon. Or coffee. But mostly bourbon.

The lake view and Charlie were absent. Charlie was bone fishing in the Bahamas with Sergei. The lake view? — it was late on a moonless night. So great room windows were a curtain of black, creating an envelope of privacy Mandy had come to cherish after New York City and, further back, the endless social whirl of Connecticut. More distant in faint memory, the simple charm of a little town in Quebec. The vivacity of a mother too early gone. When they returned to her roots from time to time, and immersed themselves in a *joie de vivre* so difficult to describe and even more difficult for many to understand.

Now, with the first serious quartered logs on the fire, heat oozed across the floor. Mandy refreshed drinks before settling into her own favorite corner of a sofa, the one usually shared with Tommy, who really did understand *joie de vivre*, even if he acquired it from totally different circumstances. She resisted the urge to speak of the pride and comfort she felt, to spare the feelings of a guest snared in the opposite end of the spectrum. Trust would have to come in baby steps. Tommy would have to earn his own.

For several minutes, they gazed at the fire in silence to allow the events of the evening to calm.

When they exchanged a smile, Mandy said, "So. Your son. He's six?"

Nikki brightened. "Yes. Cyrus became six a couple of months ago."

"An unusual name, Cyrus."

Nikki nodded. "Cole demanded it. I had just given birth, and was trying to decide which of my relatives to honor by sharing the name. But Cole insisted on Cyrus, and often calls him 'Cy.' Many people think it's because it's so similar to the company, CySafe, but that's not why. I'm certain of it."

"He never told you why?"

"No. Just that he had his reasons, and that was that. I guess whatever name I might have come up with wouldn't be very good anyway." She paused to look up, a hint of defiance in her expression. "But I was both hurt and puzzled at once, but he had a phone call and then a meeting he had to go to, and the topic was closed. I discovered two days later that he'd ordered the name on the birth certificate even before telling me."

"Wow."

Nikki shrugged and looked down again. "A name is just a name, Mandy. But it was then I realized that Cole was going to be absolutely in charge, completely control my life, the way he does with the company."

Fury ripped through Mandy's mind. *Seen this before, the ultra-alpha males, charming their way into total control. A neighbor, and a friend, and that high end prostitute, the one whose name escapes me...*

Mandy took a breath to remain calm, professional, try to make a difference. "That's so sad. Could you share what you mean by his corporate control?"

Nikki's expression was a curious mix of melancholy and defi-ance at once, a distant look in her eyes, as if she was somewhere beyond caring. But not quite. There was a flutter of impatience, uncertainty.

Mandy leaned forward. "Please, speak freely."

Nikki's eyes rose. "*Merci.* Um, please, um, do not think me, well, impertinent..."

"Not at all. I'm your friend."

"It's just that..."

"Go on."

Nikki looked away, paused for several seconds, and then her

gaze returned. "I... I... Well, I am wondering at this moment if I have not made a mistake, that I shouldn't have involved you and Tommy... Perhaps it would be better if I just, well, returned somehow and try to make it better."

Seen this before, too. More than once, even with college friends. Mandy leaned further forward to focus her attention on Nikki. "Well, of course you can, if you wish. I wouldn't want to cause you any harm."

"*Merci beaucoup.* I'm sorry. I am just now so confused. I only know what people say about my husband's business. He doesn't tell me anything." She paused again, looked away, then came back. "Please. What would you do in such a situation?"

Mandy smiled. "Continue to be brave. My father would al—ways remind me, whenever I was scared or anxious or nervous, to be brave. He would always remind me, *steady, strong, serene.*"

Nikki nodded. "A wise man, your father."

"Yes. He was. I honor his memory by leaning on his wis—dom."

"*Je comprends.* And, then, please tell me, what professions are you? Surely you must have a career, a position somewhere."

Mandy nodded. "It's rather difficult to explain. We, well, sort of help people when we can."

"You are solicitors, lawyers?"

"No, not at all, but please believe me that we can help you."

"And Tommy, he is—"

"Rather like a modern Robin Hood."

Her eyes widened. "As in the storybook character?"

"Yes. And he's very good at it."

Nikki seemed bemused. "And you are — what was she called?"

"Maid Marian?" But which version? The chick, the hand—maiden, the pampered princess, the warrior?

"Ah, *oui.*"

Mandy laughed. It didn't matter what anyone thought.

"More or less, I'm afraid. Tommy and I are partners..."

"I see. Please don't misunderstand, Mandy. I'm very isolated from family, friends." Her voice softened and she looked down in shame. "Even the people in the band. And now they are gone." She took a breath and looked up and into Mandy's eyes. "Please. I must know for certain. Can I really trust Tommy? After Cole and then Uncle Louis —"

So easy to wear a gentle, relaxed, confident smile. "Tommy? Oh, yes. Absolutely. We're quite close. And I can assure you..."

A gust of cool air swept across the floor. The kitchen door, creaked open and closed firmly, the way a guy arrives. Nikki was momentarily startled.

Mandy chuckled. "And speaking of the prince of thieves, *that* will be Tommy."

CHAPTER SEVEN

Nikki abandoned a relaxed posture to sit rigidly upright on the front edge of the chair. As Tommy burst into the room, she was on the verge of standing before taking a cue from Mandy to remain seated.

He rubbed his hands together to dispose of nighttime chill, his smile wall-to-wall and bright blue eyes sparkly in the dancing light from the fire.

A potent blend of joy, lust, and possessiveness heated Mandy's cheeks, unabashed and unapologetic. She struggled to keep a straight face while she mimicked a gooey southern drawl. "Well, well, look what the cat dragged in. Been out there honky-tonkin' again, you cute ol' rascal?"

Codependent? More like keeping up.

"That I have, for true. Yes'm, for true." He raised his arm and displayed Nikki's bag. "I believe this is yours?"

She beamed as she clutched it tight. "Oh! *Merci, merci beau−coup!*"

Tommy continued to play along. He aimed his outstretched arms toward the fireplace and feigned surprise at the crackling blaze. "Well, now. Looky here. All right, all right," he drawled, a relaxed look of approval in his eyes. "Half past twelve, toasty fire and two lovely ladies. What more can an ol' boy ask for? And ex−pertly done, too. A regular girl scout."

Mandy chuckled. "Yep. All fluffed up with pride and eager to tell my tale. But if you'd rather go first, I'm sure Nikki wouldn't mind."

The warmth had the desired effect on Nikki, who picked up on the game and waved her hands. "Oh, absolutely. Mister Robin Hood gets to go first."

"Somebody been bandying around that name again?" He turned to Mandy. "Tsk... will some people *ever* change?" And then back to Nikki. "You're doing okay? And your boy?"

"I'm good. And grateful. Thank you. My son is asleep in the guest bedroom."

Mandy said, "His name's Cyrus, Tommy. And he's just so precious. He truly deserves to be with his mother."

Nikki was leaning forward, her posture a good sign. Comfortable, relaxed, looking like she felt secure. "*Oui*, he sleeps. *Merci*, Tommy for your kindness in giving us shelter." She glanced at Mandy and seemed to sense her place by settling back, a distancing kind of move toward the edge of the stage.

Tommy continued to smile at Nikki. "I just bet he is. Likely takes after his mother." Nikki blushed. "My, my, is that scotch I see?"

Mandy rolled her eyes, plucked the bottle from the coffee table and waved it in the air. "We've saved you some, well, a little anyway, but you'll have to bring your own glass. Pour yourself a scotch, big guy, and set a spell."

"No problem," he said in the sort of cordial tone that went with a party just getting under way.

Mandy offered the bottle. "And if you'd like nibbles, you're definitely on your own. We're on a strict diet of alcohol and conversation."

He chuckled, splashed whisky in the glass, and plopped down on the sofa just beyond Mandy's curled up legs. "After that dinner at Billy's I'm not entirely sure I want to eat anything more tonight. But the stage is yours, so go for it. I'll just set here real quiet and sip whisky."

And he kept his promise, listening patiently while she recounted their escape from the bar.

"...So instead of trying to drive your ratty old truck, we bumped into Ken and Jamal on their way into the bar, called in a favor and Ken let us get into his patrol car. He gave us a lift home while you guys made sure Louis and the others were on the road. I mean, the escape thing was gorgeous, Tommy. Scary and perfect all at once."

Tommy always seemed to know the right moments to ladle out praise. "Nice call. Ken's a good man. A toast's in order."

Nikki raised her glass in salute while Mandy poured another drink for Tommy and offered it to invite a clink of glassware.

Mandy's eyes sparkled. "So, c'mon, Tommy, don't keep us in suspense. How did it go?"

Tommy's storytelling tone went for casual, routine, no big deal. He used a poker to stab at the burning logs while relating the events in the dance hall. After returning the tool to its rack, he rubbed his hands together near the hearth and said, "...So I handed the wager money to Chet, who first waved it off, but I said it was tide-me-over and he was okay with that."

Nikki asked, "*Excusez-moi*, I don't understand. What is this wager money?"

"We had a bet going about whether I could get the people at the dance to participate. Our friend, Chet—"

"The very large man?"

Tommy explained. "Yes. He's a bit down on his luck at the moment, so I decided to help him out."

Nikki's nod was enthusiastic. "That's very nice of you."

Tommy tugged the envelope from his pocket. "And because Louis left in a huff — didn't want our filthy money — Billy gave it to me to pass along to you. There's extra because he passed the hat at the bar."

Nikki protested as he placed the envelope in her hand, "Oh, no, no. I can't possibly accept."

Mandy waved off her protest. "But you *must* take it. You've come in with just the clothes on your back, no resources at all. Trust me, we've both been there, done that, and every little bit helps." Satisfied, she turned to Tommy and gave his glass of Macallan an extra splash. "Perfect! And you? You get extra for doing the right thing."

Tommy answered with his enigmatic Cheshire Cat smile.

Nikki studied the contents of the envelope. "This is so funny. I mean, the last thing Uncle Louis needs is travel money. Please, let me explain. I am married to a very successful businessman. My uncle is — how do you say...*oui*, opposite, and the folk band would never survive without my husband's financial support. My husband, he tries to buy my happiness because he knows it is the one thing I love to do most, to dance."

Mandy let the sip of scotch linger for a moment on her tongue before releasing it to a larger sense of comfort.

Tommy said, "Well, you're certainly a good dancer. I understand why your husband supports the band, but not clear about why you need to escape."

Mandy turned and glared. "Gosh, Tommy, don't you recognize abuse when you see it?"

Nikki came to the rescue. "A perfectly fair question. Permit me to explain, please. You see, my husband is the sort of man who is accustomed to getting everything he wants and controlling everything he has."

Mandy nodded. "So many men are." A glance at Tommy. "Well, present company excluded."

Nikki continued. "At first, it was such a fairy tale. He the shining knight in white armor, me, just a country girl with a simple life. At first, it was a bit frightening. I was unsure. But soon, I was so swept up in the romance of it all that it was not so very long before we were married. Only later did I discover that he had seen me somewhere and literally bought his way into my life, by giving many luxurious gifts to all those around me, who could influence me. So things are not always as they seem."

Mandy gently probed. "And after you were married?"

"He decided everything, where we lived, how we lived, what I wore, what people we would socialize with. My entire former life, my friends, my family, ignored, discarded. It was so very sad. Terrible."

Mandy murmured. "I can hardly imagine. And so what hap— pened?"

"I tell my husband how miserable I am, and of course he gives me a very long lecture on how good I have it now, not to worry about such things, he is the husband, the person in charge. But of course that is what he is in business, and so he is accustomed to getting his way."

Mandy turned to Tommy. "So? What can we do? What about some sort of immigration, or a protection-from-abuse or— der?"

He shrugged. "Tough to make the case for a green card be— cause she's Canadian."

Mandy nodded. "How about a PFA? I know the local judge is out of town, but surely the district magistrate can issue a tem— porary PFA. Nikki, did the abuse ever become physical or threatening?"

Nikki's head shake was firmly negative. "No, not really."

Tommy asked, "Was there any time you felt your life... No? I see." He turned to Mandy. "Which is exactly why it's going to be tough to get a judge to go along. Still —"

Nikki interrupted. "No. I am sorry, but there must be no scandal. Not even a little bit. It would go very badly for me. My husband is a very powerful businessman and could easily influ— ence an American court. But if I return to Montreal, I will have no chance at all. His permission for me to dance would be done, for good, and Cyrus would never be allowed out of the country again."

Tommy asked, "What business is he in?"

Nikki seemed astonished at the question. "Why, CySafe, of

course. He is *the* Coleman Savage, one of the wealthiest entrepreneurs in Canada. And the U.S., too." Mandy and Tommy
exchanged glances of ignorance and Nikki explained. "CySafe is
one of the world's leading software companies in the internet security field. Perhaps the most famous. They have offices everywhere, an enormous corporation."

Mandy winced. "Oh, of course, I should have realized...
You'll have to forgive me, but if Mister Savage is so controlling,
and surely he must realize you're unhappy, then why would he
allow you to travel?"

Tommy's eyebrows rose. He'd sensed a red flag, too, but
while she was eager to dismiss it and find a rationale, he'd probably stick it in a back pocket and putter with it later.

Nikki explained. "He has an arrangement with Louis. Uncle
Louis, the minder. I am allowed to dance, but I must not run
away. You see, my son must remain with his father — "

Tommy grasped it. "And if you leave, you never see your
child again?"

"Exactly so. You understand! Thank you!"

Tommy swirled the last of the scotch in his glass. "But this
time..."

"*Oui.* Cole must attend a conference in Europe and our tour
itinerary is already arranged, here in the U.S. Uncle Louis
promised my husband to keep a close watch, to ensure our return."

Mandy leaned back. "So that explains it. You're on the way
home, your band picks up one last booking, I just happen to get
involved—"

It was Nikki's turn to lean close, to touch the hand, to smile.
"But of course. And I am eternally grateful! And I loved the way
you dance."

"I haven't had the chance for quite a while. It was *so* much
fun. I hope you weren't embarrassed."

"No, no, not at all." She fell silent, pensive and then her

voice went soft. "It was a good moment, *oui?* For just a brief time, we entertained and everyone was dancing and happy. I know the other dancers enjoyed it so much. But now? They probably hate me. With good cause, I'm certain."

"I'm so sorry," Mandy said. "But you know, you did the right thing. It's done, you're with friends, you're safe. I'm sure we can figure out something."

Nikki shook her head. "You don't understand Cole. He is re−lentless. He will send men to find me. He will never stop look−ing. I fear that I won't ever be able to perform again."

Tommy shrugged. "Maybe we can help with that."

"*Merci*, Tommy. Mandy here has spoken very highly of you."

Tommy chuckled. "Yeah, well, she's no slouch, herself. But getting back to your predicament..."

Mandy fought the instinct to squirm in feigned embarrass−ment, and went for a leadership posture instead. To win Nikki's trust, she'd have to not play second fiddle to Tommy, but missed a cue to speak up. The conversation went sideways.

The last of Tommy's scotch vanished into his throat and it was too late to pour another. "I suppose a regular old divorce is out of the question?"

Nikki's smile withered. "Cole would never consider it."

"Tommy, we just have to do something."

"Got a Plan B, do you?" With a simple gesture of his hands, he handed the lead role to Mandy and encouraged her to take it.

Oh, perfect. Tommy would participate because that's what Tommy always did. But mostly he was going to give her the helm. A break from troubleshooting had come to an end. It was going to be another team project. And it was going to take some planning. But maybe Tommy would be willing to offer some quiet advice on the side and be comfortable in the second chair.

Charlie would growl, but come around. Sergei would be en−thusiastic if it came with a chance to damage something. Lucy would support Tommy without question.

But he was correct when he teased her. There would defi—
nitely have to be a Plan B. Nikki's eyes, and and expression of
hopefulness. Tommy's eyes, and that cute little grin. He proba—
bly already had an idea, but... And then one of her own arrived.

She turned to Nikki. "Have you ever been to the Bahamas?"

CHAPTER EIGHT

Great Exuma International Airport, The Bahamas

Tommy thought the child was a bit small for six, tending to-ward the frail and pale of city kids who grew up pampered and soft, then got the big chairs in the corporate board rooms and ran the world. And now the kid stood silent in new duds picked out by Karen, the magical steward and den mother of Tommy's corporate jet.

Pale blue shorts, red sneaks, a bright blue T-shirt with some sort of funny picture on it, maybe a size too big, the sort of col-ors a group of women would pick out if they wanted to pretend to be a boy. Not terrible or silly. Just not properly badass, like the guys used to wear while roaming the Teche.

So little Cyrus looked down at his new costume and then up, an expression of uncertainty, hopefulness, maybe just a twinge of embarrassed.

Tommy didn't have a vote in it either. But he was the only other guy in the cabin of the Gulfstream, creeping off Runway Twelve and into a narrow taxiway. And he got the hint.

He said to Cyrus, "It'll do, for temporary, anyway. It's really warm outside and you'd sweat like crazy in the clothes you boarded in."

The boy nodded.

"No worries, buddy. We'll get you some gear *you'd* like in a day or so, once we get where we're going. Ever been in the Bahamas before? No? It's not half-bad."

The boy's attention returned to his mother and as he leaned harder into her leg, a comforting arm wrapped his shoulder. Nikki might have been the go-to mom, but Mandy and Karen were working hard to spread maternalism around. And thick.

Tommy put on a patient smile and bent down to peer through the window as the jet made a second sharp left turn. The ladies had better get in their best mommy licks now, because even though they might be headed toward Mandy's place, there'd be a collection of machismo.

The Gulfstream entered an asphalt corral stuffed with single engine craft in a neat row at Odyssey Aviation, tucked off in a corner of the airport never visited by commercial passengers. A marshaller directed N226TK to a stop and Karen unfurled the stairway to the tarmac.

Cyrus separated himself from Nikki and lingered just long enough to reach out and grab Tommy's hand.

Tommy nodded and cocked an eyebrow. "C'mon, let's catch us a nice little ride over to a spot where we can find us a hotshot helicopter pilot name of Frisco."

Cyrus beamed and together they descended ten steps to where the ladies watched while bidding farewell to Karen.

A pair of extended golf carts zoomed forward to collect the four passengers while three ground guys transferred luggage from the jet. Fifty yards to the left of the yellow aviation services building, a pure white JetRanger awaited, the pilot doing a preflight walkaround. As the little caravan closed the gap, the boy's grip on Tommy's hand tightened.

Tommy said, "Ever fly in a helicopter? No? Well, that fellow yonder is Frisco, and I'm willing to bet at least a quarter that he'll let you ride right up front. You okay with that?"

Cyrus shook his head, uncertainty in his eyes.

"Yeah, I would be, too. But trust me. Frisco is a first-rate pi—lot and it'll be good. C'mon. Let's go say hello."

From Nikki, a smile of approval. From Mandy, a shake of the head and roll of the eyes. "The guy thing, right?"

"Well, yeah, sure. Of course. That okay with you, Cyrus?"

Cyrus shrugged.

Tommy said to Mandy, "Well, there you go." He turned to Cyrus. "And later you'll get to — "

Mandy interrupted. "— have a *really* nice bowl of ice cream." She shot a glare at Tommy. "There's just no need —"

No, probably not. Best save mention of Charlie and Sergei for later.

A wiry man with a deep tan, untamed blond hair thinning away from the brow and wall-to-wall sunglasses strode forward.

"Hey, Frisco, where y'at?"

"Doin' fine, Tommy. Just fine."

They exchanged grins and handshake.

"Lookin' real good, buddy. Real good."

"Hey, Tommy. Who we got here?"

"This here's my little buddy, Cyrus, who's visiting with us for a few days with his mom, Nikki Savage."

Frisco grinned even more and squatted to shake Cyrus' hand. "Pleased to meet you. Any pal of Tommy's is a friend of mine." The women approached and Frisco stood. "Hey, Mandy, real nice to be flying with you again."

Mandy beamed. "Likewise. Gee, Frisco, how do you manage to stay so young-looking?"

"Life is good, Mandy, real good. Four years, six months and thirteen days."

"Outstanding! Frisco, you've already met Cyrus. This is his mom, Nikki Savage."

"Pleased, ma'm. Let me check to make sure your gear is se—cure and then we'll be on our way."

Tommy offered to help, but Cyrus held fast and Frisco

waved him off. Frisco *was* looking good. Four years, six months and thirteen days clean of all the demons that trailed him from battlefields in Iraq and Afghanistan through a pair of military hospitals and life under a California freeway bridge. Somehow he'd connected with Charlie and a second chance after Lucy hired him for short hops on a Bell JetRanger she'd picked up somewhere. It was only a million-three, she said. But Frisco fell in love with the chopper and it gave him new life and purpose.

Now he was cool, charming, bronze and all kind of suave.

Frisco called out. "Looks like we're ready. Hey, Cyrus, you want to ride up front? Best view."

The boy looked to Tommy, who replied with a wink and a nod.

"Awright," Frisco declared to Cyrus. "Let's get you buckled up — don't want you falling out, now — and get a headset on so we can talk as we go."

The boy turned, smiling for the first time. *Give'm a thumbs up.* Plus the nod and expression of assured approval.

Passengers flinched at the sharp beeps from the battery switch and the sequence of clicks and clacks that preceded the low growl of startup. And then the winding rush of a jet engine and the rising whir of rotor blades on the steady runup to full power. Frisco tugged a tan glove onto his right hand to grip the cyclic and used his left to dance across an array of switches above, all the while giving Cyrus a running monologue of the checklist through the headsets.

"Okay, buddy, we're good to go." The first nudge into a hover.

After a slow drift forward and an exchange with the tower, Frisco turned the aircraft in a complete circle, checking for clearance, and then grass and pavement raced past and away in the steady ascent into flight.

In a few minutes the helicopter was over water, about every shade of turquoise imaginable. Lighter in the bays and across the

sandbars, darkest where the Caribbean settled in to serious busi—
ness of being a sea. And sparkly, the reflections of sunshine scat—
tering like diamonds across countless little waves.

Mandy and Nikki were seated together and combatted the
noise with a communal silence, leaving Tommy to his own
thoughts.

Frisco was taking the helicopter the long way around, a little
further off the string of the Exuma chain than necessary. No sur—
prise. As a pilot, he might have been a little shaggy around the
edges, but he also knew how to lift Mandy's heart.

Yep, a long, gentle banking turn to the right and there it
was, shimmering in the cheery light, perched at the top of a low
hill of fuzzy olive green. A sprawling building in white and pale
yellow.

Tommy no longer needed to admire the view below. He
peeked to the left.

Nikki was leaning forward, eyes gobbling up detail of every—
thing in three directions, a gasp at the concept of paradise. *"In—
croyable, tout simplement incroyable."*

Mandy's satisfied smile settled on a point halfway between
mirth and smug. It was the same expression she used every time
she caught sight of her place in the sun, perched high above a
sweeping pure-white beach, one of several that came with an is—
land presented by Walter Campos as a gesture of gratitude.

"*S'il vous plaît.* What is this island named?"

In the headset they heard Frisco's chuckle. "That'll be
Mandy Caye, ma'm."

Nikki's eyes widened and a smile bloomed on her jaw. "Real—
ly? The same as your name?" And then the realization began to
set in. *"Oh mon Dieu.* It is *your* island, and that must be your
house. It is so, so very..."

Tommy laughed. "...So much work to clean. Six bedrooms
and a whole mess of bathrooms, big ol' kitchen, dining, lots of
spaces to loaf, plus the deck, the tower, and that there, Cyrus, is

a genuine freshwater swimming pool. Comes with thirteen beaches, caretaker's cottage, usual accessories."

Just beyond and behind oversized sunglasses, Mandy's expression was serene.

Frisco made a low pass, banked left and slowed to approach the airstrip south of the house. He might be on the payroll managed by Lucy, but he knew how to please the boss.

Ten minutes later, Tommy tugged the last of the bags from the chopper and repeated an invitation for Frisco to join them for dinner.

"Thanks, buddy, but I gotta get back for a flight north to round up some guys on a fishing trip. Lucy's keeping me pretty well booked, which I'm not complaining about. Like to stay busy, and nothing better than being in the air. Next time, maybe. Hey, Cyrus, nice flying with ya. You take care, okay?"

And with that they all stepped back as the doors closed and the engine throttled up.

The walk to the house was less than a quarter mile up a sand road, but ended after just a couple of paces when a stream of epithets tumbled down the hillside.

Mandy sighed. "Okay, Nikki, don't be scared. That's just part of the crew." She turned to Tommy and cocked an eyebrow. "I wasn't expecting Charlie and Serge to be picking us up. They're usually out fishing, aren't they?"

Tommy shrugged. "Awful nice of the fellas to skip and meet us instead."

A golf cart careened through a curve and raced toward them.

"Goddammit Sergei, slow down! You'll flip the sonofabitch for sure!"

While Nikki's eyes widened, Mandy cocked her head and narrowed her eyes. "Yes. Isn't it? Frisco couldn't possibly have..."

The golf cart fishtailed through another exchange of profanity.

Cyrus peered out from behind the safety of his mother's right hip.

Tommy said, "Not to worry, Cyrus. The gent with the 'stashe is an old cowboy and the big guy gives new meaning to the word 'badass'."

Mandy slowly shook her head. "...But I'll bet Cesar might have radioed ahead if someone *asked* him to."

Tommy shrugged and then stepped to the side to wave as the golf cart skidded to a stop.

The passenger growled. "God damn Russian..."

Mandy bowed her head and muttered. "Ukrainian."

Nikki said, "Sorry, but I don't—"

Tommy called out. "Ukrainian, Charlie. *Ukrainian.*"

Mandy sighed and said to Nikki, "Never mind. It's not im–portant. The angry one is Charlie Burke. The big one is Sergei Yenchenko, a legend in his own mind. Charlie is self-reliant, no-nonsense, mostly grumpy. Serge is fearless, egotistical, a genuine soldier. And a notorious lecher."

Charlie eased out of the vehicle and hobbled three steps away. "Yeah, well, I don't give a hoot in hell whether he's Ukrainian or Lithuanian or Romanian or whatever other god–damn country they got in Europe. He don't drive worth a shit."

Yenchenko glared. "We are at bottom of hill, *da?* Cart does not roll over. You are alive still. *For next few moment, perhaps.*"

Tommy stepped into the war zone. "Nice seeing you boys, too. Now put on some proper manners and come say hello to our guests."

Heads turned. Tommy leaned close to Sergei and whispered, "Proper manners, Serge. Keep it under control. No drooling, okay?"

Yenchenko grinned and very softly said, "But she is nice morsel, eh? Who is small boy?"

"Her son."

Sergei cocked an eyebrow. "She is married?"

"Yes."

"A pity. But perhaps she is not so —"

Charlie snorted. "Mind your manners, you Commie son of a bitch. Ladies and children present."

Tommy looked toward Mandy, standing a few feet away with crossed arms. A gesture of helplessness was met with a forced smile that said she was running low on sympathy and maybe the best thing to do would be to get up to the house and a calmer sense of gentility.

Tommy said, "Okay, guys, I'd like you to meet *Mrs.* Nikki Savage, who is Mandy's guest and her son, Cyrus, who's six and probably just a bit overwhelmed by the situation. Probably could do with a big ol' bowl of ice cream, isn't that right, Cyrus?"

The boy answered with a bashful nod.

Charlie studied the child. "Don't talk much, does he?"

Yenchenko laughed. "Small boy is perhaps most afraid of strange old man who speak like drunken sailor."

"You know, Tommy, one day I'm gonna get me a twelve gauge and perforate this noisy old bastard..."

Yenchenko grunted.

Mandy interrupted. "Tell you what. Let's load the bags on the cart and Nikki and Cyrus and I will drive up to the house, and you three can spend the rest of the day down here trying to kill each other. Or you can walk up and maybe, just maybe, we'll let you in."

Tommy, Charlie and Sergei exchanged glances.

Yenchenko clapped his hands together. "Is good. We make short walk for cold drink, hear story, make good lies, *da?*"

Tommy nodded. "Works for me. Charlie?"

Charlie scowled. "Yeah, well, I'm good with it." He waggled a forefinger in Yenchenko's direction. "But so help me, I swear to God...."

Tommy patted him on the shoulder. "Yeah, I know, buddy. I know, I know."

CHAPTER NINE

Mandy Cay, The Bahamas

Mandy's eyes scanned the rooms. The house was more than empty. It was amazingly clean, everything in neat, shiny, polished, unwrinkled perfection. It could have been a set for luxury furnishing interiors, the kind of house nobody has, because nobody ever lived there.

Amid effusive compliments from Nikki, just a half dozen steps inside the door, melancholy fluttered through Mandy's mind.

Lucy really had moved on.

Mandy turned to Nikki. "Please, make yourself comfortable. All the guest rooms are to the left, each with its own bath. Pick whatever one you wish. Kitchen's over there, lots of places to sit, inside, on the deck, and the view from the observation tower is amazing."

Nikki's eyes gathered the personality of the space, just as she had done at the cabin, while Cyrus seemed to be focused on the sweeping panorama beyond the walls of glass, the constant delightful afternoons of the southern Exumas.

"I'll show you to the guest wing, where you can freshen up, and then I'll see what we've got for drinks and nibbles. Don't worry, Cyrus, I haven't forgotten about ice cream."

As they went, Mandy searched for any remnant of Lucy. A

forgotten hairbrush, scrap of paper, an imprint left by a shipping carton on the carpet. Nothing. After leaving Nikki and Cyrus to settle, she made a closer inspection on the return path. Not a whisper that any person had ever been in the house.

Until the kitchen counter. A plain white business envelope with her name on it and a cellphone for a paperweight. She rolled the phone over in her hand. Ordinary, the kind you could get anywhere. But of course, it wasn't. She laid the phone to the side and opened the envelope. A smile briefly formed on Mandy's jaw as she unfolded the note and read it.

Thank you so very much for your hospitality. It was time to get my own place, a nice one, on the beach. Dad joined me in Providenciales. Had the place professionally cleaned, hope everything is where you'd want it. Use phone to connect when you can. See you soon. L.

With a soft sigh, Mandy folded the paper and closed her eyes, misting as much out of joy for Lucy as for the loss of a house guest. Lucy, who would have been welcomed as permanent, had always said it was for a little while, until things settled, until her own emotions were sorted out, until she got issues out of her system.

Provo. A couple of hundred miles, southeast. With Bug. She'd made peace with her father at last and now... For a moment, Mandy laughed. Those two, teamed up. Now *that* was a scary thought.

But then the melancholy of the empty nest returned and she sniffed twice while reaching for a tissue.

Tommy's soft voice arrived from behind her. "You okay?"

Mandy nodded and passed the note.

He cocked an eyebrow, read it, and said, "A good thing."

"Yes. It is. I'm very happy for her. She didn't say a word about moving out when we were in Argentina."

"That's Lucy. All business, hardly anything personal. The guys say she did it a week ago, brought in a cleaning service. The crew that sets up houses for video ads, I guess."

"The place is just spotless, Tommy. I mean, almost *too* perfect."

He nodded. "Anyway, the guys said she called earlier today
to have them stock the fridge. Local fare."

"Which is why they didn't spend the day fishing. No wonder
Charlie was growly. Only hurricanes keep him off the water."

"For true. I can organize some sort of dinner. Where's our
guests?"

"Getting settled. We'll have to get them some clothes, es-
sentials."

"Tomorrow."

She turned to survey the kitchen. Lucy had it rebuilt after
Mandy mentioned that it wasn't yet feeling like her home, and
described her mother's kitchen from a warm memory. Lucy,
Charlie and Sergei had the work done as a surprise and now it
was time to emotionally claim it. "Yes. Tomorrow. Have the
guys calmed down?"

Tommy nodded. "Yeah. You know how it is. Two big roost-
ers and one small coop. They're good. Dinner for six?"

Mandy dabbed her eyes with the tissue. "Yes. That's fine. I'm
okay. A little tired maybe, but nothing an evening here won't
cure."

* * *

They took their meal in light evening air on a broad deck
that wrapped around almost the entire house and overlooked a
small freshwater pool just below. Beyond the observation tower,
the narrow dock lunged out into the pale blue water, punctuated
at the end by a cabana, all of which was aimed at a searing ball of
orange that promised a spectacular sunset.

Tommy had spared no effort on an elaborate feast organized
around guava, rock lobsters and a conch salad. But it starred

generous portions of grouper that Charlie and Serge had caught six miles offshore, supplemented by johnny cake and mounds of pigeon peas cooked with rice, tomatoes, onions, salt pork, and spices.

Sergei took charge of guiding Cyrus through the complicated meal and made an elaborate show of presenting a guava and coconut duff that he prepared with an intensity and flourish that Mandy half expected would drive Tommy crazy in the kitchen they shared.

Nikki and Mandy freely ladled out applause and praise, although the chardonnay from the States did not wear a favorite label.

The sun delivered the anticipated show at day's end. Charlie and Tommy cleared the dishes and came back with French brandy and Barbados rum and set up conversational shop in a nest of deck chairs twenty feet away.

Nikki returned from guiding a yawning six-year-old to a bed and repeated her story to the group. Ever the suspicious retired U.S. marshal, Charlie poked and prodded for clarification on several points, but it was obvious he was testing for inconsistencies. Evidently satisfied, he allowed the conversation to drift into the casual lore of the island and the lifestyle surrounding it.

When glasses emptied for the final time, Nikki excused herself for the evening. All three men stood to bid her a good night.

Charlie remained on his feet. "Well now, I believe I'm gonna fetch me a proper sippin' whiskey. Serge, you want some of that potato water?"

Yenchenko grunted. "*Da, da.* Is good plan. And for you, Koshka?"

Tommy grinned and waved him off. "I'm good. Mandy?"

"Not for me, thanks. I've had enough." More than enough, actually. When Charlie went on a bourbon roundup, a challenging discussion would soon occupy the corral of his experience in law enforcement, and he had more red flags in his holster than anyone else on the team. She stole a glance at Tommy, whose placid smile suggested she'd be very much on her own. Which was the way she wanted it.

Charlie set up his glass and the bottle on the deck railing and then used it like a bar. Shelf space and something to lean on. Yenchenko ignored the glass riding the neck of the vodka and drank directly from the bottle.

As was his habit, Charlie tugged the rimless glasses from his nose and inspected them for the dust or grease that was never there, then returned them to his face, and used the thumb and forefinger of his right hand to tidy his thick brush mustache.

Mandy discreetly inhaled a fortifying and calming breath and she was grateful for the puff of an offshore breeze that billowed her hair.

Charlie took a sip of bourbon, parked the glass back on the railing with care and crossed his arms. "Well, now, Tommy. We seem to got us an interesting situation. Yessir. Real interesting. I thought we wasn't gonna get involved in any domestic stuff."

Tommy leaned back in his chair. "You should be directing your comments to Mandy. Her op."

Heads turned. Not so long ago, she would have looked for a crack in the floor in which to hide. Today she surprised even herself by sitting up and a bit forward in chair, ready at a mo-ment's notice to be on her feet, toe-to-toe with Charlie.

Mandy opted for a disarming, pleasant, but firm, smile and a direct gaze into Charlie's squinting eyes.

He blinked. "That so?"

"That's right, Charlie." The urge to stand was strong, but she crossed her legs instead and kept her hands on the arms of the chair. "And I think we should help Nikki."

Charlie turned to Tommy. "You good with this?"

"Absolutely."

"And you both know that you're walking into a minefield of 'he-said-she-said' and this could turn real quick into a kidnap beef."

Mandy's gaze remained steady. "Absolutely."

Charlie sighed. "You're both out of your god damn minds."

In unison, they replied, "Absolutely."

Charlie appealed to Yenchenko, whose expression remained bemused between belts of hundred proof vodka, right from the bottle. "C'mon, Serge, bring these two back to reality."

Yenchenko shrugged. "Wolf may be old, perhaps little bit slow, but — " He tapped the side of his nose " — there is scent of something more. And perhaps it is good for Mandy to take turn at helm. We all get chance, yes? Is democratic way."

Charlie scowled. "Humph. Last time you was in favor of democracy, you was the only one without a loaded gun."

Tommy began to speak, but Mandy raised her hand to cut him off and focused on the ex-marshal. "In or out, Charlie?"

"Well *in* o'course. Somebody's gotta carry common sense in their saddlebag. Probably oughta take a break from the boat, anyways, just so's we don't run out of fish in the damn ocean."

Mandy leaned forward and parked her forearms on her knees, hands clasped together. "Actually, you can fish all you want. Little Cyrus would probably love to learn how, and I'd really like if you'd stay close. Protecting witnesses used to be your specialty. You're probably the most qualified person here for the task."

Yenchenko was tapping the end of his nose with a fingertip, looking intrigued but separating himself from the fray.

Nothing quite like a rising sense of confidence, especially with these three. She said, "And because Charlie makes a good point about how this could turn out to be a giant headache, I'd like to find out what's going on for ourselves. If it is just a squabble, maybe we can mediate to a positive solution. If it's more, then we can go on to other alternatives."

Tommy said, "Yeah, I got the sense that either way, Nikki's husband will show up looking for her."

"Exactly, Tommy. Which is why you and Serge should go back up to Jack's Ford, see what's going on. I don't mind Ken Pollard and even Chet Towers for backup, but I'd just as soon have you guys out front." She paused. "Um, if that's okay?"

Yenchenko waved the empty bottle in the air. "*Da, da.* Of course. Old wolf must hunt with pack to remain fit."

Tommy chuckled. "Speaking of Chet — "

Mandy nodded. "Exactly. Which is one of the reasons we're flying down to Provo tomorrow to say hello. Are there any questions?"

Yenchenko and Charlie exchanged shrugs and decided it was a good time to head down the path toward the caretaker's house they shared.

For several minutes Tommy and Mandy sat in silence in the soft light coming from the living room just on the other side of the glass wall.

Satisfied they were alone, she bit her lower lip. "Did I come off too strong? They're probably —"

He said, "No. I didn't think too strong. Well, not *too* strong. Strong, though."

She leaned back and looked at the sky. "Yes. I came off too strong."

"I liked the part where you said, 'In or out, Charlie.' That was pretty good. Got their attention."

"I practiced that line, you know. I was saving it up for tonight."

"I didn't know. But it was a strong line."

"I knew it. I was too strong."

"With those guys, strong is good."

She sighed. "But it's not going to work with Lucy, is it?"

"No. Probably not."

"How will I know?"

"Well, Mandy, if you work it just right, she'll probably say 'yeah, sure.' And if you don't, she'll tell you to go to hell."

"Gosh, thanks."

"It's strong advice. But not *too* strong."

"And if I blow it?"

Tommy chuckled. "Well, you could have a Plan B. But those things do reduce the incentive for a good Plan A."

"Seriously?"

"Yeah, sure. Everybody says so. No Plan B is kind of like walking a tightrope, a hundred feet in the air, without a net. You make darn sure you don't lose your balance."

"Kind of like slogging through a mucky field in the pouring rain?"

He brightened. "There ya go."

"Uh-huh. Would you mind terribly if I *don't* mark these words of wisdom down in a notebook?"

He shrugged. "Not at all."

CHAPTER TEN

Leeward Highway, Providenciales, The Bahamas

Lucy Tramanian leaned forward at a conference table just large enough to accommodate three chairs, one of which was occupied by Mandy Owens.

Her eyes were bright, eager, cheerful, and she wore a smile to match. Since they'd last talked at Mandy Caye, she'd discarded beach bum casual for upscale professional, wore her hair in a sophisticated style and had decorated an office in a cross between Manhattan and Grand Cayman.

"So I bet you think you came on too strong with the guys, right?"

Mandy nodded.

Lucy laughed. "Okay, so here's the thing. There is no such thing as too strong with those guys. Tommy's okay, but Charlie and Serge can be *so* intimidating. Charlie has that glare — yeah, you know what I mean — and Sergei? You'd have to climb a ladder to stare him right in the eye. I once wanted so bad to poke him in the chest, but the best I could do? Well, it would have been kinda embarrassing."

The conjured image was hilarious, and both women enjoyed a hearty laugh.

"So Tommy said that if I came on too strong, you'd tell me to go to hell."

The coffee pot gurgled to the end of its brew cycle and Lucy rose to find a pair of mugs. "He's right. Well, I mean, if *he* comes on too strong I *do* tell him to go to hell, but that doesn't apply to you." She filled oversized mugs with coffee and opened the door of a cabinet fridge.

"Still taking extra cream?"

Mandy considered the likely potency of the brew and nodded.

"Well, I think it's great that he's giving you the point on this one. You know Tommy. Jumps right in, flies by the seat of his pants, makes it up as he goes. Never a thought about alternatives."

"Exactly. I was more than annoyed about no Plan B in Corrientes. The dress was a mess."

"The David Aire? With the neat swirl at the —"

"Yep. Ruined. But I wasn't in much of a position to say much after ruining the phone."

Lucy laughed. "Dad'll get over it. Especially when Tommy hands him five grand for the damages. Which Tommy will do, and without complaining." She took a sip of coffee, but this time there were no awful doughnuts in the other hand. She'd remade herself for the third time that Mandy knew of, and looked more polished and confident than ever. When they first met, she'd been billed as everyone's favorite kid sister. Now she was a financial force to be reckoned with and building yet another empire.

"So here's the thing. I'm a smart person, Mandy. Almost as smart as you — no, don't protest, it's true — and we're both more than capable of running a casual op. I mean, consider the scale of what we've got, between banking, investments, now getting into air services... But you know what? If we're strong, then we're bitchy. If guys are strong, they're admired."

Mandy sipped her coffee. "The way it is. Unfair, sure. But reality. So we just focus on the job, do our best, let it go."

Lucy cocked an eyebrow. "Me? I'd rather kick some ass. I did my retreat thing, spent a lot of time walking the beaches at your place, finally decided I was just hiding out from myself. So I went to New York to put some finality to my relationship with dad."

"How'd that go?"

"I was expecting ugly. You know how he is. Instead, I found a broken down old man on the skids. I did strong, Mandy. Now he works for me. His business was a disaster, fading fast, and he wanted to retire. I bought a house with him, can you believe?"

Mandy shook her head. "Talk about a one-eighty."

"Yeah, no kidding. He drove the real estate people nuts, but we were looking for more than a house. A house on the beach you can find anywhere," she said with a wave of her hand, "but this, this was what we needed."

"It looks like it was once a hotel."

"It was. Colonial genteel, just a few dozen rooms, lobby, oth−er space. But a first-class electrical system with way more air conditioning than was ever needed. Until now of course."

"Mainframe?"

"Yep. Dad got us solid connectivity, a Class C I-P block with satellite uplink. I can run the bank in Cayman from here, along with TKA Air, dabble a bit in the markets." She lowered her voice and filled it with pride. "And Nyx is back."

Nyx. The goddess of night, the handle Lucy used while in−stilling fear in computer networks around the globe. Her screen signature, the panther with the glowering eyes. The mask she was wearing when fate brought her and Tommy together. Yenchenko might be a legend in his own mind, but Nyx was the real deal. "Does Tommy know?"

Just as she shrugged, a tiny red light on the wall began to blink in methodical pulses.

Of course. The button on the lobby desk with the little sign that said "Press for service." The very one she'd tentatively touched when she arrived in the foyer of an unobtrusive office building identified only by a little plaque to the right of the door. TKA

Management Services Ltd. The lobby was intended to look like it was routinely staffed, but probably never was. She had waited for several uncertain minutes until Lucy appeared to greet her and guide her to an interior elevator, then up to the third floor and the inner sanctum of an enterprise revived in the wake of stealing a fortune from five megalomaniac business executives.

Mandy said, "Probably Tommy. I sent him on a shopping er—rand for our, um, client."

Lucy lifted a remote, and a monitor on the wall came to life. Tommy stood for a moment and then paced back and forth. He gripped several shopping bags in his left hand, but the labels weren't visible.

"Looks like mission accomplished. Oh. Before I forget, Lucy, I have to ask. Whose idea was it to renovate the kitchen at Mandy Caye?"

Lucy smiled. "Well, mine, actually. But I checked with Tom—my because it was supposed to be a surprise and he was good with it. Is that okay?"

Mandy watched Tommy drift around the lobby and twice resist the temptation to press the call button again. "Oh, yes. I really was surprised. I had just sort of casually mentioned my mom's..." Realization set in. "But *of course*. Getting a look at what it was like and how to at least suggest it would have been child's play for Nyx."

Lucy's cheeks reddened and she shrugged.

Mandy said, "Thank you. It meant a great deal to me."

"No, thank *you* for letting me crash there for a while. I was a mess, a total wreck. Charlie and Serge were like surrogate fa—thers and came up with those dozens of crates of books, so I got the whole business of just loafing with some reading off my bucket list."

Mandy laughed. "You're too young to have a bucket list. Not even thirty."

Lucy pressed a pair of buttons of her own and what must

have been an alert sound caught Tommy's attention. He went to what was probably a locked door that had released and was now ajar. "Yeah, well, you can never start too early with a bucket list in the business we're in. But anyway, Mandy, I'm so very grateful for your hospitality. It was the perfect therapy."

Tommy disappeared through the door and Lucy switched the monitor to the surveillance camera in the miniscule corridor where the elevator door magically opened. He looked around, spotted the camera and waved.

Lucy sighed. "Charlie would have covered his face and Sergei would have shot the camera to pieces. Tommy waves. Go figure."

Mandy basked in a deep, warm pool of pride. "Yes. That's Tommy, all right."

Lucy chuckled. "Yeah. No Plan B. We'll have to organize one for your op, just to annoy him."

Another alert from a service button, this one audible. The outer office, with all the signs of an absent secretary. A secretary that never existed.

"That's a door and a lock that nobody's ever gonna bust through," Lucy flatly declared. "Not like that suite on Wall Street. Never again."

Mandy nodded understanding while Lucy stood and crossed the room to unlock the entry with a mechanical device reminis–cent of a bank vault door. Life's lessons. You get burned, you learn to wear gloves.

She locked it again after admitting him.

"Hey, Tommy. Looks like you've been doing a little shop–ping." Lucy took half a step back to appraise him. "Like the haircut. Is that sort of a retro scruffy look?"

Tommy sighed and turned to Mandy. "See what I put up with?"

Mandy laughed. "Lessons in humility are challenging to some."

Lucy waved a directional arm. "C'mon, Tommy. Grab a seat, I'll fetch you a coffee. Good stuff, out of Honduras. Right, Mandy?"

Right, if you like it incredibly strong, bitter, and are into overdoses of caffeine. "Absolutely."

Lucy shrugged. "Sorry, no pastries. I've reformed. Well, just a little. And selectively. What's in the bags?"

Tommy parked the bags on the floor next to the open chair at the table while Lucy poured coffee and refilled Mandy's cup before she had a chance to protest.

"Clothes for a six-year-old boy, something a guy might wear."

Lucy nodded. "Ah, so the client is a kid?"

Mandy said, "And his mother."

Returning to her seat, Lucy sipped and sighed satisfaction. "So, Mandy, tell me more." She remained focused on Mandy for another repetition of the events in the past couple of days, punctuating the presentation with nods and polite exclamations. When Mandy finished the story, Lucy said, "Okay, so you're cool with the concept that domestic issues can get really tricky, right?"

Mandy nodded. "I am. I just get this sense that there's something more." She looked toward Tommy, cocking an eyebrow. "And so did Serge."

Tommy said, "I agree. So Mandy wants us to look into it."

Thank you. Mandy turned her gaze to Lucy.

"Oh, absolutely, guys. I mean, what's the worst that can happen? We get our hands a little dirty, walk away. So, Mandy, who's the husband?"

"Some sort of businessman, I gather prominent, by the name of Savage."

Lucy's eyes widened. "*Coleman* Savage?"

"Yes. Why?"

The look of astonishment withered into a chuckle. "Wow,

you sure can pick 'em. Cole Savage is the CEO of a multinational company called CySafe. They specialize in network security,
dabble in software engineering and development, and there's
hardly a personal computer in the world that doesn't have some
influence by their work. Savage is the darling of the tech world,
a big time player, and quite the philanthropist, too. Runs a big
foundation oriented to helping Third World poor. Very big on
kids, women's rights, health. Lot of money sloshing around."

Mandy nodded. "So I'm getting this nagging sense..."

Lucy leaned forward and touched the back of Mandy's hand
to offer reassurance. "Oh, no, not at all. It's the guys who make a
big show of that stuff that can be the worst on the home front.
It's definitely worth a look. I'll be glad to help."

Tommy spoke. "Sounds like a challenge, being on the frontline of internet security."

"Absolutely, Tommy. CySafe is only ten times tougher to
crack than the NSA, CIA, DoD and half the agencies in Europe
all rolled into one. Nobody's ever done it that I know of."

Mandy could not avoid a sigh of disappointment.

Lucy remained focused on Mandy and a sly smile crept
across her jaw. "Which, of course, doesn't mean it *can't* be
done."

Tommy said, "There's also one more thing."

"There always is with you, Tommy. So, okay, tell me."

"A guy who helped us out was a victim of a phishing scam.
Lost fourteen grand."

Lucy's jaw visibly tensed. "My favorite cause. Okay, gimme
the details and consider it done. Your friend will get his money
back, plus a dividend, and some nasties are gonna be hurting
when it's over."

Mandy said, "Nyx is evidently back, Tommy."

Tommy grinned. "Nyx never left."

CHAPTER ELEVEN

Near Jacks Ford, Pennsylvania

Tommy was glued to his chair and lost in an imaginary con-versation. *You say you sit in a bar all day long, eating and drinking as much as you want, just in case somebody shows up?*

Yeah, that's about it.

Jeez. I'd kill to get a job like that.

Billy delivered another of the house specials. Burger in a bas-ket, hold the gravy on the fries, coffee black. The imaginary dia-log in Tommy's mind dissipated. *No you wouldn't.*

Billy wiped his hands on his apron, leaving enough grease stains to qualify for an EPA inspection. But not the Board of Health. They knew better than to show up at Billy's. "You want ketchup for them fries? I mean, the local guys go for gravy, but city people are into ketchup."

"Is that a fact?"

"Well, yeah. Everybody knows that. Maybe you're tryin' to disguise yourself as a city person, visiting or some shit."

Tommy thought about it for a moment. "No, actually I was trying to project the image of one of those Old West gun-slingers, just waiting for the punk rival to show up so I could drill 'em with three or four rounds from my trusty forty-four six-shooter."

Billy stared for a moment. "Yeah? Naw. You ain't gonna have no shootout in my place." A pause. "Are ya?" Another pause. "Nah, you're just givin' me some shit. No need for that, Tommy. You know what?"

"What?"

"You're fuckin' bored, that's what. Your ass's been in that chair for a day and a half, almost two, and they ain't showed. Be–cause they ain't gonna show. I know it, and you know it, and that's just the plain boring fact."

"You think?"

"Yeah, pal. I think. Okay, the tab is still on the house because I owe you for that thing with the guy and all, but this goes on much longer and I'm gonna have to pull the plug and start marking it."

Tommy grunted. "Hate when that happens. First class meal like this? Shoot, your bar might go under if you keep giving it away like that."

Billy scowled. "Don't be givin' me no shit, Tommy."

Tommy leaned forward and lowered his voice. "Okay, Billy, back to the bar. Four suits from out of town just came in. Your six o'clock."

One guy looked like an accountant, maybe a lawyer, confi–dent stride like he was a higher-up and team honcho. To the rear, a thin, shorter guy, probably the driver. And in between, two middle-aged guys in suits a bit snug in the chest. Muscle that the lawyer-accountant type could call upon to make a point by bending pennies or crushing ballpoint pens.

Billy gestured toward the platter he'd just delivered. "Want me to clear the food?"

"No. Leave it. They're going to the bar. You might want to put in a call to Ken Pollard."

Billy rubbed his nose with the back of his hand. "Figure you're gonna need an extra hand or two?"

"No. More like keeping Sergei from getting carried away."

Billy nodded and retreated to his usual post, made a call, and turned his attention to the new arrivals.

The driver-type hung back. He had nothing but what looked like a strong craving for a cigarette, an itch he couldn't scratch. He kept patting his shirt pocket to make sure it was still there, all the while rolling a lighter around in his left hand. He would not be a problem.

The lawyer-accountant guy sported a tailored suit, fifty-dollar haircut, two-hundred dollar shoes, an expensive-looking attache case, probably didn't pack a piece, but was loaded with swagger. Lawyer maybe, but not a CEO type. Either Savage was waiting in the car outside or he sent the flunky squad. The lawyer-type did the talking to Billy.

The two muscle guys stood around trying to look tough in a room full of guys who just came off hard hat job sites and didn't really care who got in the way of a swinging fist. Six-one, maybe six-two, got in some gym time, both working hard to keep the jacket closed to hide the shoulder holsters, wraparound shades even thought the room was dim. And they were probably recent graduates of Tough Guy Sneer School. Ex-military or wannabe, with the parade-rest bit and hands behind their jackets rather than in front. Tommy guessed Yenchenko would go for the slightly taller guy with the skinhead look. He had the most hardware under the jacket. The other guy, flattop hair cut and only one weapon within easy reach, would be Chet's target.

Billy dried a glass with a bar towel and nodded his head to direct the lawyer guy to Tommy's table. The tough guys tagged along behind to form the classic entourage that VIPs organize for themselves. They pulled up a few steps away and went for the intimidation circle tactic, but spread themselves too thin and ignored their backs.

The lawyer guy pulled a business card from his shirt pocket and introduced himself. "Mister Kane? Good. My name is Michael Barnett." He had a lot of teeth, like a shark has a lot of teeth. "I'm an assistant to Mister Coleman Savage, and an attorney."

Well, surprise, surprise.

Barnett pointed to the empty chair opposite Tommy. "May I?"

"By all means." Tommy watched him park the case on the table and leave a gaping hole in the perimeter that neither of the tough guys attempted to fill.

"May I come straight to the point, sir? Mister Savage be—lieves in directness." He pointed to the ignored meal. "Sorry to interrupt your meal."

Tommy adopted an attitude of indifference and felt a tug of guilt that the unwanted burger and fries were cooling on the ta—ble to an even further point of unpalatability. "I'll bet you are. Okay, I'm listening."

Barnett's smile became forced. "I understand you may have some information to share on the whereabouts of Dominique Savage, the spouse of Coleman Savage."

"Actually, no."

"Curious. I must be misinformed. I was advised by Mr. Louis Boulanger that you were a participant in a recent confrontation during which Mrs. Savage may have been separated and possibly kidnapped from a folk dance group that performed here."

Tommy nodded. "Oh, yeah, come to think of it... But no, afraid I can't help you."

"You don't know where she is?"

"I meant that I wouldn't share it with you."

Barnett leaned back, steepled his fingers and tapped them lightly on his lips. "I see. You probably realize that Mister Sav—age is a prominent businessman, and perhaps suspect that those who interfere with his private life tend to become involved in complicated situations."

"Is that a fact?"

"Yessir. I'm afraid it is. But rural folk such as you and your friends likely don't appreciate the gravity of the situation."

Tommy toyed with a french fry. It was cold. "Yeah. Kidnap—

ping's a pretty serious charge. Maybe we ought to call the local cops and let them look into it."

Barnett leaned back shifted to a patronizing smile. "Well, Mister Kane, there's no need for creating a public situation, is there?"

Tommy cocked an eyebrow and leaned forward. "Mrs. Savage do this sort of thing often? Run off, I mean?"

"I assure you Mr. and Mrs. Savage have a warm and loving relationship."

Tommy said, "Oh, that's good. I was getting the sense that she didn't care for the hubby very much. I hear it happens sometimes, with the big dog, with a lotta bark. 'Course, she mighta been one of them trophy wives, you know, arm candy with not too much between the ears, if you know what I mean."

Barnett pulled forward again and resting his arms on the table, his smile as icy as the look in his eyes. "And sometimes little people get involved in the wrong way. Mrs. Savage has some personal issues that make her, well, vulnerable."

"Under a doctor's care? Shrink maybe?"

"I don't think that's a matter of your concern. But, as I said, Mister Kane, we believe in being direct and candid. We want the woman — and the boy — back, without any publicity, and quickly."

Tommy resisted the urge to take a big bite from the hamburger and chew it noisily. "Odd that ol' Mister Savage didn't show up himself."

"Mister Savage is a very busy man, sir. He has many, many capable people to manage assignments on his behalf."

Tommy chuckled. "So Mrs. Savage is not only a little nutso, but just an errand for you guys, too, eh?"

The smile evaporated. Barnett reached for his case. "Very well, then, Mister Kane. Because I understand you're closely involved with this and may be able to assist us, we're prepared to offer you something of a financial incentive." He snapped the

latches to the case, and opened it, blocking the line of sight be—
tween the two tough guys and Tommy's gun hand.

Barnett opened his palms to signal he wasn't about to try a
threatening move, slowly reached into the case and withdrew an
envelope, which he held aloft.

"An incentive?"

"Yes, Mister Kane. How about, say, five *thousand* dollars."

Tommy laughed. "You're joking."

"Very well, then, let's make it —"

Tommy wore a grin of amusement and motioned to Billy.
"Let me buy you guys a round. Cold beer? They got a good
draft here..."

Barnett glared as the tough guys took half a step forward.
"Twenty thousand. Take it or, uh, face the consequences."

Tommy sighed while Chet put a gun to the head of the driv—
er and backed him out of the room. Yenchenko stepped in, a
twelve-gauge pump looking like a child's toy in his hand. For a
huge man, he could move in near silence, a trait that kept him
on top of the situation in Central American guerrilla warfare.

Tough guy number one began to turn, only to be clobbered
by the butt of the weapon and go down with a yowl. The second
man turned to find the business end of the shotgun nearly
touching the end of his nose.

Barnett leapt to his feet as if to protest.

Sergei waggled a finger of warning. "*Sadis', pridurok.*"

Tommy unfurled a small calibre throwaway pistol from a rag
in his pocket and slipped it into Barnett's case. "He's not a mo—
ron, Sergei. He's a lawyer."

"What is difference, Koshka?"

"Exactly." Tommy stood and stepped around the table.
From the doorway, Chet Towers closed in fast, drawing his pis—
tol as he charged across the floor. "I know, I know, you've always
wanted to kill a lawyer. But not today, all right? Michael, I'd take
my friend's advice and sit down." Barnett obeyed. "Good boy.

There you go."

Yenchenko peeked. "There is gun in case, Koshka."

Barnett's eyes widened and while his mouth opened and closed, no sound came from it.

Tommy feigned astonishment. "Well, my, my, my. So there is. Let's just move this briefcase out of harm's way, okay?"

"That...that's not... I don't own..."

Tommy sighed. "Lawyers. Always messin' with the truth. Never could trust what they had to say."

Chet said, "I seen it right off, Tommy. Won't take a minute to find out if it's registered. 'Course, if it isn't, this guy's in a world of hurt."

Ken Pollard and a young patrolman arrived and Pollard called on Yenchenko to stand down. They both drew weapons.

"You have suspect?" Sergei asked Pollard.

"Yeah, yeah, I got 'em. Cuff 'em, Dave."

Sergei backed down and handed over his weapon. Dave disarmed the two tough guys and took possession of the weapon in the briefcase.

Barnett launched a protest. "I am an attorney, officer, and we've been assaulted and threatened by these people. I am a Canadian national and insist that the consulate be contacted. I demand they be taken into custody and I'll be glad to press charges."

Pollard sighed. "One thing at a time, sir. Let's get some identification going and then we can sort this out at the station. But I gotta tell you, Mister Lawyer, that — just for openers -- I'm looking for concealed carry permits on three handguns and if you fellas can't produce 'em, you're probably facing some serious charges, no matter where you're from. Now. We got a little custom in this country called Miranda rights, so if you'll be patient for a second, I'll read them to all three of you at the same time, okay?"

Barnett seethed. "And what of these men? Threats, intimidation, assault...."

Pollard remained unflustered. "Well, I tell ya. Chet here is with Customs and Immigration, so he's got the power of arrest. And the way I hear it from a couple of witnesses, you come in here to threaten one of our local people and a friend come to his rescue."

Barnett muttered an obscenity.

Pollard turned to Sergei and Tommy. "You guys best head on out of here. Best way to defuse a situation in a bar is to get everyone on their way, all right?"

"Fine by me," Tommy said. "I was just trying to get some lunch here and..."

"Yeah, I know, pal."

Sergei spoke up. "And I come to bar to have drink with my friends, but now we are sent away."

Pollard shook his head. "High price of coming in for a cou−ple of shots with a loaded twelve gauge pump."

"It is for hunting only."

Pollard sighed. "Not the way it's been modified. C'mon Sergei, it's a friggin' riot gun."

Tommy chuckled. "Yeah, but it's real good for squirrels and such."

"Go home, Tommy. Party's over."

CHAPTER TWELVE

Trudeau International Airport, Montréal, Quebec

Tommy and Sergei declined an invitation to wait in the Sky−service private lounge, preferring the open space of the main lobby of the fixed base operator. Aircraft arrived and departed on Runway 24L, just beyond the taxiway and the nearly vacant apron.

Tommy settled into a light gray boxy armchair while Yenchenko's body consumed much of a darker vinyl sofa next to it and within reach of a flock of complimentary magazines from the varied charter services that arrived and departed at the airy and spacious facility.

Sergei stretched out, hands clasped behind his head, and studied the bright, high ceiling as if an in−flight film would mag−ically appear if he stared long enough.

Tommy said, "Okay. So what's on your mind?"

He grunted. "In old day, we make our way to target, orga−nize effective frontal assault, capture target, take what we wish and make depart. Now we travel like thief, like small mouse afraid of light."

Tommy shrugged. "Her op, her plan."

"*Da, Da, konechno.*"

"But...?"

Yenchenko shifted his weight. "Sergei is good soldier, obey order. But we are comrades, eh? And so perhaps I am permitted to say it is small amount difficult for me."

"It's not a bad plan."

"But dangerous for woman, I think. We make confrontation at bar, and all goes well. But now they are like foxes, wait for us to come, perhaps with trap."

"She did well in Argentina, and before that, the thing in the Balkans."

Yenchenko fell silent for several moments. "We are two old wolf, Koshka. Not weak. Wise. We have hunt many time, have good instinct, make quick adjustment. Mandy is very brave, very strong. But yet she is woman, and we must think of her safety. Perhaps become small distraction. Small distraction make big in-terference with focus in field."

Tommy chuckled. "So deep down, you're just an old fash-ioned guy. This isn't a combat zone, Serge. Times have changed. It's all suits and ties and high tech. All we're doing is a simple breaking and entering, a little burglary, a little intel gathering. Leaving a calling card."

Sergei scowled and shrugged his way into retreat. "Of course. What could possibly go wrong?"

An attractive and well-groomed redhead approached from the sedate reception desk about twenty feet away. She wore a conservative navy suit, a cheery smile and the demeanor of someone who understood the whims of the very well-to-do. Customer service with grace and style. "Mister Kane?"

Tommy displayed an easy smile to click into character.

"I'm so sorry to interrupt, but I just wanted to let you know that your party will be arriving in just a few minutes. They're on final, and the pilot has been directed to taxi directly here. May I have the valet get your car?"

Tommy brushed away an imaginary wrinkle in his shirt. "Thank you. Sergei, be a good fellow and meet the valet outside, would you? Miss Owens does not like to be kept waiting."

* * *

Yenchenko accepted the keys from the valet and tipped too generously, but forgivably. Unaccustomed to flamboyance, he had a tendency to overdo it. But the valet didn't complain.

Together they watched N226TK float down on a gentle approach and roar past, right on time. Cesar picked up the first taxiway and swung the Gulfstream around onto a long taxiway parallel to the runway, turning at last into the apron and guided by a marshaller guided the jet to within a few dozen yards of where they stood.

The steps unfurled and Karen descended, as if to test their stability, waiting at the bottom. Just a little pause. Mandy's entrance. Somewhere between a movie star and a princess, chin high and looking serene despite being bundled for the chill, her eyes dim behind designer sunglasses.

Yenchenko sighed. "You are most fortunate man, Koshka. Such woman is most rare."

She was playing the part of corporate queen, a role that came as naturally as sunrise on a cloudless day, that still moment of anticipation preceding the golden warmth spreading out like butter in a skillet. Mandy paused for a moment for a courtesy exchange with Karen, beaming satisfaction and a little sunshine of her own.

"Yeah," Tommy said. "One of a kind. Okay, enough drooling. Let's get this show on the road."

No cheery wave this time, no jolly hellos. Tommy doubted there were surveillance guys within a hundred yards. But if Lucy and Bug had taught him anything, it was that tech could be tucked anywhere and public places were always a stage, if only for dress rehearsals.

And she was perfect for the part, with a wardrobe that could turn her into anything, always classy and always gorgeous. More like Beacon Hill than the Garden District or French Quarter.

Yenchenko cracked a knowing smile and turned to service as a chauffeur. Tommy approached the aircraft with a blank leather day planner and accepted the carry-on bag from the ground guy, gesturing deferentially toward the limo.

A faint bow, a placid expression. "Nice to see you again, Miss Owens. I trust you had a pleasant flight?"

Her best imitation of a patronizing smile. "Very nice, Tommy. Thank you."

"Allow me, ma'm." He opened the door for her, allowed her to settle and delivered a leather notebook with blank pages inside.

Sergei popped the trunk and placed her bag inside. He scampered around to the other side and got in, put the vehicle in gear and they were away.

Mandy's shoes were off and she was rubbing the left one. "These used to be perfect, Tommy, but all this casual time is killing me. I think my feet are getting fat."

Tommy grinned. "Still look great to me."

She sighed. "You lie. You never look at my feet. Hi, Serge. I like your uniform. What do you think about my feet?"

Yenchenko chuckled as he cleared the exit to the airport. "I am most pleased to examine feet at any occasion."

"There," she said to Tommy. "You see? Never a straight answer from anybody." She perched her sunglasses on top of her head.

"Shades look good."

"Think so? They're Dior and I didn't have much time to choose. I had to make do with a Neiman Marcus outside of Chicago, so I spent kind of casually." She ended the sentence with an upswing of her tone that made it sound more like a question than a statement.

"I'm impressed. Sergei's impressed. I bet the service reps at Skyservice were impressed."

"I sure hope so. I've been on the run all day. Karl had a little trouble getting the codes right on the badges and cards and there was no real way to test them."

"How is Karl?" He was old-world, old-fashioned, old school. And the best forger on the continent, with a high-end clock restoration business in suburban Chicago as a cover.

She rummaged through her bag. "As courtly and well-mannered as ever. I so wanted to buy one of the clocks in his shop, just to applaud his restorations. But there was no time to choose, I'm afraid."

Tommy nodded. "Another time."

"Oh, gosh, that is just *so* bad." She dug deeper into the bag. "I'm beginning to think it would have been so much easier if Savage had showed up, convinced us that it was just a spat, and we patched things up. But some guys just have to push our buttons."

"We didn't mind. Kind of fun pushing back."

Mandy seemed to ignore the remark. "Ah, here we are. Passports, identification cards, gate cards and these should at least get us through the front door. Lucy says they're using a hundred and twenty-something encryption or something and embedding it into a chip was chancy."

Tommy studied the materials. "Karl does nice work."

"He *does*. But he keeps buying these exotic pastries from a bakery just up the street in Geneva, one of the best in Illinois, he says."

"And so naturally you have to..."

"That's right." She looked down to her toes. "Maybe that's why my feet are getting fat."

Tommy leaned over for a closer look and she lifted a leg to make it easier for him. "Hm. Older maybe, but not fat."

She recoiled. "What's that supposed to mean?"

"They say that when you age, your feet kind of spread out, get a little wider, flatten."

Her eyes narrowed. "You're a real help, aren't you? Serge, on the way can you find a decent shoe store? I'm in the mood for some extra wide Jimmy Choos and a chance to really stress Tommy's credit card."

"Serge, try *L'Oiseau Tonnerre*, on Duluth. If that doesn't work, maybe *Boutique le Marcheur*?"

Yenchenko navigated the limo into urban traffic. "Perhaps. But John Fluevog is better choice."

Mandy's eyes widened. "How do you guys know the shoe stores of Montreal?"

Tommy chuckled. "Like I once said, we used to be big league spies. Spies know stuff."

Yenchenko nodded. "*Da, da.* Of course. To gain favor with female target, espionage agent must sometimes buy fancy shoe."

Mandy sighed. "Never mind. We haven't much time and have to get to Westmount before shift changes. We're headed to the thirty-six hundred block of The Boulevard."

Tommy said "Pricey neighborhood."

"Mostly ungated, but Coleman Savage is the exception." She tugged satellite images from her bag and repeated details harvested by Lucy the night before.

Tommy leaned against a swerve of the limo as Yenchenko pushed it through a looping interchange and onto Route 520. "So there's a guy at the gate, with the house on a circular drive, out of view from the street itself. Single lane drive."

"The gatekeeper is Francois... yes, here it is. Francois Duran. CySafe HR records have him as a new hire, just this past week. Savage himself is out of the country, just like your lawyer guy suggested. Lucy has had no luck yet finding out where."

"And the plan?"

Mandy smiled and gathered the materials back into a manila folder. "The minute we get to the driveway, we have to let Lucy and Bug know so they can flip the switch and reroute the outbound calls to Luce. Duran is so new he probably doesn't really know anyone yet. But we can't tie it up for too long because while Bug alters the line, inbound calls won't work."

The multi-lane highway cut straight through something of an industrial district, the lanes divided by a stiff fence-over-con-crete barrier. To the side, a frontage road served pockets of fran-chise businesses and the yards of the Canadian National railroad. "What's the probability that the office will call the guardhouse?"

"I'm hoping for minimal."

"And your Plan B?"

She laughed. "I just *so knew* you were going to ask. If there's a glitch, we crash the phone system for the whole neighbor-hood."

The limo rolled on, heading northeast into an increasingly developed margin of the city.

Mandy consulted instructions on a notepad in her lap. "Bear right at this big interchange, Sergei. You're going to follow Fif-teen South, toward Montreal, Centreville and Pont Champlain."

They shifted from one highway to another, virtually identi-cal, that gradually descended into a concrete canyon. Tommy inspected his CySafe identity badge. No way of knowing how faithful it was to the originals, but Karl's usual nice touch was there. It was just a little worn around the edges, smudged with the faint layer of dust and air grease that suggested routine wear and tear. He emptied his wallet of the identification of a com-pletely fictitious person and replaced it with that of Roger Howe, a special assistant to the vice president of operations at CySafe, and most likely a subordinate to Mandy. Whoever she was for the next couple of hours.

Following Mandy's instructions, Sergei gently guided the limo onto Exit 66, toward Chemin Queen Mary and Chemin de la Cotê Saint Luc. A merge, a left turn and ten minutes later, they were cruising up The Boulevard. Mandy brought the cell phone in her hand to life.

"Hey, Luce. Yep, almost there. Serge? Slow it down... Yes. I see it. Two stone pillars and an iron gate."

The limo paused for a car going in the opposite direction and then crept into the driveway apron.

Mandy said to Sergei "Okay, one quick honk of the horn." To Lucy on the phone. "Yes, here comes the guard. Anytime. Good? Okay, here we go."

The guard approached the driver's side of the limo and Sergei rolled down the passenger window. Tommy smiled at the uniformed gatekeeper and gestured that the person next to him was calling the shots. On his chest, the name tag said "F. Duran." Late twenties, cordial but not chummy, polite but not deferential.

"*Pardon, mais je dois voir l'identification.*"

Tommy nodded. "*Bien sûr. Nous comprenons.*" He displayed the badge hanging from the lanyard around his neck.

Francois' eyes focused on the card. "*Et la dame?*"

Tommy took the cue and got out of the car, led Francois around the trunk and opened the door for Mandy to exit. Not the slightest hint of reticence, but not overdoing command either. She introduced herself as Alicia Craig, executive assistant to Coleman Savage and displayed both the badge on the lanyard and a walleted credential to prove it.

Francois tried for English, but Mandy gave him a VIP smile and continued the conversation in French. "You're the new fellow, aren't you? Yes? And doing very well, I can see. Of course, we're aware that Mister Savage is away, but we have some special materials to be delivered to the house."

The gatekeeper was only slightly cowed and spoke apologetically. "I'm afraid I must check with Mr. Savage's security people. I hope you understand."

Mandy beamed. "Excellent, Francois. Please, make the call. But first, as you must know, I need to apply my card to the reader just to the right of the gate. To feed the chip data into the security office."

Comforted, Francois led Mandy to the reader and watched her put it into the slot. A tiny light switched from red to green.

Francois said, "*Je vous remercie. Je serai un moment.*" And he reached for a conventional wired phone, tapped in a number and waited.

In the earpiece, Tommy heard the same as Mandy and Yenchenko. Lucy's voice, posing as the security official, verifying the card data, and directing Francois to allow the vehicle into the Savage compound high up the hill and around a slight curve.

The massive iron gate swung open as Tommy got Mandy back into the car and then settled himself. The guard waved the vehicle forward. To her credit, Mandy played it out, just a routine checkpoint in a business that treasured checkpoints. *First class nerve, absolute aplomb.*

CHAPTER THIRTEEN

If it looked big from the gate, the mansion up close was immense. Towering stone with incredibly tall windows, shrouded in gloomy mature trees, leafless and gray for winter, complete with a raw, biting breeze curling around the corners. She tightened the grip on her collar.

Mandy bit her lower lip and slowly shook her head. "Tommy, I'm reminded of a castle, something out of Normandy."

He seemed unimpressed, like it was about to be just another routine breaking, entering, a casual little burglary, maybe enjoy a glass of wine along the way.

He said, "Ever done this before?"

"No. Well, when I was quite young, a couple of my friends and I broke into Mister Johnson's shed. He supposedly made home brew, some sort of a moonshine."

"And how was it?"

"It turned out to be a five gallon can of kerosene and a case of empty wine bottles. So I guess it doesn't count?"

"You'll be fine. Trust me. Just bear in mind that this is a guy who monitors everything. The house might be vacant, but..."

She dug into her bag. "I know, I know. Lucy gave me one of her father's magic thingies to detect —"

Tommy grinned and held one aloft. "Brought mine along, just in case."

She sighed. "Do you always have to think of everything? I mean, how am I supposed to run this if you're always one step ahead of me?" She found the black box at last and tugged it from the bag. "Never mind. Two is probably better than one anyway."

Sergei chuckled. "Teamwork. Is good, eh?"

Mandy turned to Yenchenko. "You've got packing cartons, in the trunk?"

"*Da, da.* Of course. I remain here, guard vehicle and observe perimeter while you make robbery. If it is your wish, okay?"

They reached the entry and Mandy paused before inserting the key card into another slot with a blinking red light. She touched her phone and Lucy's voice was in her ear.

"Okay, Lucy, we're at the front door, ready to go in. What happens if the code is wrong?"

"It's not wrong."

"Yes, but just in case..."

Lucy sighed. "It's the correct code for this time frame, Mandy. Look, that's an older Mercer-Watts reader, one of their better models. If once the diode goes green, you can manually punch in an override that should shut down all the interior sur−veillance."

"Should?"

"Well, you know how it goes..."

Tommy and Yenchenko exchanged smiles. *They'd probably go in with spray paint and a shotgun and take out the gear like cowboys in a bar fight.*

"How long will we have?"

"Twenty, maybe twenty-five minutes tops before whoever's at the operations desk can respond. So don't mess around, okay? You've studied the floor plans, you have the gear, you know what to do."

The memory of her father's voice. "*Steady, strong, serene. You're an Owens girl...*" *Yes, daddy. I am.* She thrust the card into the reader. A second that took a century. The light went from blinking red to solid green. Just beyond, a faint click. A nod to Tommy. His hand on the doorknob. Twist.

Open.

And the most comforting breath of the day. She glanced at her watch. *Twenty minutes.*

Tommy grinned. Sergei tugged his favorite AK-47 from the front seat of the limo and inserted a clip of ammunition. In the earbud, Lucy signed off. *To avoid being overheard if there were any surprises.*

Tommy gestured an invitation for her to enter first, but she waved him forward. In the foyer, just as Lucy had described it, a panel of lights, the business end of the Mercer-Watts system. None lit. Unless Savage had a secondary unit that he'd installed on his own, they had successfully committed a felony.

The shell of the mansion might have been century-old archi-tecture, but the interior was contemporary. Quality, but simple lines, sort of boxy, elegant but without a stamp of personality, rather like a set or stage. And despite a color scheme that tended toward warmer shades and hues, it felt cold as they drifted from portal to portal and peeked into the adjacent rooms.

Mandy whispered. "Tommy, do you think I need more clut-ter at the beach house?"

"Clutter?"

"Yes. Mementos, knick-knacks, some artwork, maybe. You have some nice stuff on the cabin walls, shelves, just kind of around."

"Most of it was there when I arrived. The rest I picked up at the furniture place and an antique dealer just outside of Jacks Ford."

"I think I need more clutter."

He shrugged. "So go to a clutter store in Georgetown, shop online, or maybe try the straw market. They've got a lot of Chi-nese imports with a sort of Bahamian look. And why are you whispering?"

"So we won't be over..." She raised the volume of her speech. "I suppose it wouldn't make any difference. Okay, there's sup—

posed to be an office, just beyond the library. Should be that way. Bedrooms are on the second floor, both wings of the house. I'll do up, you do down."

Seventeen minutes left.

Tommy nodded and went for a look while she gingerly climbed carpeted stairs that swept upward from two sides of the hall, encircling an enormous chandelier. Four of the bedrooms were decorated identically and looked unused. Made-up beds, drawn curtains, empty closets and bureau drawers. For guests, and judging from the condition of the rooms, not very often.

A child's room. Little boy blue. Perfectly neat and tidy. The maid did quality work. Or the child was totally repressed. As–sorted toys, well organized, on a bank of shelves. *Wonder which is his favorite?* She took a guess and went for the stuffed bear clos–est to the bed. Large walk-in closet. Winter wear, again so nicely arranged that it was possible to conclude it was just for show. *Look further.* Boxes in back storage. *Summer things.*

Mandy decided to go for those that seemed to have the most wear, probably his favorites. *Had he outgrown them?* She held a pair of pants and then shirts up to guess. They seemed okay, and the pile on the floor began to grow.

From a polished teak dresser, she harvested underwear and socks, then went for a couple of familiar pairs of shoes. At last, she gathered them up into two stacks and hauled them one at a time into the hallway and parked them next to the door.

The last bedroom had to be the master. Her watch told her she had thirteen minutes left.

Just inside the door, her eyes surveyed it with care. Bath–room, double sinks, lots of mirror, very corporate look. The bedroom seemed more suited for a guy than feminine, but Nikki didn't seem to be that kind of girl. Her choices would have been more earthy, simpler.

The pieces were adding up to an impression that Cole Sav–age either got his way on everything, or that Nikki wasn't as

homespun as she'd presented herself. While the tug of a control—
ling Cole was strong, her instincts as a reporter kept reminding
her that things are not always as they seem, to stay open-mind—
ed.

Closets always tell the truth.

And the Savages had much more than a closet stuffed with
hangers. A pair of doors opened into another entire suite. His
side, rows and rows of suits, jackets, shirts, all reminiscent of an
upscale men's department in a sophisticated store. No labels.
Custom made. Complete racks of evening wear. Opposite,
dozens of pairs of polished shoes glistened beneath shelves of
folded sweaters and accessories.

*Okay. Wealth on a grand scale. A guy with a dollar sign, some
digits and about ten zeroes.*

She circled back to the closet entry area and crossed a portal
into Nikki's collection. Long on dressy, short on casual. Lots of
space between hangers. No wrinkles here. Just a couple of labels,
both better ones, but not much in the way of variety. It was al—
most as if this was all for show, that day-to-day wear was...

Tucked away.

In the furthest corner of the area, just past folk dance cos—
tumes, the sportswear that seemed to fit Nikki's personality. By
comparison to the rest, not much. Pants, tops, sweaters, some on
hangers, some folded on shelves. Casual shoes, a common brand.

Mandy took half a step back. *How to choose?* She pictured the
scene at the dance in Jack's Ford. Nikki's style. And one by one,
pieces assembled into three piles on the floor.

Tommy's voice startled her. "Take care. We can't have it
all."

"I know, but..."

"Just enough to tide her over, make her and Cyrus feel com—
fortable. Money's not the point here."

"I know, but..." She held two hangers aloft. "Would you go
for this top? Or this one?"

He shrugged. "Either one works."

"You're no help." She shook her head and dropped both into the pile. "Anything downstairs?"

"Personal papers, an appointment book, small phone book in the desk. Some business reports."

"How about recordings, CDs, that kind of thing, of the band?"

Tommy held several disks in plastic sleeves aloft.

"Great. Did you..."

"No. I took pictures, left everything the way it was. You about ready here?"

Mandy studied the pile. Eight minutes left. It was going to be tough to fit it into the trunk of the limo, large as it was. Maybe her empty carry-on could be stuffed solid and carried in the back seat. "Yes. I think so. What's in the sack?"

"Hair brushes, cosmetics, woman stuff from the bathroom." He glanced at collection of clothing at her feet. "Better clothes are at the front of the closet."

"Those are *costumes*, Tommy. The things she has to wear to please her husband. This is what she wears when she wants to be herself."

"Okay, but we'd better get a move on. Lucy said —"

"I know. Twenty minutes. Just wish I had more time to get a read on their relationship."

Tommy reached down and came up with an armload of apparel. "We don't need to black bag to accomplish that. We're just here to plant the flag, make a point." He turned to walk away.

She harvested the last small bundle to follow. "You're okay with that?"

He chuckled. "After the incident in the bar? Oh, yeah." He paused and eased the pile onto the bed. "Almost forgot."

"Lucy's calling card."

"Yep." He tugged a folding business card from his shirt

pocket, made it into a little tent. "Which pillow?"

"I'd say his is on the left, hers on the right."

Tommy moved left.

"No. Make it on her side."

He grinned. "Yeah, good call."

Dead center in the middle of the pillow, a simple white card with the silhouette of a panther, with glowering eyes.

Mandy smiled. "Nice. Elegant, even. C'mon. Let's get out of here."

At the front door, Yenchenko stood guard.

"Okay, Sergei. You and Tommy get the boxes going and I'll keep an eye out for anyone. No, I don't want the gun. Put it back in the car."

He shrugged and complied.

While the men hauled flattened boxes into the house, Mandy checked her watch. With four minutes left, she put in a call to Lucy.

"Okay, we're just about done. How do I turn on the system again?"

"I can get it from here. So how'd it go? Did you remember my card?"

"Tommy left it on Nikki's pillow in the bedroom. Hope that's okay."

Lucy laughed. "Excellent. You okay after commanding your first felony?"

"I'm good." The first of the boxes of clothing arrived. "Got a bunch of stuff for Nikki and Cyrus, and Tommy came across some handwritten documents. He took pictures."

"Perfect. Hope they turn out okay."

"Say, I was wondering. Do you think I need more clutter at my house? I mean, it seems kind of sparse. You know, memen—tos, trinkets, some sort of art."

"Hm. Not sure. Charlie knows a guy that can give you a stuffed marlin for the wall. They're always decorative."

"Which wall?"

"You've got a point. But you know, in all the time I spent there, I didn't feel like it was sparse."

Another round of boxes arrived. Yenchenko was showing off his weightlifting skills.

"Really?"

"Yep, really. I mean you've got like a dozen sofas and twice as many armchairs in there, plus all the deck stuff."

Mandy conjured images of the rooms. "Wow. You know, I never really counted them."

"Trust me, I never felt like I was in a warehouse."

Tommy displayed a thumbs up sign while Yenchenko closed the trunk.

"Okay, we're done. You can turn everything back on again. See you soon, Luce."

This time she had to get her own door, but didn't mind. "Lucy says Charlie knows a guy with a stuffed marlin for the wall."

Tommy cocked an eyebrow as the limo began the descent down the hill toward the gate shack. "Which wall?"

"You know, that's exactly what I said."

Francois opened the gate and stepped out to wave farewell.

Tommy and Mandy waved back and when the countdown reached zero, the car turned right onto The Boulevard.

She said, "Poor Francois. In a day or two, he'll be out of a job. Shamed. Disgraced. A potential career in tatters."

Yenchenko said, "Collateral damage. It happens. Too bad."

Tommy nodded. "Bothers me too. Serge, are we getting soft in our old age?"

Two sedans going in the opposite direction raced past. Mandy looked over her shoulder to see them swerve and skid to a stop in the driveway.

Sergei made another turn. "Guard remains alive. So, yes. We become soft and sentimental."

Mandy scowled. "It's not right."

"Lucy can look into it, maybe come up with some sort of anonymous reward."

"Yes. Something to ease the pain."

Tommy said, "Yeah, something with a lot of zeros after a dollar sign."

Yenchenko sighed and shook his head as the car picked up speed on the highway. "Such sad little army. Koshka One, Koshka Two."

CHAPTER FOURTEEN

Mandy Cay, The Bahamas

Barely specks on the beach below, Nikki and Cyrus knelt in the sand. The glass doors were fully open and a light Atlantic breeze wafted past, barely strong enough to ruffle hair.

But it carried the scent of the sea to Tommy, and right away that made it a fine day. Good coffee, good weather, Charlie just to the right. A day starting off on the right foot.

Tommy said, "Sand sculpture, maybe."

Charlie shook his head. "No. A castle or some kinda fort."

Tommy hoisted the mug to his lips. "Pretty sure of your—self."

"Kids his age don't know nothin' about sculpture. They do forts and shit."

"You read up about that on the internet or something?"

Charlie grunted. "Nah. I was a kid once, same's you. That age, you did forts and castles and shit. Everybody knows that."

"Yeah, but today, probably without much success. Where they're working, the sand's too fine and way too dry. Plus the kid doesn't have a pail."

"Whaddya you need a goddamn pail for?"

"To pack sand in, get some good shapes going, kinda like bricks and such."

Charlie grunted and sipped his coffee. "I suppose that's what city people do when they go to the beach. Look for every kind of shortcut."

"Pails are good for fetching water, which is what Nikki and Cyrus need to do if they want to get any further than a pile of sand."

"Hey, Tommy, all they gotta do is move maybe twenty feet closer to where the tide's coming in, they'd have all the wet sand they need. Make themselves a first rate fort."

"Or an outstanding sculpture of a big ol' gator comin' up out of the water, jaws wide open, goin' for some poor ol' hog that got too close — "

"I'm tellin' you, Tommy. Kids do forts and stuff like that. I ain't never known a kid to try his hand at bein' some sorta sculp—tor guy."

"No gators?"

"No. Especially the kind that piss in a mug and call it cof—fee."

Tommy sipped outstanding French Market and scanned the wisp of a line separating sea from sky. If nothing else, the coffee insults were always original and had been since they day the cab—in keys fell into Tommy's hand.

Charlie asked, "You miss it?"

"Miss what?"

"Roaming. Puttin' the bow toward the horizon, heading off to nowhere in particular."

The Alden yawl. The fifty-footer that for a time was a quest that got completely out of hand. "Nah. My recollection was the roaming was trying to keep one step ahead of contract killers. Besides, Mandy's not a roamer."

Charlie nodded, but remained focused on the beach, a good hundred yards below and to the right. On the deck to the left, Yenchenko snoozed on a lounge chair, a pale walrus that had beached itself to look vaguely obscene. Behind, Lucy and Mandy were assembling some sort of lunch, bouncing through a deco—rating dialog. "So, you're settling, then?"

Tommy chuckled and hoped the heat in his ears didn't show.

Charlie said, "Yeah, well, hearin' all this talk about knick-knacks and bric-a-brac and what-not, I'm thinkin' she's putting down some roots. You always know a woman's settling in for the haul when they start puttin' stuff on the walls."

"That so?"

"That's what they say."

Tommy glanced at Charlie. Shorter, rounder, grayer, hair-line receding, the mustache thicker. "How about you? The care-taker house seems a good place to settle."

Charlie grunted. "Ain't got no junk on the walls. Got no time for that shit. And settle's a relative term, Tommy. Bed, roof, somewheres to cast a baited hook, that's all and old cowboy like myself needs. Now, Sergei, there, he still has to get in some action, raise a little hell. Kinda like you, I reckon."

They stood silent and casually eavesdropped on the discussion in the kitchen, punctuated by the clatter of utensil and bowls.

Charlie spoke in an apologetic tone. "Shoulda never said nothin' to Lucy about that stuffed marlin."

"It's okay."

"You think Mandy's maybe, well, a little angry about the other day?"

"No. Why?"

"She seemed angry, is all. I mean, if there's a problem, I can, well, you know, kind of mosey along."

"Nah. She was just trying to be strong. Guys like you intimidate her. You know, street smarts and experience and such."

A faint smile formed on Charlie's jaw. "Yeah, well, women like her intimidate a lot of guys."

"You think?"

"Oh, yeah. I think. Even fellas like you."

Nikki and Cyrus relocated sand sculpture efforts closer to the incoming tide, where it would be easier to pack. Tommy chuckled. "You might be right about that."

"I *know* I'm right. Been around for a little while, you know. Now, take Nikki, yonder. She's a nice lady, all right, a good mom so far's I can tell. All kinda charm, smarts. And, yeah, she proba– bly could intimidate some fellas. But, trust me, she ain't in Mandy's league."

What was left of Tommy's coffee had cooled to the point of unpalatable and he gave up on it. "How's it going?"

"Hard to tell. Things just don't feel right. I seen more'n my share of damaged women. Scared witnesses, anxious wives, vic– tims of all kinds. Nikki's doing a first-rate job of keeping it under wraps. Either that, or something don't add up proper. Keeps to herself a lot, though."

"Yeah?"

"Yeah. Now, the kid, he's all kind of withdrawn, don't say hardly much at all. Been tryin' to occupy him with a little fishin', just some surf casting and such."

"That's nice. Thanks, Charlie."

"Ain't nothin'. Anyways, he mentions his father often goes off on fishing trips. But he don't never take the kid. Can you get your head around that? They don't seem to do much fami– ly-wise. Now, that's the sort of thing you'd expect from a big time business nut. So how comes he's so hot to get 'em all back in the barn? It just don't add up logical a'tall."

The cold coffee was at least moist on the tongue. "Posses– sions. A front. Like wall decorations. He didn't even show up himself to negotiate. Sent a lawyer, couple of goons."

Charlie grunted.

"Yep, so we went up to his place in Montreal, snagged some clothing and stuff, mostly left a calling card. Game on, buddy, game on."

The background noise had evaporated. Tommy turned to discover Lucy stepping forward, coffee pot in hand.

"You guys want refills? We've got lunch together, in the

fridge. Mandy went down to the beach to round up the guests."

The two men exchanged a glance. Good coffee to one, dish – water to the other. But Charlie extended his hand and invited a fresh round, which Lucy poured without comment.

Sergei rolled onto his side and Lucy groaned as she covered her face with her hand. "Oh, man... That is just so disgusting. Some people should never wear Speed-Os. Ever."

Charlie snickered. "That bikini you wore around here weren't a whole lot better."

"Hey, I worked my ass off to get into that suit. And it looked real good."

Tommy tried to conjure the image of Lucy in a scanty bikini but couldn't make it.

Charlie shook his head. "Yeah, we knew. And it *did* look real good."

"The suit?"

He sipped. "Your ass."

She sighed. "Well at least mine was covered. Serge's... Never mind. Tommy, see what I had to put up with? I mean, Mandy's got thirteen beaches on this island and every time I went out to get some sun, that just happened to be the place they wanted to fish that day."

Charlie was on a roll and kept tossing the dice. "I bet Bug don't like it when you wear that thing at your new place."

She fell silent. "You've got a point."

Nikki stood when Mandy approached and brushed sand away from a bikini that left little to the imagination.

Lucy sighed. "Wow. I'd kill to have legs like that."

Charlie shrugged. "Seem kind of scrawny to me. You did a lot of working out, got fit."

Lucy began to throw up her arms in dispute, but realized she was still holding the pot. "Length, Charlie. *Length.* Look. She's almost as tall as Mandy. Guys will just never understand."

Tommy laughed. "None of us are using a ruler, Luce."

She pouted. "That's because you're all tall. Well, except for Charlie." She shifted to that voice that blended gooey with im‐ pudent and a sweet smile. "Who's just *so* cuddly and cute and fuzzy." At his glare, her bawdy laugh came from the belly. "Now, moving on..."

Fearless meets fearless, like always. Tommy said, "A good idea."

Charlie nodded. "A *real* good idea."

Lucy turned and her flip-flops slapped the ceramic floor tiles on the way to the kitchen. Both men followed.

"And no watching my ass," she called out.

Charlie muttered, "God damn smartass."

Tommy smiled while she returned the carafe to the cof‐ feemaker, turned to face them and leaned against the counter.

Lucy said, "So, same as before, CySafe is gonna be a tough nut to crack. Layers and layers of security, all kinds of authenti‐ cation. About the loosest point, maybe the proverbial Achilles heel, is the security system at the Savage house."

Tommy said, "I'd believe that. It was pretty easy."

"That's because my father and I spent six hours working out the encryption. Plus, he flew it to Karl Felchin to make an out‐ standing counterfeit card for the reader. Personally. Which is a lot for him. On your jet. On your dime."

Tommy waved his hands in submission. "I meant to say *you* made it pretty easy."

"No you didn't, but that's okay. I understand. Trust me, get‐ ting into business matters with CySafe is not going to be so sim‐ ple. But you guys are probably running on a tight time frame, so naturally we're — "

Charlie shook his head in disbelief. " — probably just itching to show off. Ain't no system in the world that you two can't open, easy as popping the tab on a can of cheap beer."

Lucy smirked. "Well... You know how it is. Talent comes with a great ass."

Charlie sighed, Tommy went for a knowing smile, and Lucy shifted gears.

"Okay. So what we know is all the usual public relations bull—shit. The stuff company puts out on its own newswire to feed the media. And politicians who need an excuse to take bribes from the Savage interests. Nothing I haven't told you already. We found a back door into human resources, which is where Mandy got the stuff on the gate guard — "

Tommy interrupted. " — Who, by the way, will probably need a little help."

"Yeah, he got like *fired* about five minutes after you guys left. I'll find some cash, work out a nice little severance package for him and tweak his employment records. Trust me. By the time I'm done, any military intelligence agency in the world will hire him."

"Thanks. We felt kind of bad."

"More likely *Mandy* felt kind of bad. You guys probably didn't even think about it." She took a breath. "Anyway, Savage does seem to drop from sight now and then, so we have our work cut out for us there. The desk calendar might help, espe—cially if we can get into his phone. He's gotta be working from somewhere."

Charlie said, "The kid says he often goes on fishing trips. But always by himself."

"Okay. Some guys need to get away, think and stuff. I can have a look. But I'm telling you, Tommy, this is a company that specializes in electronic privacy. There's really no way to speed things up just because we're nice and friendly people just trying to break into their records for a look around."

"Anything new on Chet's case?"

"Working on it. I finally got ahold of the logs and it looks well-organized, using Tor."

"Which is?"

"A vast network of relays that encrypt and move internet

traffic through a maze that's hard to track. You know, the dark alleys of the net, the stuff that doesn't Google. Dump it in, zip around and it eventually pops up somewhere you don't expect. Handy when you do dark pool trading like we used to, but a genuine pain when you're on the other side of the fence. The exit nodes have been fairly well identified, so now it's just play—ing whack-a-mole. If you're interested in illicit drugs, extremist groups, some really awful porn, I can fix you right up."

"No thanks."

"You know, Tommy, Dad says sometimes you gotta put some eyes on the ground. He can rig surveillance boost, but it still takes people to put legs on the gear."

Bug probably had a point. In the old days, the most effective intelligence work was sourced to good street observers. Charlie and Sergei would be the first to agree, and Bug himself was grounded in Old School. As a reporter, Mandy might very well have cultivated a cadre of sources, people who knew people.

Tommy glanced at Charlie, whose expression was a hoisted eyebrow of affirmation.

Lucy shifted a stack of plates and software to a more conve—nient location to serve lunch. "Of course, that's probably some—thing you might want to suggest to Mandy when you get a chance."

No question where the order of things was parked. Lucy was using him as a suggestion box because she'd fully committed to supporting Mandy. For just a moment, the temptation to put the ball back into Lucy's court flashed through his mind. But she had her reasons, so he let it go.

The door opened and Nikki and Cyrus preceded Mandy into the room.

Mandy was overdosing on the pleasure of being the official hostess. "Okay, you know everyone here, except for our very best friend, Lucy Tramanian."

Lucy waved, then squatted down and extended a hand. "Hi,

Cyrus. I bet you're already into video games. Isn't it funny? Me too. I'm Lucy. Second shortest person in the room."

CHAPTER FIFTEEN

West 36th Street and Sixth Avenue, New York City

Mandy glanced at her watch. Right on time. As they exited the taxi, Tommy handed the cabbie a pair of twenties and de-clined change.

She turned up her collar and clasped it tight around her neck. "It's reminders like these, Tommy, that I am so absolutely grateful for the island. Good to come back to the city now and then, just for the, well, atmosphere. Now, you have to promise to be nice. My guy is a little eccentric, but an old friend. And a good source. Or at least was."

Tommy smiled and adjusted his sunglasses. He had been smiling ever since the evening walk on the beach when he sug-gested they pool old resources and lean toward a conventional approach than relying on a running audio feed from Lucy.

They had paused at a favorite spot on the sand, the one with the odd rocks and the log that washed ashore, to take in the fad-ing light of day. Lucy had flown out, the guys were probably swapping lies over hard liquor and Nikki was settling Cyrus down for the night. Balmy air caressed their skin and the sea surged forward in a desperate attempt to reach their bare feet but not quite making it. He had been smiling in the moonlight when she gathered perspectives. His gentle suggestion had made a lot of sense, and even now the softness of it warmed the mem-ory.

She had said, "Lucy will have her hands full dueling with CySafe."

"For sure."

"And we leaned way too hard on her last time."

He had picked up a tiny shell, a scallop. "We did. I'll take the blame for that."

"And we both know a lot of people."

"We do."

"And we're good at this sort of thing."

His smile had expanded as he passed the shell to her hand. "We are."

"And so are Sergei and Charlie."

"For true."

The little shell had a chip on one edge and she returned it to the sand. "Do you always have to be agreeable?"

"Absolutely."

The reminiscence warmed her on a chilly Manhattan side–walk.

Tommy was still wearing that same enigmatic smile, despite the harsh intrusion of the city. A sense of confidence surged through her as they navigated through pedestrian traffic on the sidewalk.

The restaurant was still as crowded and noisy as ever, the pa–trons still on the energetic side, working people a few steps above those lined up at a nearby fast-food franchise. A quick scan of the seats at the bar, then the gauntlet of leers along a row of tiny two-chair tables on the window side of Thirty-sixth.

Tommy trailed, and the temptation to peek at the expression on his face was strong. Ten years ago, he might have been one of these guys, a little scruffy, a little buzzed on beer and a lot of midtown brash.

Emerson Barr, by contrast, was a rumpled, round guy with dark hair desperately in need of a comb. He was focused on guarding the empty chair at his table from marauding patrons rearranging seating to match party size. When they made eye contact, he leaped to his feet, catching a wobbling soft drink in the nick of time. He gobbled up half a dozen paper napkins to wipe his hands, pushed his glasses back up high on his nose, and said hello.

Emmie hadn't changed. A little more wrinkled, a little more plump, but a genuinely nice guy who'd managed to merge geek and journalism into an enviable career.

Tommy looked terribly smug, and the sunglasses only served to inflate the image of a manager, an agent, a bodyguard, the burly guy who shooed away the paparazzi. While Emerson shook hands with Mandy and gestured for her to be seated, Tommy looked for a third chair. The neighboring tables had just been merged and one seat was open.

"May I?" he asked the guy at the edge.

"She with you, man?"

Tommy's grin went just a little more sly. "Yeah. She's with me."

The guy laughed. "Take it, man. And I promise not to grab any video, even if you guys are famous or something."

Tommy chuckled. "Or something."

"Hey, man, maybe I will shoot some video. Like, put it up on my feed, you know?"

Tommy peeled a pair of fifties from his hand and dropped it on the table. "No you won't. Lunch is on me, fellas."

The guy leaned back, grinning admiration. "Nah. I guess not. Very cool, man. Very cool."

Mandy cleared her throat to interrupt. "Tommy, I'd like you to meet Emerson Barr, who's an expert on tech companies and what they're up to. Emmie, this is Tommy Kane, a friend and associate."

They shook hands and settled. A waiter appeared, gathered beverage orders for Mandy and Tommy and offered menus. Emerson waved him off and wearing an eager smile said, "I know it's been a while Mandy, but I bet you're still a fan of Bronx Burgers. Am I right?"

"Absolutely. With onion rings, please."

Emerson turned to Tommy. "Make it three?"

Mandy shook her head. "No, not for Mister Hold-the-Guacamole. Try the Brooklyn instead." She turned to Emerson. "He's from Louisiana, so...."

Emerson continued to shine brightly. "Oh, yeah, definitely."

The waiter seized an opening to display incredible menu memory. "Grilled onions, Cajun seasoning, steak sauce, crispy bacon and cheddar cheese. Includes lettuce, tomatoes and your choice of fries or onion rings or sweet potatoes."

Tommy grinned. "I do believe I'm burping already." He turned to the waiter. "Two Bronx, one Brooklyn, then. Onion rings all around? Yes? Good."

Emerson's overeager smile retreated into a placid grin. "So, Mister Kane, what business are you in?"

Tommy took off the sunglasses and tucked them into his jacket pocket. "Occasional helping hand."

"Ah, I see. One of those temp services?"

"You could say that."

Emerson nodded and spoke to Mandy. "I'm afraid I live in the tech world. Don't follow the other corporate lines at all. So. How have you been? It's been a long time. Haven't seen you around. Where are you working?"

Mandy took center stage. "Well, I've kind of been out of the business."

Barr nodded. "I heard you might be taking a break. Something about being had on a bad piece about a financial scandal that really wasn't. The rumors were it was some sort of a scam run by the infamous, mysterious Nyx. Most of us didn't buy it. Although there's been some recent talk that Nyx has reappeared, but you know how it is with rumors. You're on your own, then?"

Mandy said, "Actually, I got lucky with some investments,

now just kind of kicking around, travel, that sort of thing."

Barr glanced at Tommy. "Got some good tips, eh? Lucky you. Half the companies going strong today, you could have picked up stock for a song just a couple of years ago. I bet you timed it just right."

"Yes. I was fortunate. So, how about you? You're looking quite well."

Emerson blushed. "Aw, you're still the kindest person I ever met. I still owe you for standing up for me back at Northwest−ern, that business with Carl Jorgenson. You know, he got canned from that talk show he was doing, but I heard his father got him a slot somewhere in D-C. Anyway, I'm still plugging along at *Tech Times*. Investigative stuff mostly."

The burger platters arrived and each was big enough to serve four or five starving ironworkers. Tommy looked like he was trying to figure out which face of the mountain to assault first, but the waiter had been kind and cut hers into manageable pieces.

Emerson dug in with gusto and chewed hurriedly to punctu−ate bites with monologue. "Tough to stay with it... keeps evolv−ing... lot of fronts... customers want convenience, toys... secu−rity's a big thing... lot of cybercrime...."

Tommy listened while working through a field of carbs, salt and cholesterol. He nodding when Mandy floated a prompting question and Emerson was eager to share what he knew. Half−way through the platter, Mandy knew she was not going to fin−ish and would refuse leftovers to go.

She washed it down with an overpriced iced tea. "So I bet companies like, say, CySafe are doing quite well."

Emerson dabbed his lips with a napkin. He was down to the last couple of onion rings. "Definitely. They're more business oriented than consumer, but do have a line of software that home internet providers offer customers. Trust me, Mandy. Anybody who doesn't have protection on their phones, tablets, laptops, even appliances? Just asking for trouble. Not just spam. All kinds of malware, fraud, ransom-ware. Global epidemic."

Not to mention Lucy. "So CySafe is a major player?"

The final two onion rings vanished. "One of the biggest and most respected. Canadian company, based in Montreal."

"You don't say?"

"Yep. But they have branches all over the world. That's Coleman Savage's company. Now, there's a guy who's gone from nearly nothing to incredibly wealthy in just a few years. Stun— ning. But you used to write business, so you'd know that. And the success piece has been done at least a couple of dozen times in all the major pubs, TV, so on."

She allowed her shoulders to slump and her tone to wither into disappointment. "Really? I heard he's quite the character, a real eccentric. Disappears for weeks at a time."

Emerson laughed while Tommy pushed his plate away, about two thirds empty. "No, no. Anything but eccentric. Smooth, polished, sophisticated. The company grapevine says he's a regular control freak, high standards, no excuses for bad performance. Model of PR, the kind of guy who doesn't cam— paign for spots on the non-profit boards. He gets invited."

Mandy shrugged. "I guess I got some bad information. Something having to do with dropping out of sight for periods of time, nobody knows where."

Tommy spoke up. "Maybe he's off on some hunting or fish— ing trip somewhere, just to get away?"

Emerson shook his head. "I wouldn't peg him as the out— doorsy type. But the hard-core billionaires do kind of hide out in their own little world. And it's not uncommon in the business for intensive, extended brainstorming, especially when there's a new product in R-and-D."

Pretending the lunch had lost its appeal, Mandy eased her platter to the side. Halfway would have to do. "Oh, gosh, that was a great treat. But I am just so stuffed. Emmie, you said 'nearly nothing.' I always had the sense that Coleman Savage was one of this brilliant dorm rats that came up with an incredible concept, got some backers, did the IPO thing and ran with it."

Emerson leaned back from an empty plate. "More like immigrant family makes good. The background is somewhere in Eastern Europe, first to the States after World War Two, then to Montreal. The grandfather set up some sort of a mom-and-pop office equipment company, Sauvage Office Products. That's with a "U" later dropped to make "Savage". Late forties and fifties, I think. The father tinkered with some business machines, got a couple of patents which he sold to the big manufacturers, just before the internet came along. So they were doing okay money-wise when Coleman joined the business and the rest is history."

Mandy asked, "Sauvage? That sounds more French than Eastern European."

The waiter arrived to clear the plates and deliver the check. Tommy snagged it and volunteered to pay. "A lot of refugees with a dream, a satchel and a hard-to-spell name Americanized, simplified, tried to adapt back then. Especially out of the Slavic and Baltic states."

Emerson nodded. "My own grandparents did just that. Barr is just a shortened version of Babaritcovitch, which is just as well, because the full name would never fit a single line in a newspaper byline and would have made my life in a classroom just terrible."

Emerson had a point. Her mother's maiden name was a mouthful and even if it was French, it was much more comfortable in exurban Connecticut to have a simple American name, preferably with English colonial roots. Tommy had probably experienced the same thing. On the other hand, Lucy didn't seem to care. Emerson Barr was just a regular guy, one of the Winnetka Barrs, who normally would have gone Ivy League. But he had stayed close to home to be spared dorm life, which gave him more time in the computer labs, a tech because he was comfort—able there, and certainly didn't need the minimum wage student-aid wages. He became the go-to guy for *Daily Northwestern* staffers with personal computer disasters and discovered he could write tech as well as fix it.

Now he was older without having aged, but the reporter in him could resist no longer. "So, Mandy, what's your interest in all things tech?"

"I might have a piece going, but still have some — well, a lot of — research to do." It was a weak lie and she knew it as soon as it tumbled out.

Emerson cocked his head. "But I thought you said... Oh, I get it. You're doing okay, but now you're bored and you're try—ing to work your way back into the game."

She laughed. "You are just so perceptive, Emmie. Yes, it's been way too long and, well, I'm still not sure."

"So, mum's the word then?"

"Yes. I'd be, well, grateful. Oh, I don't know. It's not much of a piece." *C'mon, Emmie. Catch the hint. Try harder.* "And it prob—ably won't work out, at least for me." *Not sure. A little more.* "If it fizzles, I'll share what I've got. Maybe you can turn it into something."

Emerson toyed with the straw in his empty glass. "Nice. Thanks." He glanced at his watch and from inside his jacket his cellphone buzzed. He excused himself and checked a message. "Sorry, I've got — "

Mandy waved a hand of understanding. "Of course. Been there, done that. Tommy, are we good?"

"Yep, I believe so." He flagged the waiter and thumbed off four twenties. "Don't need any change, thanks."

Emerson Barr seemed amused. "Interesting. No credit card."

Mandy laughed and lightly tapped the back of Emerson's hand, allowing hers to linger as a light caress of friendship. "He's *such* a Luddite. Refreshing in a way. It's been just lovely seeing you again, Emmie. We'll have to do better at staying in touch."

They stood. Tommy put the sunglasses back on, smiled and said, "Cash always works. And never leaves tracks." He extended a hand. "Nice meeting you, Mister Barr. Good luck with all your projects."

CHAPTER SIXTEEN

Near Jack's Ford, Pennsylvania

Tommy found Mandy on the living room floor, halfway between the sofa and the card table, an island of eye candy in a sea of paper. She sat cross-legged surrounded by stacks that nearly circled her.

Even dressed down, she looked mighty fine.

Her hair was piled up in a disorganized bun that was crumbling fast and the pencil holding it together wasn't up to the task. She wore jeans worth looking at and his old Navy sweatshirt, way oversized on her. The one he once used as a disguise on a black bag job at the old Willow Grove Naval Air Station. A memento she must have found in the bottom of a closet.

Reports, bound and unbound. Brochures, some slick and glossy, others kind of ratty. Stuff clipped together in black clamps with silvery ears, stuff stapled in the corner, stuff just loose and raggedy.

"Got a coffee, here. Fresh made."

Mandy tugged another pencil, which she'd been biting in the middle, from her teeth and tossed it on the floor. "Ah. A prince among...well, thieves. Sorry I didn't leave you any, but I've already been through a whole pot, I think."

She blew a stray strand of hair from her cheek and sampled the coffee. "This is the one thing I don't miss about reporting. Digging through tons of corporate compost on the proverbial hunt for something that doesn't add up. She held up a legal pad. Got a ton of notes, and no, it doesn't add up."

Like the analysts at Langley. Same mundane work, round the clock. Maybe with better material to start with. Maybe not. After lunch with Emerson, the remainder of yesterday had been tag-along as she called in markers from former colleagues. Media people, who'd been only too glad to have someone drain some of the stuffed file cabinet drawers. Corporate reports and data handouts that they knew they'd never need, use or want, but stashed anyway. Like nervous squirrels in autumn, she said, the baggage all reporters tend to lug around.

Tommy surveyed the scene. "How long have you been at it?"

"Four this morning. I know, we got in late, but I couldn't sleep. So I grabbed a piece of toast, did coffee, and started digging through all the junk. These two are junk, these are just company B.S., these might have value but probably not. This little pile is worth a closer look. But nothing really jumps out. Your shredder would probably cower in anxiety as we speak. If you had one."

"No need for a shredder."

She stretched and stifled a yawn. "I know, I know. No records, no documents. Nothing electronic. Nothing on paper either? C'mon. Maybe a secret vault, bank box, stash someplace?"

"Nope. Keep life simple."

"There are guys in monasteries with more stuff than you have."

He sipped his coffee. The usual, just the way he liked it. "Yep, and look at all the stress they're under."

She leaned back against the front edge of the sofa. "Funny. *The Case of the Anxious Abbott.*"

"More like *The Case of the Mundane Monk.*"

Mandy sighed. "Which is what all this is turning out to be.

The usual filings, everything neat and tidy. The memoranda and reports, with tons of tech gobbledygook that I can't begin to grasp. No idea how Lucy does it. And of course, all the goo on Mister Good Samaritan himself. The only thing it's missing is a snapshot of him walking on water."

PR types, running a con. Theirs is legal. Mine could could get me put in jail. Tommy shrugged. "There *are* guys, you know, who are driven, high achievers, do a lot of good, but people being people are imperfect. Doesn't make them Evil Incarnate."

"Maybe so. But I keep coming back to the way his people handled the visit to Billy's. Like she was a stray heifer that need‑ ed to get back in the barn or something. And since then, nothing about Nikki and the child missing, vanished, anything." Her ex‑ pression was halfway between a scowl of annoyance and bleary-eyed exasperation. "And more than one source talked about Sav‑ age periodically just dropping out of sight, but nobody's saying where he goes or what he does. It's like they're hiding some‑ thing, Tommy."

"Maybe it's time to take a break, get some breakfast?"

She lit up with sparkling eyes and a sunny smile. "I would *love* breakfast. What do you have in mind?"

He scratched his jaw. "I dunno. Puffin Diner. Waffles, ba‑ con, mess of eggs."

Mandy gestured toward her body. "Like this? No makeup? My hair? I couldn't possibly — "

"Folks'll figure you been workin' hard. Nobody's gonna care. Least of all — "

She waved him off. "Okay, that's just wrong on at least three counts, so you may as well just avoid the 'oops' and either think about warming up a skillet or give me thirty minutes to get my‑ self together. And that smirk makes it thirty-five. Your choice."

* * *

Frannie poured coffee and drew an envelope from her apron pocket. "Fellow in a suit, with a fancy car, a city guy, left this with Arlene at the register."

The return address was the corporate offices of CySafe. No postage, and his name was handwritten in the middle.

Mandy cocked an eyebrow and glanced around the room, probably to see if anyone was watching. "Well?"

Tommy showed Mandy the simple message on the stationery inside. It said, "$100,000 US" and a ten-digit phone number. "Looks like we got us an auction going."

She peered at the phone number. "Washington. Probably their offices somewhere along Georgia Avenue, Northwest. The tech hive. What do you want to do?"

"Eat breakfast."

Frannie delivered juice and table goodies for the waffles that she said would be along shortly. "You're lucky. It's a slow day and Ernie had just enough batter left before the kitchen shifts over to lunch."

Tommy asked her, "Recall when this got dropped off?"

"Day before yesterday. Guy looked like one of those big-city real estate lawyers. Kinda young, on the lanky side, cocky, nose high in the air."

Michael Barnett was shorter and stocky, middle aged. So after he got bailed out, the front office sent another emissary to deliver the latest offer. At least they were still thinking cash and not bullets.

Frannie tidied up the flatware, still rolled up in a napkin, on Mandy's side of the booth. She lowered her voice to confidentiality "Certain amount of talk around town that you've kicked some big dog in the shins, Tommy, just so you know."

For sure. He glanced toward Mandy, whose impatient facial expression urged him to share news.

Frannie fiddled with her pen and order pad. "Have anything to do with Billy's the other day? Heard there was some kind of a showdown."

Tommy said, "Yeah, well, we had a chat with some people."

"And that thing with Chet?"

"Yep, got some people working on it. Complicated stuff, tracking these guys down, but we'll get there. Promise. He doing okay?"

"Yeah, fine. You know how Chet is, Tommy. He doesn't care about the money so much as he wants someone's hide on the crapper door." She paused to muster candor. "Look, I don't mean to tell you your business, Tommy. I'm sure your techie friends are good at what they do. But where I come from, you don't bag the buck until you get on to trackin' him."

Mandy said, "Don't worry about it Frannie. It's going to be fine."

"Uh-huh. Well. Chet's not the kind of fella who'd ask and I'm probably speaking out of turn. I'll just get your platters. They should be ready."

He appealed to Mandy. "Chet said — "

"I know."

"These things just don't — "

"No, they don't."

"Lucy's probably going as fast as she — "

"I'm sure. Tommy, we're all getting a little frustrated. We pushed their buttons, they pushed back, now we're running in circles."

"Like a dog chasing its tail."

She sat back and gestured with her fingers in the air. "Yup. Round and round. With the meaningless stuff they want us to have. Not what we want to know."

Like grandpap once said. "An ol' hound dog chasin' its own tail ain't getting no closer to that damn rabbit." Or buck, as the case might be.

Frannie returned with the platters, which she warned were hot because they'd been in the pickup window under heat. And an apology. "Look, Tommy, I didn't mean to — "

He offered a patient smile. "It's okay. And I sure didn't figure on giving you the ol' bureaucrat shuffle."

"Thanks, it's just that — "

Mandy chimed in, a pat on the arm, soft and reassuring. "Of course. Perfectly understandable. Things are okay?"

Frannie shrugged. "I believe they'd be a whole lot better if this business got cleared up. Chet doesn't say much. Not that kinda guy. But I know it's chewing on him something fierce and, yeah, well I'm in love with the big lug."

Mandy gave her attention back to Tommy, her smile saying it all.

He said, "Maybe we can ratchet things up a little. Get it all back on the square."

Frannie grinned. "Thanks, Tommy. I just knew — Oh, well, I'll leave you two to your breakfast. Eat, eat. Before it gets cold. More coffee?"

Tommy looked at Mandy. "No, thanks. I think we're good."

As always, she used her knife to put a little space between the scrambled eggs and bacon and the waffle. She once explained the move would keep the pool of syrup from fouling the egg but just soften the bacon. The eggs, showing the specks of dill, made it just to the edge of the dish and to his recollection had never spilled over. Habit. Practice. A smart move she'd done many times.

Like his own grandpap, who'd step out onto the porch of his shack, a familiar side-by-side shotgun on his arm. And the dogs that mostly slept when not chasing their own tails on the dirt road, they'd snap right to attention. Time to get down to busi—ness, get the nose to the mud, pick up a track and get on with fetching supper.

Tommy didn't separate a thing on his platter. His eggs were sunny up and he'd carve off a hunk of waffle to mop yolk in easy circles, saving the bacon for the end. She was right. They were chasing their tales on the stuff that CySafe wanted folks to know and it was coming onto time for the answers to nagging questions.

He swallowed a wad of egg and chunk of waffle. "I'm thinking we're going to up the ante, deal a fresh hand. Only this time, we're going to get some help."

She looked up. "Not Charlie and Serge — "

"Not yet."

"I'm not so sure I might like where this is going. 'Yet' is a dangerous word with you guys."

"All three of us have worked with people, mostly floaters, sort of freelance types, occasional mercenaries, professionals. I'm thinking that Serge's people are mostly jungle rats, and my old crew was mostly Europe and Central America. But Charlie used to work with a guy, a skip tracer, who had a really first-rate crew. Here in the States."

"Used to work?"

"Well, yeah. I mean, Charlie's retired now and doesn't have much of a call for that sort of thing."

She began to tap the tip of the knife lightly on the remains of the waffle. "I'm listening."

The plan was obvious and relatively routine. But he cautioned himself to watch how he said it. "So I'm suggesting we set up maybe a floating box, real unobtrusive, tag along and see where Savage goes. If he's just a guy on a vacation, and this is just a person with a misguided sense of values, then, okay, we'll have to deal with Nikki on it and maybe get ourselves out of the line of fire."

Her eyes narrowed. "I didn't think we were in a line of fire."

He shrugged and gestured to the envelope on the table. "That's just a friendly howdy-do. Maybe nothing, but — "

"Go on. What's a floating box?"

"Loose street surveillance, passing the target along from point to point, old fashioned espionage work. If you get a good

crew, they do a whole lot better than electronic stuff. The peo—
ple element, you know."

"Ah, of course. Stake-out on wheels."

"Yep, sorta. Anyway, just an idea."

If she had noticed the effort to play a secondary role, she was
being very subtle about it.

"And you suspect Charlie's people would be good for it?"

"From what he tells in stories, anyway. I don't know them
personally."

She glanced at the envelope, then stirred a folded piece of
bacon in the syrup pond on her platter. "Do you think it would
be better coming from me, or you? No, wait, never mind. I'll
dial, you talk. It's what you do best."

CHAPTER SEVENTEEN

Near Harrisburg, Nebraska

Nothing. Nothing ahead. Nothing to the right or left. And certainly nothing behind. Except for dust. If nothing else, Mandy decided, the topography of western Nebraska was con−sistent.

And worrisome. For miles, the tires of the rented SUV crunched a blend of gravel and fine dirt in a westerly line with−out a street sign, a traffic sign or any sign of human life. Just twelve hours earlier, Lucy reported she was very gingerly work−ing into CySafe's system via access records first. Finally daring to go for archived files of building access, she'd discovered a pat−tern of absences by Savage. And six hours earlier, Charlie set the Nebraska meet.

Now there was nothing.

Mandy studied directions. "Tommy, do you think we made a wrong turn? According to the lady at the courthouse, this is sup−posed to be a county road, like a highway."

"No other turn to make. First right, then west to the fourth intersection, on some sort of a curve. She specified four-way in−tersections."

She said, "It's been a mile since the third. And I'm not so sure it was an intersection as much as it was a dirt turnoff into a field or pasture. This is supposed to be Canyon Road, but I sure haven't seen a canyon. Just empty land. Flat. Nothing."

He chuckled. "Goes kind of up and down in a gentle roll."

"Like an ocean in dead calm. Okay, slow down. She said there'd be a slight rise and the main road — if you can call this that — bends just before a stop sign for the opposite direction."

Tommy reduced speed. By the time Mandy looked up, the back side of a stop sign shimmered in the sunshine of a completely cloudless day. Even the sky had nothing.

He pulled to the side and stopped.

"I wonder if that road goes on to maybe a hot bath and a heated swimming pool somewhere."

Tommy checked his watch. "We're a little early. We could go thirty or forty miles and see."

"I'll be patient. Now what?"

"We wait."

They stepped out into air that was milder than expected, taking in a panoramic view of...nothing. Scrubby grass, a few utility poles, the road on which they had just travelled, narrowing to a dot on a horizon line that might have been drawn against a ruler.

"Wow. Welcome to Banner County, Nebraska. So this is where Charlie's buddy hangs out? Do they arrest people for running this stop sign? If you ran the stop sign and there was nobody within ten miles, would it — "

"Make a sound?"

"No, silly, break a law, for which you'd be captured, jailed, released on bail that you'd skip and then Charlie's guys would come along, on a herd of thundering horses, ten-gallon hats and canvas dusters flapping in the wind."

"I don't think running a stop sign was ever a hanging offense."

She leaned into the hood of the car. "I dunno, Tommy. Frontier justice, podner, frontier justice."

He chuckled. "This is more like the scene from *North by Northwest*, with the crop duster."

"Don't be ridiculous. That's only in the movies."

He pointed east. "Really?"

Just a dot in the sky. Floating forward at a steady pace, in a straight line, not like a bird in flight. Following the line of the utility poles, over the open pasture. Coming fast.

"Should we hide? Or wave?"

"Neither."

"But there's no gasoline truck for it to crash into and burst into flames. In the movie — "

Tommy leaned against the vehicle, arms crossed, like he was waiting for a bus. As the chopper slowed, the thutter-thutter hammered the air while her heartbeat pounded her ribcage. It lowered, a giant insect examining them as potential prey. The fields in Corrientes surfaced in her memory, the blind sense of flight, the ripping of the barbed wire, the driving rain. *At least Hector Suarez couldn't get a chopper in the air.* Maybe it was Charlie's friends. Maybe it was Savage's people. Within her, an overwhelming sense of panic surged, of being exposed in an open place with virtually no place to hide.

Tommy seemed to sense her anxiety. His placid expression was unchanged. "Steady, steady."

The helicopter roared overhead and followed the road they were not supposed to take. The sound faded into the gentle whoosh of the wind pouring across the plain. Silently, the aircraft pressed on, toward a distant low hill, and seemed to vanish into thin air.

Relief. Probably just one of those agribusiness execs checking on his flock of ranches. She said, "You've done this sort of thing before."

Tommy dug into a day pack for field glasses. "Yeah, but last time they were armed to the teeth with anti-tank gear and there really was not much of a place to hide." He gazed at the horizon and pointed to grey movement. "Dust cloud. Here they come."

He handed the glasses to her. Two headlights, some sort of at truck, bouncing along over the sandy road. A tower of dust in the air behind.

"Congratulations, Mandy. You passed inspection. Any of that coffee left in the Thermos?"

"Probably. Just wish I'd have packed something stronger."

He smiled. "You're doing fine. Just don't hesitate to take charge of these guys. Be strong, take charge."

Mandy sighed. "Strong is one thing. Getting killed in Nebraska is something else. It would be years before they found my body."

A dust cloud boiled from the horizon, high into the sky. In the center of it, headlights jiggled as the truck bounced along the gravel road. Suddenly, a second vehicle pulled out from behind the first. They charged as a braced pair. "Tommy?"

Coffee splashed into the tiny cup in his hand. "Hm?"

"Just wanted to confess. I, um, don't have a Plan B. I didn't think it would be... But, anyway, if you'd like to, you know, maybe come up with something?"

He shrugged. "It's only a rendezvous. Nice and private. With a pack of really bad dudes, guys that've been thrown out of everything. Including prison. Half a dozen, I bet. If they had biker types in the Old West, this'd be them. Range bums, the worst you'd ever find in the darkest shadows of a scummy saloon. The kind that go for women and children first. Us and them. In the middle of nowhere. Nobody else for five, ten miles. What could possibly go wrong?"

Her mouth was agape. When she realized it, she closed it tight and narrowed her eyes. "I've heard about guys like you. The ones who told the scariest story around the campfire just before all the little kids had to crawl off into their pup tents."

He sipped coffee and chuckled. "Yep. And then have to listen to the sounds of all the creepy-crawly spookies in the woods. All kind of nasty. Boogiemen, big time."

Mandy shook her head, struggling to contain a grin and resist the temptation to sock him one, right in the shoulder. "I bet you were a really rotten kid. Legendary."

The big SUVs were coming fast now, gray dust billowing in their wake.

"Oh, yeah, awful. Hope those boys slow down a mite before they get too close or we're both gonna choke on that dust."

Never mind my throat. My hair. Should have brought the jacket, the blue one, with the hood.

The trucks, perhaps once shiny black and now a lightish gray to match the gravel, eased to a stop side by side about thirty yards away. From the north, the free-roaming wind of the Great Plains freshened into an icy gust that bit her face. The dust swirled and went straight south.

Or I could just be grateful for an incredibly lucky break.

Tommy screwed the cup onto the Thermos and parked it on the hood of their own vehicle, standing relaxed and casual as if this was the sort of thing people do every day. It seemed like a good idea. But she lifted her shoulders, opened her stance and cocked her hip, taking a posture of command in the middle of the road.

From the back seat of the lead vehicle, an enormous man dressed in black leather exited. Late forties, military haircut, weathered complexion. He wore a holster across his chest and had a second one low on his right thigh. A dark wide-brimmed hat, straight out of an old spaghetti western. The swagger of a professional wrestler and the cocky grin of a television game show host.

Behind, five equally big men climbed out of trucks. Combat gear, desert fatigues. Wraparound sunglasses. Two shotguns, three rifles. No smiles. More like solemn sneers. They fanned out to form a curved line and they marched like they meant business.

Her father's words. *Steady, strong, serene. You're an Owens girl.*

Mandy crossed her arms, locked deeper into her stance in the middle of the road and stared right back at the leader.

Half a dozen paces away, he stopped. The line behind him did the same, spread across the road.

"You'd be Miss Owens? Mandy Owens?"

"I am. And you are?"

He disregarded her question and tugged a paper from his shirt pocket and held it aloft to compare. Apparently satisfied, he folded it and tucked it away. "Name's K-C. And this here's my crew." He stepped forward and extended his hand. It was hard, calloused, and felt like sandpaper rubbing the skin of her palm and fingers. "Who's this guy?"

Mandy's smile was probably too patronizing. "This is my partner, Tommy."

K-C studied Kane and extended an invitation to shake hands. "Tommy Kane?"

"That's right." He was about as cowed as the bigger tomcat in an alley and spoke very quietly and steady.

He called out over his shoulder to the others. "Well, boys, this here's Tommy Kane himself." He turned back. "I've heard about you, bud. From Charlie. You're her partner?"

"Yeah, I am."

K-C glanced at Mandy and then back to Tommy, whose smile was very close to a smirk.

Tommy's tone was dismissive. "Her show, K-C. You deal with her."

K-C let the idea settle and then nodded. His attention re-turned to Mandy, waiting impatiently. "Charlie said you was something. Tommy Kane working for you? Yeah, you must be." Without breaking eye contact, he lifted his right arm and ges-tured for the others to step closer. "Let me introduce you to the crew. Your crew. This here's Frag, and J-2, and we got Brick, Dice and Jinx. We ain't too big on regular names."

Mandy relaxed and shook each hand in turn. "I can see that."

"These guys are the best in the business. Mostly high end skip-trace, now and then flat out surveillance, video records, lot of FISA court stuff. So Charlie said you had some kind of target, somebody you want followed?"

Mandy pulled a manila envelope from her bag and handed it to K-C, who in turn removed several sheets of paper and a photograph and passed them around to the team. Brick was about to return it but Mandy directed the file to K-C. "Keep it. So here's the thing. The guy is headquartered in Montreal. Drops out of the public eye regularly. Our people have managed to crack part of their system and have just learned he skips checking into the office once a month, every month, like clockwork. Nobody knows where he goes."

Our people. Nyx and Bug. Working together. Scary thought, even if they were on the same team.

"And you want to know where."

"Yes. Only, if he follows the pattern, he's taking off tomorrow. If it's not possible — "

K-C shrugged and stuffed the papers into his jacket pocket. "No problem."

"Okay, I suppose I should ask about your fee? I mean, day rate, expenses?"

K-C shook his head. "On the house."

"Nothing?"

"That's what on the house usually means."

"I don't understand. We have an operations budget and — "

K-C smiled. "Just returning a favor. When Charlie calls, he always goes to the front of the line. He sprung Frag — he's my little brother — from a military prison a few years back. Kid got a raw deal, life term, that kinda thing. So we owe Charlie, big time, ain't that right, Frag?"

Frag looked down and glumly nodded.

"Yeah, so we got this one for ya, Miss Owens." He thrust his right hand forward.

She accepted and shook it. "Mandy. Friends call me Mandy."

CHAPTER EIGHTEEN

Township Road 3010, Near Jacks Ford, Pennsylvania

From a plain foam cup, Tommy finished Frannie's to-go cof—
fee. It was cold and bitter, appropriate for sitting just off a two-
lane asphalt four miles north of town.

His truck was tucked into a stand of scrub trees just past the
apron of a logging road, barely dirt lines in the gray, misty for—
est. A complete reversal of yesterday, on the deck at Mandy's,
lounging in eighty-degree sunshine, part of an audience of four
watching a performance of French Canadian folk dancing orga—
nized by Mandy and Nikki.

Part party, part performance, actually. Mandy'd found some
recordings of authentic music, peppy, happy stuff that seemed
more appropriate for cozy nights in a Quebec bar than Carib—
bean sunshine. And so Nikki, relaxed and delighted, taught
Mandy more complicated dance steps. The guys stretched out in
easy chairs on the side.

Nikki said it was cute how Cyrus was just one of the guys,
mimicking everything Tommy, right down to the style of
shades, khaki shorts and color of polo shirt, standard wardrobe
on the island. Charlie and Serge knew better than to tease.

In yesterday's sunshine on Mandy's island Cyrus had been
hanging with the guys while Mommy was dancing. Tommy had

asked, *"Puis-je vous offrir un verre?"* The child eased out of his shell but didn't want milk or expect a couple of fingers of Scotch. Iced tea seemed like a plan. Cyrus was way underage for the usual beverages that Charlie and Yenchenko preferred. But they went along, just so the kid could be one of the men.

Now the men were out there, hidden along a stretch of road where the trees came right up to the pavement. Outside, the fog turned into mist, almost enough to suggest windshield wipers. Raw, cold, November weather, the kind that just demanded a den or maybe Billy's, but not a remote spot out on a road that was ninety-nine percent deserted.

Couldn't ask for a better spot for a trap.

Tommy tapped the steering wheel to the memory of the dance tune, a reel that must have gone on for about ten minutes. The crackle of radio traffic in his ear clicked him back to reality.

K-C was still a couple of miles north. "Two vehicles. Black SUV, tinted windows, your way."

Tommy sighed. *Here we go.* An annoying interruption to a Bahamas party, the news from Lucy and K-C arriving during supper only a couple of minutes apart. Savage had dispatched a crew. What they didn't know was K-C's people were now tag— ging along.

Two clicks of a mike, opening and closing. Then three clicks. Charlie and Serge had also heard word from K-C and were checking in from similar spots several hundred yards up the road.

Except for a thin frame of light, and pavement directly ahead, Tommy was cloaked by pillars of dormant tree trunks, black with the damp, muted by the foggy mist that clung to the side of a ridge, gradually sloping upward from behind to directly beyond. All in the eerie silence of late autumn, the day or so be— fore deer season opened, when this same spot would be packed with pickups and guys in searing orange vests and hats.

K-C's voice. "Half mile, forty, forty-five, closing steady."

It was time. Tommy grasped the riot gun from the passenger seat and slid out into the wet air, chambering a round as he stepped toward the road. Left, right. No traffic. Across the gravel shoulder, onto the firm footing of pavement. The dashed line marking the center. He turned, took a wide stance, and focused on the end of curve. Hundred and fifty yards.

Snipers like Ian Wells would prefer a scoped rifle, from somewhere up on the side of the hill. Yenchenko, a trusty AK-47 on full auto. But Charlie had a point. Nobody argued with a short-barreled twelve gauge pump.

Tommy loosened his shoulders and brought the weapon up, aimed high and across his chest.

The sound of tires on wet asphalt. Around the bend. One, then another, bunched tight. Headlights stabbed at the mist. Brakes. Slight skid to the right. Dead stop, fifty feet. Right rear door opening. Slight guy, dark overcoat. Barnett. Two more from the lead vehicle, four from the secondary. Who wears sunglasses in the rain? Right hands inside jackets.

In his ear, double click from a mike. Triple.

Barnett approached cautiously, hands in the air. "I'm unarmed, Kane. You're making a mistake. A really big mistake."

Tommy aimed directly at Barnett's chest. "That so? Tell your boys to show their hands. They'd better be empty, or you're about to become roadkill."

Barnett seemed to suppress a laugh. "I don't think so, Kane. I think you're one guy in the middle of nowhere — "

The roar of pickup trucks, the screeching of tires desperately clutching at the wet road. Heads turned. Charlie out of the truck with a twelve gauge.

Barnett scowled. "You're joking." Then his eyes went to Yenchenko, who'd spun his truck to block the entire road and who rose like a breaching whale. The AK coming, ready, as he rounded the hood of the vehicle, abandoning cover to pounce on the furthest of Barnett's men. Swing of the rifle butt into the jaw, and down the guy went.

"Nah," Tommy said. "We ain't joking."

More SUVs rushed into the scene, and big men tumbled into action, drawing an assortment of weapons as they flooded the confrontation. K-C. Frag. J2. Brick. Dice. Jinx.

Charlie barked. "Show me your goddamn hands! Right now! Your hands! Yeah, you! Get 'em up!"

Yenchenko came forward like a tank in battle, clobbering the guy who didn't obey, using his enormous hand to push heads down and drop Barnett's crew into kneeling positions.

Tommy grinned at Barnett and strode forward. He reached into the lawyer's coat and patted him down for weapons. "You just don't get it, do you, Michael? We don't want your kind around here. You come down here with a bunch of second-rate pansies, you get squashed. I'd sure wish you'd get the message. Nikki's not in the area, she doesn't want to go home, and your Mister Savage is just gonna have to accept that."

Barnett adjusted the fit of his suit. "And what you don't get, Kane, is that Mister Savage is a very powerful man who usually wins."

"Except for today."

K-C's crew began the process of binding the Canadian team with white plastic disposable cuffs, roughly shoving them into prone positions as they did so.

Barnett smiled as he brought his wrists together in front of his chest. "Very clever trap, Kane. You were waiting for us. How did you know we were coming?"

Tommy grunted. "No, no. Hands *behind your back*, Michael. Always behind the back." Barnett complied and Tommy walked around to make the cuffs fast. "There ya go, buddy. We've got a pretty solid intelligence network. We stay informed."

"Don't get *too* clever, Kane. Ours is likely much superior to yours."

Tommy chuckled. "Yeah, I guess that's why you're the one

standing in the middle of the road in handcuffs."

Barnett shrugged. "And of course, then there was your visit to Mister Savage's residence. Very obvious criminal act, break— ing, entering, burglary of prized family possessions."

Tommy stepped back and cleared the chamber of the shot— gun. "If that's what you think, Michael, how come you didn't call the cops? You know, things could get a lot easier if you'd just ex— plain all the secrecy. We might be able to come up with some sort of truce."

"And Nik — um, Mrs. Savage?"

"Probably not on the table. I'm telling you, Michael, I do be— lieve she's quits. If y'all got some kinda separation or divorce of— fer, I'd be happy to pass it along..."

"Mister Savage is not interested."

"Well, that's too bad." In the earpiece, a message from Chet, five miles out. Traffic coming. Tommy called out to Charlie, Serge and the K-C crew. "Hey guys, let's get the road cleared, wrap it up."

Charlie pointed to the prisoners. "What you want to do with these? Me, I can see dumping 'em out here in the woods, maybe they'll get lucky and deer hunters'll find 'em before they think they're venison steaks on the hoof."

Yenchenko shrugged. "We leave no prisoner. Shoot them now, dump into ravine, two hundred meter southwest."

As cold as it was, beads of perspiration formed on Barnett's head, like he was struggling to mask real fear.

Tommy sighed. "Stuff them in K-C's van for now, get the vehicles off to the side. Don't need to look *too* suspicious, now, do we?"

Frag and Brick prodded the prisoners back to the last van in the traffic jam. The rest squeezed other vehicles tight into the logging road entrances punctuating the stretch of highway. While Frag and Brick puttered with what looked like the final leg of changing a spare tire on the van, everyone else stepped into the trees and waited. A pair of big trucks and two cars passed.

While Sergei slung the AK-47 over his shoulder, Charlie cleared his shotgun and muttered, "I s'pose we ain't gonna stop in town for road coffee."

Tommy said, "Not a bad idea. Got a long trip ahead."

Yenchenko cocked an eyebrow. "Montreal?"

"Yeah. All kidding aside, it's probably better to give those boys a lift home."

Sergei's eyes were as friendly as an Arctic wolf. "I make no joke. We are eight, so to dig grave to hide body is not difficult task. They kneel, round to back of head, we fill hole, done. We go to Billy's bar, eat, drink, share story about hunt."

Charlie sighed and turned to Tommy. "That's what I like about this clown. A genuine humanitarian. Goddamn Russian."

Tommy shook his head. "Ukrainian, Charlie. *Ukrainian.*"

"Yeah, yeah, whatever."

Sergei looked astonished. "So. I ask. Which is smaller price. Eight bullet or drive to Montreal?"

Tommy said, "Probably depends on how much you eat."

Charlie added. "Or drink."

Yenchenko shrugged. "*Amerikanski.* So soft, most disagree—able. So. It is as you wish. We go to Montreal, dump these idiot, make return to boat where it is warm and we fish."

K-C stepped into the area. He was about six-three or four, maybe two-forty-five and had the gait of a former defensive line—man. And he looked up at Yenchenko.

"Hey, Charlie."

"K-C."

"You still got some moves, man. Like old times. And this has gotta be your big Russian buddy."

Tommy said, "Ukrainian."

"What?"

Tommy smiled. "Sergei Yenchenko is Ukrainian."

"Yeah, sure." He turned to face Serge. "Nice workin' with you, buddy. Heard a lot of tales about you."

Sergei had several inches and eighty or ninety pounds on K-C, who now looked like a regular guy. Yenchenko shrugged, but shook hands anyway.

K-C went into full grin mode. "Hey, and what Charlie says about you is true, man. One ballsy dude. Man, I wished I coulda seen it from the beginning. So where's, uh, Miss Owens?"

Tommy said, "Didn't make the trip, K-C. But you guys did great, picking up on a possible problem and following them all the way in. You did the right thing, and we owe you one."

"Nah. Was worth it, just meeting her. Be a long time before I forget her, standing there in the middle of the road, staring me down. Man, she had *me* half scairt, wonderin' what I'm gettin' my butt into."

Tommy smiled. "Yeah, and you definitely look like the kind of guy who don't scare too easy."

K-C shook his head. "And you guys work for her? That's gotta be somethin' else. Damn. I don't believe I ever met a wom-an like that before."

Charlie shrugged. "Yeah, I prob'ly shoulda warned you."

K-C chuckled, smiled in a distant kind of way. "Oh, yeah."

Tommy shifted his weight and used his toe to stab at a bro-ken tree branch. The guy was right about Mandy, and had no clue about Lucy Tramanian, methodically peeling away the lay-ers of Savage's security, finding the pattern of Savage's mysteri-ous travel that put K-C's crew on the track.

Charlie said, "But, anyways, thanks a bunch for helping out. We're obliged."

Tommy decided to help both men when the conversational pause opened and began to widen. "So you were making progress in Montreal?"

K-C nodded. "Yeah, but we might be blown. Your target hit the local airport and flew out on a private." He dug into his fa—

tigues for a wad of paper. "We persuaded the FBO people to give us a copy of the flight plan. Your guy went to Spain. Don't sound like a fishing trip to me."

Tommy accepted the photocopy of the required materials filed by the pilot, which was on behalf of CySafe Corporation. *Ibiza?* A playground for the beautiful people, big on noisy bars, bawdy beaches, scanty bikinis and all kinds of booze.

K-C continued, "But now the dudes in the van are witnesses. They can finger us anytime. Tell Miss Owens it was a bad break, but the change in plans mighta done us in."

Tommy passed the plan to Charlie, who looked like he was reading it with great care, but more than likely it was just for show.

Yenchenko grunted. "Thirty minute only. Then no witness."

K-C shook his head. "Sorry, friend, we track people. We don't snuff 'em." He turned to Tommy. "Is this Russian guy for real?"

Tommy sighed. "Ukrainian... nah, never mind."

CHAPTER NINETEEN

906 Rue Belmont, Montreal, Quebec

Tommy looked up. He'd scribbled Lucy's directions on a scrap of paper and had spent the last thirty minutes trying to de-cipher it. "Yeah, Serge, this has gotta be it. Just ahead, on the left, right past that little construction area."

Yenchenko paused at a bilingual stop sign partway out into the road.

They had just passed a construction office trailer stabilized for the long haul and an area cordoned off by four-foot welded wire fencing. An assortment of construction supplies were neatly organized inside.

Further along, mostly commercial vehicles parked head-on into the row of low buildings. Vans, pickups, small box trucks. The working guys who kept the glamor buildings, fronting on boulevards to either side, humming along. To the left, brown brick, maybe some kind of a warehouse. To the right, a parking garage wall punctuated at regular intervals with huge square ex-haust vents.

"*Da, da*. Of course. Here is good place for you to depart."

Tommy opened the passenger side of the white van. "Meet you just on the other side of the boulevard, dead ahead."

Yenchenko gestured him out. "*Idi seichas, bystro, Koshka.*"

Beyond, the routine urban mid-morning traffic. In the closed space behind the seats, Barnett's men, bound, gagged, thirsty, hungry and probably bruised from the long drive north. In the rear view mirror, black SUVs with Quebec plates waited.

Tommy walked toward the intersection. Yenchenko eased the van forward and the SUVs followed close behind, both ig—noring the stop sign. The van eased left and stopped in front of a side alley leading to corporate parking for CySafe Corporation. A towering brownish glass block reached into a rich blue sky. The SUVs followed to seal the entrance. K-C's men alighted to the pavement and scattered.

Tommy had just passed the entry to the parking garage on the right when Sergei turned off the van engine, got out and strolled toward the intersection, ignoring people in the area.

Astonished faces. Voices of objection. Several vehicle honks. A uniformed guard, scampering from a doorway beyond, waving his arms. Yenchenko didn't even look. Just marched forward and into to the boulevard against the flow of traffic. He thrust his hands out left, igniting blaring horns, and paused for a moment on a wide median with low shade trees. Then his right hand came up to cause a round of screeching tires and even more honking as he marched with indifference to the far side.

At the intersection, the traffic signal was in Tommy's favor. Halfway across the wide boulevard, he glanced as four guys in—spected the vehicles, opening doors. At least Barnett's boys wouldn't toast in the sunshine. From the opposite side, he watched the action unfold. More guys, closer look. They opened the rear doors of the van. From his left, a limo swept forward. Charlie at the wheel, Yenchenko up front. The rear door opened and he settled into perfect climate controlled comfort.

Lucy looked up from her ever-present electronic pad. "Hiya, Tommy. Wow. You could use a shave and a change of clothes. So did you guys have a fun field trip?"

Tommy said, "Ruffled a few feathers, but nobody got killed."

"Great. We're trying to ruffle a few more. Charlie, could you make a left up here, then maybe pull over, close as you can, to the curb?"

She tapped on her little screen, glanced out the window, tapped again. The limo swung left.

A glass boxy skyscraper shimmered in the sunshine. The usual flags, corporate, Quebec, Canada, fluttering light in the swirling breeze of the street. Above the focal point of a line of plate glass doors, the stylish letters unabashedly identified CySafe Corporation, with smaller letters stretched underneath declaring this was the world headquarters.

Charlie asked, "Whereabout?"

Lucy looked up. "This is good. Hit the blinkers for a sec." One more firm tap on the tablet screen.

Tommy said, "So. Cole Savage's little sandbox. Doesn't look all that impressive to me."

Lucy wore a patronizing smile. "Trust me. It's a friggin' fortress. You gotta remember, Tommy that this is the operations center for a company that specializes in security. They've got a reputation for being showy about it, just as a marketing device. By comparison, the NSA nest down at Fort Meade is like a newspaper on a park bench."

"You sound impressed."

"Damn straight, I am. Which is why dad and I are taking this in baby steps. Remember the stories you used to tell about Doc's old place in the desert? Yeah? Now picture one of those, maybe a four footer, and all you have to do is pat it on the head and scratch its tummy."

Tommy nodded. "Got it. Who we waiting — "

Doors opened. Two men and three women in corporate wear, looking like they were right out of the executive suite. And right behind, a squat little man, thin hair just this side of bald, wearing a utility workman's jumpsuit.

Bug.

He carried a soft tool bag overflowing with plastic-handled screwdrivers, pliers, testing gear and strode to a telephone com—

pany van illegally parked in front of the building, marked off with traffic cones front and rear. And a manhole, with the lid pulled to the side, the reason every passing cop would take a look and roll on. Bug stowed his equipment in the truck, then used a combination of a crow bar and manhole cover hook to seal up the hazard. He checked for passing traffic and crossed the street.

With two guys up front, the van pulled out into traffic and sped away.

Lucy opened the door for her father. Charlie brought the limo to life.

Tommy waved. "Hey, Bug, been a while."

Lucy directed Charlie to roll into traffic.

Bug grunted. "Yeah, Tommy, you got that right. You still owe me five grand for that phone Mandy dropped in Argentina."

"Can I write a check?"

Bug scowled. "Uh-huh, sure, and then you can shove it right up your ass."

Tommy turned to Lucy. "Pay the man."

Her eyes widened in protest. "What do I look like, some sort of piggy bank?"

Tommy pictured the private bank in Grand Cayman that Lucy had bought just to stash the cash and said, "Well, as a matter of fact..."

Yenchenko chuckled. "When I am small boy, Sergei has bank for coin. It was jungle animal, *slon*, big gray animal with long nose."

Charlie muttered, "Elephant."

Sergei brightened. "*Da, da!* To get coin, boy hold bank upside down by ankle of animal. Shake most vigorously, until money fall out."

It was an image that brought laughter from all the men in the car, while Lucy's face reddened as it settled into her palm, and her head shook slightly from side to side.

When laughter withered, Tommy turned to Bug and Lucy.

She said, "Well, since you guys decided to poke Savage in the eye by dumping off his people in the alley, dad and I thought we might try some new tech inside the castle."

Bug leaned forward. "Yeah. So I've been tinkering with a modified RX-D78, running two-point-five gigahertz on a secure eight hundred-oh-one band. Maybe we can filter out most of the crap and tune in to the right lines inside. Got a helluva range, those seventy-eights. Buildings from that era, they've usually got the com circuits in the first level basement. Couple of flashes of ID, bing-bing-bing. We can tune in later, from the home base."

Tommy stared for several long seconds.

Now it was Lucy's turn to laugh. "No, you don't have a clue what he just said. Don't even try to talk your way out of it."

She was right. About all he could do is smile and settle back for the ride out to the airport.

* * *

Twenty-three minutes later, Lucy conferred with the valet at Skyservice tarmac, signed paperwork, and handed the guy the keys to the limo. Tommy had found his aviator sunglasses and a broad, relaxed grin. Behind him, the Gulfstream sparkled in the late morning sunshine, and Karen was waiting at the foot of the steps.

He gestured toward N226TK. "C'mon, boys, lemme buy you a first rate breakfast. Steaks, eggs, big ol' mess of hash browns, hotcakes, whole bucket of real good coffee."

They trooped forward, lugging small duffels, mostly weapons and a change of skivvies, and climbed aboard.

Lucy brought up the rear and greeted Karen. "I think I've rounded up all the strays. They're in a partying mood."

Karen glanced at Tommy, then back to Lucy. "I can see that. And you?"

"Me? I'm going back to Provo. I've had enough of being mommy, er, Mandy for a day. Now I've got to sit with this guy for the next hour and bring him up to speed on where he's going next."

Karen smiled. "Lucky you. Your usual fruit bowl for breakfast?"

"You are *so* thoughtful. And gallons of coffee?"

The way she and Charlie loved it and Serge could tolerate. Still, Tommy kept grinning. "C'mon ladies, let's get this bird in the air."

Lucy nodded toward him but spoke to Karen. "This is what happens when you mix too much adrenalin and testosterone."

Karen's smile was placid, calm, diplomatic, and she followed them up the steps and secured the door.

* * *

Wheels up, steady climb on a long, sweeping turn toward the south, through clear air and finally leveling off at 38,000 feet. Two carafes of coffee, the high test favored by the others and French Market, just the way he liked it.

Lucy unfolded her portable office, the dark brown leather case that was as standard on the jet as seats and glassware. Toward the aft galley, Charlie, Bug and Sergei shared campfire tales of the hunt, the score, the little triumph that revived adventure in their lives.

She basked in the comfort of coffee that would bite the toughest men hard, and reviewed notes she had scribbled in actual ballpoint pen on a legal pad usually reserved for doodles.

She gave him a direct look. "So is the adrenalin getting down to normal? We've got some serious shit to go over."

"Yep, no trouble. Some of the crew was wondering why Mandy didn't make the trip."

Lucy smiled. "No brainer. Somebody had to keep an eye on

Nikki and the kid. She speaks French, I don't. And most of all, I don't do kids. Besides, dad wanted to try out this new toy he's been working on for weeks and Mandy's not all that strong on tech."

The scent of steaks and eggs was drifting through the cabin and he realized it had been almost a day since he ate last. Karen served the guys in the back first, and then delivered his platter and her fruit bowl, refreshing the coffee cups.

"You know, Tommy, that stuff'll kill you. You're living much too dangerously."

"Yeah, I'll make a point of reforming tomorrow, maybe the day after. So how's the CySafe thing going?"

She used a knife to subdivide an enormous strawberry. "Steady, but slow. Just about the time I get feeling lucky, I re– member being nailed by the SEC and pull back. Maybe I'm get– ting old."

"No, Luce. Just wiser. Trust me on that. I think about it ev– ery time I step out into a highway with a shotgun to face down a speedy truck."

She chuckled. "Tommy, you are just so full of shit... Okay. So here's the thing. I'll spare you the play by play since I know you can't stand tech talk."

"Thank you."

She targeted a chunk of melon. "The OK Corral incident in Jack's Ford wasn't a total loss. Charlie's guys got us a destination and it was pretty straightforward to roll back through the flight ops archives to see the pattern. Third week of the month, off to Ibiza, where, it turns out, he has a villa just on the edge of the party scene. I don't have our guy down as a jet setter — his bio makes him out to be a lot more stuffy than I'd find interesting, the charity work is all goody-two-shoes, and I'm still working on his financials."

The ribeye was tender, juicy, a melt-in-the-mouther. The best way to make it last was small bites, slowly chewed. "And so, do you think hes got a mistress stashed in Spain?"

"Well, it's the sort of place where you could find that sort of thing in any bar, on any beach, and especially at the better clubs. Which is opening up a lot of trails to follow, long distance. Just cross checking hotels, resorts, flights in and out, for a matching pattern is gonna be a bitch."

He chuckled. "One little hurdle at a time."

"Yeah, well, speaking of hurdles, your buddy Chet's not as innocent a victim as he sounds. I got the emails, Tommy, and it wasn't one of those things where you accidentally click on an at—tachment and the malware rolls in. He was chatting with one of those 'lonely Russian girls' that was probably some chubby little pimple-face in a boiler room. And he got caught. They're work—ing out of a data center in suburban Chicago, and I'm guessing you guys are gonna want to pay a visit."

Tommy sighed. Not news he welcomed. "People do stupid things, sometimes. So what's your suggestion? For Mandy, I mean."

Lucy chewed some citrus, cocked an eyebrow and smiled. "Attaboy. You're finally learning that this time out, the girls are running the show."

CHAPTER TWENTY

Mandy Caye, the Bahamas

A lounge chair under a giant orange umbrella. A couple of fashion magazines, two months out of date. A soft drink, starting to go warm, a drowsy sensation of being lazy — with permission.

Mandy yawned. *If you've got to be alone, this is the perfect spot to do it.* Caressing ocean air, probably hovering around five knots. The little waves, tickling the beach. How long had it been, where was it, what was she doing, the last time she felt completely away from it all? For a rhetorical question, it was rather silly.

She wasn't the only one on the island.

Mandy shielded her eyes from the sunshine to scan the beach. A couple of hundred yards to the left, nobody. Past the dock and the thatched-roof cabana on the right, more beach, but partially blocked by palms hugging the shoreline. Beyond, another quarter-mile of sand, another point, another beach.

Nikki and Cyrus had gone for a long walk to relieve a creeping sense of boredom, the high price of indolence on an island.

Paradise. I made a promise to myself to always savor this.

Not so long ago, the island had a different name, wearing an opulence that seemed obscene, the vehicle for Walter Campos to stick it to a rival in a breathtaking collision of enormous resources over a simple grudge. The kind of grudge that ordinary people carry around day after day, an itch that only guys like

Campos can really scratch.

Which he did. A stunning *gotcha!*

Mandy sighed. *And he used me to pull it off.*

Which was okay. *Because I wanted to beat her just as badly.*

And then the moment, on the yacht off Cayman, when Walter handed over a fistful of paper, title, deed, permits, the legal things. A gift of paradise, a tip of the hat, the kind of thank-you that only billionaires do. Then he sailed off in his yacht for some time in Greece.

Once again, she scanned the beach.

Nothing but paradise. Tommy had the the Pennsylvania land, the cabin, the hideout in the woods with the big porch and the charming little kitchen and the lake with the path all the way around it. She had the island, hundreds of acres, beaches, a mansion and a guesthouse and even an airstrip. A big, spacious kitchen filled with all the conveniences and a fridge and freezer stuffed with food. Food that Charlie and Serge and Tommy helped get, because they knew the route to town, to the market.

The boat.

The boat that was tied up at a dock fifteen miles away, at a marina near the airport. Which technically meant she was marooned. In Paradise. Which wasn't, because...

Tommy. It all meant nothing without Tommy.

Mandy stretched and pulled herself up out of the lounge chair, gathered the warm glass and dumped the remnants of the drink. She stuffed the magazines into her beach bag, still unread. And the phone, just like the one she'd dropped in the drainage ditch and ruined.

How could you be marooned when you can call Lucy anytime and have a Frisco's helicopter here in a few minutes?

They'd all be back late today. It would be noisy and teasing and laughter. And good food, probably barbeque by the pool. Fine scotch, smooth rum and silky bourbon. Stories of adventure. Life. Not alone.

She could not resist a smile and a chuckle as Lucy's text message echoed in her mind. "Guys kicked ass. All fine, headed home."

Home. To paradise. The sweep of bright whites and blues and horizon from there to there. From just past the palm tree point, Nikki appeared, walking in child steps, hand in hand with Cyrus and without even thinking, her thought process slipped back into French, native for them, heritage for her.

* * *

Kitchen conversation was built on exotic salads they made for themselves while dancing around the subject of Cole Savage. As a matter of teenage grooming, Mandy had been taught not to pry. As an element of her career as a New York reporter, she'd poke a fearless question at anything. Courtesy to keep her guest comfortable, curiosity to try to assemble a puzzle of seemingly disjointed data about Savage and his business empire.

Nikki had not been much help. She professed total ignorance of CySafe, Savage's business, his money, how it was spent. She had to know something, but had either turned a blind eye to it or was genuinely kept in the dark, marooned in a marriage many people would consider a paradise of comfort and convenience.

And little Cyrus, so terribly withdrawn. If Savage was so disinterested in his own child, why did he care so much about getting them both back? Into his net. His trophy case. The secretive world that increasingly seemed to be his trademark.

"The kid don't seem to be interested in fishin'," Charlie had said. "What kid don't like to fish?"

Well, me for one, and Tommy for another.

Sergei was puzzled, too. "Boy say father make many trip to fish. But never take boy. Very sad."

Lucy had discovered the trips were not to some remote trout stream, but touristy Spain, courtesy of K-C and his band of outlaws. K-C. Scary guy, but quick to change direction and turn the hunt into the trap in Jacks Ford. And even apologetic that he thought their cover was blown. Didn't matter. A trip to Ibiza, would be fun. A getaway with a gun.

Then Lucy could resume work on Chet's problem, the phishing scam that wrecked his life and whatever remained of his relationship with his ex-wife.

The boy stabbed idly at the salad.

Across the table, Nikki said, *"Cyrus, vous devez manger votre déjeuner."*

Mothers had the same problem everywhere. Mandy said, *"C'est bon. Peut-être que je peux préparer autre chose."*

Nikki waved her off. It was a mom-to-child teaching moment and alternatives were not going to be on the agenda, like the cookies that Lucy used to overload the pantry when weaning herself from doughnuts and dropping twenty-five pounds in the process. By ignoring the cookies.

Cyrus fussed in his quiet little way. Nikki's patience was wearing thin. *"Je suis vraiment désolé...*

Mandy shook her head. *"Ça va. Ne vous en faites pas."* It really was okay, no big deal. The conch wasn't all that great anyway, the lettuce was getting old and the tomato was overripe.

Everyone was getting bored with paradise.

The deck of playing cards. In the kitchen drawer, the one stuffed with the miscellany to be organized, some day but not today. Cards. A fun and simple way to — *how did Tommy put it? Yes. Pass some good time* — while away an hour or so.

Mandy kept the conversation in French. "You know, Cyrus, when I was your age, we used to play a wonderful card game. Called Go Fish. Have you ever played it?"

He shook his head while Nikki looked up and smiled.

"Ah, well, it's a lovely day to learn."

Nikki brightened even more. "Absolutely! It is such fun!"

Plus a good way to get past a so-so salad and an excuse to reduce the stash of cookies. Which would be used to keep score, maybe serve as prizes that Cyrus could easily win.

Conversational French was one thing, but explaining card game rules in six-year-old speak proved more challenging. Mandy was grateful for Nikki's help in describing the variation called Canadian Fish.

Probably better coming from Mommy anyway. They were so tight-ly connected. Clinging together in a lonely world, where there was only a chance to dance.

The first round of five cards each were distributed and Nikki walked Cyrus through the concept. Mandy played with grandiose ineptitude, making sure the child easily won points and a half dozen cookies. Cyrus soon seemed to be having a good time, gaining self-assurance and even laughing now and then.

Nikki whispered counsel in his ear.

Cyrus grasped his cards with both hands and spoke with all the smugness of a guy on a roll in a casino. *"Mlle Mandy, avez-vous des rois?"*

Kings. *"Oui, j'ai deux."* She tugged a pair of kings from her hand. Kings. Actually, she had three. Tommy, who didn't fish. Sergei, who fished like it was hand-to-hand combat. Charlie, filling the role of the father she missed so much.

And Lucy. Who loved to go after a different kind of phish—ing, the kind of crooks and thieves that lurked throughout the internet, the sly scams used to con innocent people out of all their money.

Phishing.

The purpose of CySafe was to block phishing and other cy—bercrime. Reports said they were better at it than other compa—nies providing protection to millions of computer users, large and small.

Phishing.

Cyrus had said his father often went *fishing*, but never took the child along. But the trips were to Ibiza, an island playground off the coast of Spain. Why *fish* in the Mediterranean instead of the Caribbean? Software. Some sort of technology involved with *phishing*. Some kind of a super-secret breakthrough. *But why go anywhere?* Savage had a fortress in Montreal.

Mandy's mind groped through conversation with Lucy, rattling on about background information she'd been sifting. Savage wasn't native Canadian. He came from immigrant stock, post-war refugees from Eastern Europe. Originally to the United States, then to Canada, name changing for the usual convenience along the way. Why *ever* hadn't she paid closer attention?

Because it was no big deal. Millions of people moved around just after World War Two, trying to piece their lives back together, start fresh.

Somewhere in Eastern Europe. *So easy to call Lucy, ask her to repeat it. And look dumb. Focus. Focus. Focus.*

Lucy had said, "That's a city in Eastern Europe."

Yes. Savichi. In Belarus. Which was once part of the Soviet Union.

Russia.

Like China, India, Denmark. Where Lucy said they had some of the best hackers in the world, running enormous enterprises built on... *phishing*. Mandy's mind raced to...

But what if CySafe was the culprit, not the guardian?

Cyrus spoke with soft deference. "*Mlle Mandy? C'est à ton tour.*"

She could not suppress a smile. *Go phish.* "Oh, gosh, yes, Cyrus, it certainly is my turn."

CHAPTER TWENTY-ONE

C'mon. Dance with me. Tommy saw Mandy's hand gesture. Floating fingertips. An expression that was all kinds of sultry.

Party music of Trinidad thundered across the deck and rico‐ cheted off every corner of the island. And likely made waves fif‐ teen miles offshore.

Tommy prodded shrimp on the grill. Yeah, he thought, one of those parties that nobody ever forgets. A bunch of grownups, who should know better, acting like a bunch of kids, who don't. Shoulda seen it. Little things coming together in a big ol' gum‐ bo pot and bubbling up into... *party.*

C'mon. Dance with me. Mandy wiggled, waggled, laughed lustily. Hair splashed her face and her eyes sparkled like sunshine on morning dew. At the dance halls, back in the days when he was hanging out in the bullpen or even at Billy's on Saturday nights, it was all steps prescribed and practiced. In the open space beyond the grill, it was free form, the impromptu moves of young club people. Spring break beach stuff. Or in the big clubs with a lot of strobes and lasers in weird colors. Totally uninhib‐ ited.

Grandpap once said it best. "Don't show up to my party, 'less you plannin' to *dance.*" And there it was, in the center of the deck. Nikki on the left. Lucy on the right. And Mandy in the middle. Bodies plugged into a jolly bundle of soca recordings found in a storage box. The song was *"Mo'Fete."* Couple of hun‐ dred volts, a lot of amps. "Nobody leave, nobody go," repeated dozens of times. "Are you ready to go home? No! What time is it? We don't care!"

C'mon. Dance with me. Grin, smirk, grin some more. Her gaze locked onto his eyes to flirt without shame. Her arms wove enticement and her torso seduction, and he replied with a pheromone-filled smile from behind the grill.

It got started with five-gallon buckets of enormous shrimp they'd picked up on the way to the island. Then Charlie and Sergei mentioned they'd found and restored an old barbeque grill in a shed at the caretaker house. Now those shrimp simmered summertime easy, summertime slow. In a sauce he learned working short order grill at a bar in Belize, the kind that bites back when a guy sinks teeth into it.

Soca music, on a sound system that Lucy and Bug resurrected, a father-daughter thing with a bunch of growling, barking, sidewalk superintending, teasing, laughing. Whole lot of decibels, vibrating right through the deck boards and up into the legs and hips of carefree dancers. Even little Cyrus was going to town, jumping around like little kids do.

C'mon. Dance with me. Arms up, high in the air, swaying to and fro, enticing him forward. Mandy drifted into a reverie, her body turning, twisting, turning, the bewitching heat of movement pouring over him, making him sweat, dissolving resistance.

Sergei showed off bartending skills he'd once used on a espionage assignment in Monte Carlo. Continental cocktails from recollections probably just little foggy, but that was all right. Charlie wanted bourbon straight up but got something blue with a bunch of fruit and an umbrella perched on top.

Eyebrows went up when Bug began to nod in time to the music and showed off a tentative Brooklyn boogie. After Charlie sucked enough of the potent beverage through a straw, he got his toe to tapping and tried a not half bad shuffle himself.

C'mon. Dance with me. Mandy cranked up allure even more. Tommy hoisted barbeque tongs as his last holdout defense. She pouted. She shook her head. And she went to The Look, the one she saved up for when she really wanted him to knuckle under and follow.

Why not? Maybe a few conservative heel-and-toe steps, line style. Mandy laughed and her fingertips caressed the air, begging him to keep coming. *Okay, a few moves from the old Mardi Gras days.* The kind that came easier when half buzzed on a couple of quarts of beer and were gratefully forgotten the following day.

Sergei filled a glass with vodka and chugged it like water. He nodded, gave Tommy a thumbs up, and began to clap in time to the intense, sizzling beat.

Let go, let go. Tommy stepped and strutted like a drunken moth who'd found too much candle. And when he was close enough to hear her, she laughed again and said, "This is called Plan B."

Song after song, pounding inhibition into indifference. On and on and on, tumbling back to the Saturday night dancing of youth and the wild college parties of turning twenty, pushed fur-ther and further from any sense of propriety by Mandy, who knew a lot more about dance than she'd ever let on before.

When it was done and breath settled, easy laughter skittered across the afterglow, the golden and pink time after sun settles into the sea. Sergei reset the bar and the focus turned to food, a feast of a different kind of fun.

The shrimp had survived and shimmered in the fading light. Mandy drifted close and wrapped her arms around his bicep.

"You did well, big guy. Splendid." She leaned forward to peek into the grill. "Oh, wow. The shrimp looks divine, a work of art, stunning."

He chuckled and turned a shrimp. "Me, I looked like an id-iot. That's okay. Now, you were looking good. *Real good.* Better than these shrimp, even. Up in Jacks Ford, you were amazing. But tonight? Dang. Probably illegal in most of the hemisphere."

She giggled, the coy little giggle she always used to brush

away a compliment and keep it at the same time. "The thing about you, Tommy, is that you could sweet talk your way out of a felony arrest. And..." She paused. "Yep. There it is. Right on cue, that cute little smug grin of yours that just gives you away every time."

He feigned a sigh. "Darn. You know me much too well."

"I don't know you well enough. I want to know you better."

"Well, yeah, but there's a bunch of people watching. And I believe these ol' shrimps are just about perfect." With a large sheet cake pan in one hand and tongs in the other, he began to harvest his culinary crop.

She reached out. "Here. Let me hold the platter while you shovel the goodies aboard."

"I've got it okay."

"That's what all the strong guys say before the platter some—how shifts and all that gorgeous shrimp tumbles down to the deck where it — "

She was right. It *was* a guy thing, enduring the precarious, resisting the loss of control. His entire career had been shoul—dering the load, flying solo, directing others only when he re—quired an extension of himself. The dance at Billy's was being a good sport, pitching in to help her win a bet, showin' off. Tonight she'd drawn him out of his comfort zone and into her—self. "You've got a point."

He handed her the platter.

She grasped it with two steady hands and held it perfectly level. And she shrugged. "It's what one partner does for the oth—er. Now you can focus on presentation. Oh, gosh, they look just *so* good. I just know it's going to be a best ever."

He transferred shrimp to the platter in deft, sure motions. The others had retreated upstairs to gather side dishes and as—semble at the big round table in the observation tower.

"You know, Tommy, we're going to have to talk later."

He chuckled. "Oh, yeah, I bet."

"About Spain, silly. Ibiza to be exact."

More shrimp built columns and rows. "I heard, from Lucy."

"You heard a little. There's more. Look, if you scooch that third one from the left over just a bit, you'd have a much better presentation."

"You think? I always thought asymmetrical was okay."

"Nope. Sorry. I was always into balance. Just scooch the third... ah, there you go."

He grinned. "Happy?"

"Immensely."

Shrimp continued to populate the pan, with a lot more care than ravenous appetites required.

Her hands remained steady, firm. "Tommy, I'm going to need some help."

"Okay...."

"Since we're all together, we're going to have to organize some sort of plan. Nikki's not been much help, but I understand. Cyrus is always nearby and she might not feel as candid as she could. But I also don't think she knows much of anything. Cole keeps her at a distance, but on a tight leash. It just seems so odd."

"Okay...."

"But I'm not sure how to organize the others, direct them without annoying them or hurting feelings."

"They're very good at what they do, Mandy. Solid team. You know you can count on them."

"Right. And they'll do whatever *you* want."

With the bottom of the pan covered, he began a second tier, working from the middle outward along the center line of the pan. "They go their own way, know a lot of people, but when it comes to crunch time — "

"They follow you. *Always.*"

"So you want me to kind of step back?"

She wore an undecided expression. "Not so much that as...

Okay, honestly, I don't know what to suggest to them. I could sure use a little guidance here."

"Well, you're going to need a crew. And don't suggest. Just define what you think you'll need and let them do the rest."

"How do I — "

"Just have them brainstorm for... Hm. Let's see. Okay, a jack-in-the box, maybe two, couple of dingalings, half a dozen lifters, and a really good ghost. Plus some first class paper. A sitter. And a honeypot."

"I have no comprehension of what you just said."

"I could explain, but..."

She looked around at the empty deck. "I know. We're out of time and the shrimp will be getting cold."

Tommy said, "Trust me. It's what partners do."

"I should write this down. I'll never remember."

"No. You've got to rattle it off, ding, ding, ding, like you do it all the time."

He repeated the list.

"You're sure?"

He nodded while lining shrimp into neat rows.

She drew a breath and exhaled. "Okay. We'd better get up there with the main event. Otherwise there'll be all kinds of talk."

He gently laid the last shrimp on the platter and closed the grill. "Probably already is."

She extended her arms to offer the platter. "Here. You probably want to carry this. It's your presentation."

"Nah. Go ahead. It's your party."

Charlie and Bug had rigged some torches and Lucy and Nikki delivered bowl candles and platters of steamed vegetables, peas and rice and johnnycake to a round table, high in the tower where the view of paradise and the horizon was three-sixty.

Tommy trailed Mandy into a round of oohs and ahhs, laughter and banter, and he paused to capture details and commit them to memory. Happy faces, glowing in candlelight. Lazy surf, lapping the shoreline below below. And the fine scent of salt air on a whispering breeze, refreshing and flowing free.

CHAPTER TWENTY-TWO

Mandy settled in her chair and idly turned the stem of a wine glass as night deepened all around the glow of the table. It was good food, but even better company.

Especially Tommy, she thought. To her left, he worked patiently to converse with little Cyrus, explaining in Cajun French the food and traditions of the Caribbean. With any luck, the French-Canadian child would understand and feel welcome.

Lucy delivered the chilled guava duff they'd concocted that afternoon. Nikki had been eager to learn but was still very much the tentative guest and gave much of her focus to her son.

Now Nikki was the first to excuse herself. Cyrus had begun to nod off, overfed and worn out. He leaned into his mother, who said in French, "It's very late. Way past your bedtime."

A murmured protest was met with an affirmation from mom.

Tommy leaned over and whispered man-to-man reassurance. "It's okay, buddy. Tomorrow you get to do it all again, okay?"

Cyrus managed a nod despite drooping eyelids.

Nikki held her son tight, smiled and gently said, "*Merci, Tommy. Tu es un bon ami.*"

Mandy guessed what he was probably thinking at the sight of the mother-son moment, of how it would be wonderful to have a moment like that just once more. And he was not alone. Still, his patience and tenderness... It was impossible not to reach out and caress his shoulder blade while Nikki bid farewell.

She refilled her glass from a chilled bottle of a soft Pennsyl‑
vania wine that he'd found and occasionally smuggled to the is‑
land in the jet. When she looked up and around, there they all
were, the entire group together at one place, one time. Free
spirits so distinct in heritage, character, personality. Fiercely in‑
dependent, people who made their own rules and their own way.
Tommy's people. Her family. Stories were retold, teasing punc‑
tured exaggerations, and when the conversation began to dissi‑
pate.

Tommy said, "Mandy, earlier you said something about
Spain, something new that's come up?"

They listened politely while she summarized her thoughts
about phishing and the possibility that Savage was involved in a
good but secretive way, or in a bad and conspiratorial way.

Lucy cocked an eyebrow, leaned forward, looking intense,
and rubbed her jaw with her thumb and fingers.

*This is dumb. She's already figured something better. She's al‑
ready talked to Tommy about it, on the flight down.* Embarrassment,
not having thought it through well enough. "Okay, it was just an
idea, a theory. Kind of brainstorming. You know how it is when
you lay on the beach too long."

Lucy waved her hand. "No, no. Not at all. It's plausible. First
off, companies like CySafe are always developing new software.
Applications, upgrades, patches. Innovation lives in the pipeline,
and for all the obvious reasons it's always under wraps. Not only
is the usual competitive edge involved, but the coding is ex‑
tremely vulnerable to, well, outside tampering. It has to be kind
of open, because teams of engineers and programmers are in‑
volved. Trust me, all the black hats in the world would love to
get a peek at this point."

Tommy folded his hands on the table. "So it's a good bet
that they've got a hot project going — "

Lucy waggled a finger. " — but, Tommy, Spain doesn't fit.
Their R&D is based in Montreal. There's a data center near

Toronto, but that's it. The rest is sales, marketing. And there's no operations unit of any kind, by anybody I know of, on Ibiza. Plus, I really doubt that they'd farm out something on that kind of level to an outside unit."

A sense of relief flooded through Mandy. "So the second alternative?"

Bug started to answer, but Lucy got there first and said, "Yup. That's where I'd dunk my doughnut." With a faint wince, she turned to Bug. "Um, wouldn't you say, dad?"

Respect. According to Tommy, all Bug ever wanted was respect. Well, money, too. But mostly respect. Lucy probably realized she erred and tried to make amends. Okay, not the worst situation. They were still trying to work things out.

Bug let the slight pass. There was a time when Bug would respond by stalking off and then the phone wouldn't work for a year. Now he went paternal, like the old days he often spoke about, like the underbosses of organized crime who ran the neighborhoods of his youth. "Yeah, a good bet, maybe. The scenario might be that he's just testing stuff with hacks for hire. But any munchkin engineer can do that. Your guy? He don't do that shit. He's a *pezzonovante*, a big shot." His voice went to a sneer and spat every syllable. "A genuine god damn CEO." He shrugged. "Which o'course, is just a thief in a two-grand suit. So, yeah, kiddo, you might be right."

Mandy said, "Lucy, you mentioned you'd been researching immigration on the family's migration?"

"Yep. The Savage is a modification of Sauvage, the name the grandfather took when he emigrated first to New York, then to Canada." She tugged her tablet from her bag and swished through several screens, the whitish glow giving her a sort of spooky look in darkness that had somehow managed to sneak in after dusk, while no one was paying attention.

She smiled as she found the file. "Yeah, here we go. Okay, the grandfather was Cykiel Savitsky, eastern Ashkenazic Jewish family. When he got to the States, like a lot of immigrants, he Americanized the name. First into Savitz, then simplified it into Savich."

Mandy rolled the words around in her head. Savich, Sauvage, Savage. It seemed logical.

"So Cykiel set up shop, office supplies and equipment, more than likely the business he was in pre-war. The son, S-zzz.. S-zzz. Sorry, too much wine. Okay. C-z-y-c-z-a. He took the busi—ness into some innovative office machines for the time, got cou—ple of patents. Under the Anglicized version of that complicated first name: Cyrus."

Mandy looked at Tommy. *Cyrus*. She could see it in his eyes. The reincarnation of the father. Pieces were coming together.

Lucy skimmed through several screens. "And then comes our guy, Coleman, who made the right call when tech came along, the rest being history."

Mandy nodded. "And where did you say the family came from?"

Lucy looked up. "Well, the name Savitsky is supposedly a habitational name for people from Savichi, in Belarus. Don't know if it's for real or not."

Yenchenko cocked his head and spoke in a casual tone. "*Da*, Savichi. Is well known in Belarus."

For once Lucy seemed to be caught off guard and asked, "How so, Serge?"

"Savichi is in Minsk Region. They make small farm, quiet life. Most ordinary. It is unique, of course, because it is one hun—dred kilometer downwind from Chernobyl. So small farm be—come waste area. Only now do some people make return. But most fear for Cesium poison."

Tommy said, "I don't see a connection with the reactor crisis and internet crime. What's the connection with CybaSlave?"

Mandy chuckled. "Yep, too much wine. It's *CySafe*, Tommy."

Lucy sat up. "Tommy, what did you just say?"

"CySafe."

"No. Something else."

"Oh. CybaSlave, I guess. I mispronounced — "

She waved him off. "CyberSlave."

Mandy shrugged. "And that is...?"

"Old nemesis. From way back. Every time I'd get into some – thing kind of interesting, it seemed CyberSlave was nearby or had been there. Used to call him C-S for short."

Tommy said, "I still don't see the connection."

Lucy leaned back to reflect on a puzzle taking shape. "Okay, so here's the thing. CyberSlave was still active when I closed up Nyx, doing his stuff. Leads from Chet's phishing thing go to 'CySla2' which was just one of those handles you see all the time. Until just now. He's evolved."

Mandy chuckled. "How do you know it's a he?"

"Because the work is good, but kinda sloppy. I'd get there and find a mess. Never picked up after himself."

Tommy glanced at Bug and then Sergei. "I suppose people could read something into that."

Lucy ignored the remark and spoke to Mandy. "So now I'm beginning to wonder. What's the difference between *CyberSlave* and *CySafe*?"

Shrugs all around.

The time was right. Mandy shifted to the front edge of the chair and leaned forward, looking first to Lucy and then Tom – my. "Well, why don't we ask Savage himself?"

Chuckles and smiles.

Lucy cocked her head. "You're serious."

"How hard can it possibly be?"

Tommy had the decency to look like he was giving a plausi – ble idea serious attention.

Charlie's eyes narrowed. "Okay, Mandy, right off, I gotta ask."

"Okay, ask."

"Is this worth it? I mean, you're gonna need a crew. It'd be a fraction of the cost to just re-lo the kid and the mom, new iden‒tities, all that. And nothing to reload Chet's bank account and fix his credit score."

Mandy said, "I'm sure that's true."

Bug drummed his fingertips on the table. "So, yeah. Who needs the hassle? Sometimes you gotta choose your battles, maybe take the easiest path."

Steady, strong, serene. "I think it's worth it. Sometimes you just have to know. But you're correct, Charlie. We'll need a crew. A jack-in-the box, perhaps two or three, several dingal‒ings, half a dozen lifters, and a first-rate ghost. Not to mention first class paper, a sitter and, of course a honeypot."

Tommy nodded approval. With luck, their eyes were on him while she exhaled relief during the pause around the table.

Lucy spoke first. "Well, right off, I'd go with Lester Finn. He's the best I know, especially if you're doing casino work. If our guy is in Ibiza, I don't suspect he'd be a club guy, but more of a casino guy."

Tommy said, "Serrano, maybe?"

"No. He's in jail. Italy, I think."

"Can we spring him, Luce?"

"Doubt it. He was running an art scam."

"Who was the mark?"

"The Vatican. Some sort of cardinal."

"Ouch."

"Rubin Ward's pretty good, and then there's Misty."

"Who?"

"Misty Caldwell." Lucy spread her arms wide. "You know, the one with the really big — "

Mandy winced.

" — smile? No kidding, Mandy, she's got a wall-to-wall smile. That's three. Which is more than enough."

Bug aid. "I can handle phones. Yeah, yeah, Charlie, don't

gimme no hassle. I still got some moves. Plus I know a coupla guys. Plus Luce is good on the wire, so we oughta be okay."

Charlie said, "And then there's K-C's guys. I know, Mandy, they was frettin' about being made, but for a pounce-and-grab, they oughta be okay."

Mandy nodded. "Any thoughts on a ghost?"

Tommy and Sergei looked at each other, did that little what-the-hell shrug.

Yenchenko continued to look at Tommy. "Ian Wells."

"Retired, Serge. He's got that vineyard in France."

"Koshka, as always, you know not so much. Wine is perhaps mere cover for contract work."

"No, I heard he was out. Done. Besides, he was expensive."

"We make offer. You must pay for talent, da?"

Mandy turned Sergei. "Are you sure?"

"I am."

"Okay. That's good enough for me. Tommy, think you can charm him out of retirement?"

Tommy grinned. "I can try."

Mandy said. "Okay, for paper, Karl Felchin as usual. I'm sure he can get us whatever we need."

Charlie raised a hand. "I'd do the babysitting for Nikki and the kid. I'm guessin' you want to be a player, and it's about time they learned proper American food."

Lucy's grin was wicked. "Oh, yeah, I'll do the honeypot. We'll need a black hole for both Savage's people and Chet's phishing guys to fall into. No trouble at all."

Mandy leaned back, uncertain about what sort of game she'd launched, but knew Tommy would fill in the details later. She stole a glance at Lucy, whose smile was one of complete satisfaction. "I guess we're good to go, then?"

Lucy said, "Sounds like you've got it under control. You're still sure you want to do this? I mean, Charlie has a point..."

"Oh, yes. Absolutely." *Jack-in-the-box.* People who created

electronic surprises. *Dingalings*. People who did phone work.
Lifters. Big guys, who lifted weights and other problems. *Ghost*.
A sniper, the scary guy who... Hopefully didn't kill anyone. A
babysitter, of course. And paper, the usual forged documents.
Honeypot. Some sort of electronic trap.

Lucy picked up her tablet. "Okay, then. I'll have Cesar prep
the jet, find you a hotel, and I know you'll want to spend a some
time at Bergdorf's. This is early winter, Tommy, and spring lines
aren't out yet. So it's gonna cost. Even if she is a perfect six.
With long legs."

Tommy chuckled. "Yeah, for true. No problem."

Charlie interrupted with an exaggerated yawn. "Well, I reck—
on I'm gonna turn in myself. Long day for the geezer in the
group, and I plan to get in some fishin' tomorrow."

Bug sat up. "Yeah, yeah, that might be good, lay over for a
coupla days, learn how to do that shit."

Lucy said, "G'night, Charlie. I'll make sure the coffee's good
in the morning." She glanced at Bug. "Before *we* shove off.
We've got a lot of work to do."

Bug scowled and tossed his hands in the air.

Tommy winced. "'Night, Charlie. You done real good the
past couple of days. Real good."

Sergei had laced his fingers behind his head. "*Da, da, to—
varich*. Perhaps I teach you how to catch nice fish."

Charlie paused and his eyes narrowed. "My ass. That'll be
the god damn day."

Mandy drew a breath. "G'night, Charlie..."

Charlie turned to walk away and muttered, "God damn Rus—
sian."

Three voices called after him. "Ukrainian!"

Charlie departed with a dismissive wave of his hand. "What—
ever."

CHAPTER TWENTY-THREE

Castillo de los Reyes, Ibiza, Spain

Tommy sprawled on a first class lounge chair to snag Mediterranean sunshine. Just a touch up on a tan that surely must have faded in the week between islands.

On an island stuffed with luxury, Lucy could sure pick top of the line. As a travel agent, she'd have set popularity records with the first-class crowd, especially the prices she got. But the hotel, probably not. Reservations didn't even know their booking system had been hacked.

And just the right room. Third floor front, in a sloping line of terraces off the face of every room. If it had been a sports stadium, which it resembled, it would have been good seats to watch the game. A few feet away, Mandy coated herself with tanning lotion in all the places not covered by a swimsuit. Which was most of her body.

He said, "You know what?"

"Mm?"

"We ought to send Luce a postcard."

"She wouldn't wish she could be here, Tommy. She'd hate it."

"What's wrong with a little stylish? I mean, the view from here..."

She tossed a towel at him. "I feel like a neon goldfish in a very small bowl. This visibility game is just surreal. I should have hired about a hundred people to comb the island for Savage and sent *him* a postcard. 'Here to have wonderful time...kicking your butt.' You know what? I'm not even going to ask you to do my back. The thought of them photographing my bottom is disgusting."

"Your plan."

"I know, Tommy. Lucy just went with the whole Ibiza thing and organized details without any discussion." She paused and tried to mimic Lucy's voice. "I'll book you into Castillo de los Reyes. May as well start with the best."

Tommy adjusted his sunglasses for a better view of the second building on the left. Several guys had managed access to a fifth floor balcony and set themselves up with cameras and lenses the size of cannons. "I dunno. Seems pretty aptly named. Castle of the Kings works for me. On a scale of one to five stars, I'd say a solid eight or nine. Usual boutiques, restaurants, but a top-end casino for high-rollers and a private club just ideal for the diamonds and cocaine crowd."

Mandy muttered, "Yes. Like those who snort through twenty-four karate straws. I can't imagine how dancers in strip clubs manage to block out the ogling by dirty old men."

"Or dirty old paparazzi."

Mandy's elegantly simple plan was working well. Instead of sifting for Savage on an island of permanent Spring Break, let him do the work of finding. Make some waves, make a splash, attract attention. And while the others did the groundwork, they could start with a little shopping in New York.

About five days of it. A phone call from the flight north, a car at Teterboro, a straight run to David Aire's design house in the Garment District. A summer collection still behind locked doors and runway models that looked like six-foot pencils.

Swirling the scotch and taking a sip, Tommy peeked at more guys on the balconies who were watching Mandy apply lotion.

She said, "Thanks for not saying anything about the dress in

Corrientes. David is an old friend, and would have been crushed."

In New York, he'd stepped back while Mandy rummaged through racks with David. They did the little beg-and-protest thing, and gee, imagine that, ol' David could get a wardrobe to—gether by the day after tomorrow.

Bergdorf's came next, for accessories. David tagged along to organize what was going to go with what, and deliver a stern lec—ture on last season's swimwear, scrounged from deep storage and which, at the right moment, might appear magically in the clear—ance bins after the first of the year.

Tommy said, "I think the salespeople were impressed. The floor manager was impressed. Lucy was thirty thousand dollars impressed. And maybe any of Savage's hounds, if they were on the scent."

"Exactly. If not, no big deal. Ostentatious takes practice, you know. I thought you did okay for being on your own on Fifth Avenue. You know David would have — "

He chuckled. "Yeah. I'm sure. All I needed was to costume myself as a Very Big Timer in a city of Big Timers."

She smiled. "I really liked that navy polo. It worked so well with the slacks. Okay. Paparazzi or not, I've got to go over docu—ments from Karl. They look fine, but, well, when I sent Sergei out to Illinois pick them up, I didn't know it was a touchy situa—tion."

"Yeah. Some sort of falling out a couple of years ago. Some—thing to do with a shaky Norwegian passport, I think. Still you handled it well."

She set the bottle of lotion to the side. "You know, if you lay like that for too long, you're going to burn. Or they'll think you're dead. But I'm glad you think I did okay with Serge and Karl."

Tommy chuckled. "You're getting good at staring down the big guys. I loved that 'darn it, kiss and make up' part. Deep down, Serge is a pussycat."

"I wasn't worried about Serge. I was worried about Karl."

He shrugged. "Don't. Karl's been drooling over you since the day you first visited his clock shop out there in corn country." Mostly, it was nice not having to intervene and smooth ruffled feathers. Almost like a regular vacation. Except for the guys on the balcony, jockeying for position along a white railing handy for supporting telephoto lenses.

"Tommy, I'd really like to organize my things here and stretch out, but I don't know whether to lean over facing them or away from them. Suggestions?"

"Profiles always work when someone's admiring your body."

"Are you speaking from experience? Wait. Don't answer that. I'm already learning more than I want to know." She circled her chair and opted for profile.

"Such as?"

"Oh, the little things. Like why Cesar suggested Sky Valet at the airport here. The way Lucy set up the timing with the car, so we'd have to linger a little in the VIP Lounge, all because this is where more upscale travelers go, where we'd have a much better chance at catching the attention of paparazzi."

He smiled. "Details count. Remember the couple that landed just ahead of us?"

"The famous rock musician and his film-star companion? The ones that sponged up almost all the photographers and raced off to ostensibly hide from the media?"

"We got their usual room."

She nodded and hunted through her bag. "No wonder about the big scene at registration. How can you lay so still with cameras clicking away?"

"Well, we may have caught the attention of photographers looking for publicity table scraps, but it's a game of subtlety." Just a few, gambled on unfamiliar faces but nevertheless a couple reeking of money. When they formed a manageable parade through Ibiza Town, Serge could play a sloppy little game of shake-the-tail to fluff up credibility and encourage aggressive shadowing. It was entertaining before the easy run north on Carrer de Ses Feixes to the hotel.

Tommy opened his left eye. Serge was on a balcony one floor above the paparazzi, scanning the area with field glasses.

Mandy found some sort of thin skirt and wrapped it around her waist. She settled into the lounge chair to study a folder full of documents from Karl.

He said, "You're not going to get much of a tan wrapped up like that."

"I know, and it's also hot. But those guys over there, looking at my body from the feet up? It's just wrong. Plus, there's Sergei. I could fake it for the photographers, but I have to work with Serge. Trust me, Tommy, being glamorous is not all it's cracked up to be. How long do you think we have to keep this up?"

"Depends on how resourceful those paparazzi are."

A soft knock on the door to the suite interrupted.

She cocked an eyebrow. "Room service? Your turn?"

"No idea. Flip for it?"

She rolled into a standing position. "No need. I need a break from prying eyes anyway. Maybe wiggle my behind on the way out. Hm. I could wave. Make an obscene gesture. Say, I bet we could, and it would do one of those viral things on social media. What do you think?"

"Actually, it's probably all online now." She padded away. Tommy strained to hear soft conversation but soon gave up. She returned with an envelope and card in hand. "We're in luck. Or, rather, one of those photographers works for Savage. The bell—man delivered an invitation. Cole would like us to join him at a benefit casino event tonight. Black tie."

"That didn't take long. This the sort of thing that happens when you don't tip the bag guy enough."

Her phone danced from vibration. "Hi, Lucy. Okay... Okay...

Yes. We just now got an invitation. Really? Terrific! And our jack-in-the-boxes?" A pause. "Yes, got it. Thanks a bunch. Bye!" She disconnected. "Well, well. Not only did we hear from Savage, but Lucy just discovered he owns the hotel through some sort of a bashful trust connected to his foundation. And his benefit events are regular as clockwork, once a month. The invitation says nine o'clock. But I'd say nine-thirty or quarter to ten would be better. What's your preference? Craps, roulette, cards? Oh, wow. Yes. *Baccarat.* Right out of James Bond. Now *that* would be elegant."

Tommy smiled. "You watch too many old movies."

* * *

Shower, shave, short nap and a long wait while Mandy converted from lounge chair eye candy to the upper crust of elegance. Worth it, though. David Aire's signature raspberry, what he'd called a cap-sleeve knit. Form-fitting was understatement. Countless sequins sparkling with the faintest move. A hair style that belonged on the cover of a fashion magazine.

She stepped to the center of the room, practicing a toned-down runway walk, and did a couple of turns for his benefit.

He took in all the lines and curves. "My, my, my. When I was a kid and the prettiest girl in the parish stepped in, the boys'd say 'she sho' sucked up all the eyeballs tonight.' Which is what you're going to do, for sure."

"And what about all the older guys?"

He laughed and exaggerated his native drawl with a gravelly dose of dirty old man. "Why, they'd say, 'c'mere, sugar, and put yo' finger in mah coffee."

"Uh-huh. Part of the fun of being with you are Idioms on Parade. So. What do *you* say?" She turned again. "Too much?"

"Any more and they'll call the fire department. And then the TV news people. Dang, I truly feel sorry for all the women in the casino tonight. They're going to be jealous, big time."

She smiled satisfaction and slithered over to do the mandatory adjust-his-tie thing. It was perfectly tied, absolutely level, precisely correct. But she tweaked it anyway, like she always did as a wish of good luck just before she gathered up her bag, a tiny one this time, on the way out the door.

"Got Bug's little toy?"

Mandy unfurled a hand. A tiny speck of black on a forefinger. "I'm really nervous about this, Tommy. About losing it, about transferring it, about whether it sticks, or even works."

"You'll be fine. Compared to what the better intelligence agencies have, that's a big ol' clunker, a sure-fire."

She studied the spot. "Amazing. Looks like a tick or something, makes me want to wash."

"And one of the reasons I got out of the business. You can't compete with the nano-tech in the field."

"*The Washington Post* would probably love a carton of these."

He chuckled as he opened the door. "*The Washington Post* probably buys them by the case from Amazon. Just remember. Don't scratch your ear or fiddle with your earring unless you really need — "

"I understand."

The elevator whooshed in silence to the casino level. She did the little mental focus thing he'd seen in stage performers, politicians, business executives before the big speech, athletes before the big game. The car stopped. She drew a breath and, just as the door opened, she went from being Mandy the Friend to Mandy the Star.

CHAPTER TWENTY-FOUR

Coleman Savage was not as imposing as she expected. A bit shorter than Tommy, and perhaps an inch or two taller than she, in flats. On the thinnish side, with disorganized hair looking out of place with his tailored suit. Cordial, but intense, perhaps ill at ease with social conventions.

The reception hall was populated with opulence. It ranged from mature British conservative to Hollywood outrageous, with the former likely grateful at the absence of media and the latter wondering where it was.

Tommy dug right in with his boyish grin and eager hand—shake, treating all the obstacles on the path to Savage as if they were old friends who hadn't seen each other in a while and would certainly catch up later. He was laying on the deference thickly, causing Mandy to wonder when he would say, "And al—low me to introduce the princess and, no, you needn't bow or curtsey."

But it was forgivable, only an act, an entrance in which she was supposed to claim the spotlight. And avoid looking up, into the high ceiling or the balcony or some secret shadow. Ian Wells lived up to the expression "ghost." He was somewhere, but nowhere visible.

Mandy focused on smiles and hellos and *it's ever so delightful to see you* and an occasional *lovely to be here tonight*. Tommy did the steering, patiently but methodically crossing the hall.

While sharing a greeting with a middle eastern couple, she

heard Savage from the right side of her turned head.

"Welcome. So nice of you to join us tonight, Mister Kane. I've heard so much about you."

"Thank you, sir. I'm surprised that you recognize me."

"I make it a point to know who's staying in my hotel, Mister Kane."

Mandy brought her head around and looked just slightly down at Savage, a nice, full, eager smile while the two men shook hands.

Tommy said, "Allow me to present Miss Amanda Owens, who — "

Savage's hazel eyes locked onto hers and his expression shift-ed into plastic corporate patronization. "Of course. A pleasure, Miss Owens."

Mandy extended a hand and hoped he wouldn't kiss it. His handshake was anemic and brief. "Mandy. Friends call me Mandy."

Savage nodded. "As you wish, Miss Owens." And then his focus switched off and attention returned to Tommy.

Tommy was sliding easily into his Texas oilman thing, the casual ooh-and-ahh phony astonishment that made a person wonder how many bulls had just left deposits on the spot they were standing. Savage was giving the summary tour, pointing to the varied facilities that extended from the huge hub in which they were about centered. A subdued hall with table games. A more neon fluorescent room with slot machines. A closed entry to a lounge with doors and a wall unable to contain the thud of the Balearic house music so popular on the island. Flickers of light from strobes and lasers skittered out onto the carpet.

The reception hall had a classic medieval Spanish look to it, more Castilian than Balearic, and the masterpieces in ornate frames on the walls were all knockoffs. Which did nothing to contain Tommy's projection of awe and amazement nor to contain – wait for it – yep, there it comes.

"Boy, it's just all kind of fantastic. I oughta buy me a couple or three, just like it. Now, Cole – can I call you Cole? Good – you don't suppose..."

Savage's smile was a perfect example of acid annoyance. "No, it's not for sale."

Mandy stepped in close to take Tommy's arm and do the usual gentle chastisement. "Now, Tommy, you can't just run out and buy everything you see."

Tommy looked taken aback. "How come? I mean, it's just business."

"I'm sure Mister Savage adores his little hotel. Isn't that right, um, Cole?" Before he could organize a reply, she pressed on. "Say, I'll bet the fishing is probably really good around here. Do you fish, Cole? I mean, the eating kind, not the cheating kind."

Savage's jaw tightened.

"Yeah, Cole. S'pose I wanted to get me some fishin' time. Y'all got good sport fish hereabouts? Them really big ol' rascals?"

A loud argument erupted a dozen feet away. Tommy, Mandy and Savage turned to watch. A boisterous, pugnacious man, looking like he'd had a few beverages too many, grappled with a hotel staffer and the woman he was with. Rubin Ward calmed down, gestured he meant no trouble, and Misty Caldwell appealed to the hotel guy that things were under control, and all her husband wanted was to say hello to Cole Savage, an old friend.

The hotel guy looked to Savage, who nodded approval.

Rubin straightened his jacket and brushed his lapel, then lurched forward. Misty scampered to keep up, her hands clutching the skirt of a creme-colored brocade gown.

Ward's arm came out. The lurch turned to a stagger and, just as he might have tumbled to the floor, he crashed into Savage, one arm in front, the other across the back of Savage's neck, grabbing at the jacket collar. Cole tried to pull away. Misty tugged at Rubin's arms.

Mandy gasped. *The collar, the collar! Get to his collar!*

Too late.

From all directions, hotel security pounced and pried the couple off Savage amid noisy objections, a string of profanity, and horrified shock from a ring of witnesses.

In moment it was over. Rubin Ward and Misty Caldwell were unceremoniously escorted from the hall, and probably the hotel.

Savage straightened his jacket, forced a smile and raised his hands to signal all was well. "Nothing to be alarmed about, ladies and gentlemen. I want to thank you again for coming, and I think it's an excellent time for our evening's amusement to begin."

After waving toward the gaming rooms, he turned back to Tommy. "Now, Mister Kane, I know you're not here to shop for hotels, perhaps not even to gamble."

Mandy stepped forward and interrupted. "Allow me to fix your tie, Mister Savage."

Cole raised his hands but hers got there first and gently adjusted it.

She displayed an earnest, calming smile. "It's all right. Tommy's is always a disaster and he doesn't even have to fend off drunks." She stepped back and opened her palms as if to frame the view for a camera. And to show Tommy the little black spot was no longer on her fingertip. "There. Perfect."

Savage's nod of gratitude was as forced as his smile. He motioned for one of the staff. "Okay, honey, why don't you try your hand at some of the amusements? Mister Kane and I have a matter to discuss." The hotel guy hovered patiently, and Savage spoke to him while looking straight into her eyes. "Felix? Give this lady five, no, ten thousand, and show her to the casino halls. I wish you good luck...*Miss Owens.*"

He turned his back to her and gave all his focus to Tommy. Felix motioned with his arm and she followed his direction.

She peeked into the table games room, but declared it would require too much concentration and skill beyond the comprehension of a simpleheaded woman. Ignoring an intense urge to raise her arm and scratch an ear or caress an earring, she chose the slots room, dark and noisy with the competing tunes of temptation. A sedate sign adjacent to the portal said *Sala de Máquinas de Azar.*

She said, "Thank you, Felix." He replied with a faint, firm smile and drifted back to his post.

At a cashier's cage, she placed ten thousand Euros on the counter and received a player's card. If nothing else, she could kill time while Lucy tuned in to Cole's bow tie to hear the latest offer for Nikki's return, then perhaps pick up clues on his other contacts before the little battery gave up the ghost. A ghost. Like the one hidden somewhere, who could have shot that arrogant bastard and put an end to the entire matter.

Steady. Strong. Serene. She turned to face a dozen aisles of massive video screens, illuminating faces that already looked so bored, their bodies just darkened whispers on molded chairs, comfort for the indolent wealthy.

A soft voice, to her left and slightly behind, said, "Tough to choose, ain't it?"

Startled, she turned. And relaxed. "Hi, Lester. You look very handsome in black tie."

He shrugged. "Ain't much. Hard to find a size for a little guy like me. And a tough town to pinch it."

"You did very well."

Lester Finn chuckled. "You done better, out there. Nice move. A lotta pros, they couldn'ta done better."

"You think so? I was *so* nervous."

"Nah. Looked good. You could have a great career in body work if you wanted."

"Gosh, thanks! My confidence could use a boost just about now." She drew a fortifying breath. "So. I have ten thousand Euros to spend. What sort of machine would you recommend?"

Lester pointed left. "Over there, you got your cheap seats. Buck-a-spins, stand-alones with frequent but small payouts. And some local network progressives, but even the jackpots ain't nothin' to crow about. Ten grand, maybe."

"So I should ignore them."

"Yeah, unless you wanna spend half the night spinning." He pointed right. "Now them, in the second to last row, those are wide area network progressives. Them babies is tied in with other casinos, around Europe, maybe the world. Hundred a clip."

"So I could shoot my wad in a hundred spins?"

"Or you could get, you know, *lucky*. Luck is a random thing, always a surprise."

She smiled understanding and studied a largely empty row of seats. "I see. What are the odds, anyway?"

He shrugged. "For these people, nobody really knows. The talk is fifty million to one, though."

She nodded. "Well, then. Since it's Savage's money and I'm really annoyed with him just now, a determined hundred spins seems like a good bet. How about you?"

Lester chuckled. "Me? I'm strictly a nickel-and-dime kinda guy. Win a few, lose a few. Pocket change. I'm gonna go for a couple of the cheapies over there."

She raised her voice above a whisper. "Good luck! And thank you for your suggestion, Mister Finn."

He began to step away. "Yeah, yeah. Try one of the Megabucks games, go home early." Finn glanced around, left to right, then up and left to right. And he stepped away into a drifting crowd of people with time to kill and money to burn.

She went with the flow, casually examining the garish promises of thrills and excitement, finally succumbing at the fourth unit from the end of the row. A second screen above the machine proclaimed, "Jackpot! Currently 1,914,971.32 Euros!"

About $2.1 million, US. Why not? Mandy slipped into the seat and skimmed through the instructions, easy enough for mindless amusement. And she began to play. Two spins. Four. Eight. Ten. Fifteen. Twenty. It was so easy to become captivated, addicted. She sat back, stretched, slowed the pace. At the end, on the opposite side of the aisle, Lester had settled on a machine to use and methodically touched it for a spin with his right hand. His left reached into his pocket. And returned with a piece of candy, which he popped into his mouth and continued to play.

Mandy's shoulders slumped. Twenty spins. Twenty-five. Another pause, another stretch, another look around. Lester's left hand went back into the pocket. Mandy turned back to the machine and pressed the button. The icons and images danced and rolled.

Jackpot! A blaze of light. Wince. Turn away. Jump back. Some sort of loud alarm. The jackpot sign flashing wildly, heads turning, people gathering. *Can't someone turn this thing off?*

A blur of people, closing in. Lester, gone, vanished. Hotel staff, forming a protective ring. Congratulations without smiles. Assistance in standing. An escort back to the cage.

The clerk, a young woman who earlier looked terribly deferential but bored, now beaming with excitement. A phone call. A flood of paper pushed toward Mandy. Pen. Signature.

Alternatives. Annuity? Direct deposit? No and no, thank you. "I'm sure cash will be fine." A flurry of guards. The audience at a distance, muttering to themselves. Looks of admiration. Looks of envy. Into a narrow hallway, well lit, terribly silent. Footsteps tapping on a hard floor. An office. Table, two chairs. A guy coming through a door, studies the paperwork, excuses himself. Beyond, some sort of vault. A couple of minutes, feeling like a couple of hours. Where's Tommy?

Two guards, big guys, guns, into the little room. The guy

from the vault, with a huge canvas bag. Another. Right behind, another guy with a cart, stacked with bundles of cash. The counting, in tens of thousands, distant, an echo. She felt herself nodding, but at last the numbness went away.

"Miss? Are you all right? Can I get you something to drink? Would you like to sit? Take a moment?"

Another deep breath. Make a smile. "You're very kind. I'm afraid I'm not used to this sort of thing."

The counting guy smiled. Patience. Understanding. "No one ever is."

Mumbling something about how she could manage. The casino guy laughing, saying it was two bags and weighed fifty pounds. Not to mention security.

Scampering through the corridor, into another, to a side entrance and cool, soft air. From a distance, the thud of Ibiza's party music, the glow of light from people having a good, simple time. The car swept in from the right. A stretch limo. Sergei rolled out of the driver's seat and opened a door for her. She turned to watch him open the trunk and collect the bags of cash from the guards.

Opposite her, a row of smug smiles. Rubin. Misty. Lester. And next to her, Tommy, grinning.

Mandy asked. "Cole Savage?"

"Two million, one hundred and thirty seven thousand dollars and change poorer. And he made an offer, which we can refuse."

"And Ian?"

Tommy said, "Probably halfway to the airport."

She nodded. "Where Cesar and Karen are waiting..."

"I'm sure. I heard you had fun with Plan B."

"Yes. And I'm still a little numb."

CHAPTER TWENTY-FIVE

920 Pratt Blvd., Elk Grove Village, Illinois

All the doors were closed and the windows up. But it didn't matter. Raw November breeze found its way to Tommy's hands. He knew complaining was out of the question. Anyway, stake-outs and idling vehicle engines were incompatible.

Mandy was bundled in layers in the back seat, wearing a hat and hood. The best part of her face, a rosy pink, peeked out from a mound of fabric. Her arms were wrapped tight around herself and she was probably keeping her fingers as comfortable as possible by tucking thick mittens into the armpits of a down jacket.

Next to her, K-C passed time by thumbing through a list of warrants for Cook County, always available to pick up a few ex-tra dollars by collaring some dummy who believed everyone had stopped looking. His team was scattered around the area to serve as eyes and ears.

Yenchenko had the wheel, upon which he drummed the fin-gertips of his left hand. Probably a veteran at Siberian winters, he'd likely find this weather to be downright balmy.

From the left, Jinx and J2 strolled across the parking lot with two white paper sacks and a gray cardboard tray stuffed with foam cups.

When they reached the van, Tommy rolled down the win-dow to accept stakeout-style breakfast at half past nine in the morning. He had to pull off a glove and loosen his jacket to reach his wallet. He asked Jinx, "What's the damage?"

"Don't worry about it."

After Sergei snagged a cup, Tommy passed the food to the back seat. "Too late. I already got my wallet. So how much?"

Jinx shrugged while Tommy passed the food into the back. "Twenty-two fifty. And the lot count across the street is the same. No departures, no arrivals."

Tommy harvested a twenty and a five and told Jinx to keep the change.

Mandy leaned forward. "Are you cold, Tommy? Your hand looks like you're cold."

"Nah. I'm good. I was just going to remark on what a nice mild autumn day it was." He tugged a cup from the cardboard tray and Sergei did the same. Yeah, the coffee was ice cold. Wonderful. Yenchenko poured it into his mouth and passed the empty cup back to Tommy.

Mandy unwrapped some sort of sandwich and stared at it as if it were a refugee from a dumpster.

Jinx was unapologetic. "What can I say? It's fast food from down the street. Only place we could find."

"This is not food. This is awful on a bun, with some sort of goo oozing onto my mitten."

K-C chuckled. "Now, now, boys and girls. It's just a typical stakeout. Trust me on that. We do it all the time."

She held the sandwich aloft, a plaintive look in her eyes. A shrug and a look of encouragement was all he could muster. "Don't think about what it looks like. Just wolf it down, chase it with coffee, burp once or twice and let it decompose in your bel—ly."

"You're a real pal, Tommy. Times like these I wish Karen would be catering the stakeout. A fruit bowl, maybe a frittata, or some of those marvelous muffins from the aft galley. She could deliver them, I bet, and we'd have a much better way to pass the time of staring at a bland building with a nearly empty lot on the side." She took a breath and bit in like a kid dealing with a de-spised vegetable trying to focus instead on the building.

Bland was an apt description. One story, some sort of gray brick, a bashful sign in front that said "CSIT Research," now and then a car passing by. The handful of people inside would probably be comfortable, with food and certainly hot coffee.

And if Lucy was correct — which she always was — they'd be cackling away while stealing thousands of dollars from hap-less people around the world. The progress report was all tech-no-babble, about onion networks and some sort of a back door into the Tor network.

Lucy had snickered. "Those people think they're hidden, but they're not. The algorithm they use to bounce through a labyrinth of servers was just so easy to unravel."

Mandy, nearly as lost as he was in the details, had asked, "So what does that mean for Chet Towers?"

Lucy's triumphant response was, "Thanks to the Tor node at MIT, where the techs have more reputation than skill, we know exactly where they are." She had displayed a screen map showing the building, that same one that sat directly right across a road from where they parked, froze, and waited for Lucy to trigger the raid.

Tommy decided Lucy and Bug just might have an edge over good, old-fashioned street work. They were warm, glowing in the success of the tiny bug Mandy tacked onto Savage's bow tie. In its brief lifespan, it tagged along with Cole to a private meet-ing with a band of Russian-speaking guys getting a regular re-port on cash flow from bleeding accounts of prominent busi-nessmen. The bug went dark without names, but the trail brightened. Now, Tommy knew, Mandy was mentally fondling the comfort of a breakfast delivery from Karen, who was likely also warm and happy in a fixed-base operator lounge a dozen miles away. The notion began to appeal to him as well.

K-C grunted. "Speaking of delivery, who's these guys? About two o'clock." He tugged his pistol from the shoulder holster, flicked off the safety and chambered a round.

Everybody tracked two men wearing baggy overcoats and dark suits as they approached from the right, crossed in front van at about twenty-five yards, paused to scan the perimeter and then eased toward the van on the driver's side.

K-C gripped the pistol on his lap. "Don't look like cops or guards."

Yenchenko spoke quietly, with resignation. "*Nyet.* Not po-lice, not soldier, not guard, not target. They approach like wolf. Wolf which has found dead animal. Cautious, wary. Like all good Russian intelligence officer."

Mandy dropped what remained of her sandwich into the sack. "You're certain?"

"*Da, da.* Of course. Quick, quick. We must hide weapon, prepare to talk."

Hints tumbled together into a mosaic. Lucy's mention that, without evidence, she *felt* an electronic tail but dismissed it as old paranoia. Three parked vehicles out there that just *felt* wrong but he didn't mention because it would seem like... yeah, old paranoia. Two guys, walking up to point blank range. Tommy said, "Probabilities that they're hitters?"

Sergei chuckled. "*Nyet.* They come to make dialog."

Mandy said, "You're sure? I mean — "

Sergei shrugged. "If they are assassins, we would be most completely dead already."

The men were within ten feet when Yenchenko lowered the driver's window and waited. Raw cold air rushed in to attack complacency. While the second man hung back and continually scanned the area, the older of the two approached.

He wore an ill-fitting inexpensive suit with a white shirt, taut over a rounded belly, and a tie with several food stains partway down. After a faint bow, he smiled, the way a guy does with a winning poker hand. He seemed as though he wanted to tip a hat, but wore none, and the light breeze ruffled thinning brown hair, combed straight back.

"Hello. Good morning. A most pleasant good morning to all. Please. Excuse our interruption."

Catching a glance from K-C, Tommy slowly shook his head.

The guy gave his attention to Yenchenko. "*Tovarishch Sergei Il'ich Enchenko?*"

"*Da. Eto ia.*"

The guy took half a step back. "*Tovarishch Sergei Il'ich, voz– mozhno, vy mogli by prisoedinit'sia k nam dlia korotkoi progulki?*"

Sergei nodded and the guy opened the door to the van. They strolled out to the sidewalk, and then the guy gestured with a hand and they went east.

Mandy leaned forward. "Tommy?"

"Russian SVR. Sergei's been made. He's been an outlaw, un– der their radar for a long time. Looks like they want to set some– thing up. Recruiting, maybe, bringing him in from the cold."

"*Recruiting?* Or are they taking him into custody? Or worse?"

Tommy shrugged. "Maybe."

"And we did nothing?"

"Serge wouldn't want to screw up the stakeout. So he went quiet. Besides, not much he could do. Two vehicles, eleven o'clock, another at one, and the third in the parking lot dead ahead looks wrong."

K-C's jaw momentarily dropped open, then closed tight. "My guys could — "

"I'm sure. And we'd have a firefight in the middle of a subur– ban industrial park and way too much to explain later. These guys just don't throw up their hands and wait for the cuffs, K-C."

Mandy bit her lower lip. "Help me out, here, Tommy. What do we do?"

"We wait. Maybe they'll come back with warm coffee and a couple of decent sweet rolls."

K-C passed time by releasing and reinserting the magazine into his Browning, periodically sneaking a look at the targets Tommy identified.

She sighed. "I just don't understand how you guys can take this so calmly. I'm in a mild state of panic and... Oh, never mind, I'm sounding silly."

Tommy leaned back in his seat. "Don't worry about it. The people you and I have dealt with as a team are your normal everyday criminals. The intelligence community is a whole different league, with different rules. Maybe there's something bigger than the hacker house across the street. That there's a Russian interest in what's going on."

Yenchenko reappeared, alone. The eleven o'clock car rolled slowly to the street, made a right and was gone. Seconds later, the one o'clock did the same. And just as Yenchenko opened the door, the one in the lot backed out and went the opposite way.

Yenchenko's expression was somber but unafraid.

Mandy exuded sympathy. "Oh, Serge, whatever happened?"

He waved it off.

Tommy casually said, "They found you at last?"

"*Da*. It is so."

"All good things come to an end. No big deal."

Mandy's eyes widened, but a slight shake of the head from Tommy caused her to pause and say nothing.

"As you say, Koshka. They are Section S, SVR. Mere errand boy, but I do not wish to break them into small pieces and damage progress we make."

"Restraint is good, Serge."

"So. The agent with whom I speak is recruiter, but not as you might suspect, Koshka. We make casual talk about small matter, become comfortable, relax. He is not so good as I, of course, but I am patient with him, okay? He brings message only."

Mandy said, "Which was?"

Yenchenko chuckled, but kept his eyes straight ahead. "He say — I make translate, yes? — he say, 'I am sorry, but I have bad news. Our cousin has taken ill and would be gladdened if you might visit him. First, you may offer a prayer for him.'"

Tommy nodded. "New York center?"

"*Da, da*. I ask if it is crisis, and yes, he say, most seriously. I explain I am with colleagues on small assignment. He say it is permitted for leader of team to attend to cousin. But Sergei must pray alone."

Mandy said, "I have utterly no clue what's going on."

Yenchenko turned to face her. "I most strenuously regret in-convenience. We must make brief visit to New York."

Mandy looked to Tommy. "How soon? I mean, we've just got set up here. And as cold as it is, and as bad as the food is, we're getting close to busting the guys that stole Chet's life sav-ings. Serge, I appreciate your situation, but — "

Tommy interrupted. "Serge has no real choice. He's been doing a good job of staying off their radar, but the game is over. The big dogs want to talk. About what, I don't know."

K-C gently cleared his weapon. "We can hold down the fort for a couple of days. They won't even know they're being watched. If these guys are as dedicated to their computer stuff as you say, you folks can do what you gotta do, get back, and we'll pick it up from there."

Mandy sighed. "Lucy's about to dump bait into the trap, a file to prove these are the thieves."

Sergei again apologized. "Most sad to leave good bait in trap, make depart with no reward. But perhaps there is more. These errand boy, they know nothing. New York may give better clue."

"I understand, Sergei. And I appreciate your situation. I just can't help but wonder what would happen if we ignored them?"

Tommy said, "Not a good plan. If we upset a Russian intelligence op on U-S soil, they definitely won't take kindly. It takes a lot of effort and resources on their part, and — "

Yenchenko's voice softened and lowered. "It is like hunter who sneak up on big sleeping wolf and then kicking it. You must prepare to run very fast and hide well. But, Mandy, you are lead—er. You make decision. We follow."

Mandy looked out the window and fell silent for several sec—onds. "Well, it might be nice to get back to the city for genuine New York coffee. *Hot* coffee."

CHAPTER TWENTY-SIX

8-10 Columbus Avenue, New York City

Granite blocks soared to the sky, but were modest in a ring of Manhattan skyscrapers. Bits of greenery struggled to soften the gray building, a losing cause against the urban reality of a venerable gothic revival property of the Roman Catholic Archdiocese of New York. Massive black iron gates flanked entryways, spread wide to show the Church of St. Paul the Apostle offered a spiritual embrace.

While Lucy chattered through an earbud about the building, a postscript to the inflight briefing, Mandy took in the view from the car at the curb,. She began to raise her arm to adjust the earpiece. *Oops. Don't. Somewhere out there, Ian Wells is peeking through a powerful scope and somebody might get killed by mistake.*

"Yes, got it, Lucy. I've been here more than once."

"Really? As in — ?"

"As in research for a piece I did some years ago on the centennial of the so-called 'crime of the century.'"

"In a church?"

Mandy found relief in a moment of laughter. "No, actually, the interior design was by Stanford White, a flamboyant architect of the day, who'd seduced a young socialite and was murdered by the woman's high-society husband. I always found a certain irony in that. But, meantime, he lined up a who's who of ecclesiastical art for the interior decoration. Mostly Byzantine styles, but it's definitely museum grade. Got me interested in art, though."

"Wow, cool." Lucy turned an aural page. "Okay, so these guys are pretty slick, using the daily twelve-ten Mass to hide in a crowd, then linger for the rendezvous. One-thirty makes a lot of sense. There's probably a few people hanging around for confession and whatever they gotta do after to make things right. So, yeah, about perfect."

Easy to say from the comfort of a computer in the Bahamas. A lot different in the city shade on Columbus Avenue at the threshold of Big League espionage.

Tommy had the steering wheel this time, with Serge as the front seat passenger and Mandy alone in the rear of an oversized SUV delivered to Teterboro for the ride into midday midtown. At least the men couldn't see the increasing twitching of her knees or sense the growing anxiety in her chest.

In a private moment on the flight, she'd said to Tommy, "Look, you're much better at this than I am. I'd really prefer to defer leadership to you, if only to make some sort of dumb mistake that gets a lot of people killed."

"Nobody gets killed in a church," Tommy had replied.

"You haven't been in New York for a while, have you?"

Now Sergei opened his door, just a crack, before turning to her.

"You are ready?"

Knees shaking? Check. Stomach churning? Check. Anxiety peaking? Check. "As much as I ever will be, Serge. Tommy, you're being unusually taciturn. You're sure about this?"

"Remember when I said nobody gets killed in a church?"

"I just knew there was a catch."

"Yeah, well, I lied. If anybody might be a target, it'd be me. There's some old grudges with these guys, so I'm better off out here."

She nodded. "Well, I suppose that's some measure of solace and encouragement."

"Best I can do. Look, you're doing great, everything will be fine. Just drift in like a citizen off the street, take a spot near the back, let Serge do his thing."

She stepped out, onto the curb next to a directional parking sign for Lincoln center, made something of a showy farewell to the passengers in the vehicle, glanced at an open box truck making a delivery or who-knows-what just ahead of them, and marched to the church entry.

Tommy pulled away from the curb and into traffic, heading toward Fifty-ninth Street. She paused and drew close to Yenchenko, who bent down to hear. "Is Tommy okay?"

He shrugged. "Of course. Why?"

"I don't know. He just seems very quiet, like there's something I should know, but don't."

"It is nothing. All goes well."

She sighed. "You're a poor liar, Sergei."

"Perhaps. This time, he is not leader. Perhaps he wish not to interfere. New for him, I think."

"But back in the day, you were a leader. It must be difficult."

Yenchenko shook his head. "*Nyet.* I am always soldier who follow well, but like old wolf, know good place to survive and keep comfort. So I am most okay, *da?* You must have no worry. I have your back. Now, we must move forward. Our position here is most exposed, and it is expected there will be those who watch from building nearby."

Among them, Ian Wells, with a sniper rifle.

"Just don't break anything. Or anybody. Okay?"

Sergei laughed. "*Da,* of course. You are boss, I make good behave."

Up a dozen steps to the landing under an enormous blue and white relief sculpture over an equally enormous pair of wooden doors. Past a small gift shop in the narthex, her footsteps self-consciously becoming lighter on the wood floor to muffle staccato echo. Flanking a baptismal font were confessionals on the left and banks of candles on the right in a vast open space, traditionally the standing-room-only area for those outside the faith and now a block of negative space, that from a design standpoint, made what was beyond special. A sea of polished wood pews shimmered in the soft light cast by illumination of a stunning array of Catholic icons, murals and LaFarge stained glass windows that soared toward the vaulted ceiling. With the desired effect, too. Humility.

Above, the distinct lighting, which still reminded her of fourteen three-tier wedding cakes in two rows, floating in the air and glowing with promise. Just enough illumination to see, not more than necessary to create a sense of calm. If the art along either side of the nave was spectacular, the pews were spartan. Plain, hard wood, simple and punctuated by scattered silhouettes of heads and shoulders of people looking for emotional comfort, inspiration, or courage. Or other spies.

All of which would be helpful just about now. *Pick a pew, any pew, look like you're reasonably devout.* Third one to the left, a couple of spaces in. Time to sit quietly and wait for whatever happens. Admire the art again. Enjoy the silence. The absence of all things electronic. *Steady, strong, serene.*

Sergei Yenchenko eased past, moving like a cat, more with a sense of respect than wariness, a casual visitor choosing a seat at random. Her eyes tracked him to a pew about a quarter of the way back from the front and on the right. A much smaller silhouette shifted sideways to allow Serge to sit.

Their exchange was subtle and she struggled to eavesdrop on a conversation well beyond reasonable range. Mandy allowed her mind to roam through memories. In the tradition of French-Canadians, her mother had been Catholic and supposedly fairly serious about it before it faded in the more secular lifestyle of upscale Connecticut. She speculated about why her mother might have let it go, or had to let it go, or perhaps how strong it was in the first place.

Ahead, the meeting of the two silhouettes was certainly any–
thing but theological. To all the players in this game, a church as
lovely and purposeful as this was merely a convenient ren–
dezvous to plan bad things. It seemed rather wrong, rather sad.

Tommy. How difficult it must be for him. As complicated
and even dangerous this had become, he had put himself in the
second chair and somehow managed to bite his tongue when he
and the others could so easily make decisions and form plans. It
had even become troubling, like he was holding back to let her
fail, then rush in to rescue her. Yet what Serge said made more
sense. They had all gathered round in support of her, confident
that...

Exactly. Now was not the time to fail. Problem was, she had
no idea what she'd need to do.

A soft voice slightly behind and to the right, jolted her back
to reality. "Excuse me?"

More like jumped out of her skin.

"I'm sorry. I didn't mean to startle you."

She whirled. A priest in vestments, kind of on the youngish
side, Latino, hopefulness in his eyes.

"Are you waiting for the sacrament?"

Mandy struggled to steady her breath and push her heart
back down into her chest. "Sorry?"

He smiled. "Reconciliation. Confession? I only ask because
there's just a few minutes left and I have other appointments."

Mandy stammered. "No, no. I'm fine, thank you." Which, of
course, was hardly true. If anything, she could admit to sort of
perpetrating a fraud on the entire meaning of the sanctuary in
which she so casually sat. And perhaps wonder what her mother
would have said.

The priest smiled. "Happy to hear it. Please, take your time
and enjoy our hospitality. Is there anything I can do for you?"

*Other than tell me how to manage Russian spies somehow involved
with our little caper?* She displayed a warm smile. "No, thank you.

You've been most kind."

He pulled away. "Have a wonderful day. Again, sorry to have intruded. God bless."

Mandy closed her eyes as he drifted off, and when she opened them again the two silhouettes were strolling toward her. She slid right, to the end of the pew, ready to greet, stand or flee, whichever would seem the most logical.

I know, Tommy, I know. No Plan B. Focus, focus.

A middle-aged man, late fifties, maybe, balding, with what few hairs on his head combed straight back. Blue suit, white shirt, red tie. Some sort of tiny lapel pin catching the light from a nearby chandelier.

Sergei spoke in a soft, easy voice. *"Tovarishch Glukhov, ia predstavliaiu nash lider, Miss Amanda Owens."*

Bright blue eyes, warm smile, on the eager side. If he was surprised Sergei was working for a younger girl, he didn't show it. A very slight bow, never losing eye contact or expression. And in nearly accent-free English, he said, "How do you do, Miss Owens. A pleasure to meet you."

As they shook hands, Serge continued. "Comrade Pavel Glukhov is assistant deputy director with *Sluzhba Vneshney Razvedki*, the SVR."

How coincidental. The Church of St. Paul the Apostle. The introduction of Pavel the Spy.

Glukhov continued to smile, this time with an edge of patience. "Which in your language means approximately the Foreign Intelligence Service of the Russian Federation. The equivalent of your Central Intelligence Agency, Miss Owens."

Mandy had found her way to standing and stepped out into the aisle just as Glukhov tried lean in and place his left hand on the back of the pew. It would have blocked her exit and forced a position of dominance.

Instead, he adroitly withdrew to allow her a stance of equal footing, hopefully disarmed by her open smile.

"Mandy. Friends call me Mandy. I *do* hope we can be friends."

"As do I. Comrade Sergei and I for many years are friends. Even as young officers with the KGB. Well, perhaps with some rivalries, eh, Sergei? But time heals many wounds, and good friendships endure difficulties and misunderstandings."

Mandy glanced at Sergei's bland reaction. "A good thing. Grudges can be so heavy a burden, Mr. Glukhov."

"Pavel. I insist." He waved his arm. "It is appropriate that we should become acquainted in such a place as this. The Catholics seem to thrive on forgiveness, of letting bygones be bygones, of looking forward to being a cooperative family."

"I suppose that depends on sincerity of penance, Pavel."

Glukhov chuckled and turned to Sergei. "So, we see you are correct, comrade. She is not only beautiful and intelligent, but formidable and strong as well."

Yenchenko wore his best told-ya-so smug grin.

Glukhov looked around. "Very well, Miss — er, Mandy — it is as you say. But perhaps we cause a small disturbance in this place, and should adjourn to a location of more candor and comfort. May I invite you to join me and some colleagues for tea?"

Mandy looked to Sergei, who nodded.

Glukhov caught the exchange. "And of course, Comrade Yenchenko is invited as well, perhaps to give counsel and translation as needed, perhaps to provide a sense of security, eh?"

"That would be lovely. Shall I call for my driver?"

"Mister Kane? No, that won't be necessary." He raised a defensive hand. "Yes, yes, we know Mister Kane. To have both Kane and Yenchenko working for you suggests a great deal to me, Miss Owens. I apologize. *Mandy.*"

"Such as?"

"You are possibly much more, shall we say, influential than we might have anticipated. Yes. An afternoon of pleasant surprises Shall we go?"

A gauntlet was the last thing Mandy expected. Sergei's subtle gestures on West Sixtieth identified half a dozen men on both sides of the narrow street looking like they were killing time or waiting for someone.

Who are these people?

As they progressed, the men began to follow.

And somewhere, probably high, was Ian Wells, the ghost with a sniper rifle and probably a silencer just as big. She could touch an earring, touch off a hail of gunfire and people would die. She found the prospect terrifying, not reassuring.

At last, the building entrance. An unsmiling guy ahead of them paused to open the door. *Down the rabbit hole, like Alice.* More men, groups of two or three, talking, watching. Three women browsed bright shop windows across the immense lobby of Time Warner Center, tracking them as they passed.

C'mon. Paranoia. This is silly. But when she saw faces a second and third time, it wasn't so silly. It was like walking through an empty parking garage, late at night, with the sound of footsteps following in shadows. At least there was Sergei, but he was un-armed, and there was no communications with comforting voic-es. Just the echoes of blurred conversation, footsteps, the soul of the building itself. Alone. Alone in a crowd.

Someone along the route spoke to his shirt cuff, and within moments of arriving at a bank of elevator doors, the one Pavel chose magically opened. A younger man, who looked like he worked out a lot, stepped into the lobby to hold the door. He stepped back into the car, sandwiching her between two guys in the back and himself at the floor button panel.

The elevator door whispered closure. The car didn't move.

CHAPTER TWENTY-SEVEN

10 Columbus Circle, New York City

Pavel Glukhov said, "I apologize. However, security is most crucial. You, of course, are not wearing any transmission or se—curity device? Good. So then it is only a brief inconvenience that these officers do electronic scan as we ascend?"

Yenchenko's eyes narrowed, but he nodded and raised his arms. She could not see the control panel, but only heard the soft whine of the elevator and the steady upward motion high into a tower.

The men with scanning wands turned to her, their eyes ex—pressionless.

Sergei had been correct when he casually mentioned during the drive into the city, "Security will be most tedious. Do not object, do not complain, do not try to defeat process. You will not be damaged. If anything is amiss, they will walk away."

Airport security checks could be less embarrassing. How she'd come to accept the luxury of Tommy's jet as just a matter of routine. Walk up, say hello to Karen, get aboard.

Mandy lifted her arms and chafed at the sensation of flat wands rubbing up and down against every inch of her body, hair to toe and back again, wondering whether Pavel took pleasure in watching. So she made firm eye contact with him, as if being in—spected like a piece of meat was routine. A placid smile of toler—ance ended when they motioned for her to lower her arms and the men returned to a position of parade rest.

The car shuddered, slowed, and, a couple of seconds later, the door opened into a small foyer. The fifty-fourth floor. Several numbered doors. The guards formed a new perimeter near one of them.

Again, Pavel gestured with his arm. "Please. This way."

Mandy took a deep breath and followed Pavel across a beige carpet, with Yenchenko right behind. The guards stepped away to allow Pavel to unlock the door. They entered a pool of light pouring through a wall of glass twenty feet away.

Pavel said, "The security detail did not disturb you? Good. They are *Spetsnaz*. Efficient, but not so accustomed to diplomatic courtesies."

Sergei asked, "*Zaslon?*"

Pavel shrugged, but didn't deny it.

Sergei turned to Mandy. "Special forces team. *Zaslon* are most elite. It is signal we are in most delicate circumstance."

Mandy surveyed surprisingly contemporary décor, perhaps Scandinavian design. Kitchen and dining to the left, a corridor probably leading to bedrooms or offices on the right. From a chrome and gray leather sofa and matching chair, three men rose to their feet.

Sergei hung back to serve as a translator while Pavel beamed in the manner of a servant and ushered her to introductions.

"Miss Owens, I have the honor to present Yevegeny Ledovskoy, first deputy director of SVR Directorate S."

She shook hands with a stone-faced man, about sixty, stocky, with thick gray hair, bushy eyebrows and eyes as warm as ice. In her ear, Yenchenko whispered, "Illegal intelligence, mostly to recruit spy, prepare for assignment."

Pavel continued. "And Aleksei Pichushkin, first deputy director, SVI Directorate I."

A taller, gaunt man with dark hair, combed straight back, and very dark eyes that reminded her of a shark. Yenchenko advised,

"Technical. How you say? *Da*. Computer service division, analy–sis of intelligence data and make daily report to president."

While smiling and shaking Pichushkin's hand she asked Sergei, "President?"

"*Da*. President of Russian Federation."

Pavel continued, "And, of course, Vasily Tvardovsky, first deputy director of FSB."

He, too, was polite but only marginally so. Another bland handshake formality, eyes searching her face for hints, clues, anything.

Sergei said, "*Federal'naya sluzhba bezopasnosti Rossiyskoy*. Fed–eral Security Service. Counter-intelligence, state security, an–ti-terrorism. Formerly KGB. These are most high-ranking offi–cials."

Three-for-three, seemingly uncomfortable with the situation but not the kind of guys to be trifled with. Not politicians or diplomats. Seasoned professionals. Alpha males. The kind of guys Tommy could probably handle. One, she could charm. A pack would be a challenge

Pavel launched a brief exchange in Russian with the deputies. Yenchenko began to translate.

Mandy raised a hand to interrupt. Body language said it all. "I know. They're waiting for the guy in charge."

Right on cue, a slight man entered from the corridor, mid-fifties, rimless glasses, about five-eight or five-nine but in self-as–surance, the tallest in the room. His arm rose as he closed the gap between himself and Mandy. A widening smile, the kind saved for greeting old friends at reunions.

"Good afternoon, Miss Owens." A two-handed handshake. Mandy responded by making it four. "I am Viktor Kozyratkin, first deputy director of the SVR. And I am most grateful you ac–cepted my invitation. I apologize for all the — what do you Americans call it? Oh, yes. Cloak and dagger. Matters of state security create inconvenience."

Not just for this guy. For her entire digestive tract, which seemed to be knotting up below a growing tightness in her chest. No chance to step away, pull it together. *Just fake it, best you can.* She laid her most gracious smile on him. "I'm very pleased to meet you, Mr. Kozyratkin. Thank you for your kind invitation. And no trouble at all with your precautions."

"Excellent. And Comrade Sergei Ilyich!" He reached past Mandy to shake Sergei's hand, gripping Yenchenko's forearm with his left as he did so, the politician's power handshake to pull into a guy hug complete with a pat on the back. "The years have been kind, old friend, but it has been much too long."

Kozyratkin and Yenchenko exchanged pleasantries in Russian and Serge turned to Mandy. "Comrade Kozyratkin is equivalent of American deputy director of CIA. Long ago, he was *rezident*, directing espionage operations in Washington and New York. He report directly to president of Russian Federation."

Kozyratkin shrugged to feign modesty. "And so, you see, from myself and my colleagues here, we have a security concern, because none of us are supposed to be in your country, and we would prefer the American FBI not be aware, yes?"

Mandy chuckled, as much out of unease as cocktail party charm. "Oh, absolutely understandable. Travel can be so complicated these days, Mr. Kozyratkin."

"Viktor. Please call me Viktor."

She felt calmer now, her belly relaxing, her shoulders softening. They weren't street thugs. They were the cream of Russian intelligence, and civilized. And so her smile was genuine. "Mandy. Friends call me Mandy. Can we be friends?"

"I should hope so. Please, take a seat. Pavel has prepared tea and some refreshments. We have much to discuss."

While Pavel vanished to assume the role of waiter, Mandy picked the nearest boxy chair and, as she settled, the men eased back onto the sofa, leaving the dominant chair for Viktor.

Pichushkin provided a thick manila folder, which Kozyratkin

gave a cursory thumb-through and set aside. He leaned forward and folded his hands together. "So. We represent various branches of Russian intelligence and are also here on behalf of the Federal Service for Technic and Export Control — which concerns itself with information security and protection of our country's technology — and the Federal Ministry for Internal Affairs and the *Politziya*, the Russian Federal Police."

Not bureaucrats. The guys who called the shots. Mandy nodded. "And would it be reasonable to say you have some issue of substantial concern?"

Viktor seemed relieved, but it was artificial, just a move in the game. "Precisely so."

"I'm flattered that you might think an ordinary American such as myself could be of assistance."

Viktor leaned back as Pavel returned with a large silver tray bearing two pots, six empty cups and a platter of pastry. "I as-sume, Mandy, that black tea is acceptable? It is Russian Cara-van."

"Lovely. Thank you." Pavel poured a small amount of *savar-ka* from the small pot into each of the cups, then topped off the tea concentrate with steaming water. Mandy declined milk and sugar as a courtesy to her Russian hosts. Pavel nodded and with-drew.

They'd spared no effort on food to accompany tea.

Viktor picked up a small plate to serve her. "Please. We have some *ptichie moloko*, or Birds' Milk Cake, which is very sweet. Some Alenka chocolate if you like, very popular in my country. And of course *vatrushka*, which I confess is my favorite, and pleasant with sugar and jam."

Mandy ignored everyone else in the room. "*Vatrushka* would be very nice, thank you."

Viktor prepared pastry for Mandy, passed it, and invited the others to indulge. Without looking up, he said, "And no, not for a moment do I think you are an ordinary American, Miss, er,

Mandy."

She held steady and softly replied, "What makes you think so?"

Eye contact returned with a smile. "Quite simply, you are the leader of a small unit of troubleshooters, independent of government, unaffiliated with the American government. What some might see as, shall we say, renegades, outsiders, those who answer to no one."

"So you say."

He continued as calmly as if he were discussing the best way to find a parking spot in midtown Manhattan. "We aware of your group. Our intelligence suggests that, in addition to Comrade Sergei, you have with you Tommy Kane and several others who might be considered irregulars, including a person codenamed Nyx. We don't know the identity of Nyx, but have seen his work. Most impressive."

Mandy contained a blush by focusing on the gender assumption of Nyx. "And what brings you to me — us — today? Surely the entire intelligence apparatus of the Russian Federation can manage quite well."

Sipping tea and taking tentative bites of pastry, the others observed with apparent unease.

"Yes, of course. Our agencies have considerable resources. And, as with your own country, budgetary limits and priorities as well. We are the same, eh?" He paused for a sip of tea and when he spoke, it was with a much cooler tone. "It's a very complicated and troubled world, Mandy. I'd prefer to focus on more substantial matters."

The *vatrushka* was delicious and a sense of deep calm saturated her mind. "Perhaps you could explain?"

Viktor put his partially-consumed dessert on the table, took a sip of tea, and abandoned the cup. "Of course. Your group is researching a band of internet hooligans, *kiberprestupniki* — cybercriminals — presently operating in the United States. While

the scale of the criminal activity is global, it is most seriously af-
fecting some parties in my country."

Mandy nodded and echoed Viktor's actions with cup and
plate. "I'm afraid that our effort, on behalf of a friend, was bearing some fruit when our paths crossed. We'd very much prefer
to continue."

"I see. Please. What, then, is the connection with CySafe?"

CySafe? How did they... Be candid, tell the truth. "That's very
preliminary, with no evidence to support a connection." The image of Nikki Savage flashed through her mind. "In fact, it began
as an unrelated matter. Could you elaborate on the impact within your country?"

With a glance, Viktor polled the faces of the men on the
sofa. Scowls all around, but no outright objection. Probably
weren't in a position to do so. For the first time, Mandy saw the
spine of a white ring binder on edge, stuffed between the arm of
the furniture and Ledovskoy's thigh.

Viktor momentarily laced the fingers of his hands behind his
head before abruptly leaning forward to tap fingertips together
just above his knees.

He's impatient. Uncertain. Stay steady.

Viktor paused for a moment that seemed to last forever, then
said, "Mandy, what I share with you now is most sensitive information, and your confidence would be appreciated."

"Go on."

"Within my country, there are powerful people, persons with
great wealth and influence."

"Oligarchs?" *Plutocrats with pull. Every country has a few.*

Viktor cracked a faint smile. "Let us say, people who have
the ear of our leaders, including the president. Losses are severe,
and ongoing. Our president has insisted we take action to stop
it. And so it has become an annoyance, distracting us from more
important work. Perhaps you may be of some assistance. I'm
certain that we can accommodate any reasonable fee for service."

A couple of million here, a couple of million there... Chet's fourteen thousand dollars seemed almost ridiculous in the grow−ing scale of things. *But maybe, just maybe... Oh, gosh, Tommy's go−ing to just kill me...* "We'd be more than pleased to assist for no fee, a gesture of friendship."

Viktor's smile suggested he was genuinely pleased. "Most thoughtful, but I insist on payment for services. I suggest a part−nership, merge forces. For our part, I would welcome Comrade Sergei's return to our fold. He could be perhaps a deputy direc−tor, a very good position. As you Americans say, let bygones be bygones, all is forgiven, come home."

A flutter of conversation in Russian erupted among those on the sofa. The tone suggested displeasure, even protest. Viktor squashed it by raising his hand. Mandy turned to Yenchenko, who had the most votes in the room.

With no expression whatever, Sergei calmly replied, first in Russian, then English, "A generous offer, but I am, of course, Ukrainian."

Viktor shrugged. "A small inconvenience, easily corrected in the files. You can be one of us again, yes?"

Mandy bit her lower lip. *What a terrible offer, what an awful predicament.*

Yenchenko shook his head. "*Nyet*. I am *Ukrainian*, not Rus−sian. And my loyalty is to Mandy Owens. And so, it is impossible to accept."

Whew. Well, maybe. Showdown time. Mandy sat back to offer Viktor a slight shrug of apology and spoke in a soothing, gentle voice. "I'm sorry. His decision. Sergei is a valued member of *our* team. We all look out for one another. It's the only way we sur−vive."

Viktor made a fist and with it tapped his lips and jaw, the warmth gone from his eyes, his smile evaporated. He turned to his associates and spoke in Russian. They went back and forth, sometimes talking all at once, and voices began to take on an edge of frustration and exasperation.

Ledovskoy pursed his lips, stood for a moment and handed the binder to Viktor. His face was deep red and his jaw tight, as though what he'd just done ran against every instinct and train—ing he'd embraced for decades. But he said nothing, and retreat—ed to the sofa.

Viktor studied Mandy's steady gaze, then abruptly held the notebook aloft for Yenchenko to deliver across the coffee table. "My colleagues are dismayed. Disappointed. There is much work in this material, the efforts of very skilled intelligence offi—cers in our cybercommand."

Mandy accepted the binder. "I shall treat it with the respect it surely deserves."

Viktor tilted his head back and took a deep breath. "I sin—cerely hope so, Miss Owens. If your unit matches reputation and is successful, my government will pay the sum of ten million dol—lars, US, deposited in a bank of your choice. If not? Well, such is an option that speaks for itself."

Mandy looked at the cover of the binder. "*Delo Reziume - Syny Chernobyle.*"

An inquiring glance to Sergei as the sensation of suffocation eased and air flowed easily into her lungs. The big, lovable Ukrainian translated. "Case Summary – Sons of Chernobyl."

CHAPTER TWENTY-EIGHT

Mandy Caye, The Bahamas

The sun hung low in the sky, easing down behind distant, puffy clouds. Orange spewed in all directions, a warmup for what Tommy thought would be one of those great sunsets that came with her island.

Evening air whispered across the cove below and washed up into faces finishing supper on the tower. It billowed Mandy's hair and the light gave her a glow that made everything right with the world.

Nikki was tending to little Cyrus, which seemed more and more to be her full-time job, and Charlie'd tossed the last of a bourbon into his throat and yawned. Bored, most likely, not having Serge around to ignite some sort of snortin' match. Charlie's loss was Lucy's gain. Sorta. She'd have to put up with Yenchenko for another day or two just to get the notebook from the Russians translated.

Tommy wasn't sure who'd kill who first.

Table talk between the women seemed strained, like they couldn't get on the same wavelength, like Billy's, the cabin, even the first few days on the island. Maybe it'd dragged on for too long. Maybe Mandy was just tired.

Maybe a few ounces of Macallan would do the trick before an early lights-out.

Charlie yawned a second time and called it a day. Earlier,

he'd tugged Tommy to the side in the kitchen to grouse about how he didn't want to speak poorly of a guest but for sure she was either dumb as a rock or holding onto a secret tighter than bark on tree. Didn't matter much. Nikki made her good-nights, too, and ushered Cyrus off to bedtime, where she'd read to him a bit and then vanish until morning.

Alone again, Tommy and Mandy savored evening air and the sound of the sea caressing the beach. The sun dropped out from the clouds and tumbled in for the night, one last gorgeous spear of light shooting high in the sky before it all went blue.

"Doing okay, Mandy?"

"Hm? Oh, yes. Fine. Great meal, big guy. A best ever. Where'd you learn to grill grouper that way? No. Wait. Not really sure I want to know."

Her voice crossed his ears like the gentlest fingertips on a shoulder rub, low and silky and intoxicating all at once.

She sat upright. "I should get these dishes."

"I got 'em."

"You cooked. It's only fair."

"Nah. You've been doin' some first-rate showdown diploma—cy and all. I'll run these puppies into the kitchen, fetch a couple of glasses and that bottle of 30-year-old we save for special."

A full moon was partway risen, filling the sky with its magic glow proving that the sun didn't own the sky. And all that glow seemed to land right on her face. When she looked up, it made her eyes sparkle.

"You know what, Tommy? I'd very much like to go for a walk. Nice, long walk on the beach."

"A thinkin' walk? I surely do under— "

"No, silly. A walk with you. Just you and me and the beach. It seems like ages since we've had a chance. The long way, around the east side. Along the edge."

He nodded. "A talkin' walk. First four beaches before that little cutoff?"

"Kind of. And a together walk, too."

On the beach, they tugged off dock shoes and dug toes into the sand, still warm, still soft and still hers. They marched hand in hand toward the sea, turning left when the ocean found their feet.

After a hundred yards, she paused. High above and behind her, the house with the three-sixty view, a castle a million miles from any kind of trouble or sadness or anger. Ahead, the endless ocean, running quiet with moonlight kissing the waves.

"Oh, gosh, I do love it so." She thrust her hands into the side pockets of white shorts and lifted her chin to enjoy a breeze caressing her hair. "I could spend forever, right here, and it wouldn't be long enough. It's like wrapping yourself in paradise and never having to let it go."

She fell silent while tiny waves lapped the sand. Finally she turned. "Tommy, how do you do it? Handle it, I mean. The pressure, the complexity, the anxiety for the others?"

Easy to be flip, to be modest, to dust it off with male bravado. But it was a sincere question, deserving candor. "Not always easily. It gets hard, sometimes."

"But you manage."

"Let's walk a bit." They strolled for fifty yards in silence while he confronted candor. "Long time ago, working solo, I didn't care. Live or die, no big deal. Now it's different. More careful, maybe. More thoughtful. But it's still the action, the thrill of being out on the edge. Adventure's a crazy addiction."

"Does it matter whether justice is served?"

He chuckled. "I know. That's your thing. I try to accommodate, best I can."

After a few dozen paces, she paused again. "And I'm grateful. But just now, I'm not so sure where justice is. This all started out as such a simple thing, helping a frightened mother and child. I'm sure it was one of those 'yeah, the rookie can handle it' situations, just to be nice. But now it's a mess. And I'm tired, burned out. And scared."

"Never thought of you as a rookie, Mandy. And scared? It sure didn't — "

She laughed. "Oh yes, scared. Right down to my heels, all the time. That's what I've been, from Nebraska forward."

"My old grandpap used to say, 'if you ain' scared, you ain' doin' nothin' worthwhile.'"

"Well, I'm not so sure about worthwhile. Savage was just a dime-a-dozen jerk, but I was just so livid. And the jackpot in Ibiza was just surreal and then hauling off all that cash. I was ready to stuff it in my bag and the guy says I was going to need help because it's two sacks, twenty-five pounds each, and customs and immigration is surely going to be intrigued. Thank heavens for a private jet and Lucy's bank."

"A millionaire moment."

"Which I actually felt guilty about."

He asked, "How so?"

"The Foundation. So here's Mister Save-the-World with his *de rigueur* foundation to leverage a tax break, which is involved in this Sons of Chernobyl bunch the Russians have down as terrorists, connected to a string of casinos."

"String?"

"Yes, five altogether, Lucy says. All the upscale playgrounds. She thought that networked slot machine must have been connected, and it was. So, lucky me, I let Lester help me out by clipping them for two million. Foundation money, allegedly to feed starving kids in the Third World. I was half tempted to turn the jet around and take it back when she told me on the flight."

He paused to gather a few shells to toss at the surf. "Of course, maybe the starving mouths that were being deprived was the Russian pals to feed whatever habits they have."

"Exactly, Tommy. *Dachas* for the porcine."

"Is Lucy looking into that? Where the foundation money goes?"

She sighed. "There's only so many hours in the day, and we both know that breaking into secure systems to roam around is a baby-step kind of thing."

"So you've just scored two million that otherwise would have prevented poor children from some terrible disease — maybe — and then you went right to the stakeout."

"And it was, well, kind of sporting, camping out in the parking lot near Chicago, but just so terribly cold. At least I felt like a regular spy or something. And then New York. Gosh, Tommy, I was so nervous that I was about to step on a trigger for World War Three... I was sure it would be just some kind of a field agent or something and here's the top brass of Russian intelligence, the guys who answer only to one of the most powerful men in the world.

"Serge said you were magnificent. He's never seen anyone play those people so well. You got one of the toughest guys in the trade to fold."

"On a very weak bluff."

"But you got the piece to the puzzle that made Lucy's whole day. She's still probably cackling, even if she does have to put up with Serge while assembling it into the answers we need."

Mandy lingered at a spot where shells tended to wash ashore and gathered a few. "I know. The Sons of Chernobyl. A cyber-terrorist group dedicated to robbing the plutocrats of Russia and all the incidental Chet Towers of the world. Blah, blah, blah. So the Russian government wants to pay us ten million dollars to take care of a political annoyance, so they can get back to the routine business of causing chaos around the world. It just doesn't seem worth it. I mean, who needs the crummy ten million? Not us, that's for sure."

He shrugged. "We could put it to good use, maybe. Help some people out. What we usually do."

She discarded the shells, all of which were broken. "I thought about that. Poor Chet. Right. We're trying to bring down a group of criminals that bagged him in a trap he shouldn't have gone near in the first place. And Lucy's showing us evidence that he's doing it again, striking up a relationship with some sob-story woman in Russia. And is actually just a group of clowns in Chicago. Should Frannie know? It'd hurt her terribly, but..."

"Yeah, I know. It kinda sucks."

"Thank you for that." She sighed. "Chet really deserves what's coming to him.' Plus, I'm worried about Lucy. She and her father have been putting in huge time on this and the strain is beginning to show."

"Like last time?"

"Hard to say. But she was actually happy to know the people tracking her were only Russian intelligence."

He said, "Yeah, until she picked up on just an incredibly intense effort by CySafe to discover the identity of Nyx. She said she's walking some sort of electronic tightrope with some kind of exotic trap. But the tracking's coming so hard and fast out of Montreal that she's worried."

"It's not fair, Tommy. It's always been some sort of a game for her, but this is serious. And you and I both know that if we pull the plug on the operation, she can go back to a nice, easy life for herself. Manipulating currency markets, dabbling in real estate, that sort of thing."

"And the guys?"

She shook her head. "None of them are getting any younger. Ian keeps talking about this year's vintage on his farm in France."

"And Nikki?"

"Nikki. You know, Charlie really is perceptive. Did he share what he thought with you? Yes? Good. I was just so optimistic, and even thought, well, with two million dollars from Cole, and a little help from Charlie and Lucy, she could have a nice, new life and that would be that. I even thought, wow, if I could engineer Cole's arrest and imprisonment, her problems would be solved."

They stepped gingerly through a single-file path around a point and down onto the second beach, this one nearly a quarter mile long, sheltered by a roving band of sandbars just offshore.

He said, "And now?"

"I don't know. It's like Charlie says. Nothing there and sponging or doing an incredible job of hiding something and playing us for fools. She's awfully nice, but so totally helpless. I thought a first she was uneasy about being the proverbial stranger in a strange land, uncertain, even frightened. Then I began to think she was just very shy and quiet, and then I wondered if she was withdrawn, with serious emotional problems."

"Except for dancing."

"Yes. Well, even very socially awkward people have outlets where they can open up. But this is unreal, like she's deeply troubled, and I couldn't tell whether Cole is responsible or protective or sheltering. But lately, I think responsible. Still, she seems so indifferent, just sort of going with the flow."

"Taking an emotional break, needing time to think it through?"

"Too much time. Too... well, I can't seem to put my finger on it. More like she's hiding something."

"We can certainly keep an eye on the situation."

She sighed. "I don't know. It's just bothersome, that's all."

"Maybe you've grown?"

"How do you mean, Tommy?"

"Well, you were always top-of-the-line, maybe didn't quite believe it, but you're stronger now, more aware of your own abilities."

"Think so?"

He said, "Know so. What would you like to do? Your call, anything you want."

"Besides unload the entire project and just spend the rest of my life with you in paradise?"

"We'd be bored after the first fifteen or twenty years."

She pulled up and tugged on his hand to draw him near. "I know. And you're correct. As much as I hate to admit it, we're two of a kind. You've gotten me addicted to crazy schemes and madcap adventure. It's entirely your fault. Don't even try to deny it." She looked away for a second and then moved closer and spoke in a very soft, almost apologetic voice. "Can we make a deal?"

"Sure."

"This whole thing has gotten so out of hand, and I'm very anxious about making a mistake and having it blow up in our faces. I'd very much like to step back a bit, share the load. Not a 'you or me' but rather an 'us.' Do you think the others might be okay with that?"

"They'll understand. Especially when situations get fluid. They won't have to worry about stepping on toes."

Her smile was one of relief. "Exactly. If we stay with this case, it's going to get very complicated very quickly. I'd be up for it, but only with you as partner, not crew. You're very good at this sort of thing, intuitive and experienced."

"I'm flattered."

"Well, don't let it go to your head, big guy. You're still just a good ol' boy and I'm still the baddest bitch on the beach. Who just happens to know a shortcut back to the house. Where they keep the single-malt scotch."

CHAPTER TWENTY-NINE

Charlie took a long pull of his morning coffee and half-sighed, half-scowled.

Some things never changed, so Tommy smiled. "Yeah, bud—dy, I know. Tad on the weak side, right?"

"I didn't say nothin'."

"Facial expression counts."

Charlie set his jaw. "Don't neither. I known fellas who got real fine news and stepped on by a cow at the same time. You can't grin and get stomped by a heifer all at once. You get things settled up with the boss?"

Tommy cocked an eyebrow.

Charlie grunted. "Yeah, I reckon so. Seen you two comin' up that back path from the long beach."

"So, we just went for a walk. Nice friendly stroll, maybe."

"Uh-huh. That's first class horseshit. You two don't need walks to get all romantical. Mostly when you got business to set—tle."

Thirty feet away, Mandy energetically organized seat pillows around the big table on the tower, tidying up for company.

"How can you tell?"

"Hell, boy, look yonder. She's gone from tighter'n a spool of barbed wire to all kinda pretty glow. Good thing, too. I been gettin' sorely tempted to smack you aside the head with a two-by-four and put things to right."

Tommy laughed. "Hey, hey, now. It was her turn, her op,

her call. Not my place, not one bit. And don't kid yourself, bud—
dy. She's done a first-class job, too. But maybe she doesn't want
to be too autocratic. Maybe she wants everybody to participate
fair and square."

"Tough on her, though. And that's a fact."

A surge of anger crawled up the back of Tommy's neck. "I
know what I'm doing."

"You sure?"

"Giving her a chance to step out front, take charge."

"You're trying to turn her into another you, maybe? Look,
bub, she ain't crazy, like you. And that, well, yeah, that real
clever *Ukrainian*. Yeah, yeah. I heard about New York. Don't
matter. Serge is still a dangerous fella, like you in a lot of ways.
Which is good if you're some citizen in a mess of trouble and
need a hand. But Mandy's decent people, Tommy. Ain't like us.
Smart, pretty, all kind of class, just the nicest gal. You can't pull
her down to our level, my friend. You gotta climb up to hers."

"You think?"

"I think."

"And of course, you're right."

"You bet your ass."

Mandy paused at her task, shielded her eyes with the palm of
her left hand, then waved, her face stuffed with joy. In moments,
Frisco's helicopter roared past and began the turn to descend to
the island.

Charlie watched the aircraft bank right and cross the line of
the beach. "Lucy, Bug and Serge?"

"I believe so. She's bringing a big ol' sack of those sweet rolls
you favor, from that bakery in Georgetown."

Charlie studied his empty mug. "Yeah, well, you might be
decent at sweet-talking Mandy, but with Lucy on the island, I
know there'll be a decent cup of coffee."

And there was. Forty-five minutes later, the buffet was laid
out, pots of fresh coffee for all tastes included with platters of

eggs with sausage and bacon, decent *blini*, bowls of fruit, and a field of pastry. Laughter, comfort, the whole team pleasant and happy.

When Mandy had gently eased everyone into the new working arrangement, she gave the stage to Lucy.

"Okay, I'm gonna spare the technical details." There was a light round of applause, which was a shame. All hunters like to tell their tale, but none present could appreciate one of the most stunning achievements in wiretapping and computer hacking. Bug, who never ducked a chance to brag, went for modest and tossed the credit back to his daughter.

"Let's just leave it at we're into their system, found a way to beat forty-ninety-six RSA encryption and pretty much have the run of the place. There's a definite link to the data center front near Chicago."

Nikki registered no reaction.

Lucy continued. "So, okay, I'd heard about Syncher but, hey, there's a lot of creeps on the net. So when I tracked the email involving Chet to them, it was no big deal. But Mandy, your stuff made a lot of difference filling in the blanks."

Sergei said, "Standard field note and analysis. SVR tracks terrorist type group called Sons of Chernobyl, activist relative of victim of power plant disaster. They steal from capitalist pig connected to plant and make huge profit anyway, despite suffering of people. So it is form of revenge."

Mandy "Which brings us to Savage."

Lucy chewed and swallowed a danish. "Who also has connections, the Savitsky line. And he's got some past, too, having spent a little time on the hacking circuit before going sorta totally legit with CySafe, the best cover I've ever seen."

Tommy said. "A security firm, fronting a crime network?"

"Looks that way. And I'm betting Savage is involved."

Tommy refilled his coffee cup. "Smoking gun?"

"Smoking *cannon*, Tommy."

They exchanged a glance and with the faintest nod of her head toward Nikki, she inquired whether if candor was all right. He turned to Mandy, who signaled approval.

Tommy asked, "Care to elaborate?"

"Okay, so we're getting a real strong sense that tucked inside CySafe, in a special R-and-D section that's limited to a handful of people — Cole included — is the cybercrime unit, with varied names depending on perspective. I think this the one feeding Sons of Chernobyl via the foundation. There's two plausible paths. The first is cash flows through CySafe and gets laundered with tax write-off contributions to the foundation. Then it could co-mingle with the casino operations, a pet project of Savage that most people don't know about. The second possibility is that it goes directly to the casinos for laundering, then to the foundation, again for a tax write-off. I kind of prefer the latter because it's simpler, but either way it would take time to sort out."

Charlie stabbed a sausage and took a bite. "Well, I don't know a thing about all tech hoo-rah, but what I'm hearin' is that you know, but can't prove nothin'. His word against yours and that fella's got a bigger rep than anyone here. You gotta bag that scumbag red-handed or you ain't got squat."

Lucy's tone took a patronizing edge. "Charlie, I'd love to have black-and-white proof, but we're walking on friggin' eggs here. I've got a lot of access, but I'm assuming they're security conscious, read their logs, look for traffic that doesn't seem logi—cal. We can only go so fast."

Mandy came to her defense. "And I think you've gone ex—traordinarily far. No sense in taking any more risk than we have to. We're going to have to help carry the ball."

Yenchenko was smearing fruit preserves on an array of *blini*. "*Da, da*. We must have plan, make good trap." He wolfed down an entire *blini* in one bite. "A pity we cannot use Wells."

Mandy turned to Nikki. "Please. Isn't there *anything* you

might know that can help us out? I mean, I assume you still don't want to return to him and you've said you don't want to be always looking over your shoulder. Anything at all?"

Nikki looked like she was trying to focus for ideas, but finished with a helpless smile. Maybe she didn't understand. Tommy repeated the question in French.

Nikki shrugged. "*Je suis désolé, mais je ne sais rien au sujet de son entreprise.*" She wrapped a maternal arm around Cyrus. "We are afraid, and do not know what to do."

Same excuse, but unwilling to do anything.

Mandy ignored raised eyebrows around the table and patted Nikki's arm. "Don't worry. We'll figure something out." She took a breath and turned. "Okay, Tommy, I think we're going to need one of your specials. It's time to somehow wrap this up."

Tommy chuckled. "Got maybe a Plan A, but no Plan B."

Mandy replied with a sly smile. "Why would you ever waste time organizing Plan B? You're a Plan A kind of guy."

Nikki seemed to be struggling to follow English in too many variations and showed all the signs of giving up on trying to comprehend. Little Cyrus had become fidgety and bored with an extra sweet roll. His plate was only half empty and he silently appealed to his mother.

She stood to excuse herself. "I think he wishes to play on the beach. And I am sad to say I am not more helpful. So, we excuse ourselves, okay?"

No dissent from the team. Mandy did the little maiden aunt thing and brought a smile to the boy's face just before he wheeled and scampered across the causeway to the stairs leading down. Nikki followed, her step quick to keep an eye on him, but not frantic.

Charlie muttered, "Yeah."

Sergei and Lucy exchanged looks that said, "Amazing. But what are you going to do?" Tommy shrugged and Mandy sighed.

After a few reflective seconds, discussion resumed.

Lucy said, "Look, I really think we have to start with their operation near Chicago. You guys were planning a raid anyway, and K-C's people are still doing stakeout. I'm betting the people inside are small fry, easily overpowered."

Tommy said, "Yeah, but there's probably a whole bunch of computer equipment, which we'd have no idea what to do with. I'm betting it's not just pulling the plug."

Mandy said, "Which is why we're going to need Lucy on this one. We're going to need everybody."

Charlie asked, "And Nikki?"

Mandy pursed her lips. "We can't babysit any more. I don't know that it makes any difference anyway."

Charlie said, "But she's the client. I thought the whole deal was to work out some kind of deal with this Savage guy, or at least set her up with a fresh start."

Tommy said, "Still possible."

Mandy sighed. "For now, I'd like to give her the benefit of the doubt. But realistically, where is she going to go? And who's going to find her here?"

Lucy rubbed her jaw. "I dunno. Savage's people have been pressing hard. It was bad enough with the Russians, but these guys? I'm just glad we set up a honeypot in one of the NSA units to slow them down. But sooner or later the people at Fort Meade are going to pick up on an aberration and CySafe's engineers are going to get past it."

Mandy and Tommy looked at each other.

She said, "Got to risk it. For at least a day or two. What could you and Bug do with the equipment outside of Chicago?"

Bug shrugged. "Maybe pick up a high-volume data line, three or four actually, link'em, shoot a relay. Maybe some satellite time?"

Lucy asked. "One of the television birds? We could mask it as network back channel feed."

Bug said, "That'd work, kiddo."

Lucy nodded. "Dump it into that spare I-P block in Cayman, lock it down. If they know we have it, they'll probably put their priorities on recapture and leave us alone."

Mandy said, "What will we do with the people at the data center? We can't just cut them loose."

Sergei drummed his fingers on the table. "She make good point, Koshka. Perhaps our prisoner are clever, take opportunity to escape. SVR director would be most displeased."

Tommy smiled. "Put them on ice for a few days, then deport. Well, rendition. Do a transfer in, say Berlin. I don't think the Germans will mind very much. They never do, and I know some guys. Meanwhile, we need to get Savage and his pals pointing fingers at each other."

Charlie shook his head. "Calling it awful tight, boy."

Mandy said, "I agree. You're really going to have to build motivation under Savage. I mean, you can promise him anything, but he's a cool customer and not about to panic."

Tommy hoisted his coffee cup and sipped. "Unless he reads about himself in the newspaper. I haven't seen a bad guy yet who likes a spotlight peeking into dark shadows."

Mandy said, "Oh, Tommy, that's just so mean."

Lucy looked puzzled.

Mandy said to her, "Emerson Barr, *Tech Times*."

"I haven't seen it in years. The name is only vaguely famil-iar."

"Tommy wants to use Emmie, who's an old friend, to plant an article and rattle Savage. Tech companies, in particular, are fairly volatile on market rumors and Savage would know that. He could loose millions on a whisper."

"Cool."

Mandy sat back and toyed with her juice glass. "Sorry, it's the sort of thing that just rubs me the wrong way. I was once a jour-nalist, after all."

"Yeah, but this guy, Barr, he's with the press, right?"

"Well, yes."

Lucy shrugged. "Then who cares?"

Mandy said, "I do, but I'll live with it. And what about some sort of a calling card?"

Tommy said, "We ought to do it in person this time. We *could* start by setting up a face-to-face with Savage and Nyx."

Lucy's eyebrow jumped and she silently bit her lower lip.

Mandy said, "No. No way should we put Lucy in harm's way."

Tommy was undeterred. "I said *Nyx*. Not Lucy. You'd make a very fashionable hacking queen, I think."

Mandy waved her hands in denial. "Oh, no. *No, no, no.* No way could I talk my way through tech stuff with a guy like Savage. Uh-uh. Sorry."

Bug said, "We could do a wire and an in-ear. Lucy could coach you. Yeah, yeah. On the fly."

"And if they do a sweep for devices?"

Bug shrugged. "So gimme one of your favorite underwire bras, overnight. I can rig it."

When everyone smiled, Mandy's cheeks went pink.

Lucy said, "C'mon, Mandy, it's just a bra. Be glad he didn't ask for panties. I did one of those once, remember, Dad? I was sixteen, and you worked it into the elastic around the legs. Man...talk about pinch in all the wrong places..."

Amid full-bore laughter, Mandy's face and ears were beet-red, and she shook her head in dismay.

Bug said, "Plus an earring. One of them big gold ring ones. They won't pay no attention, especially if they're wondering how they're gonna frisk your — "

Mandy waved him off. "I've got the picture, Bug."

CHAPTER THIRTY

920 Pratt Blvd., Elk Grove Village, Illinois

The squat gray CSIT building hadn't changed in the past couple of days, but Mandy was grateful the weather was milder and the coffee not as cold. This time, no awful-on-a-bun.

Brick and Jinx somehow managed to get a to-go container of yogurt with a nondescript berry flavor in a sort of pinkish-bluish tone. It was palatable.

And this time, instead of a truck full of tough guys unable to confess any discomfort under any circumstances, it was just Tommy, who was his usual coffee-only, and Lucy, who remarkably spurned the opportunity for a doughnut and went with the yogurt.

Lucy scrapped the last of it from the cup with a tiny plastic spoon. "I'm thinking like raspberry, maybe, but there's a lot of blue in it."

Mandy nodded. "Always chancy, the mixed berry. Sorry they didn't have rib-eye and potato flavor, Tommy."

He said, "It's okay to rough it once in a while. Maybe next time."

Lucy finished and returned to her electronic pad. "Nothing yet from across the street. Probably taking some sort of break during their daily spam run."

Mandy sighed.

"Hey, you gotta be patient. Techies are human, too. They

goof off, they drink coffee and eat crappy food, sleep, tell sexist jokes. Not like those big-league spies you ran, right, Tommy?"

"Oh, absolutely. Focus, discipline, concentration, better catering…"

Lucy laughed. "Yeah, and they fold when the first smart woman comes along, pulls their chain. Gee, Tommy, think about it. Mandy trots off to Ibiza, comes home with the all-time carry-on. Bundles of hundred-euro notes, fifty pounds of cash just the right size for those big safe-deposit boxes at our bank in Cayman."

He shook his head. "Everybody returns with souvenirs."

"Yeah? Well, then she goes one-on — what, four? — with the head honchos in Russian intelligence and comes away with a note to die for. I mean, Sergei couldn't believe it. Like, really stunned. He's translating the junk and muttering all kinds exple-tives, and I just want to get the meat off the bones. That stuff had leak-it-and-you-die stamped all over it. *Sovershenno sekretno.* Which means 'top secret," and it's on almost every page. I had to load him up with high-test coffee and sweet rolls just to keep him on track."

"Sergei? I find that hard to believe."

Lucy chuckled. "Yeah, well, Mandy must have really worked those guys. I mean, like blood on the carpet and shit. I've bumped into SVR people now and then, usually embarrassing little encounters in the back alleys of NSA and CIA, and they're some serious dudes. And so, really. All their stuff was just handed to you by the big dogs?"

Mandy smiled and nibbled at yogurt.

"Very cool, Mandy. Very cool."

Mandy glanced at Tommy, who was watching the industrial park building and taking Lucy's teasing in stride. "Wish I could feel a sense of triumph, Lucy. But it's the same-old same old. Fat cats with the ear of the president, caught with fingers in the dal-liance cookie jar, get burned, run to daddy, who'll put the best and the brightest in their intelligence community on bailing out a bunch of stupid plutocrats."

Lucy nodded and closed the binder. "Yeah, I hear ya."

Mandy discarded the yogurt cup and crossed her arms. "So now they've got us to do their dirty work for a crummy ten million dollars. I almost feel sorry for the gang across the street. We're gonna bust them and they're just putting the squeeze on some rich creeps who deserve to be squeezed."

Tommy cocked an eyebrow, but said nothing.

Lucy shrugged. "Cybercrime is cybercrime. They've got other victims, Mandy. Like, um, your friend Chet."

Mandy shook her head. "Who wouldn't have lost his savings if he hadn't replied to — who was it?"

Lucy rummaged through the tablet. "Sasha. Well, actually a relay remailer in Italy and one of the guys across street."

"Oh, yes. Dear little Sasha, with her gooey pitch."

Lucy chuckled. "Got it right here. Let's see.... Ah. *I am Alexandra or Sasha in short; a young, timid, yet well accomplished, blue eyed girl from Russia. I am from the city of Ivanovo, which is also known as the city of brides. I want to find someone matching my tastes and views, who can melt my heart on the first date itself with his character, looks and intelligence.*"

Mandy sighed.

Lucy said, "Plus of course, the link that poor old Chet couldn't resist. Tommy, do regular guys really fall for that shit?"

Tommy chuckled. "Don't even get me started on the way companies manipulate women, day in, day out."

Mandy said, "Not the same. I mean, this is just dumb."

"Yeah. I know."

Lucy stretched. "I can understand when some guy whose marriage has fallen apart might be feeling self-destructive, one time, but even knowing we're watching his I-P, and even with a thing going with Frannie, he just couldn't resist a second time. I blocked it, but boy, I was sure tempted."

Mandy shook her head. "So we're doing the dirty work for the Russian government and trying to rescue naughty Chet at the same time. Poor Frannie. She'd just die if she knew. Maybe we ought to just — "

Tommy lifted a finger toward the roof of the car to inter-rupt. "We promised to fix his credit and bank account. He helped us back in the bar. He might be tarnished, but I gave my word."

Lucy shrugged. "Whatever."

The radio crackled and K-C declared that everyone was ready. He and Serge would take the lead after Brick and Jinx broke through the door, with Bug right behind. The balance of the crew would handle the rear entry.

Lucy leaned forward. "Okay, they're back online. Just reiter-ate to all these guys that they're to *secure* any equipment, but not damage it, okay? Not even touch it."

Tommy repeated the order and team leaders acknowledged it. Lucy ruffled her nylon windbreaker. "I'm kind of getting used to it, Tommy. A genuine-looking FBI jacket. Perfect fit, even the sleeve length. Adore navy blue. Can I keep it?"

"I suppose you want the badge and I.D., too."

"Sure. I bet it gets me a better seat on the plane."

Mandy rolled her eyes. "All the seats on the jet are good, Lucy."

"No, no, I meant when I've gotta fly commercial. Unless, of course, you want to discuss getting into fleet charter, which I've been recommending for a while..."

Mandy said, "Probably not a good idea during a raid."

"Okay, it'll keep. Here's all the warrants. Federal, the usual charges, enough for K-C's guys to lug 'em into Chicago, get them to arraignment. Give me just a half a second... Okay, good to go. They're in the system. As John Does, but the feds can still tag them after we fill in the blanks."

Tommy gave the green light by flashing his headlights twice.

The others responded in kind while Tommy pulled a pistol and chambered a round.

Lucy said, "I suppose I couldn't get one of those, too? No. I guess not."

* * *

In less than thirty seconds, they breached the entry. Noise, yelling, orders, guns everywhere. In less than a minute, seven startled and frightened men clasped their hands behind their heads and dropped to their knees.

And in less than two minutes, their hands were securely bound behind their backs and they were lined up facing a wall in the tiny building lobby.

Throughout the building, Mandy heard doors crashing open, followed by calls of "clear" and "secure."

And just five minutes after Lucy's instructions unleashed the assault, K-C was grinning while he pulled the FBI jacket from his body and returned to his usual black-leather style. "Perfect! Nobody hurt, hardly any damage, got seven perps with some juicy warrants. We'll make a bunch of reward money, have a few beers tonight to celebrate."

Lucy and Bug were already huddled over a keyboard, taking control of the system. Lucy stuck a flash drive into a USB port and within a handful of seconds had command of the rows and rows of mainframe racks all around them.

K-C walked up, a cleared shotgun on his shoulder. "We good to go with the prisoners?"

Tommy said, "Absolutely. Nice job, fellas. Thanks for staying with it, being set to go."

"Anytime, buddy." He hoisted the faked warrants into the air. "Your gals, they done real good. First class paper here. Now, you said it was gonna jibe with the system downtown?"

"Yeah, it should. Get them on ice, treat them well. Ten

grand apiece, plus expenses."

"Sounds good to me. Okay, let's get the perps loaded up, and we'll be out of your hair. You got my card, right?"

Tommy patted a shirt pocket and smiled. The card was in Mandy's bag, but K-C didn't need to know that.

Fifteen minutes after the raid began, all that remained of one of the world's worst cybercrime nightmares were hums. The hum of the ventilation system. The hum of the fluorescent lights in the ceiling panels. The hum of cooling fans in the main-frames.

And the faint clicky-clacks of diodes winking on and off, do-ing the bidding of Lucy Tramanian.

From a few feet away, Bug finished an electronic sweep and pronounced the building secured.

Lucy leaned back from the keyboard and stared at the gib-berish on the monitor, some sort of computer commands in blue, pink, green on a field of black, frozen with a methodically winking cursor at the bottom.

Tommy's eyes were on Lucy. "Okay, so whatcha got?"

She took a deep breath. "Moment of truth. We definitely have our proof. No question this is the base of Sons of Cher-nobyl."

Mandy said. "And they are officially off line and no longer conducting business?"

"Sort of. More like on pause. The routing's connected to servers in Montreal. This monitor is where the system takes in-coming bank account data and does two things. The program tries the account, snags a few dollars, and them moves the data to an external system."

Tommy and Mandy nodded while Bug stood back, paternal pride evident.

"The one in the middle is the actual operating system of the racks in this facility. It's the central brain of the operation. And the one on the right is outflow, primarily spam, to I-P addresses and user names. It's the part of the system that sends messages to guys like Chet. Plus all the other usual junk. The lottery winning in Nigeria. The stranded relative in Indonesia. The invoice for the product you didn't order. All in all, it's pretty basic. The code is somewhat upscale, but not what I'd call earth-shattering."

Tommy said, "You mentioned data moving to somewhere else."

"Very good, cowboy. Which is why it's holding, but still alive. Kind of decision time here. If my memory is still okay, the external is a server in the farm at CySafe. Your smoking gun, Tommy. Proof that there's a relationship with *somebody* at CySafe. But that doesn't necessarily mean Savage himself."

Mandy pursed her lips. "I was so hoping..."

Lucy grinned. "Game's not over. But this is a point of no return. Three options. We could still just shut it down, pull the plug, kill it. I can wipe the entire farm here in an hour or so, render it useless and they'll have to go to a lot of work to put it back online."

"Or?"

"Or I could let it run, spend some time doing diagnostics, follow the little bouncing ball kind of thing. That might go somewhere, but it would at least prove it's a CySafe op."

"Or?"

Bug said, "Or, like we planned, we could take charge of it. Make some noise, send a message, try to rattle their cage. See if Savage himself is a player. This is where all that encryption work comes in handy."

Tommy asked, "How secure are we, really? Will Savage figure it out from his end?"

"Only if they're willing to back trace every phone line in their building and then know where to look. Like I said, dad's little goody is well-camouflaged. Eventually? Sure. Next few months? Not likely."

Mandy asked, "And you're sure we can run it remotely, in a way that Savage's people can't find it?"

"Yes. I can mask the I-Ps so we can completely clean this place out and still be up and running. Trust me. So you want to do this?"

Mandy nodded. "That's why we came this far."

Lucy beamed. "Attagirl." She plopped back down into the chair and flexed her fingers above the keyboard.

"Shouldn't we start closing this up before, I don't know, someone comes or calls someone?"

Tommy said, "I agree. Let's not linger."

Lucy waved a hand. "Gotta satisfy my curiosity. Gotta know." She took a breath and brought a monitor to life, began to type a bit too fast, cursed, and tapped on the delete key a dozen times.

Mandy said, "Take your time."

Lucy ignored her. The screen flicked quickly through a series of directories and then locked into a list of messages. She scrolled down, down, down, paused, backed up a few. "There we go."

Mandy exchanged a shrug with Tommy.

Lucy began to cackle. "Ta-da. Yes. The money's running into the casinos through a shell company in... let's see... yeah, Spain. So it gets laundered — because casinos spread around the world are good for that kind of thing — then it washes out into the foundation. But not all of it. The Sons are getting a piece, just as we suspected. Give me a day or so and I can get some good data."

Mandy tried to follow the words on the screen, which looked like some sort of a spreadsheet. "Nice."

Lucy turned to face them. "Yep. And you know what? Cole's cheating his partners, too."

CHAPTER THIRTY-ONE

Castillo de los Reyes, Ibiza, Spain

Tommy worked his way around the edges of a substantial bowl of seafood paella, planning to save the centerpiece prawn for last. Cole Savage might be a first-class sleazeball, but his kitchen set a good table.

Mandy was seated opposite Tommy at a round table on a broad open-air restaurant, about three-quarters full with guests on the well-to-do, somewhat pretentious side, behaving as though they were more concerned about appearances than the cuisine.

She'd been undecided about what to order from a card of the day's specials, finally handing the sheet back to the waiter and declaring she'd have the same as Tommy ordered. The seafood paella hadn't disappointed, although the squid seemed a bit overdone.

He said, "So you're okay with it?"

"The view? The plan? The bugged bra?"

"The paella."

She gently relieved a mussel shell of its meat. "It's fine. I think the saffron and the paprika works well together. Why?"

"You could have ordered anything from the menu, you know."

"Paella was a good idea. Glad I went with your choice. It's delicious, I was famished, and I'm afraid I'm wolfing it down.

Was there something — "

"No, no. Nothing wrong with it."

She put on the brakes by taking a sip of wine. "What, then?"

"Never mind. It was... well, ridiculous."

A sly grin spread across her face, her eyes sparkled and she leaned forward. "Oh, this I have to hear."

The big centerpiece prawn was a tempting escape. "Nah, it's nothing."

"Tommy, how can we be partners if we don't share? Gosh, men. Always having to be the filtering agent. How about letting me be the judge if it's ridiculous?"

Yeah, boxed in. "You won't laugh?"

She turned her attention to a chunk of monkfish and sliced it into three pieces. "Of course not."

"You will."

"Nope. Promise."

"You're sure?"

"Yes. Tell me."

"Okay. When we ordered, you were taking your time and I went for the seafood paella. You seemed interested in other choices, but went with the same thing."

"So?"

"The other day, Charlie said he thought I was trying to make you into another me, which maybe you were doing by ordering the same thing."

She stared for a moment, then laughed. "And he would be so wrong. You're right. It *is* ridiculous. Pass some of that seasoning. It needs a touch more."

"You said you weren't going to laugh."

She shrugged. "I lied. Get over it."

"Doesn't exactly encourage candor."

"Oh, gosh, Tommy, I have nothing against lying. Just as long as it's done honestly."

He stabbed the prawn. "I've been had."

"Yep. But you're not the one with a bug in her bra." She tapped her sternum twice. "Hello, hello? Is this thing working? Agent Thirty-four-B, checking in. C'mon, Tommy, finish up. I want to go deal with Savage and then get Lucy and her father off my chest."

Twenty yards away, Savage was the focal point of conversation around a much larger table. Six others listened, sometimes spoke and most of the time didn't look too happy. Savage gestured for waitstaff, and the departing plates and bowls looked half full. Another hurried instruction and the chief waiter refilled wine glasses around the circle.

Mandy had been watching Tommy sneak glances toward Savage's meeting. "What do you think?"

"I think it's time." He dabbed his lips with a napkin and dropped it on the table. A waiter appeared within seconds, delivered the check, and Tommy signed for it. "You ready?"

"Can I be scared?"

"Absolutely. Just don't show it."

She pulled her hair back away from her ear and started to reach for an earring. "Oops. Almost forgot." She held her palm open and up, turning it from side to side as if to display she had nothing in her hand. "Wouldn't want to have Ian shoot you by accident. Okay, let's turn Lucy on and get into it." Her hand went to the ring on her right ear, as if she were just checking to be sure it was well connected. After a moment of listening, she nodded. "Yes. We're live, Tommy. No more bawdy jokes about Lucy in a swimsuit."

Not much more to do than take it. And take comfort in knowing things were back to normal.

Mandy chuckled. "Just kidding, Lucy. Yep, here we go."

They moved toward the target. He said, "Just stay natural, like we're headed for an evening out, just happen to bump into old friends. And whatever you do, don't forget to..." He brightened. "Well, well, if it ain't our old buddy, Cole Savage. Howdy, there, sport. Looks like you got some friends after all." He turned to Mandy, "Just hold on, for a second, honey. I oughta buy these boys a round."

Savage showed a faint smile on a tight jaw, like a guy trying to make the best of hemorrhoids on a hard chair. But only for a moment, because he stood to shake hands and then changed his mind about the courtesy. "Good evening, Mister Kane."

Tommy pulled a wad of cash from his side pocket and peeled off a pair of hundreds. "Let's get some good stuff in those glass—es. Oh, hey, I ain't interrupting some kinda meeting or nothin' am I?"

Savage cocked his head. "Not at all, Mister Kane. These are some business associates of mine and we were just enjoying — "

"Yeah, first class meal. Had me some of that pay-ella. Mighty tasty. O'course, problem with that seafood stuff is it sure enough gives me gas. Ain't that right, Mandy?" Before she could speak, Tommy turned to Savage and rolled on. "By golly, don't rightly know where I forgot my manners. You remember Mandy Owens, don'tcha, buddy?"

Savage turned to shake her hand and his eyes locked onto hers. "Ah, yes. Miss Owens. Very nice to have you with us again. Of course, I'm not so sure I'd say the same for my casino manag—er."

She replied with a disarming smile and shifted to a confiden—tial tone. "It's Mandy. And please excuse my friend. He's had quite a lot to drink."

Savage seemed to ignore the remark. He gave a quick scan of the men at the table. "Or is it perhaps — what was that? Oh, yes. *Nyx*."

"I'm sorry, I don't know what you — "

"Please, Miss Owens, or whoever you are, don't trifle with me. It doesn't fit the sort of person who can stroll onto a casino floor, pick a slot machine, do twenty-five pulls and beat fifty-million-to-one odds."

Her smile widened and light sparkled in her eyes. "Twen–ty-six."

"Ah, of course. Twenty-six pulls and two million euros, cash, and then just walk away. Rather nicely done. Frequency over–ride? Back door into the random number generation software? Local, or remote?"

"We all get lucky sometimes. Look, Mister Savage, I really don't want to intrude on your social gathering here, and Tommy and I were just — "

Savage chuckled and gestured toward the seat he'd just va–cated. "No, no, I insist." He raised a hand and motioned for the waitstaff to bring another chair. "I think you know who these gentlemen are, and why we're here tonight."

Three of the men shifted to make space when the extra chair arrived, and Savage put his hand on the back of it. "Oh, dear. I'm afraid we don't have a seat for Mister Kane. Do you think he'll mind? Think he can stand on his own?"

Tommy grinned. "I'll be just fine."

Savage glared, his renowned self control looking frayed. "Yes. I'm sure you will be. You should be careful, Mister Kane. Too much alcohol makes you look ridiculous. You can wait qui–etly wherever you'd like, or I can have some people escort you out."

"This is good."

"As you wish." Savage turned back to Mandy as they both settled into seats.

Mandy managed to cling to the bluff, acting like queen of the hive and adroit with the prompting coming through the faint wire from the earring into the tiniest earpiece they'd ever seen. The one they nearly lost when she dropped it into a thick carpet two hours earlier. But now it was where it belonged and the om–nidirectional mike in the bra gathered all the tech talk and fed it smoothly to Lucy, several thousand miles and a satellite skip away.

The pace picked up and he suspected they were testing her with irrelevant stuff and flat-out false junk for her to correct and explain. After ten minutes of warmup, it sounded like they were getting into the nitty-gritty, the part where she was holding all the cards and they were more than a little annoyed.

She masked delay between hearing and speaking with a serene, contemplative air that came off as being incredibly smug and haughty. It was wearing on Savage's demeanor. He was getting caught in the middle, translating what Mandy said into Russian and then turning increasingly strident questions into English. No need to understand the shop talk of hackers with big league systems. Body language and tone said it all.

At last Savage appeared to be satisfied that he'd encountered a rival from a dozen years ago face to face. He held up a hand to quiet the others, especially two guys directly opposite him and Mandy, who looked angry enough to do something stupid. If they were armed. From Tommy's vantage point, it was difficult to be certain.

"You'll pardon my caution, Miss Owens. You're quite the surprise. I'd always pictured Nyx as being short, dumpy, a bit unkempt."

Tommy struggled to suppress a smile, thinking about how well that must have gone over with Lucy. But Mandy registered no reaction.

"Mandy. Friends call me... no wait. I guess Miss Owens is appropriate, isn't it? But, anyway, no offense taken. Stereotypes are easy, but unpredictable."

Savage relaxed and fled into reminiscence. Code names Tommy couldn't recognize, but Lucy probably knew well. "Ah, yes. The follies of youth. When we were loaded up with caffeine, sugar, and a passion for the summits of digital mountains. Still using that old warehouse?"

Mandy needed no time for a prompt. "No, it's long gone. Just a vacant lot in Allentown. You know, Pennsylvania."

"Yes, of course. So you've moved on to — where exactly was that, again?"

Mandy offered the most innocent smile, leaned toward Savage and patted the back of his hand. "Why, into your worst nightmare, Cole. The girl in the white hat. Who's not only in your system, but has control of it."

Savage's hand found the stem of a wine glass and his grip tightened around it. "That's a dangerous place to be, Miss Owens."

Mandy shrugged it off. "Actually, I find it rather, well, *elemental*. But you and I both know that this particular visit to Ibiza isn't one of your monthly status reports. It's because you're scared, and you don't know what to do."

The hands of the two angry guys began to move, ever so slowly, toward the insides of their jackets.

Savage nodded. "Let me tell you something, Miss Owens — Nyx, if you like — about what happens to people who interfere with my business. They get crushed. But because I admire your work and respect the initiative, I'll make an exception. You return control of our project, give back the two million, hand over my wife and son, we'll let you go."

"And the alternative?"

Savage raised his glass, as if making a toast, and smiled. "Well, like I said. You're just one little annoyance against an entire corporation. We'll never stop looking, and one day we'll find you. You'll not only get crushed. You'll get killed."

Mandy bowed her head and nodded. She looked up and used her right hand to pull the hair back across her ear.

Savage's glass exploded. Shards and wine spewed across the table. All that was left in his fingers was the stem.

Stunned and shocked, others at the table tumbled backward, scrambling to get to their feet. In quick succession, five more glasses shattered in a clockwise pattern, coating the tablecloth with wine and crystal. The last left additional spatters across

Savage's chest, but he remained motionless, uncowed in a hushed patio of silent, staring patrons.

Mandy's expression went to sympathetic. "Oh, dear. And that was such a lovely jacket and tie. And the shirt, too. I do hope you can get that cleaned." She stood, leaving him holding the stem of the glass. "Well, it's been lovely chatting with you, Cole, but I'm afraid we have to go. Thanks for your offer and I promise to give it some thought. Really, I will."

His eyes narrowed. "You do that, Miss Owens."

Tommy fell in next to her as they strolled away, dozens of sets of eyes following them toward the exit.

She squared her shoulders and lifted her chin, a smile of sat-isfaction on her face and her eyes sparkled.

"Oh, gosh, Tommy, that was *so* much fun. I thought sure I was going to have to replace this dress, but Ian... he's really that good, isn't he?"

"He is. And he's an expert with that specialized ammunition..."

"I mean, the way the glasses just exploded. Pow, pow, pow. It was amazing."

"Serves them right for putting a marginal vintage on the ta-ble."

"For the first time, I really understand the thrill you must feel. I mean, so, so very cool." She made a fist and used a fore-finger to create an imaginary pistol. "Pow. Pow. Pow."

He chuckled at the way she savored an adrenalin rush. "Yeah, you did good. Scared me, even."

"Did I? I mean, I don't think it was as good that thing you did in Salzburg, at that bakery near the monastery..."

Tommy guided her to the waiting car and opened the door for her. "I dunno. On a scale of ten, that was maybe a four or five. Tonight you were a definite eight, pushing nine."

She sighed. "Oh, yes. Pow, pow, pow. So incredibly... *Exquis-ite*. What's next?"

CHAPTER THIRTY-TWO

101 West Congress Parkway, Chicago

Mandy watched the Immigration and Customs Enforcement duty officer examine credentials. They stood in a lobby of a nine-story building near the heart of the city, with Charlie lead—ing an entourage of special agents.

Charlie shifted from indifferent courtesy to impatience. "There some sort of a problem? Should we be dealing with your supervisor, maybe make a couple calls to Washington?" He turned to Mandy. "Alice, you go ahead and call our friends at Homeland, tell 'em we're having some sorta problem here."

The officer interrupted. "Not necessary, sir. I can do that myself. I appreciated that you understand security related to sen—sitive cases." He picked up a phone. "I'll have verification in just a..." He looked puzzled and tried the phone again. And again. "I'm sorry, sir, but there seems to be a malfunction..."

Bug and Lucy had struck once more.

Charlie scowled. "Always something. Alice, give this fella your phone so he can make the call, do what he's gotta do, and let us get on with our job."

Mandy felt pompous in a conservative blue suit, ultra pin—stripe, not badly tailored for off-the rack, accented with black rimmed glasses with dummy plastic lenses. Her hair was tied into a tight bun, which saved the chore of a long wash and blow dry in the cramped lavatory on the jet. She struggled with a

sheaf of files, finally handing them to Sergei, posing as a translator for the State Department team. From her bag she pulled
phone and passed it to the flustered officer. "You just swipe and
press..."

The officer glared. "I know how to use a smartphone, miss."
Smarter than you think. Certainly smarter than you.

He tapped in the number, listened for a moment, identified
himself, read data from the credentials, and summarized the papers he had been handed. It looked like Lucy put him on hold.

Charlie turned to Tommy. "Jimmy, when we take custody of
the prisoners, I want you to be sure to contact the liaison with
CIA and NSC, get them to give the green light to ticketing at
O'Hare."

"Yessir," Tommy said.

"And Alice, you make certain that there's both CIA and State
people at the door to take custody. I don't want none of that
nonsense like last time, okay?"

"Yessir, no problem."

Charlie turned back to the officer. "Any luck, son?"

The officer was about to speak but held up a finger to gesture he'd finally connected. Several muttered affirmatives later,
he disconnected, returned the phone and then the credentials so
carefully crafted by Karl Felchin the night before. "And here's
your paperwork, sir. The elevators are just to the right. Please
proceed to the sixth floor, see the man at special detention, and
you should be good to go. My apologies for the delay."

Charlie responded with a look of annoyance but Tommy
stepped forward and smiled. "No trouble at all, officer. These
things happen. If you'd like, I can contact your maintenance staff
to look into the phone service..."

The officer waved him off. "I'll send a messenger, have the
tech guys look into it. It's been up and down, some sort of network thing. Again."

Mandy nodded understanding, and fell in with Tommy to

follow Charlie to the elevator. Yenchenko brought up the rear.

* * *

At a long conference room table befitting of a special assis‐tant to the Secretary of State, the seven detainees from the sub‐urban data center sat opposite Undersecretary Charles J. Burke, flanked by Mandy on the left and Serge and Tommy on the right.

Mandy played her part by blending recollections of corpo‐rate attorney behavior, memories of a couple of icy federal pros‐ecutors, and Tommy's style playing the role of an associate suck‐up named Jimmy. She spread the counterfeit files out in front of her.

Tommy did likewise, while Yenchenko positioned himself slightly behind. Charlie folded his hands on the table and stud‐ied the captives, left to right.

Two seemed sullen, bordering on arrogant, but the others wore shades of confusion and anxiety, caught without passports and visas five thousand miles from Moscow but nevertheless treated with the sort of dignity they wouldn't find in a Russian jail.

Charlie identified himself in a stern but folksy way, and in‐troduced the others. Yenchenko gave every appearance of being friendly and concerned as he translated, comrade to comrade, smoothing idiom into understanding, the only real pal they had in the room.

One of the sullen ones, who seemed to be the unofficial lead‐er, stared at Tommy and Mandy. "You were at the attack on our office. Surely you must know..."

Tommy said, "You got it, buddy. I set it up, and now I got you by the short hairs."

The leader seemed to struggle for calm and explained they did, in fact, possess passports and H1-B visas, which they kept in

a small office vault for safekeeping. He said it was all a misun—
derstanding, that they were consultants on an important project
for a large company, and surely the corporation would be able to
send a lawyer to help clear things up.

Charlie tapped the tip of a pen on the stack of paper in front
of him, nodded, and abruptly said,. "You fellas being treated
okay? Yeah? Good. Anyone thirsty? I could surely use a cup of
good coffee, but you know how it is. All they'll have around here
is some kinda water in one those plastic bottles. Say Alice — no,
Jimmy — why don't you see if you can fetch some bottles of wa—
ter for these nice young men? I was about to ask Alice, you see,
but these days in America, the gals get all kinds of upset about
being the people who take care of refreshments, and Jimmy, he
don't mind on account of he's after my job. Ain't that right, Jim—
my?"

Tommy smiled. "I don't know what you mean, sir, but I'll be
glad to get water. One for each? Yes? Good." He stood and left
the room.

Charlie waited until the door closed behind Tommy. "Well,
fellas, here's what it comes down to. That nice young man who's
just left is what they called a *liaison.*" He repeated the word very
slowly, lingering on every syllable. "Now, that's a fella who wears
a coupla hats. In his case, one of them happens to be the Central
Intelligence Agency, and they're just all kinds of upset about the
things you fellas have been up to."

Three of the men reacted to Sergei's translation with alarm
and objection.

Charlie motioned for silence. "Now, now, no need to get
into a bunch of denials here. We got a whole truck full of evi—
dence, all kinds of tech stuff. It's the sorta stuff that usually gets a
federal grand jury real excited and throwing around a mess of
paper that'll, in the end, mean some hard time in a United States
penitentiary. Maybe, just maybe, one in some hot, miserable
place with a bunch of people who'd eat softies like you alive.

And, yessir, that fella Jimmy's gonna be the guy to do it."

The men exchanged glances. Genuine fear filled their eyes.

Charlie rolled on. "Now on the other hand, Alice here, she's looking at the practical side of things and she's been making a case for some sort of, well, creative solution."

After translation, the sullen leader invited elaboration.

"Well, sir, I'm glad you asked that question, because to me that shows we might be able to work something out here. Now, everybody who searched that building you were using swears on a stack of Bibles that there weren't any passports or visas, and there hasn't been a single American company or organization that's stepped forward to claim you. So that leaves you boys on the hook, hangin' pretty high in the wind. But Alice says this entire business can be put to rest if you're all willing to get on a flight — we'll pay the bill — and head on home."

Tommy returned and distributed a bundle of plastic water bottles.

"Thanks, Jimmy. I've just been explaining to our guests here what the situation is, and we're looking for some sorta indication from them what they'd prefer to do."

The sullen one spoke and Yenchenko translated. "They express sorrow for confusion and wish only to return home."

Tommy looked surprised. "Absolutely not!"

Charlie narrowed his eyes into a deep frown. "You got problem with that, Jimmy?"

Tommy struggled with exasperation. "With all due respect, sir, these men are complicit in an enormous cybercrime ring, stealing millions of dollars from innocent people, the elderly, the poor. American citizens, sir."

Mandy sighed dismay at her arbitrary, inflexible colleague.

Charlie studied the faces on the other side of the table, then turned to face Tommy. "No disrespect taken, son. And I recognize your point of view. The law's the law, and we're a country of laws. And justice, too. Now, we could make a point of shipping these young fellas off to some mean, nasty prison for an awful long time, make everyone in your sphere happy. But we got a situation here, what with the Secretary trying to improve rela-tions with the Russians and all, and he's lookin' to me to see if we can settle this kinda quiet-like."

The translation led to faint nods and hopeful expressions from the hackers.

The sullen one, looking a lot more eager to please, promised mercy would go a long way with all of them speaking kindly of their American hosts, that they'd never again succumb to bad in-fluences, and would be grateful to be reunited with families.

All of which was a load of baloney, but it was what Charlie wanted to hear.

Charlie gestured recognition of a reasonable offer and told Tommy it was a good idea to play ball, maybe choose battles more worthy of being hard-nosed. "Myself, I'm inclined to think that these fellas just might prefer to go, real quiet, back to their country and nobody'd need to spend a lot of money making an example of some small-fry criminals. Which is gonna suck up a lot of time and expense to prosecute, if you get my meaning."

Tommy shook his head, pursed his lips, and folded up the documents in front of him. "But sir... uh, never mind."

Charlie turned to the formerly sullen one, who seemed anx-ious to know if the ruse worked. "Well sir, do you think we might have a deal here?"

An expression of relief, an eager statement. "Absolutely. Thank you, sir. We are most grateful."

Charlie nodded. "Alice, you'll take care of logistics?"

Mandy said, "Yessir, right away." She picked up her mobile phone and called Lucy, ordering tickets on the next flight out of O'Hare. "Excuse me, sir, there are no direct flights from O'Hare to Moscow. The best she can do is a change of planes in Berlin, at Tegel."

"I see." Charlie looked hard at the leader. "Well, now.

Berlin. You'll be outside of our jurisdiction, o'course. So I'd feel a whole lot better if I had your word as a gentleman that you'll make that Aeroflot flight out of Berlin."

Sergei translated. "Yes, yes, of course, he says."

Too easy, too quick. Of course he was lying. Mandy said, "We should expedite this, sir. It's one-thirty now and the flight departs a little after three."

* * *

Customs and Immigration was only too happy to clear seven cases with no effort and provide escorts and drivers to move the hackers from downtown to the Airberlin gate in Terminal Five at O'Hare International, eighteen miles away. They flashed a barrage of badges at TSA's security and breezed straight to boarding, with Mandy and Sergei doing the honors of seeing the thieves embark on an overnight flight.

Mandy pretended to take a phone call and excused herself for a moment, stepping half a dozen paces away and turning her back.

Sergei stepped up to the leader, now looking more cocky than sullen, and spoke in Russian. "I have family who were from Chernobyl, so I am a friend, yes? You have been caught in the center of a very poor scheme, comrade." He handed the man a packet. "Here is some material a friendly member of my unit has found that might be of assistance. I regret I did not have the op-portunity to present it to the legal team. It would have changed the direction of the case. But such are fortunes of the shadowy world in which we find ourselves, yes?"

The man accepted the packet and slipped it into the carry-on bag in his hand. They turned, had their boarding passes scanned and were welcomed to go down the ramp to the waiting plane.

Mandy completed her faked call just in time to see them march away. "You gave them the file from Lucy?"

"*Da, da*. Of course. He does not look, but puts in bag."

"However, he will have plenty of time to study it on that long, long flight. Sure hope it works."

Yenchenko chuckled. "It must only make suspicion. In busi—ness like ours, suspicion is all that is needed."

"Kind of a shame that they'll all be arrested."

"They are thief. They must pay for crime." His mood brightened. "And now, our task is completed, eh? You make very good official of government. Perhaps I buy you shabby lunch in airport restaurant, yes?"

"That, Sergei, is the best idea I've heard all day."

CHAPTER THIRTY-THREE

655 W. 34th Street, New York City

The hollow hum of humanity drifted among an ever-changing chorus of mostly electronic sounds, video sound tracks, and cellphone ring tones. Tommy surmised it was just another typical day for the Jacob Javits Convention Center, this time for the tech industry.

Crowds floated along ephemeral boulevards and avenues, periodically huddling around company booths to evaluate offerings of the annual event called *TechSpo New York*. Tommy and Bug floated, too, hunting for Emerson Barr, but trying not to be obvious about it.

Bug was better at the game. He cast an experienced look at the latest gadgets of his trade, mostly surveillance and security gear, but ignored consumer goods altogether. Stands were defined by rectangles of blue fabric hanging from metal poles, the most modest of which were perhaps eighty or ninety square feet with a table or two and a worn-out sales guy glued to a chair with a couple of brochures on a skirted table. More elaborate exhibits were huge constructs of customized glitter with perky gals who were living proof that there was life after cheerleading.

Tommy's eyes roamed exhibits with zero to fragmentary recognition of what he was looking at, other than it wasn't his style. He spent most of the hour analyzing the convention layout for possibilities as a dead drop, which were fair to decent, or for eluding a tail, which were excellent, depending on the aisle.

Mandy and Lucy worked the other side of the hall. While only Tommy and Mandy could recognize Barr on sight, Lucy and Bug tagged along out of professional curiosity. For them, it was a field trip, a chance to get escape the mundane routine of electronic breaking and entering. And get to play a bit part in the field for Mandy.

They watched a demonstration by a guy evidently looking for trade with private investigators. He had some sort of a tiny parabolic mike and bragged that it could isolate and eavesdrop on a conversation a hundred and fifty yards away without being noticed.

On the outer edge of about fifteen listeners, Bug was unim—pressed. "Old technology," he advised Tommy. "We was doing that stuff eight, ten years ago. And in Central Park, on a Sunday. But, see, this ain't about the crap in the booths. It's who's in the aisles. Discreet place to do business, screw over your boss, net—work for better jobs. Most of the guys, they already do the stuff on display. They're just keeping an eye on everybody else. It's the guys who *aren't* here that you get nervous about, because they're probably half a dozen steps ahead of what you got."

"So a kind of casual convention, then?"

"Yeah. Lucy liked to visit a lot when she was a kid, mostly because she'd ask some asshole questions he couldn't answer, give'm a rough time. I didn't mind. These outfits put millions into R-and-D, marketing shit, and like that, and then dump some clown in front of people. People who know more stuff about the biz than all of government intelligence agencies com—bined."

Tommy's tone was a bit too patronizing. "Impressive."

Bug sensed it. "Hey, we all got our professional circles. Lotta new faces, people coming up in the trade, though. Glad I got out when I did."

"*Sort* of got out."

"Yeah, sorta. Nice being off the street, always chasing around. The phone ringing off the hook, some hurry-up tap, drop everything because my job is important. And then I gotta chase 'em for the money 'cuz all of a sudden it wasn't a big deal and why should they pay if it ain't a big deal, right? Some guys, you could forward all their incoming calls to the cops, but most of the time you gotta rely on repeat business, y'know what I mean? And some of them bastards, they didn't care. They'd whack you over a five-hundred-buck tab. Yeah, so it's good now. Lucy's got me set up nice, I don't freeze my ass off in winter, I get to do specialty work, like that tap in Montreal."

"That was a good one. Really slick."

"Yeah, me and the kid, we make a good team. She comes to me and says 'Dad I got to figure out a way to listen to a comput−er from maybe eight, ten feet.' I'm thinking like hearing some−body use the keyboard, but no, she's tuning into the CPU itself, like listening to tumblers behind the dial in a safe. So it's a chal−lenge, right? Gets me going in the morning. Then I gotta figure out how to pick out a specific desk phone line and then how to hide device so's it won't be noticed."

Tommy picked up a brochure. A salesperson began to close in. He glanced at it and returned it, waving the disappointed rep back to his chair. "Which you did."

"Yeah, it worked out. Slower pace, maybe, not much action, maybe, but no rush. A guy my age? Who needs rush, right? So you know for sure your guy's gonna be here?"

"Yep. Mandy called his office, the person said he was out at the show today. Regular pilgrimage for him, she said."

"Hate those media guys. They don't know jack but think the world is entitled to what a good tapper knows, maybe spent years learning, just to sponge a buck off the backs of a working guy."

The sales rep locked on to several passersby and launched an enthusiastic pitch, tossing around tech lingo that made no sense.

Tommy chuckled. "Well, that's what Mandy used to do."

"But she wised up, got smart, didn't she? Come over to the right side of the game. So she gets points in my book for that. C'mon, Tommy, let's move on. I can't stand what this asshole is saying no more."

Bug's cellphone beeped twice and he paused to take the call. "Lucy says they spotted him in the thirty-three hundred aisle, which is, what, just a couple over from where we are. You know, pal, one of these days you oughta take one of my units with you, save having an old wire guy like me acting as some kinda secre— tary or something."

"Old school, buddy. Never trusted anything going over a wire or the air. You're living proof as to why."

"Yeah, but my shit is tight. Ain't nobody gonna hear."

Which was probably true, but old habits die hard and cau— tious field guys tend to live longer. "I'm sure. But why take the chance when I got someone as charming as you to do my work?"

Bug's eyes narrowed. "You know what I say to shit like that?"

"Not in public, Bug. There's ladies all around."

Bug muttered an epithet and pointed. "Let's go this way, save a few steps."

They turned at a cross aisle and waited. Mandy and Lucy en— tered the line of booths from the opposite end. They browsed their way to rendezvous, where the foursome chatted like old friends who'd unexpectedly reconnected after a long separation. As a group, they decided to tour the thirty-three hundred aisle, which was primarily smaller companies with software ideas, al— most all of them startups, according to Lucy.

Halfway up the aisle, Mandy noticed Emerson Barr and waved a greeting. He seemed pleased and surprised, to see her.

She made introductions. "You remember my friend, Tom— my, of course. And this is Allison Frost who apparently actually understands all of this, and her father, Jack."

Emerson looked amused. "Jack Frost? As in the — "

Bug shrugged. "My mother had a lousy sense of humor."

Mandy said, "Jack's a forensic accountant."

Emerson cocked an eyebrow. "Is that so? You know, Mandy, it just begs the obvious question. You still working on that piece about CySafe?"

She nodded, but put some resignation in her expression. "It just gets more and more complicated. Lucy and Jack are helping me understand some of the details, but you know how it is with corporate pieces. Just endless."

"Of course."

"And so, Emmie, what brings you to *TechSpo*? Something new and exiting?"

"Just sifting, I'm afraid." He turned to the others to explain. "It's like any news beat. Tech writers are always looking for the latest tidbit, eager to get ahead of the company PR people."

Tommy asked, "And what have you discovered today — or is that an improper question?"

"Not the best of year for innovation. And that doesn't make for a must-read piece in the next edition. But I still have a way to go, people to see, so who knows?"

Mandy said, "Well, we shouldn't keep you. Tommy, I'm famished, and one of those dreadful hotdogs suddenly has appeal. How about you guys?"

After everyone declined, Tommy said to her, "Maybe we'll just do some browsing on our own, meet you on the way back."

Mandy briefly pouted before returning attention to Emerson. "It was lovely seeing you again, Emmie. Hope you find a hot story."

He beamed. "You, too. Hope your piece works out okay."

After they watched Mandy walk away, Lucy and Bug drifted to a booth offering free apps for Android phones.

Emerson said, "Sure do wish her luck. They say once you get out of the game, for whatever reason, it's tough to break back in. She had a great reputation in finance, but technology is a whole different world."

Tommy said, "Yeah, she's been working hard on it. Now, me, I'm not a tech guy at all. Wouldn't know how to use any of this fancy gear."

"That's what a lot of people say, but we use it more in our daily lives than most people even suspect."

"That so?"

"Absolutely."

"Well, from what I've been able to follow, the project she's working on is more financial than tech anyway. Allison was help—ing out with some of the fancy stuff, but Jack's a first rate detec—tive when it comes to some of the games corporations play with financial stuff."

"So she's looking into CySafe financial issues rather than technical innovation?"

"Yeah, but I keep tellin' her that it's not worth the trouble."

Barr asked, "How so?"

"Well, now, I believe she got it to a point where she had a lot of suspicion that all kinds of money was being handled kinda sloppy, but couldn't prove anything. Driving the poor gal mad, you see. Now, just between you and I, my suggestion was to take all the theory over to a friendly U.S. Attorney, maybe have a grand jury get into it."

"The corporation? It's Canadian, you know."

"No sir, I meant some kind of foundation they got going. Been all kinds of talk about a string of casinos on the side, mov—ing money around to cover losses and such."

Barr cocked his head. "You're telling me that there's mis—management of — "

Tommy held up his hands. "Whoa, now. Maybe I'm speak—ing out turn here. I mean, it's her project and all."

"Of course. But maybe I could help."

"She's a proud gal, Emerson. Now, I think she might be about to give up on it altogether, which to my mind would be a real good idea. But I'd hate to, well, kind of put her into some kind of box where she didn't have a say."

"You've got a point, Mister Kane."

He decided to borrow Mandy's pet line to lather on a little trust. "*Tommy*. Friends call me Tommy. But like I said, she's getting tired of all the blind alleys and dead ends. That's for sure. Hate to see her torn like this. You know, not wanting to quit, but knowing it might not be going anywhere, leastways, where she could take it."

Emerson nodded understanding. "She's a good friend. We go way back, you know."

Tommy brightened. "Wow! Y'know, that's *exactly* what she said about you. A real good friend, from college. And Mandy and I are real good friends, too, and I care a whole lot. Just want her to be happy and not be so doggone stressed, like she's been lately. Wonder if your people might have a look around, see what's going on. Kind of on the side, y'know, sorta take the strain off, open a couple of doors, that kind of thing. Don't know if that's possible. Me, gosh, I've got no understanding of how the news business works."

Emerson's tone shifted to assurance. "Oh, we're fairly collegial. And I certainly could do you a favor and look into it. I've got some solid connections in the industry. Do you have any specifics of where this investigation is going?"

"Aw, man, sorry. I surely don't. But you know what? Ol' Jack does. Give me a couple of minutes to talk with him, kind of smooth out the path a bit, you know, see what we might be able to work out."

Tommy excused himself, and when he reached Lucy and Bug explained they needed to participate in an animated conversation, as if surprised, but not hostile. They complied, and in the end Bug pulled a folded packet of paper from his jacket pocket and put it in Tommy's hand. It went directly to Emerson Barr.

Tommy said, "Now, those folks weren't too excited, but I ex—

plained things and how you'd be all kinds of helpful if given the chance. If it's okay with you, Emerson, maybe we ought to keep this just between us. You know, let Mandy get the idea she's do– ing the thing on her own. She doesn't need to now she's getting a little help. Whole lot of pride and all that. If you know what I mean."

Emerson's eyes were already scanning the scraps of evidence Lucy had culled from CySafe records. Just enough to tantalize, prompt a shrewd reporter to make a few phone calls.

"Okay, I'll see what I can do. How can I get in touch, Tom– my?"

"Here's my card. The number's good any time of day. Just leave a message with the operator."

"Will do."

"And mum's the word?"

"Mum's the word."

Tommy thrust out a hand. "Thanks a bunch, buddy. I feel a whole lot better and surely do appreciate it."

He tucked the card into his shirt pocket and they shook hands. "Glad to help. Take care and enjoy the show."

"Yessir, I do believe I surely will."

CHAPTER THIRTY-FOUR

Leeward Highway, Providenciales, The Bahamas

Lucy turned the computer screen ninety degrees to allow everyone a good look. Title screen words were in Russian, but needed no translation after Sergei identified the emblems of the Russian Federation and the SVR. A second screen said *Terminal A, Berlin-Tegel Airport* followed by a smaller line with the date and time.

Lucy said, "This is from a surveillance camera, fairly high in the beams above passport control. Exactly how your Russian pals tapped in? Hard to say. The Germans are pretty security conscious, but when you think about it... Okay, here we go. Far upper left. There's your guys, getting off that Airberlin flight. They've cleared immigration with the stuff they found in Sergei's packet and you can tell from the track that they're not exactly hurrying to make the connecting flight to Moscow."

The seven strolled casually in the general direction of the terminal exit, but Mandy sensed they were moving with some uncertainty, not knowing if they were to meet someone or simply disperse.

Lucy continued the narrative. "Okay, so here's several men coming from the opposite direction. The SVR people were kind enough to zoom in. Wait for it... yeah, there we go. Recognize anyone?"

The men at Savage's table, when the wine classes shattered

in a series of precision shots from Ian Wells. Mandy said, "The Sons of Chernobyl. Rounding up their crew. And right under the noses of German security."

Tommy said, "The SVR has a lot of friends in the right places."

Lucy sighed. "And so do we. Must have been some kind of a bidding war to set this up. The Russians could have just waited, you know."

Sergei laughed. "It is not in Russian manner. Wise hen does not keep all eggs in same basket when fox is near, eh?"

Lucy scowled. "Whatever. We shelled out a lot of bucks for paper and airline tickets, plus a hefty gratuity to Tommy's bud—dies in Berlin. Those guys were double-dipping, taking a payoff from Viktor Kozyratkin, too. Pisses me off to no end."

The action on the screen continued. They conferred in the center of a corridor, the team leader passed materials to one of the Sons, and they left the field of view. With a flutter, a second camera cut in and they made a direct path to the airport parking area, got into three vehicles and drove away.

Charlie grumbled. "So much for the gentleman's promise." When others stared in astonishment, he added, "Just making a joke there. I was about as trusting as everyone else."

Lucy produced a sheet of paper, a printout of a text message that accompanied the video. *"Video evidence — band of hooligans arrived, without leader. Took rooms in Berlin hotel. When American unit left for homes 0600 hrs this date, were taken into custody by SVR/S, renditioned to Moscow. No documents. Regards to Owens. Await instructions. V. Kozyratkin"*

Mandy drew a breath and looked at Tommy and Serge. "Okay, okay, you were right. Just as you predicted. Once a spy, always a spy. I owe you twenty bucks."

Lucy and Charlie exchanged shrugs.

Mandy said, "Tommy's plan was to get the Germans to look the other way, let our suspects through the net but keep them on a leash, so we can use them as bait for Savage."

Lucy said, "I'm missing something."

"I just didn't give the Russians enough credit. Tommy and Serge bet twenty dollars — each — that the SVR people would handle the German Federal Police and airport security. I wasn't sure and wanted nothing left to chance."

Lucy grasped it. "So Tommy made sure we connected from our end, just in case. The Germans must have loved it."

Tommy said, "Well, in fairness, it's always good to have a Plan B, and the bottom line is Viktor Kozyratkin is getting what he wants by doing some selective sifting of the people we're putting into the net. So I'm not worried about the twenty bucks."

Mandy said, "No, no, I'll pay up. Honor among thieves and all that. I'm probably more disillusioned that Emmie Barr suc—cumbed to your temptation, Tommy. I would have thought him more honorable than that. You know, maybe offered to help, talked to me directly, been upfront."

Tommy smiled. "But it's just like you said. Catnip for media kittens. A really good rumor to get the wheels of the stock mar—kets turning with a bunch of squeak."

"It *would* be a terrific piece, Tommy. I mean, it's Pulitzer contender at a minimum, the once-in-a-lifetime career maker."

"If that's your career, Mandy."

Lucy offered a look of sympathy. "So this guy Barr will be the big hero?"

Charlie said, "Maybe, maybe not. Kinda hard to get a con—viction if the evidence is phony in the first place. I'm betting — well, all right, then, twenty dollars — that he'll wind up with a mess o'egg running down his cheeks."

Lucy said, "Yeah, agreed. He'll pay for not being honorable. Maybe even learn a lesson from it."

Mandy shook her head. "That's if CySafe, not to mention the foundation, can prove to everybody that they're totally clean.

And we all know that's not true. Trust me, this is the kind of piece that has legs. Every business writer from New York to L-A will be all over it. Not to mention the Canadian press, and they're not exactly pushovers, either. If there's a loose thread anywhere, some of those people will find it and start pulling. It could drive CySafe into ruins."

Lucy seemed dubious. "Maybe. I haven't exactly felt the Earth shudder with the news."

"Too early in the cycle. It's going to take a day for the first 'no comment' to show up."

A long, uneasy silence lingered in the room.

Mandy said, "But we can't dwell on it. We've got to move forward, and so far, so good with Tommy's scheme. It's coming together well."

Lucy said, "Did you get a chance to talk to Nikki? I mean, this is about her last chance to call this off."

"I did. And it's still the same. She doesn't want to go back to Cole. She doesn't want to be given a new identity. She doesn't want to be bought off. And of course, she's probably correct that Cole isn't about to just let her go."

Charlie said, "Well, it seems to me that we're goin' to a whole lot of work for somebody that ain't doin' much, initiative-wise."

Tommy said, "Agreed, but we took it on when we responded to her call for help. Good, bad or indifferent, we committed. If she doesn't want to have some sort of say in all this, that's okay."

Mandy nodded. "And I'd still very much like to believe that she's just pulled inward, trying to get her bearings."

Tommy said, "Sooner or later, she'll just have to accept whatever outcome there is for her husband."

Charlie asked, "Which is?"

Sergei spoke up. "Prisoner of SVR. Enemy of Russian peo–ple."

"Maybe so, but the guy's a Canadian citizen, and one of the

more prominent businessmen in the world."

Sergei seemed unmoved. "Perhaps SVR make some deal, perhaps not. Outcome of company depend on honesty. Customer make choice."

Tommy said, "It's not our problem. Savage at any time could have worked things out, made some kind of arrangement, some sort of concession. But he didn't. And he's dirty. At a minimum, he's a terrorist, at least to the Russian government. If it were the other way around, they'd be dusting off a cot in Leavenworth."

Mandy sighed. "All the stuff I was debating myself just a couple of days ago. It's all so incredibly gray. But we can't leave it in limbo. It's either in or out, and, frankly, I'm just annoyed enough to be in. I know, I know, justice isn't supposed to be about making it personal, but that's for people who enforce the law. We don't answer to any of that. I vote that we deliver. So, yes, Lucy, to answer your original question, I gave Nikki one last chance to call it off and made it as clear as I could. She wanted a couple of hours to think about it, and I let her have them."

Lucy seemed satisfied. "Okay, then, we have to organize some kind of emissary to haul the white flag. Then we have to get back to Mandy Caye to share the play-by-play with Nikki."

"You think it might help prod things along with her?"

"Mandy, I'm sure you're right, but I'd really be comfortable seeing it for myself. I'd like to give her a sense of just how seri—ous this has become."

* * *

Twenty hours later, Lucy opened a laptop on Mandy's kitchen counter. "Recognize it, Nikki?"

"*Mais oui.* It is the lobby at CySafe. All visitors and staff must pass through it. But how..."

"I've tapped into the surveillance system for the building. This is the feed from the camera near the southwest corner."

"I understand."

"Okay. Just for myself, I need to know, right now, whether you want to continue with this. Once we make our move in the lobby, there is absolutely no turning back, all right?"

Nikki reacted with an expression somewhere between anxiety and confusion. Mandy repeated what Lucy said, in French.

Lucy leaned in closer. "There could be real trouble for him and the company as well. Mandy's already explained what's involved. We're giving him one last chance, but then...."

Nikki bit her lower lip and nodded while gazing at the screen.

Mandy said, "Okay, then. Let them know."

Lucy tapped out a text message on her phone, disconnected and placed it to the side. Mandy's kitchen was just beyond the reach of direct sunshine, but the light bouncing off their shoulders created an eerie glow.

On the lower left of the screen, Charlie entered the lobby. Lucy reached across Nikki and touched a key. The screen switched to an uneven shot, bouncing up and down.

Lucy said, "Body cam. It's on the lapel of his jacket." She reached out again and brought the volume of audio up.

A receptionist wearing a maroon blazer looked up and smiled. "Yes sir, may I be of assistance?"

A hand extended, offering a business card.

"You may. My name is Charles J. Burke. I am an attorney and I need a brief word with Mister Coleman Savage."

"Do you have an appointment?"

"I do not. However, I'm confident he'll make a little time for me."

The receptionist offered an expression of sympathy. "Well, Mister Savage is a *very* busy man, I'm afraid. Perhaps someone else might be of assistance? If you could indicate the nature of your visit..."

"I'm a very busy fellow, too, young lady. You just call up to the executive suite and mention the word 'Nyx.'"

She blushed a bit and grappled for control. While she picked up a phone, she made a faint gesture.

Lucy said, "Calling for security."

The shadow of a taller man fell across what they could see of Charlie. The receptionist listened, raised a finger to put the guard on pause, continued to listen.

The receptionist placed her hand over the mouthpiece. "Just one moment, sir."

Charlie muttered. "No problem."

Her attention returned to the receiver. "Yes sir. Right away, sir. Thank you, sir." She hung up and offered a more welcoming smile. To the guard, she said, "Albert, would you be so kind as to escort Mister Bird — "

"*Burke.* Charles J. Burke."

"Sorry, um, Mister Burke." She turned to Albert and continued, " — to the fourteenth floor? Thank you. Mister Burke, there will be someone from the executive staff to meet you when you get off the elevator. My apologies for the delay."

While they watched a dull image of the elevator door, Mandy stole a glance at Nikki, who remained as impassive as ever. A profound sense of sorrow oozed through her mind. Love him or hate him, she was still watching the net softly settle around her husband's shoulders. Such an odd difference from the joy and exuberance of dance. But it was her choice and now there were larger issues in play. Nikki, she decided, was a survivor, someone who would drift off to a life somewhere, nothing fancy, just kind of empty.

The elevator door opened and the body camera stared straight ahead.

Cole Savage.

Nikki recoiled. Mandy placed her hand atop Nikki's and allowed her fingers to close into a reassuring grip.

Savage said, "I'm Coleman Savage, Mister Burke. Won't you step this way?"

Lucy, Mandy and Nikki watched in silence as the body cam took them on a video tour of the ring of executive offices guard-ing the suite of the CEO. Several people looked up as they passed, but most gave them no attention at all, continuing with various tasks.

Nikki whispered, "The door to Cole's office. I've been there several times for corporate functions."

The men crossed a broad, open space. Simple, basic furnish-ings, contemporary, leaning toward reddish woods, chrome, glass. No drapes or curtains on a wall of glass. A highly polished desk with virtually nothing but a telephone and a computer ter-minal, the one that Lucy used to listen for the security codes. Smallish conference table, five straight-back chairs. And several chairs, leather upholstery perhaps, circling a coffee table with a sofa on the window side.

"Please, Mister Burke, take a seat." When they settled, Sav-age said in an even, almost disinterested tone, "I assume you have something to discuss, a proposal of some kind."

Charlie had parked his case on the coffee table and now reached for the latches. "May I?"

"Of course."

"Well, sir. My name is Charles J. Burke. I am an attorney and chief counsel for Mister Tommy Kane, who I believe you know."

"Yes, yes. We've met. I have only a few minutes to spare, Mister Burke, so if you could come directly to the point?"

"Sure thing. Well, sir, Mister Kane and his associates — "

" — Including the genuine Nyx?"

"I believe you previously met Miss Owens as well, sir."

Savage smiled and crossed his legs. "Not for a moment do I believe that Miss Owens and Nyx are one in the same. I give them both credit for a clever little ruse. However, the time for clever is over, Mister Burke."

"I see. Well, Miss Owens did ask me to convey her hopes

that you managed to get your suit cleaned after that incident with the wine. Tricky business, having snipers around, I sus— pect."

"Your point, sir?"

"Mister Kane and Miss Owens have given your offer some consideration and are amenable to negotiating a settlement."

"No negotiations. They know my terms."

"Just for clarity, would you mind repeating them, sir?"

Savage's smile was pure arrogance and patronization. "Con— trol of the system they hacked, the two million euros they stole from the casino, and of course, deliver my wife and son."

Charlie said, "Well, sir, I'm not entirely sure they, well, Mrs. Savage, is amenable. We're wondering if you could consider — "

Savage leaned forward and made a slight jabbing motion with his right hand, the forefinger extended. Mandy felt Nikki recoil.

"I don't care what Nikki thinks, Mister Burke. If she thinks at all. She's mine, *my property*, and I demand she be brought to me. Is that quite clear?"

"Crystal clear. And in exchange for these items, you agree to cease and desist any further actions against Mister Kane, Miss Owens, Nyx, their associates?"

"Those were my terms. I'm a man of my word, Mister Burke."

Charlie said, "Very well, then all that remains is a place of transfer."

"I have no preferences. Whatever is convenient to where they are."

Charlie reached out to close his case, the sheaf of papers in— side untouched. Mandy was amused. *So much for Plan B.*

Charlie stood. "Terminal A, Berlin-Tegel Airport, near the information desk on the main level. Tomorrow, three o'clock lo— cal time. I believe we're done, sir."

CHAPTER THIRTY-FIVE

56.62 Degrees North, 8.50 Degrees West

Mandy swirled deep-red wine in an oversized glass and sa—
vored the bouquet. Seven miles below, the Irish coast drifted
past, on an unusually clear day, etched in white from Atlantic
waves crashing into the rocky shores of a series of bays.

Opposite her, Ian Wells wore a hopeful expression while
awaiting an assessment. She took a sip and allowed the wine to
linger on her palate, then sniffed again, nodded and smiled.

He spoke with a gentleman's British accent that never ceased
to enchant her, one which he said he acquired at Sandhurst
while listening to the BBC. "Well, then?"

"It's certainly a wonderful vintage. Um, let's see. Dense, vel—
vety texture. Ripe cherry-blackberry flavors, maybe with a hint
of coffee? And, I sense a bit of new wood taste, too. So my guess
would be, hm, perhaps just a bit over ten years?"

Behind her, the soft wine of the jet engines and the whisper
of air was the only other sound. They'd been in the air for just
under seven hours, with not much more than two to go to
Berlin. Further ahead in the cabin, Tommy and Sergei were
sound asleep, and in the aft kitchen, Karen was cleaning up after
a lunch of sirloin tips, baked potatoes and assorted vegetables.

Ian leaned back and swirled the merlot in his own glass. He
beamed approval. "Oh, well done. A brilliant oh-four, as a mat—
ter of fact. *Réserve privée*, from our own private stock. Over the

years, they've produced rather decent table wines, but some— times set a little aside for occasions. When I assumed ownership, I encouraged staff to lean toward higher quality vintages."

She said, "I can certainly see why. This is exceptional. Can you spare a couple of cases? I'd love to surprise Tommy."

"Of course. Consider it done."

She smiled satisfaction. "So, tell me about your chateau. It must be marvelous, owning a vineyard in the south of France."

Wells chuckled. "More like a lot of bloody work. It's near Saint-Chinian in the Languedoc-Roussillon region. Previously owned by a group of Chinese investors. Absentee landlords, actually, and, as I said, geared toward elemental table wine production."

"And you persuaded them to part with it?"

"I daresay they persuaded themselves. Extraordinary amount of effort involved in these smaller wineries, and they were long on metrics and short on diplomacy. Vast difference in cultures. The vineyard came with a *régisseur* who's family had been with the place for generations and a staff that were a bit resentful."

She nodded and enjoyed another sip of the wine. "Noth— ing worse than a grumpy steward, I take it?"

"Quite so. So when the Chinese group gave up and I had the opportunity to acquire it, the suspicions lingered. Of course, I was only a bloke with no credentials whatsoever. Not much call for burned-out snipers amongst rows of grapes, you see. Consequently, there was a certain amount of adjustment."

"What did you do?"

"I had the very good fortune to retain the services of a broker who suggested I discard the demeanor of a former military officer, accept my ignorance, and remain open-mind— ed. After a fortnight or two, we began to communicate on better than a stand-offish manner. That I knew some French was helpful, although I'm quite certain that staff understood an assortment of unfortunate British idioms bandied about at moments of disappointment."

"I can only imagine."

"Indeed. There are, of course, many Frenchmen who view the U.K. as a third-world country — not always without justi-fication — and so any foreigner running the shop is bit dodgy. I say not without justification because I had a great deal to learn, and the *régisseur*, an extraordinarily proud chap, needed the opportunity to really take charge of the place. One day he unlocked a special area of the cellar and revealed the reserve stock, quite a small lot, actually. Their special vintages that they crafted for themselves. This is one of them."

Captivated, she asked, "So what did you do?"

"Went straightaway into the fields to do grunt work with the staff, learn about the soils, the varieties, the weather, the agonizing decisions about whether to pick early or late — it greatly affects the final product, you know. Got bloody cal-louses for the first time in my life."

She nodded and continued to enjoy the wine. "So you're happily — ahem — retired, then?"

He finished his glass. "Quite so. No more contracts for this old tosser, thank you very much. The occasional ghost service for Thomas, of course, and now yourself. But I've enough blood on my hands for a dozen lifetimes."

"Or, as in the case of Ibiza, wine. That really was remark-able shooting."

He replied with a sly smile. "Trusty old Heckler and Koch. Light-weight loads, a hundred and fifteen meters. It's a splendid weapon, Mandy. I could easily teach you to do the same thing. You'll have to come out to the farm one day, try a few rounds."

The odd sensation of desire and abhorrence fluttered through her mind. She said, "Well, perhaps. I don't think I could ever do what you did for a living, though."

"Just as well. It's manageable as long as one views it as a matter of precision, just a target. The SAS thought it brilliant, but when it blurred into what sort of work I was actually doing, it turned quite tedious indeed. Eventually, it led to blowing an assignment — quite frankly froze up — and I was given my choice of the sack or twenty years hard labor of Her Majesty's pleasure. I chose the former, did an occasional contract job, just intimidation rather like Spain, to pay the bills and went on the drift."

Karen approached with the bottle of merlot and offered to freshen glasses. They both declined another round.

"And then came Tommy and Sergei."

"Right. And we were three and soon in the thick of it. Frightfully messy business. However, in the end, we departed with resources for the future. Yenchenko blew his lot, but I bought the farm."

Mandy nodded. "Well, I doubt if we'll have much trouble in Berlin. We'll be in the middle of the secure area of the airport, lots of German security people around, doing our little thing. Will you need much time?"

"Not at all. I'm quite familiar with Tegel and if the buggers haven't tinkered with the place too much, I should be all correct well before your man arrives."

Mandy's attention returned to Tommy and Sergei. "Look at them, sleeping like babies. I can't imagine how. I'm more than nervous about this confrontation. Not to mention that CySafe is pressing really hard on tracking down Lucy. She says it's getting to be a frantic game of moving honey pots or something from one server to another, but it won't be very long before Savage has a fix. And then there's the whole busi—

ness with Chet, his escapades and our promise to help."

Which was true, anxiety and stress having showed up in Lucy's voice when they spoke on the way to the waiting jet, and then again soon after they were in the air. Savage's team *had* been near, and suddenly abruptly closer. Only sheer chance in checking logs caught Bug's attention and Lucy scrambled with a quick fix. Bug muttered something about the move being so quick that it seemed like a mobile phone signal had been traced. Lucy wasn't so sure, and she steered CySafe engineers into a wild goose chase on an obscure corner of a major commercial server and bounced off into several government agencies. But, Lucy warned, with an edge of anxiety, that time was running very short, that the flow of probing from servers in Montreal was intense, and that their attention was beginning to focus on the Caribbean.

Wells seemed calm and shrugged. "Then we should be keen to tie this business off. Renditioning Savage to the Russians will put an end to the hunt. And this Chet fellow, well, I'd wager a tenner that Thomas will come up with an elegant solution to keep his word and protect your friend from the restaurant. As for Thomas and Yenchenko? Well, I daresay they've have been in enough patches to know when to catch some rest. Soldiers learn to do that, you know."

"And you?"

His smile was rueful, distant, almost weary. And most of all, enigmatic.

"Let's just say that while the H-and-K is in my kit, I've also brought along a modified MK-12, five-fifty-six, which is a bit on the pathetic side for this sort of work. Your Navy Seals fancy it, but a seven-sixty-two round is always better."

Mandy cocked an eyebrow. "Why, then?"

Wells said, "Because German security people will be armed with Heckler and Koch G-36s, and they're all five-fifty six. Wouldn't want any non-matching bullets, now would we?"

A shiver tumbled down Mandy's spine, and she found her—self nodding as if this were the most normal thing in the world, like selecting a brand of laundry detergent. She decid—ed not to press it further, and her thoughts turned to Nikki. Enigmatic was an understatement. The frantic plea for help. The big scene at Billy's with Louis Boulanger. The sudden awareness that, since that night, how he'd just sort of faded into obscurity. Perhaps he really was just a folk musician with a band.

But it rankled that Nikki would hang around, like she was in some sort of world unto herself, and then suddenly decide it was time to excuse herself to take Cyrus to the beach, or put him to bed. And how Cyrus was so very withdrawn. Still, Nikki seemed terrified of Savage, even flinched when she saw him on the monitor for the body cam Charlie was wearing.

Charlie. Mister Suspicious himself. But only slightly sus—picious of Nikki. Maybe it was all nothing. Maybe a larger justice was about to be served. *Maybe, maybe, maybe.*

No wonder she couldn't sleep.

CHAPTER THIRTY-SIX

Terminal A, Berlin-Tegel Airport, Berlin, Germany

Mandy decided the coffee needed extra cream, stirred in more than she planned and slumped in her seat. "Why is it that all airport food tastes the same, costs the same, and always makes you regret it?"

Tommy sipped from his cup. "It's an international conspiracy. A plot. To get a spot in airline terminals, food service companies have to sign an agreement to sell the same-tasting stuff for exactly five times what it's worth on the street. Or the airport management turns the space into a place that sells combs and funny T-shirts."

"Simple as that?"

"Absolutely. Everyone knows that. That's what Charlie says."

She sighed. "Give me a fixed-base lounge any day. When you roll in on a corporate, they upgrade the food. And certainly the coffee."

"People say Marché is good, but it's in Terminal D. Hard to watch Gate Nine from there."

And, of course, he was correct. There was a time, not so long ago, when the cellophane-wrapped cookie would have been acceptable as food-on-the-fly between connecting flights. Inhaled and forgotten. Now it was a waiting game and the alleged cookie endured more focused scrutiny.

Coleman Savage had tried to book a flight outside Lucy's ev–

er-expanding periphery of control, but hadn't succeeded. Not that it mattered anyway. They were in countdown mode to rendezvous. Savage's own private jet had suddenly developed mysterious maintenance issues and was in a hangar, and options out of Montreal and New York were lean. Lucy had been eager to push him into economy, but Tommy interceded and directed that there was no purpose in complicating Savage's travel any further.

Now Tommy sat opposite, at a table barely big enough for the cups and wrappers between them, nibbling on his snack, supposedly a ginger snap but more resembling an over-baked sugar cookie.

All around, the sounds of feet and luggage wheels on a hard floor, a soft blend of human voices and public address announcements suggested it was just another routine day for travelers in Berlin. Which, Tommy had explained earlier, was why airports are ideal for this sort of thing. Lots of people and lots of security. Tegel was no different.

She asked, "So how do you differentiate between your people and theirs?"

"You don't. It's much too unpredictable. So you have a couple of faces you know just in case, and wing it from there. But it sure beats meeting in a dark alley in a city you don't really know. And you're correct. This is not a very good cookie."

She'd been casually paying attention to the inbound trickle of passengers coming through Gate Nine and was soon rewarded. "Well, you're spared enduring it any further. He just went past. Very small flight bag. Looks like he doesn't plan to spend much time here."

Two quick, light taps on a microphone pulsed in her earbud. Then two more. She guessed Ian spotted him first, considering he probably had a position very high in the terminal, maybe even somewhere in the tubular framing that supported the roof. Yenchenko had spent the last forty minutes reading the same page of the *Berliner Morganpost* on a lower level bench about fifty meters from the point of rendezvous.

Tommy said, "Something doesn't feel right."

"What do you mean?"

"Can't say for sure. It's a feeling more than anything specific. Maybe I'm just getting way too cautious in my old age."

Here, there, and everywhere it seemed, police patrolled the area in pairs, but unlike American airports, they were dressed in combat gear and carried automatic weapons.

Mandy laughed. "Old age? Now you're being ridiculous."

He tapped his fingertips on the table. "Yeah, maybe so. It's just that I get the sense we're missing something. Something we should have picked up on with Nikki... Ah, well, time to get down to business. Probably nothing."

She crumpled her empty cookie wrapper and dropped it into the paper cup. "Is it okay if I'm just a little nervous? I mean, it's great to walk up to this guy and... No, never mind. I'm being sil‐ly."

Tommy did the same, only with half a cookie added to the cup, and gathered the paper from the table as he rose. "It's per‐fectly okay. There's always just a little rush of anticipation. Only this guy? Well, what could possibly go wrong?"

She nodded and followed him past a trash receptacle, where he dumped the cups. "You're right. And thanks for letting me have the lead on it. I'd really like to punch him right in the nose, but this is going to be much more exquisite."

They began to trail Savage down the corridor.

Tommy said, "Just remember, you won't actually see it go down. Make your offer, accept whatever he says and walk away."

Savage approached the information desk. People flowed left and right. Men, women, children. Young, old, professionals, travellers. Ordinary people in an ordinary terminal at an ordi‐nary airport.

And Savage, who slowed to nearly a point of standing still and began to look around. Like someone lost, someone waiting to meet a friend.

Friends like us.

Tommy and Mandy paused near an advertising display. In her ear, Mandy heard Tommy's three light taps on the tiny mi—crophone attached to his shirt pocket. To the left, Sergei ruffled his newspaper and turned a page. She craved the opportunity to look up, high, in all directions, but knew better. Tommy nodded and they stepped forward, through the flow of people, closing in on Savage.

Within fifteen feet, Mandy called out. Savage turned but didn't smile. His expression went more to frown as he looked past her and saw only routine airport pedestrian traffic.

He seemed exasperated. "It looks like you're not honoring your offer, Miss Owens."

She nodded and closed the gap between them. Tommy stayed half a step behind. "Well, I am afraid I have some bad news. Change of plans, really."

"Why am I surprised? You people have no honor."

"Well, it's just that it's become quite complicated. We spoke with Nikki, who decided she just wasn't interested in returning to whatever leash you want to put on her. And of course, the boy stays with his mother."

"Go on."

Mandy recalled a hostile confrontation from long ago, when she was riding high as a reporter. *This is just like an ambush inter—view. Step up, take control.*

"Well, somehow the *Autorité des Marchés Financiers* — I guess they just call it the AMF in Quebec — has been alerted to some potential irregularities with CySafe. The relationship to your foundation, the casinos, the Sons of Chernobyl, and there's some talk in the media that one of your divisions has been doing, well, shall we say creative research on criminal activity?"

"I don't know what you're talking about."

Fake it, fake it. Mandy offered a broad, reassuring smile. "But of course you do. It's a sad day when a secure system leaks like a sieve, isn't it?" She reached into her bag. "Here, I just wanted to share with you some of the documents — "

He stepped close. Very close. She desperately wanted to back away, but her feet were like lead, attached to the floor. He lowered his voice to a growl. "I'm sure that won't be necessary."

Push back. Harder. Steady. Mandy dropped the manila folder back in the bag. *Strong.* "That's such a relief. I was concerned that I'd be compelled to show you some embarrassing materi‐ als." *Serene.* He began to interrupt, but she waved him off. "Tommy and I were discussing it, and I thought he came up with a really first-rate alternative, something to resolve our dilemma."

Savage directed a glare to Tommy. "And what might that be?"

Mandy said, "So here's the deal. You let Nikki go, we keep the two million, and we'll return control of your network to you. That way, you'll have time to purge it, make adjustments, get it in good order before the investigation. I assume AMF is very much like the American Securities and Exchange Commission — efficient and persistent and all that."

Savage chuckled. "I'll say one thing, Miss Owens. You've got a lot of brass. I've been in business for a while, long enough to know how some people have it and some people don't. But I as‐ sure you, it's not going to make a difference. I'm well connected in Montreal and I'm sure we'll weather any difficulties that might come our way. Our reputation is impeccable, and we have many friends in the right places."

"Well, thank you at least for the compliment, but — "

Savage raised a hand. "But nothing. I want you two to un‐ derstand that no matter what, no matter how long it takes, no matter what the cost, we will find you and we will make sure you regret this little episode. I will personally take you down."

Jerk. Total jerk. Good. Easier now. On a roll. Mandy sighed.

"Sorry, Cole. It's just the other way around. Have a nice day."

Voices. Two men, behind. Closer, screaming something. *Can't understand.* Cole's eyes, widening, bigger, filled with terror.

Tommy's voice. "Gun!"

Cole, turning, trying to get away.

Gunshots. *Pop. Pop. Pop.*

Cole, stumbling, staggering, falling. So much blood.

But who....

Face to face, the barrel of the weapon coming up, aiming, the barrel so big, so black...

Two more shots, from far. Spray of red, all directions. The gunman, sinking, down, collapsing.

Sergei. His enormous body suddenly in front. Legs all wobbly, rubbery, dizzy. Arms around, turning again.

Sergei's voice. "We must go! Now! Quick, quick."

Tommy?

Tommy, tackling the second guy. Rolling on the floor. People screaming, everywhere, running in all directions. Cops, lots of cops, swarming. More shots, different. *Get away, get away.* Sergei, pushing, prodding, saying something, words spoken but not heard.

A terrible silence. A long rolling blur, people staring, moving past. *Or we're passing them, not quite sure.* A lounge. Gray chairs in lazy circles. Sitting, staring. A painting on the wall that made no sense. Sergei's voice, talking to someone at the counter, hushed voices. The room otherwise empty, no one to stare. *Take a breath.*

Sergei returned to where she sat, leaned down and placed his immense paws on her shoulders. "You are okay?"

Mandy numbly nodded. "What...what happened?"

"Partners of Savage. They scream they have been betrayed, begin shooting. So, again, you are okay? You are not wounded?"

"No. Well, not really. I'm just scared."

Sergei stood and nodded. "Is good."

"Tommy?"

Yenchenko leaned down, close, his eyes searching her face, his words strong and confident. "He comes soon. Now we must go to jet, make depart, eh?"

"Yes. That would be good." She looked down at her hands, trembling, shaking. A big glass of whisky would be even better. "Serge?"

"Yes?"

"It's not a game, is it?"

"*Nyet*, Mandy. Not game. But you are most brave, do very well, eh?"

"Tommy said we were missing something."

"Gangsters are crazy people. Who is to guess? But now it is completed. And we are alive still."

CHAPTER THIRTY-SEVEN

The Puffin Diner, Jacks Ford, Pennsylvania

Tommy admired a nice stack of waffles, couple of eggs on the side, three strips of bacon on the platter's edge. Jug of pure Pennsylvania maple syrup and a whole lot of butter oozing across all the little waffle spaces where a knife and fork ought to go. Nearby, a steaming mug of decent coffee.

What Mandy'd call a best ever, a sort of reward. That's how he'd billed it after the long flight to Williamsport and the drive back to the cabin afterward. She slept most of the way on the jet, helped by a few stiff belts of Macallan single malt, a good thing, considering.

The last leg, in the ratty old pickup with the lousy suspen—sion, was impossible for sleep and now Tommy was debating whether the truck was due for replacement. Pride was suddenly wearing thin.

Still, she'd been mostly quiet in the truck. Halfway home, she said, "I'm really sorry I got us into all of this. It seemed like such a simple little thing, and it turned into a mess. I feel like an idiot."

"Don't. You did what you believed was right."

"Didn't do it very well, did I?"

"Actually, I thought just the opposite, given all the circum—stances."

"Stumbled around. A lot."

He had said, "There's always an unpredictability, there's always the need to adapt, there's always the need to press on. Not as succinct as 'steady, strong, serene' maybe, but it's always worked for me. You were persistent. Your greatest asset."

She responded with a glum sigh. "Wow. My greatest asset? That's it?"

"Well, among other things. You know what? I think you deserve a nice Puffin Special, kind of a gold star for a job well done."

"My forehead needs a pillow more than a star. For about three or four days, maybe, in between naps, shuffling around in those big fuzzy slippers."

"Nah. Trip to town, back to normal. That's the best medicine."

She chuckled. "Doctor Tommy. Always prodding the patient. Is that your Plan B?"

"Absolutely."

Now, with winter sunshine pouring through the diner window, Mandy was looking pretty decent. The platter was promising, but the diner also had the local papers, and he knew she was still addicted to newsprint and ink.

The shooting of Coleman Savage by a couple of crazed terrorists in a Berlin Airport was splashed all gaudy-like all over the front page of the Williamsport Sun-Gazette. Big picture of the scene with a whole bunch of German police pretty much blocking the view, another of a gurney with a body bag and a portrait of Savage.

Tommy said, "Waffles are getting cold."

From behind a wall of newspaper, she said, "I know, I know, I just wanted to... oh, gosh, Tommy, what a terrible picture. Look." She folded the paper and held it out.

Tommy alternated between waffle and egg, using a chunk of bacon to puncture the yolk and spread it around. "Airport surveillance cam. They're not too flattering."

"That's us."

He peered at the grainy black and white photo. "Yep, looks like you and Serge."

She turned the page back to read. "Well, of course, the caption says authorities are looking for a mystery woman and man reported to have been speaking with Savage just before the terrorists struck. It says the one guy was killed — "

"Yeah, probably Ian. He was going down before the Germans opened fire."

" — And one was captured and was taken away. But no information about him, Tommy."

"Probably won't be, either."

"How come?"

"Because the guys who jumped in after I took the guy down were speaking Russian, not German. I'm thinking it was SVR people, there to tie up loose ends but something went sideways."

She folded the newspaper and turned her attention to the breakfast platter, poking at it with indifference.

"Thought you were hungry?"

"Tommy, I just have to read the related articles. Do you mind, terribly?"

"Nope. Maybe I can catch Frannie's eye, have her warm it up."

Mandy picked up the newspaper and turned another page and began to read. "Oh, wow... Listen. This is a sidebar on the business page about CySafe, with rumors that there were some irregularities, um... and company people deny it... but look. Again."

She passed the folded page this time.

A photo at some sort of press conference, described as "the grieving widow of Coleman Savage, Dominique, taking the helm of one of the world's leading tech firms." She was reassuring investors that rumors of problems were simply not true, and she hopes to get the company, whose stock was shaky, back on track.

He said, "Well, they're trying to stop the bleeding, fix things. Lucy made some money on that, you know."

"Really?"

"Yes. Right after Savage got shot, she shorted the stock, turned a profit of several million in a few hours."

Mandy's jaw dropped. "That's terrible... no, that's like insider trading or something."

He chuckled. "More like no rest for the wicked. I talked to her while you were sleeping on the flight. She wants to take a lit-tle time off, do some decorating at her new place. She was growling about being referred to as short and dumpy, so to her, it was just — "

" — About revenge?"

Tommy shrugged. "You never want to get on the bad side of Lucy."

"Look closer. No, not at me, Tommy. The picture. The people in the background."

In a crowd of dark-suited men, second row, third from the end. Louis Boulanger, looking eager and supportive.

Tommy cocked an eyebrow. "Our accordian-playing uncle."

Mandy carved into a waffle, took a bite and said, "In the arti-cle, it says Nikki is going to be relying on her uncle to be impor-tant counsel going forward. We never considered him."

"Shoulda." He looked again at the photograph. She was holding something in her left hand. A cellphone? All the times Nikki excused herself to tend to Cyrus, to walk on the beach, to think. The moment at Billy's when Louis turned away for her bag, that little pause when his back was turned. The loud protest, the whimpered departure. He felt his eyebrows rise.

Mandy noticed. "What?"

"We assumed what Nikki was saying was the truth."

She nodded. "They were setting up a coup. You had a hunch, a feeling."

"Probably. And I might have had a feeling, but didn't pick up on it."

"And we helped her get away with it."

Tommy began to scan the article. "Maybe. Says here she is planning to have the company endow French-Canadian folk arts, help keep their heritage alive."

Mandy slowly shook her head. "That's nice. But you know and I know we were had."

"Sounds about right."

"Does it bother you, Tommy?"

"No. Lucy says she got the money and the Russian government says thanks. Twelve million for a month's work. Not too bad. But what really bothers me is that there's never enough bacon with the breakfast special."

Frannie arrived with a carafe for refills. "So, uh, how was Berlin?"

Mandy passed her mug for a refill. "Cold, dreary. So how are things with Chet?"

She filled the cup and chuckled. "Over. He got a transfer to the west coast. I heard he was trying to reconcile with his ex-wife. It's for the best. Probably wouldn't have worked out anyway."

Tommy ignored a probing glance from Mandy. No need to say nothing about a few dumb emails.

Mandy said, "We got his credit score fixed and the money returned."

Frannie ruefully smiled. "Don't much care."

Tommy said, "Stuff happens."

"Yeah. Say, what are you guys doing for Christmas?"

Mandy's eyes had widened. "Christmas! Oh my gosh, Tommy, I haven't had a chance to do anything. Plans, decorating, gifts... When?"

Frannie shook her head in amazement. "Five days, if my calendar is correct. My stars, you two just don't keep track of time, do you?"

Tommy laughed. "I think Mandy's breakfast has gotten cold."

"I can have Ernie get you fresh or warm this up, whatever suits."

Tommy looked up and past the two women, toward the door. He motioned somebody forward and heads turned. A guy in a green uniform made his way down the aisle. He was carrying a large, flat carton.

"Mister Kane?"

"That'd be me."

"Yessir, I have a delivery for you." He passed the box and the two women leaned away to let it pass. The courier produced a small clipboard and asked for a signature. When the task was completed, Tommy handed him a tip and the happy courier left.

Mandy's eyes were locked on the box on the seat next to him. "So...?"

Tommy sliced another piece of waffle. "Something I ordered."

"Okay...."

Frannie shook her head. "Tommy Kane, you're just about the meanest old dog this side of Dallas."

Tommy looked up, then studied the box. "Well, it's not exactly mine." He pulled the box back up into the air and passed it across to Mandy, who was getting to her feet as it came in her direction.

Frannie reached in to collect the dishes and make space.

Mandy's fingers found the edges and began to open the package. Her jaw dropped open. "The gown! Tommy, how did you..." She picked up a card. "Oh, gosh, you told David! You told David Aire and — "

"Now, now, before you go getting all riled up, yeah, I did. I explained to David the circumstances in Argentina, how you were off rescuing this priceless painting. Now, ol' David's a big time art lover, you know, and it just so happens that he still had that pattern of yours filed away, plus some of the same cloth."

Her eyes were misting and she was unashamed about it. She murmured, "It's not *cloth*, Tommy. It's mulberry silk. The very best. This must have cost you a fortune."

She pulled the dress from the box to touch, to hold, to admire. An envelope fell into her hand.

As she opened it, he said, "Nah. We kinda passed the hat, shared the load, like always."

"It's from Lucy, Charlie, Sergei and Bug. And there's a picture of them, waving. I'm guessing you know what the card says."

He nodded. "You know, that can be a blessing or a curse. Anyway, I told him to hang on to that pattern, because, well, you never can tell."

Tears streamed across her cheeks and she wiped them away with the back of her hand. "C'mon, Tommy, let's go home."